1/00

Severed Threads

Kaylin McFarren

THREADS SERIES: Book #1

July 2012

Published by

Creative Edge Publishing LLC
8440 NE Alderwood Road, Suite A
Portland, OR 97220

ISBN 10: 1475186525
ISBN 13: 9781475186529
E-ISBN: 978-1-4675-2671-5

Printed in the United States of America

10 9 8 7 6 5 4 3 2 1

PRAISE FOR KAYLIN MCFARREN'S THREAD SERIES

SEVERED THREADS

"The crisp writing and sparkling dialogue will hold the interest of any reader who enjoys a good mystery story that's well told."

–*MARK GARBER,* Publisher, *Portland Tribune*

"Dive right in; the water is full of danger, intrigue, and passion. This treasure-hunting jewel of a story will hold the reader captive to the very last page."

–*LAUREN CALDER,* Affaire de Coeur magazine

"An intriguing tale of mystery, deception, and murder."

–*REBECCA READS, Austin, Texas*

"I enjoy nothing more than a well-researched, thought provoking read, and *Severed Threads* definitely found itself in that category for me."

–*SUZANNE GATTIS, Pacific Book Review*

"Sizzling adventure awaits in this wonderfully fresh story from Kaylin McFarren."

–*RHONDA POLLERO, USA Today* bestselling author

"With plenty at stake, erotic chemistry, dastardly villains, a lost relic, an unusual setting and a touch of the supernatural, this indie novel could stand on any romance publisher's shelf. The full package of thrills and romance."

–*Kirkus Review*

BURIED THREADS

"The many levels of this story will engross readers into the world of the Japanese syndicate, a Buddhist monk, and the American couple, while they quickly read to a satisfying conclusion, absorbing the culture within which the story is set along the way."

–*San Francisco Book Review*

"Buckle your seat belt, hold on tight and don't forget the ice! Another fantastic story by Kaylin McFarren."

–*B.K. WALKER, author of B.K. Walker Books*

"Kaylin McFarren delivers an extraordinary, sizzling romantic adventure in *Buried Threads* that is compelling, suspenseful, and intense!

–*GERI AHEARN, Geri Ahearn's Book Reviews*

"With 353 pages of awesomeness, *Buried Threads* is one of the best books I have read in 2013."

–*JENNIFER HASS, Reader Views*

"*Buried Threads,* an erotic thriller, combines the action and adventure found in a Clive Cussler novel, the plotting and romance of Danielle Steel's books, and the erotic energy and supernatural elements of a work by Shayla Black."

–*LEE GOODEN, ForeWord Reviews/Clarion Review*

"From geishas and Japanese street gangs to women just beginning to realize their inner strength, *Buried Threads* incorporates it all. It sounds almost too busy; but all these elements come together in a logical, satisfying progression that uses life's slings and arrows, twists and turns to provide an outstanding backdrop to what really matters: *love.* And without giving away the ending of the story (which will take many a seasoned mystery reader by surprise) suffice it to say that ultimately events come full circle, offering both a conclusion and the seeds of new experiences to come in an earth-shaking epilogue that neatly ties everything together."

–*DIANE DONOVAN, Midwest Review*

Severed Threads

A Pirate's Ditty

Two foreign, fetching, lonely souls
Did meet one day with common goals.
One lived on land, one traveled seas,
Per chanced a glance through chir pine trees.
Two hands, one touch, one swan, one rook,
A kiss exchanged, great risk they took.
Bosoms fused with mutual aim,
To share their hearts—ignite the flame.
Then torn apart to distant shore,
To bid farewell, to love no more.
How cruel this sad, divided fate,
To search once more at heaven's gate.
The blooms may fade, the skin bare bone,
But love will never live alone.
Threads severed once will bind again.
When true love's found, death has no end.

–Kaylin McFarren

"The fear of death follows from the fear of life.
A man who lives fully is prepared to die at anytime."

–Mark Twain

1

The Adventure Begins. . .

Chase Cohen tumbled over Stargazer's side and into California's cold Pacific Ocean, the riches of which he dreamed so close that he could barely breathe. Five years of diving for corporate salvage companies had taught him to engage his senses as quickly as possible—to concentrate and remain focused on his purpose. Yet every time he entered this icy, underwater world, he found himself briefly caught up in his surroundings. Off to his right, a brown dogfish approached. It hovered close by, apparently intrigued by his trailing bubbles. When he smiled and reached out, he half expected the shark-like creature to dart away. Instead, it swerved and circled around him—an action reminiscent of the daring woman in his life.

Sam Lyons suddenly dropped into view, sending the fish scurrying for safety. Hanging weightless before Chase in his black mask, wet suit and regulator, his partner took on the appearance of a dark avenger. His salt-and-pepper hair swayed in the current above his head, matching the rhythm of his large, slow-moving hands. In the muted light in the ocean, his brown eyes were tense with impatience.

He signed, "OK." Chase mimicked his action.

Deflating his buoyancy compensator vest, Chase followed Sam's scissoring fins down the length of their anchor line, and in no time, they reached the bottom, eighty feet down. Moss-covered boulders dotted the soft, gray sand. In the distance, the ground gradually sloped into an opaque, bottomless depth. For hundreds of years, the jagged outcropping just beyond them had snagged unsuspecting ships and dragged them beneath the waves. According to the coordinates on Sam's map, somewhere between the bottomless pit and mountainous rise lay a barnacle-crusted anchor and chain. If his calculations were right, below them rested the wreck of the *Wanli II*—the Ming Dynasty emperor's lost dragon ship. But aside from an ornately decorated piece of wood that Sam had acquired at a local junk shop, it was still unclear what had led him to this particular spot. Perhaps it was the drunken ramblings of the retired salvager with whom he'd kept company at the Crow's Nest bar. Or the books he pored over every night. Had he really found the mother lode, as he claimed? Chase had his doubts, but Sam's unrelenting pursuit of his elusive treasure ship gave credence to the notion that something spectacular lay buried down here—something Sam was so sure of that he'd stake his life on it.

As they swam beyond their own anchor, an occasional fish passed by. But there was nothing of interest in the gray, gloomy water. Following Sam, Chase floated over craggy bedrock into a gully of crevices extending like arteries in all directions. They signaled and nodded before separating to cover more ground, to peer into dark places, hidden nooks and crannies, where evidence or unseen creatures might rest.

For twenty minutes, they surveyed the ocean floor. They fanned boulders and crustaceans, dusting off layers of sediment. The farther and deeper they went, the muddier the frigid water grew. Chase strained his eyes and ran his hands over rocks in the hazy murk, but he could not find the anchor chain.

This is pointless! Diving 101 had taught Chase the necessity of maintaining visual contact with his diving partner and carefully monitoring his time, but growing impatience tempted him to blaze his own path. He signed to Sam before veering off and heading due north. He continued groping along, his flashlight illuminating the particulate, floating like dust in the narrow beam of light. As he mindlessly continued his search, minutes ebbed away along with his youthful enthusiasm. He'd considered circling back to catch up with Sam when something took shape before his eyes. His hand closed over the metal object, an iron ingot half buried in silt. Believing it had been used as ballast for an ancient ship, his avidity returned. He brushed the sand away, scanning for porcelain shards, chain links—anything to confirm Sam's boisterous claims. But his efforts proved fruitless. The marker stood alone—an ancient, deceptive decoy. He glanced at his watch and quickly realized time had evaporated. Worse yet, his partner had completely disappeared from view.

Damn it! Chase shook his head, frustrated by his lack of common sense. What was he thinking by wandering off? He noted the position on his compass and checked his gauge. By his calculations, he had barely five minutes to spare. Just enough air to clear the surface. To reach the ship and waiting crew.

But what about Sam?

As he curled back around to locate him, Chase's breath suddenly caught. He felt a wall hit his lungs, the stream of oxygen halt in his regulator. *What the hell*? He briskly tapped on his gauge, but the impenetrable problem remained.

Equipment malfunction? The gravity of his situation sunk in with the weight of lead. Reacting purely on instinct, Chase triggered the inflator on the buoyancy compensator in his vest. He sucked on the backup mouthpiece. Then, willing himself to sustain a controlled ascent, he rose through the swirling cloud of silt he'd kicked up from the ocean floor.

Halfway mark, he assured himself.

Out of nowhere, a current took hold, blasting him sideways into the grip of an abandoned fishing net—a ghost trap set adrift by an absent ship.

Oh, shit! Tank tangled, he struggled to break free. But the woven trap held tight. He grabbed the knife strapped to his ankle and slashed wildly above him, behind him, all around until the web gave way. With his heart pounding, he quickened his strokes.

Almost there. Almost there. Racing his small cluster of rising bubbles, he calculated his required safety stop. Miss it and he'd be facing decompression sickness and a whole heap of pain.

When he reached ten feet, he slowed his strokes and hovered. For an eternal minute of strained, rationed breaths, the silhouette of Sam's ship taunted him from above.

Come on…come on. Finally, he kicked his fins to rise. Reaching upward, he emerged in the choppy surf and spat out his mouthpiece. He gasped for air. Salty air. Air that had never tasted so good.

"Bloody wind's comin' up," the Irish helmsman barked at him. "Callin' it a day."

On board, the crew feverishly looped anchor lines. Froth-tipped waves rocked the ship back and forth, as Chase bobbed in the restless surf. He slid his mask back over his dripping, blond hair.

"Gauge is busted," Chase yelled. "Get me some new gear. I'll head down and grab Sam."

Within a matter of minutes, Chase reached the bottom. He retraced his path and spotted his partner twenty yards out.

Up, Chase repeatedly motioned.

Sam shook his head. He signaled, "Not OK." Yet rising bubbles indicated that his oxygen was still flowing.

Chase grabbed him by the harness to maintain contact.

Hang on, Sam. As they ascended, Sam began moving his arms and legs. Then his limbs went limp. After ten more feet, his regulator fell out of his mouth. Heavy lids sealed his glazed eyes, indicating he'd lost consciousness.

Come on, buddy. Don't do this. Chase's brain scrounged for information, a practice drill from the certification classes he'd taken years earlier. Classes he should have taken more seriously.

Damn it! This wasn't ever supposed to happen. Chase shoved Sam's regulator back into his vacant mouth. He pushed the purge button, forcing air down Sam's throat. Escaping air bubbled around his slack lips, a clear indication that he wasn't breathing. Chase punched Sam's chest repeatedly. But his efforts proved useless.

God no, God no. This couldn't be happening. Not to Sam. Not to Rachel's father. Not when Chase had assured her that he'd look after him.

Fifteen feet under the ocean, Chase struggled to keep his calm. He seized the lifeline and secured Sam to it. He removed his weight belt and inflated his BC. With one huge push, Chase shoved Sam upward. *Go*! Then remaining in place, he hovered—decompressing himself for the longest minute of his life. All the while, his memories filled with Sam. The only man in his life whom he had allowed himself to trust. The only father figure he'd ever known. Without hesitation, Sam had offered him a job. He had opened his home and welcomed him like a member of his family. How could Chase have been so careless? So completely self-absorbed?

His reeling thoughts centered on Sam's daughter. The moment Rachel had stepped into his life, all the bad that ever was had vanished. Of all the women he'd allowed himself to become involved with, she was the one who had found her way into his heart. How could he possibly explain this fiasco to her? What words could he use to excuse his actions? Sam and Rachel were the most important people in his life, and in a matter of minutes, that could all change.

Be all right, Sam. Please, be all right. Chase tucked away his anxieties and headed for the surface. With each determined stroke and kick, he prayed that his partner would survive. By the time he boarded *Stargazer,* the crew had already hoisted Sam onto the dive platform. They had radioed the San Palo Coast Guard station, only fifteen minutes away, and one of the crew members had taken over the helm. As they blazed a path toward shore, Chase breathed in oxygen to help purge the excess nitrogen from his system. His gut wrenched as he watched the bulky helmsman aggressively work over Sam's body. Exhaled breaths, rhythmic chest compressions. Ian's relentless attempts continued for an eternity with no visible response from Sam. Then Ian checked Sam's vitals. He closed his eyes and shook his downcast head.

Chase could hear voices all around him asking questions, but his fear muted them. He shoved Ian out of the way. "No!" He took over breathing into Sam's gaping mouth, hammering Sam's chest with his fist. "Breathe, Sam, goddamn it! Breathe!" he yelled. Chase knew that people could be revived without brain damage after as long as an hour in cold water. He couldn't give up. Not when it meant losing his closest friend.

They finally reached the dock and someone had the courage to pull Chase off Sam. Hold him at a distance as a team of professionals took over.

"Looks like cardiac arrest," a coast guard officer announced.

The words reverberated in Chase's ears. He grasped the ship's railing to keep from collapsing. He watched as they transferred Sam's spent body into a waiting ambulance. Then he forced himself to follow closely behind, his rubbery legs barely cooperating. He begged to ride with Sam, but the same officer assured him that nothing more could be done.

Chase stood barefoot in the gravel lot of the marina, watching the white emergency vehicle drive away. As soon as it disappeared from view, he fell back against a parked car. All sound had been siphoned from the air. The only thing registering was his throbbing brain and the radiating pain in his chest.

Why Sam? He was a healthy fifty-five-year-old man. He had over twenty years of diving under his belt and knew the ocean better than anyone did. With no threatening divers or reported sharks in the area, Chase couldn't imagine what had caused Sam's heart to stop cold.

What did I miss? Chase racked his brain for answers. He'd personally checked Sam's tank and regulator after picking it up at the dive shop. At the time, everything had been in working order. He was sure of it. Yet, if equipment failure were determined to be the cause of Sam's death, Chase would be held accountable. Even if the court let him off, he would always believe himself responsible.

Chase's eyes dropped to a white plastic bag, bouncing and rolling across the ground—a discarded and insignificant piece of life.

"Mr. Cohen?"

A man's voice turned him around. The coast guard officer had been making inquiries, taking statements. Checking their dive equipment. The crew members were now huddled at the far end of the dock, casting wary looks in Chase's direction.

"Would you like to come with me…to explain all of this to Miss Lyons?" he asked.

God, Rachel. The worst was yet to come. He glanced at the ship's fantail, now vacant except for Ian. The mountainous man stood hunched over, his face in his hands, sobbing.

"I'll tell her," Chase said. He waited until the officer turned and walked away. Until he was completely alone. Why had he agreed to do such a thing? Knock on Rachel's door. Tell her that he was responsible for taking away the only parent she had left.

Watch the love in her eyes turn to hate.

Although he loathed his decision, he chose the coward's way out. He flipped open his phone and auto-dialed her number.

Rachel's voice came on the line. Confident. Captivating. Unaware. "So, don't tell me. Another fool's errand, right? I swear my father will never grow up."

Chase remained silent for an eternal moment. And in that moment, he wished for the strength of Goliath—to rein in his quaking nerves, to give him the courage to spill the words that refused to form.

"Chase?" Concern edged her tone. "Chase, are you there?"

He forced another swallow. "Rachel, listen," he began in a rasp of a voice. Rusted from panic, from guilt. From disbelief. "Something happened. It…it's your dad."

2

Four Years Later
San Palo Archaeological Museum

Dread traveled on Rachel Lyons's rapidly clicking heels. With each breath, she drank in the musty smells of ancient relics and discovery. Her gaze dusted the familiar terra-cotta warriors and inscribed cuneiform tablets that lined the plastered walls. As she rounded the museum library's sharp corner, a woman's shriek and the thundering boom of falling books jolted her.

"Good Lord!" Eleanor Briggs, Dr. Ying's silver-haired assistant, clutched her chest. "I didn't realize anyone was in the building." Her eyelids fluttered beneath her yellowed bifocals before recognition took hold. "Please excuse me, dear."

"Sorry, Eleanor. I didn't mean to startle you."

"What's that?"

Rachel repeated her words loud enough for the woman to hear. "I said I didn't mean to startle you."

"Not to worry. That's what I get for not paying any mind." Eleanor's translucent blue eyes dropped to the scattered textbooks around her feet. "Goodness. Would you look at the mess I made?" Her slight frame wobbling, she gingerly lowered herself. She planted a blue-veined hand on the floor for balance and reached out to collect the nearest volume.

Rachel stole another glance at her watch and her muscles tightened. Only two minutes left. But what choice did she have? Without assistance, Eleanor might keel over from exhaustion.

"Here, let me get those for you." Dropping her briefcase, Rachel knelt and gathered the books into her arms. *Imperial History, Swift Explorations, Treasures of the Deep.*

She stacked the professor's texts on a nearby table, and then reached a hand under Eleanor's bony arm and guided her back onto her feet with care. A thirty-year museum veteran with more knowledge than the entire basement archives, the woman was an exhibit in and of herself.

"My, my," Eleanor said. "It does seem a bit harder to get up than it used to."

Rachel flashed a smile while collecting her bag. "Dr. Ying? Is he in?"

"Oh, yes—of course. Come with me."

She linked one of her arms through Rachel's and shuffled beside her down the never-ending corridor of coin collections and metal implements. Rachel battled the urge to break into a sprint.

Nearing the museum director's office, Eleanor released her hold. "Just one moment," she directed. After a rap on the door, she opened it a crack and peered inside. "Professor, excuse me. Miss Lyons is here."

Rachel slipped off her black beret and tucked it into the pocket of her tan overcoat. Noting a dust mark on the knee of her black slacks, she gave the pressed seam a brush.

"Go on in, my dear." Eleanor widened the door for entry.

Rachel edged past her guide and made her way toward Dr. Ying, a compact, sparse-haired man. He stood beside the crowded bookcase in his tiny office. Dark circles weighed heavily under his eyes. When their outstretched hands connected, crow's feet deepened behind his thick, black-rimmed glasses. He offered his usual warm smile, which today only added to her discomfort.

"I can't thank you enough for stopping by." He waited for Rachel to seat herself before rounding his desk. "We've been busy with preparations for the maritime reception tomorrow night. I hope you're planning to attend." His executive chair creaked under his weight.

"Oh, right. I'm looking forward it." *Make that dreading it.* She hated attending formal affairs, subjecting herself to idle chit-chat. At the moment, however, even banal conversations sounded more appealing than the one she was about to have.

Eleanor was suddenly at her side. "Shall I fetch you any coffee or tea, Miss Lyons?"

"None for me, thanks." Rachel watched as Eleanor confiscated a scarred, red saucer filled with cigarette butts from atop the professor's cluttered secretary. Eleanor gave him a reprimanding but caring shake of her head before she left the room. Apparently, his vow to abstain from his two-pack-a-day habit had fallen to the wayside since Rachel's last visit. At least the scent of vanilla from the air freshener on a shelf behind him masked any airborne evidence that hadn't escaped through the partially opened windows. She unfastened her briefcase and pulled out the manila folder.

Time to get this over with. With four more stops to make and a dozen phone calls to return before noon, she had barely ten minutes to spare.

"You know," he said, "I've been meaning to ask you about that old house you're living in. Have you made up your mind about selling it?"

His question threw her off balance. She rested the file on her lap, debating how to answer. "I haven't decided yet."

"Mmm..." Dr. Ying nodded thoughtfully. "Well, if you do, I'm sure it will go quickly. Your dad used to say the sea captain who built that place put his heart and soul into it."

Dr. Ying had been a close friend of her late father, so it was no surprise that he wanted to reminisce. But the subject threatened to unearth the trove of guilt she'd prefer to keep buried.

"Shall we get down to business?" She extracted his application—the first and only of his applications that had given her pause. Hall expansions and artifact acquisitions were one thing, but this project was quite another. Raising her head, she found Dr. Ying studying her over the rim of his blue, oriental teacup. "I'm afraid, professor, we...have a bit of a problem."

He sighed. "Don't tell me I missed a line or two. I asked Eleanor to double-check it for me. But then, these days neither of us is—"

"Actually," she broke in, "your grant application was in perfect order."

"Oh. Good."

"But," she quickened the pace of her rehearsed words, "as you know, the board of trustees can't be responsible for the majority of your funding. And they typically don't get involved in speculative proposals. There's no doubt in my mind that they will *deny* your request this time."

Tea spilled from the professor's cup. The brown puddle seeped toward a stack of files on his desk. He mopped it away with a scrunched piece of notebook paper as he glanced in her direction. "I'm sorry. What did you say?" His strained voice shot out an octave higher.

She swallowed. "The Warren Nash Foundation provides funds to museums to bid on collections *after* they're evaluated by official committees. Although it's common knowledge that Mr. Nash encouraged exploration projects, he never would've financed acquisitions based solely on assumptions and unsubstantiated claims."

Dr. Ying froze, bewilderment in his dark eyes. "But this...this isn't a *tugboat* we're referring to. This is history in the making."

"I understand your disappointment, especially since the board has always been such a strong supporter of your work." An attempt to soften the blow. "Our office would be more than happy to look at other—"

"Rachel," he ran over her words, "maybe I didn't make myself clear. What we have here is an incredible discovery that's going to bring international recognition to our museum...to our city and community." He took a breath, gathering himself. "Please understand...an opportunity like this doesn't come along every day. I know Sam would've *loved* to have been part of this."

Rachel's stomach churned as she realized that her father's name had just been tossed for leverage. And for what, a few gold coins and some ceramic knickknacks she could find on eBay?

She shoved the paperwork back into her file. "I don't know what else I can say, Dr. Ying. Perhaps the American Maritime Association can be of assistance."

In an instant, the man was on his feet. "If you could just give me a minute..." He pulled a worn textbook from his desk and flipped through the pages as he moved toward her chair. "This isn't a Spanish galleon, mind you. It's an ancient Chinese vessel, similar to the *Nanhai No. 1*—an eight-hundred-year-old merchant ship that was involved in arms smuggling before it sank fifty-eight meters under the Java Sea. Copper guns and cannons—which weren't uncommon on ocean-faring vessels at the time—were discovered near the wreck site. Ah...here's a sketch." He placed the book on her lap, anchoring her. "Besides a cargo of valuable tea, our ship was carrying more than 10,000 pieces of *kraak* porcelain in the lower decks as ballast. According to the historical data I have here somewhere…" He turned and briskly leafed through a hefty stack of paperwork.

"Oh, now I remember," she said. "I read about the recovery of that ship years ago. The survey and lifting cost of the artifacts alone was over ten million dollars." She set the book aside and rose. "Doctor, this sounds fascinating, truly, but like I said…"

Abruptly, he straightened. The intensity in his gaze stilled her. "The point is, Rachel, it's a phenomenal find. I've acquired an ancient manifest and trade records. They indicate the *Wanli II* had miraculously reached the Sea of Cortez before a storm ripped through her sails and buried her under the ocean. What's more, there's gold and treasure on board worth more than anything you could ever…" He pressed his glasses up a notch. "It's priceless."

Rachel released a closely held breath. She felt like the executioner of the man's lifelong dream. The same damn dream her father had held onto for most of her life. She wouldn't have accepted her exasperating job or been placed in this awkward position if not for her family's tragedy. If not for the promise Dr. Ying had made to her father years earlier.

But what if she was proven wrong? If the professor's project was more than wishful thinking? It certainly wasn't the first time wreckage had washed up along the California shore. A discovery of the magnitude that the professor claimed this was could make all the difference to San Palo's disintegrating township. "And you have proof, I assume, of everything you're telling me?" The question slipped from her mouth before she could stop it.

He nodded with enthusiasm. "I've been meeting with the lead diver from Trident Ventures on a regular basis. The artifacts he's in the process of collecting should help validate the ship's identity."

Trident Ventures. There was something vaguely familiar about the name. "So this is a reputable firm? A company that would give credence to your proposal?"

"Absolutely. But unfortunately, the owner has run into a few glitches. The cost for additional supplies and recovery equipment has slightly exceeded his expectations."

Exceeded by how much? She was afraid to ask.

"I know this seems a bit unorthodox, but he's actually due here any moment. I'm sure all your questions will be answered if you could just—"

"Wait!" Eleanor's shrill voice echoed in the hallway. "One moment, sir."

"It's all right, ma'am. I'll let myself in." The man's deep, captivating voice pulled Rachel's face toward the opening door. "Sorry I'm late, Doc, I was—" His words broke off when his gaze found Rachel's.

Her shoulders coiled. *Oh my God.* It couldn't be.

Trepidation flowed hotly into her cheeks as her gaze traveled over his face. Years had passed, yet he appeared as irritatingly handsome as ever. His sun-bleached hair still fell into a natural part above his lucid blue eyes. The ever-present five o'clock shadow rimmed his contemptuous jaw.

"Rachel," he finally said. "It's been awhile." A satisfied glow replaced his look of surprise.

She shot a pained look at Dr. Ying before facing him again. "You're Trident Ventures?"

A confident nod of his head was his only reply. Word had it, Chase Cohen, the renowned treasure hunter, was more determined than ever to leave his mark. He'd rifled ocean plots stretching from Spain to Key West, selling off remnants of other people's lives. She had hoped their paths would never cross again.

So much for that wishful thought.

The professor's worrisome voice broke the thorny silence. "Well, now that we're all here, maybe we could get down to the matter at hand."

"My thoughts exactly." Her intense stare carved lines into the professor's chin. Clearly, he was now wishing he hadn't finagled this meeting. Knowing full well the history Chase and Rachel shared, his manipulation only further demonstrated the extent of his desperation.

Chase threw on a crooked grin and sauntered across the room. He braced himself against the desk. "Did Doc show you the piece of china I found last week? Got real worked up over that one, didn't you, pal?" he tossed over his shoulder.

Her eyes raked over Chase's snug T-shirt, tattered jeans, and weathered cowboy boots, which were crossed at the ankles. His golden tan served as testament to the time he'd spent frolicking outdoors. *Some things never change.*

"Found it only ten miles off the coast. Even though it wasn't marked like we hoped, after the storm we had last week, there's no telling what's going to turn up."

This was California, not Micronesia. Every sunken ship, half-buried skeleton and carefully mapped wreck site had been fully played out. She wasn't about to be fooled or charmed into backing a hopeless cause. She stared daggers at his face, hoping he'd be forced to look away. But nothing seemed to faze him.

"Came real close to going over a sheer drop-off. Then we figured it out...where the *Wanli's* been holed up all this time. Man, I can't wait to show you—"

"How you're still exploiting what my father taught you," she finished.

"Exploiting?" Chase cleared his throat. "That's not exactly true, Miss Lyons." He dropped his chin, the tension around his eyes softening. "It's still *Miss*, isn't it?" Before she could respond, he continued. "My crew might move a little sand around, but whatever we find ends up benefiting everyone, I assure you."

Oh, really?

Rachel pulled the scarf from her neck. The arrogance in the room was suffocating. "Not everyone benefits from your actions, Mr. Cohen. All your shifting around does a ton of damage too."

"We *are* talking about diving here, right?"

She reared back. "What did you say?"

Chase coughed. He shot the professor a wary glance before returning his attention to Rachel. "I just meant that this expedition…it's important." A plea settled in his eyes.

"In that case, you shouldn't have any trouble finding someone else to help you. For future reference, gentlemen, our foundation won't be supporting *any* projects involving Trident Ventures. Good luck to you both." Snatching her briefcase, she spun on one heel and stormed out of Professor Ying's office.

As she strode into the parking lot, Rachel was agitated to see Chase following closely behind. Nearing her vehicle, she blew out a heated breath and fumbled for the keys in her bag. Just as she located them, Chase inserted himself between her and the car. She reached around him, trying to grasp the door handle. But with a flick of his arm, he deflected her hand.

She felt her entire body flush. "Get out of my way," she ordered.

"Two minutes. Just give me two minutes to explain," he implored.

"I don't have time for this." She meant it in more ways than one. His nearness rekindled the pain; it unearthed the argument she'd had with her father only hours before he died. Her thoughtless outburst had clouded his judgment and driven him to take an unnecessary risk. In her mind, there was no other explanation for his death.

"Rachel, I'm not going to lie to you. I heard you'd given up diving. That you were working for the Warren Nash Foundation. But I honestly had no idea you'd be here."

Her spine stiffened.

"And as for your dad," he continued, "not a day goes by that I don't feel responsible for what happened. Sam was a good man. Like a father to me."

She bristled. Her gaze burned with emotion. "Oh, really? Then why didn't you have the decency to show up at his funeral?"

Chase's gaze slid from her face. His brows met when he looked up again. "Look, I really wanted to come. It's just that after the investigation and everything—"

Her anger ripened. "Yeah, right." His scrawled note had left her brooding for weeks. *Something urgent came up...have to leave town.* After professing his love for her, he had turned out to be the scoundrel her brother, Devon, had painted him. Her teeth clenched at the memory. "You were a complete asshole. Now get out of my way."

Using both hands, she shoved hard against his taut chest, but he rocked right back into place. He grabbed hold of her wrists and pulled her in close. "You have every right to be angry," he said quietly. "But there was a good reason why I stayed away. Why I never called you."

An involuntary shiver ran up her spine. She turned her head and looked toward the marina, wishing the drifting fog could shield her from his soul-searching gaze. She didn't want him to see how broken she'd become. Or that, deep inside, she had never stopped yearning for his touch.

"It had nothing to do with you and me," he insisted.

She stepped back, breaking his grip. "It *still* doesn't." Venom dripped from her words.

Chase nodded slowly. "Maybe not. But right now, I need this job. More than you know." His blue eyes intensified. "What will it take for us to get past everything? An apology? You have it. My promise to stay clear of you? Done."

His words reminded her how easy it was for him to dismiss her. She'd been such a fool for allowing his charm to blind her. He obviously cared about no one but himself. And deep down inside, no matter how hard she had tried to dismiss it, they both shared the blame for her father's death. Nothing would change that.

She drew in a deep breath. "There *is* one thing that would make me feel better."

His face relaxed. "You name it. Anything you want."

She pulled back her arm and swung with all her might. Her palm connected with his cheek so hard that it stung her hand to the bone.

"Damn!" He grabbed his face, wincing from the blow.

She pressed her palms together, nursing her own pain, and addressed him again.

"I've wanted to do that for a long time. If you think you can just show up and expect me to—"

Before she could finish, he pulled her into his arms. His lips found hers, launching a current through her veins. The parking lot was spinning out of control, and he was the driving force. Her legs quivered, leaving her unsteady on her feet. When he finally lifted his head, she leaned against him, breathless, betrayed by her body's weakened state.

His warm breath brushed her cheek, lifting tiny hairs on her skin. "And I've wanted to do *that*," he whispered raggedly, "from the first moment I saw you in Doc's office."

Of course. His agenda. Her senses sobered. She distanced herself and firmed her tone. "Nice try. But you're still not getting a dime from me."

Chase bent his head and seemed to be strategizing his next move. When he looked up, his crystal eyes chipped away at her soul. "For what it's worth, Rachel, I really am sorry…for everything. Should've said that a long time ago." He rubbed the back of his neck. An emotion resembling disappointment crossed his face. "Believe me; I would've stuck around if I could have."

She was surprised by his show of sincerity. But nothing he could say would lessen the pain she still felt over his abandonment when she had needed him most.

She jutted out her chin. "It was just a summer fling. A mistake from beginning to end. We should have ended it like adults, is all."

Her final words hung in the air. A nerve jumped at his temple. "I didn't know you felt that way," he said.

Chase's kiss still simmered on her lips. His nearness threatened her resolve. It wasn't in her to be cruel, but she had hurt far too badly to back down now.

"So…now you do." The lie tasted bitter in her mouth.

Chase's eyes darkened. He gave a rueful nod. "Good thing we got that cleared up. Wouldn't want to make any more mistakes."

As he strutted toward his truck, anger gathered in Rachel's chest. Anger over his words, his deeds, his presumptuous kiss. Over the fact that for a split second, he had made *her* feel like the bad guy. Mentally, she threw daggers at his back. "Damn you, Chase Cohen."

She slid inside her silver Kia and slammed the car door, grateful that the museum's security guard was now watching from a distance. If he hadn't been, she might have acted on a homicidal impulse and run Chase over, the manipulative jerk.

In fact, it made her feel better just to imagine it.

3

Chase pulled the heavy wooden door shut behind him and waited for his eyes to adjust to the dark. Through the white spots dancing in his vision, he made his way toward the towheaded helmsman, Ian Lowe. Two months after leaving San Palo, they'd miraculously crossed paths and ended up working on one of the largest salvage operations in the West Indies. But now, they were back in the States, more determined than ever to make it on their own.

As was his usual practice, Ian was parked at the far end of the bar, beside the swinging kitchen doors. Chase dropped onto the barstool next to him.

"Whiskey," he called to the female bartender, who was busy pulling bottles off the top shelf. In his present circumstances, he'd be wise to hold onto the few measly dollars clinging to the inside of his pocket. But thanks to his unexpected run-in with Rachel, the need to quench his thirst won out.

Ian's shoulders remained slightly hunched as he rocked a raw egg back and forth in his half-filled beer mug—a crude remedy for his apparent hangover. His heavy-browed eyes studied Chase.

"Didn't go well, I take it?" The gravel in his brogue suggested he'd come straight from bed to the Crow's Nest Bar.

"An understatement," Chase muttered. "You won't believe this, but Rachel Lyons was there. Just as stubborn as ever." A glance around the room reassured him that no one in the musty bar had the slightest interest in their exchange. To his left, a young couple was sharing pancakes. In the corner, a scrawny guy was typing away. And scattered about were leather-faced fishermen who appeared to be leftovers from the previous night.

By the time he turned back, Ian had finished his drink. "Gimme another pint of wet stuff, darlin'," he sang out.

"Be right with you two," Naomi McKenzie tossed over her shoulder. She inched her way down the ladder.

"And how *is* Miss Lyons these days?" Ian asked.

"Let's just say I don't know anyone who can leave an impression like she does." Chase massaged his cheekbone while working his jaw. No doubt, the blow she'd delivered had been well deserved. Still, he was glad he'd stolen a kiss before she'd trampled his ego.

"Ah, so ya finally fessed up."

"She didn't want to hear any of it." And personally, he hadn't had the stomach to unload on her. Not with her brother, Devon, holding a world of secrets over his head. Secrets that no woman, especially Rachel, could possibly understand.

Ian pursed his lips, clearly working up more bum advice about women.

Chase quickly steered him away from the subject. "So where'd you end up spending the night?"

"Down in Whistler, acting the maggot. The skirt's husband was supposed to be gone for a good two days. Ended up climbin' out a window with me pants in tow. Swear I heard a trigger cock as I was roundin' the corner at Main."

"Shit, I hope you're not leading any of those guys back to my boat."

Ian scratched his grizzled face and then slapped Chase on the back with his meaty palm. "Maybe I should. We could knock 'em out and shake 'em for change."

A smile tugged the corner of Chase's mouth.

"That is, unless you've got a better plan, Cap'n."

"I wish to hell I did," Chase grumbled. "*Alegria's* pump's busted, fuel's nearly gone. Won't be long before someone slides right under us." He released a sharp breath and stared down at the bracelet on his wrist. Christ, he'd give anything to stop thinking about money and his fledgling business for one lousy day.

"Ah, no point mopin' about, mate. Go to yer woman. Convince her to change her mind. With her company's money, we'd be back on the water in—"

"Not an option," Chase cut in, although he couldn't deny wanting any excuse to see her again.

The day she'd walked into her father's office, grinning over new algae she had discovered, he'd been completely captivated. Sure, she was smart, sexy, and drop-dead gorgeous, with her long, cinnamon hair and moist, kiss-me-now lips. But it was the depth in her hazel eyes that had arrested his thoughts, making it impossible to throw two coherent words together. Then she shook his hand, and the softness of her skin had melted away every last ounce of tension.

Too bad he went and screwed it all up. Just like everything in his life.

"With *gobshite* bankers avoidin' us like the bloody plague," Ian persisted, "what other remedy is there?" He leaned far back in his seat, oblivious to Naomi, who was now standing behind him, trying to access the kitchen.

She shifted the cumbersome tray in her arms. "Ian, sit up. You're blocking the door."

A twinkle gleamed in Ian's green eyes as they latched onto the bartender's ample cleavage. "Not at all, darlin'. Feel free to sit on me lap anytime and rest that top-heavy load of yours." He grinned, as if his retort was among the cleverest ever spoken.

"The only thing I'm gonna be giving your lap is a swift kick. Now, move it."

The threat was a powerful one. He immediately scooted his chair out of the way. "Was meant as a compliment, ya bleedin' weapon."

Chase mentally applauded the gutsy broad.

She blew out a huff as she made her way past them. "Can't you afford any better friends, Chase?"

"Not at the moment," he replied flatly.

The scrapper Chase had aligned himself with definitely had his flaws. His mischievous flirting and sexual promiscuity provided constant reminders of why his wife and two sons had booted him from their home in Dublin ten years ago. Yet when it came to friendship, no one was more loyal or forgiving.

"Ya know, me friend, there *is* another way," Ian said. "Was in Dolan's Pub two nights ago, when this burly gent saddled alongside and offered to wet me whistle. Turned out to be a loan shark. Charges interest steep as bunkers. Still an' all, I could convince him to give us a shot."

"Yeah, he'd give us a shot, all right. In both kneecaps." Chase shook his head. "Just give me a few more days. I'll come up with something. I always do." He spoke with confidence that didn't extend past his words. His credit was tapped. Bill collectors would be calling again any day now. Everything he had was tied up in the sixty-foot Delta secured to the dock outside. If he sold his only possession of value, he'd forfeit a lucrative reward for the treasure that was sitting on the ocean floor—just out of his reach. But what were his options? At that moment, he'd sell his soul if there were a way to reel it back in.

Chase spotted the bartender chatting it up in a dark corner. "Naomi, did you forget us?" he called out.

The petite bartender sashayed back to her post. "Now how could I forget about you, sweetheart?" She flashed a smile before setting the fresh pint and amber shot glass before them.

Ian grinned. "Aren't you joinin' us, darlin'?"

"Too early for me." Naomi pushed her unruly red curls off her sweaty brow. She lifted a water bottle and sucked it down in nothing flat. Then she resumed her chores behind the bar. As Chase watched her with renewed interest, he recalled the first time he'd laid eyes on the plucky woman.

Macy's Café. Chase had joined Sam for a cup of coffee, and Naomi was sitting in the booth beside him. She ogled and fussed over the old man, who was clearly twice her age. Although Chase had gone there to discuss Sam's job offer, for the better part of an hour Naomi had given both of them an earful. He'd never met anyone who took so much pride in the amount of gossip she could spout. Aside from Ian, anyway.

"So, today's your birthday?" Chase quizzed.

Her smile brightened. "How'd you guess?"

He nodded toward the black T-shirt she wore. In white script, the words *Over the Hill* were stretched thin across her chest.

Ian nearly choked on his drink. He wiped his mouth with the back of his hand. "Here I thought you were advertising yer assets."

"God, Ian. You're such an ass." She dragged the blue towel off her shoulder and over the bar's splattered surface. "Can't you get your mind out of the gutter for one minute?"

Chase jumped in to save his friend from further humiliation. "So," he said to Naomi. "You still heading back to Alaska?"

She shrugged a shoulder. "Doesn't look like it. My sister made a ton of money last spring, but according to her, fishing's gone all to hell. With trawlers pulling in half empty, her regulars completely dried up."

For half a second, Chase saw dollar signs in her eyes and considered asking if her sister might be willing to invest in his ailing business. But somehow, soliciting money from the town's "ceiling expert" seemed a little too desperate—even for him.

"Still chartering your boat?" Naomi asked, wiping her hands on the white tied around her waist.

He shrugged and ran his thumb over the shot glass rim. "For the time being."

"My cousin, Blaine McKenzie...over there in the corner...he just flew in this afternoon and plans to stick around all week. He's looking for someone to take him out."

Chase glanced over his shoulder. It was the scrawny guy in his early twenties, hunched over a laptop computer. With his rolled-up shirtsleeves and round, black-rimmed specs, he resembled a contestant on some nerd reality show.

"That pip's yer *cousin*?" Ian blurted.

Chase actually had had the same thought. The idea that the two shared DNA was staggering.

"We share a last name, but he's a distant cousin through marriage," she replied.

The shaggy-haired kid glanced up and smiled. He seemed undaunted by the three sets of eyes that were now fixed on him.

"Believe it or not, Blaine's intellect is highly sought after," she went on. "He's some kind of software genius up in Seattle. Every now and then, he manages to fly in for a visit."

"Ya don't say," Ian muttered, returning his focus to Naomi's shapely figure.

She set Ian's empty glass behind the bar. "He's planning to stay on for a full week this time. If you're interested, he's got his gear stowed in his plane outside."

Chase had just tossed back his high-octane drink. "His *plane*?" he squeezed out, certain he'd misheard.

She jerked her thumb to the bar's picture window. "That's it right there."

Both Ian and Chase craned their necks to look. There, tethered to the dock, sat a beautiful, red-and-white Grumman Mallard seaplane, and in the corner of the room, still smiling, sat the solution to all their problems.

4

Bam-bam-bam! Bam-bam-bam!

Devon Lyons sprang up in bed. He squinted at the green-glowing clock on his nightstand. 12:45 a.m. *What the hell?* It suddenly occurred to him that Logan Tulles must have gotten his messages. He had probably come over to rage about their disastrous dilemma. But why show up at this hour? Why didn't he just call?

"Dev, it's me. Open the door!"

Selena Pollero's muffled voice jacked his scowl into a smile. A verbal assault wasn't waiting on his doorstep after all. Still, if he didn't hear back from Logan by the time he finished breakfast, he'd have to send out a search party. He tied on his bathrobe as he swept through the condo and unbolted the front door.

Selena rushed inside, her long, auburn hair flowing behind her. "What took you so long? It's freezing out there." A tight, off-the-shoulder black dress hugged her curves, raising more than goose bumps on her olive skin.

"Aren't you breaking rule number, what, fourteen on your brother's list?" Devon said, smirking. He closed the door, already imagining his hands exploring every inch of her figure. The memory of her long legs wrapped around him caused his body to ache. He seized one of Selena's arms to draw her in for a kiss.

"I'm not here for that." She broke free and marched past him.

He brushed the scruff on his chin with the back of his hand, thoroughly amused. Selena had taught him the power of impassioned stares and soft-spoken directives. Once she ended her playful taunts, her sexual appetite had been known to surpass his, which wasn't an easy feat.

"So why *are* you here?" he challenged, lips curled.

At the window, Selena lifted the edge of the beige blinds at the living room window. She seemed to be distracted by something in the illuminated street below. When she looked back at Devon, her knitted brows had relaxed a bit, but her doe eyes appeared unsettled.

"What's going on?"

"I think someone's following me again." She walked a short distance across the hardwood floor and back again. "My brother's got his guys on me all the time."

After her second trip, Devon grabbed her arm. Her pacing was rattling his nerves.

"He can't know I'm here," she insisted.

Just like his sister, Rachel, Selena had a tendency to overreact. Yet this time, fear flickered in her eyes, convincing him to heed her warning about Gabe.

"When I got home tonight, I heard him on the phone. He said you'd been messing with him. That if you didn't show up, there was gonna be one less investment broker in town." An accusation edged her voice.

Releasing her, Devon stepped closer to the living room window. He lifted the shade a fraction higher and scanned the marina. No one in sight. He blew out a breath.

"Whatever you're involved in, Dev, you gotta get out of it. And fast."

Despite the angst balling in his gut, he faced her and offered the false reassurance she sought. "There's nothing to worry about. Just a misunderstanding. I'll clear it up tomorrow, OK?" He stroked her cheek with his thumb, shielding his anxiety.

Based on Logan's recent discovery of their boss's offshore accounts in Antigua, their "venture" was suddenly showing all the earmarks of a Ponzi scheme.

Selena pulled his hand from her face. "Don't lie to me. If you're into something illegal..."

"I'm not," he told her. "I promise."

Devon hated being dishonest, and of all people, Selena deserved the truth. There was no purpose, though, in coming clean at this point—letting her know he was climbing walls over the laundered money he and Logan had entrusted with their missing boss. Should the Securities and Exchange Commission find out, they could be facing prison time. And if they didn't deliver an overdue and inflated return on her brother's stag investment, they could both end up facedown in a back alley with two bullets lodged in their brains. He squelched the thought. No need to toil over something that wasn't going to happen.

In his mind, he firmed his plan. Come morning, he'd contact everyone on his call list. Track down their firm's chief adviser. Find out where his boss, Walter Moten, had been holed up for the past two weeks.

Get this whole crazy mess straightened out.

He gazed into Selena's narrowed eyes, carefully weighing his words. "Baby, don't worry. I care too much about you to be that stupid."

Slowly, the tension in her features fell away. She shook her head and sighed. "God, you scared me. I thought the creeps Gabe hangs around with were gonna be after you next."

Devon scratched the back of his head, still tender after Gabe's cantankerous bodyguard threw him against a wall to punctuate the warning to keep his hands off Selena.

But then, some things in life were worth a few bruises. Like using his tongue to trace the delicate line on the slender neck before him.

He smiled at her knowingly. "You were worried about me, huh?"

She arched a brow. "Don't flatter yourself. I was just in the neighborhood."

"Uh-huh." As she started to walk off, Devon encircled her waist and pulled her backside against him—hard. She gasped. He nuzzled the side of her head and whispered into her ear, "I'm glad you were in the neighborhood." He felt her body melt in his arms before she turned around. She leaned in and seductively kissed his bottom lip, then his top one, taking control. And he gladly let her.

Every muscle in his body tensed at the feel of her breath, moist and hot on his skin. She closed her eyes and caressed his tongue with hers, delivering a taste of mint and desire, stripping away his restraint. He crushed her thick hair with one hand and grasped her hip with the other. A familiar, intoxicating scent filled his lungs. He buried his face in her neck, desire driving him on.

Anticipation tightened his stomach as she moved between his legs, grinding up and down on his thigh. "You *have* missed me," he teased in a low voice.

"You've got no idea." She pressed her breasts against his chest and caressed his neck. The whisper of a breath tickled his ear. "You taste so good," she hummed.

With one hand, she loosened the tie around his waist. She ran her warm palm along the inside of his leg, higher and higher, freeing a groan from deep inside. Her fingers traced the length of his erection and then locked firmly in place.

Devon stared at her parted mouth and swallowed hard.

Lifting her chin, she peered into his eyes. "Sleeping in the nude, I see. You haven't had company, have you?" She awaited his response, maintaining her grip, a playful threat.

He shook his head and smiled at the ridiculous implication. How could he be with anyone else when was all he thought of was Selena?

He ran his fingers up her back until they found a home in her soft, auburn hair. In long movements, he resumed his exploration of her mouth. The pressure of their wet kisses intensified, matching the invigorating tempo of her hand. He was left gasping for air as she drove him closer to the edge, closer to collapsing on his weakening knees.

"Slow down," he rasped, grabbing her wrist.

"Something wrong?" Coyness laced her tone.

He shut his eyes, trying to temper his libido. For weeks, he'd waited to make love to her. He needed all the strength he could muster to give her the sexual gratification she had come to expect.

"Just been waiting too long for you."

He pulled her closer and blazed a path of kisses along her collarbone. As she arched in his arms, he sucked in a strangled breath. God, how he wanted to leave a visible mark on her neck—a mark that would brand her as his own. But then she'd have to hide it from her brother's menacing eyes. Devon would just have to find another way to claim her.

He tugged down her tight black dress, pinning her arms at her sides. Free of a bra, Selena's tantalizing breasts mesmerized him.

"You're *so* beautiful," he said as he lowered himself to his knees. His tongue circled one hardened nipple, and then the other. He pulled the smooth fabric farther down, past her arms and over her hips until it pooled around her ankles. He held her hips possessively, planting wet kisses on her stomach and across the top of her black lace panties. With the fabric pushed aside, he flicked the tip of his tongue over her clitoris, drawing moans and trembling sighs from her lips.

Her hands kneaded his shoulders as he stood and regained his balance. Leaning into him, she nestled her cheek into the curve of his neck. Her warm, ragged breaths traveled like waves across his skin, flaring his desire.

"Baby...make love to me," she whispered.

Oh, hell yes. Sweeping her into his arms, he headed down the hallway toward his king-size bed. No matter what tomorrow held in store for him, he'd make sure Selena knew how much he wanted her, how much he needed her, how much pleasure he was capable of giving her.

Even if it took him all night.

5

Breathe! C'mon, breathe! Rachel's panicked mind cried out as her lungs crumpled under the weight of the ocean. She was sinking fast. Inside, she screamed for help. A scream no one could hear. She scanned the milky water for something to cling to—a way to claw her way to the surface. Then she saw him. Her father dangling in the water. Head down, arms stretched out, he was a lifeless marionette puppet. He drifted closer and closer. The pounding in her head increased, the pain in her chest grew. She didn't want to see the horror, the death in his eyes. If she didn't breathe soon, she was going to drown and join him forever.

"No!"

Her voice rang in her own ears, jolting her back to reality. Her vision clouded, she took in her surroundings. Ticking mantel clock, pale-yellow walls, curved horseshoe chair, dragonflies on a linen shade. She was in her bedroom. In the cottage. Entrenched in a blue comforter. Perspiration dampened the navy tank top and boxers now twisted around her body. Through the screen of the second-story window drifted the sound of waves crashing on the beach, like slaps from Neptune. It brought her to her senses.

It was the dream. The gut-wrenching, recurring nightmare. Magnified tenfold by her exchange with Chase.

Rachel took a deep, cleansing breath. She held tightly to both sides of her neck, wishing she could simply squeeze away the images and dread that each morning brought. If only she could end the horrific thoughts, perhaps she could regain control over her life.

She climbed out of bed and tugged the covers back into place. Then she picked up a small box of fish food from the bureau and shook it once over the goldfish bowl before dragging herself into the bathroom.

Once showered and dressed, she headed downstairs and swung open the door of her compact fridge. A quart of milk bordering on expiration, a half-empty bottle of Chardonnay, a few individually wrapped slices of cheddar cheese. Nothing appetizing, just items to fill empty space.

She flipped through the mail stacked on the white, ceramic counter. Between the catalogs and utility bills appeared a postcard reminder for tomorrow's foundation board meeting. A gathering guaranteed to be even less thrilling than the contents of her refrigerator. All conversations undoubtedly would center on highlights from tonight's stuffy cocktail reception—Mayor Potter's canned dedication, the ladies' room gossip, and who should and, most vitally, shouldn't have been wearing what. No question, she'd be wise to upgrade her usual single-shot latte to a double today, just to prevent falling asleep in the middle of the celebration.

Scooping up her car keys, she forged toward the front door. She had just grabbed the knob when the phone rang. *Sorry folks, leave a message. Starbucks takes priority.*

Then again, it might be Devon. Assuming he could be bothered long enough to call her back.

The machine's beep broke into Rachel's thoughts, and a man's voice echoed through the room. "Rachel, I'm still trying to reach you."

She froze. Her heart contracted at the familiar tone. Her father's. But how—

"I'm going to be in town for a few days. If you don't mind, I'd really like to stop by. If you get this…just *please* return my call this time, OK?" A pause. "You have my number."

Slowly, her muscles relaxed as she realized it wasn't her father on the phone, haunting her from the grave. It was her Uncle Paul, her dad's brother. A walking ghost whose voice and face bore too much resemblance to Dad's for Rachel's comfort.

Shaking off the voice mail, she retrieved an engraved pill holder from her purse. She swallowed two aspirins and clicked the container shut. Her reflection beamed on the silver casing. Only a long, peaceful sleep—or pricey Botox injections—could erase the fine lines edging her hazel eyes. Neither one was a viable option. Thank goodness for Visine—magic in a bottle. It prevented mistaken assumptions at the office or, even worse, concerned inquiries.

She shouldered her purse and opened the front door as the phone rang again. Clearly, her uncle was determined. Another ring and the hypocrisy hit her. Who was she to criticize Devon for refusing to acknowledge calls from a family member?

Reluctantly, she picked up the phone and said hello.

"Rachel, it's Lao," the man replied. "I'm so glad I caught you."

She was so relieved that it took several seconds for his name to register. *Dr. Ying.*

On a monthly basis, he had made a point of checking up on her since her father's death. But the casual use of his first name this morning and his urgent tone were uncharacteristic.

"What can I do for you, Professor?" She hoped he wasn't going to take her question literally.

"Is there any possibility you could stop by the museum for a few minutes?" He sounded preoccupied, as if troubled by something greater than her denial of his grant application.

"Well, I guess I could delay my ten o'clock—"

"Good, good. Meet me in the maritime wing outside the new exhibit hall."

"Can you at least tell me—"

Click.

"Professor? Hello?" *Fabulous.* Why on earth hadn't she kept walking out the door? The last thing she needed was to borrow someone else's trouble.

Rachel hadn't misunderstood him. She was sure of it. A quick peek inside an adjacent room revealed gold chairs and floral decorations for the planned reception. But there was no sign of Dr. Ying anywhere. She walked the entire length of the maritime wing a second time. *I'll give him ten more minutes,* she told herself.

Glancing around, she tapped her hand against her thigh in a steady rhythm. Just then, a new display caught her attention. It was an enormous photograph of recovery operations in the shallow waters of Abu Qir Bay in Egypt. The underwater view of divers at work pulled her closer. She leaned in to skim the detailed description.

Fire had ignited gunpowder kegs in the hull of the *Akron* during a battle with the British fleet. Centuries later, divers had found part of the stern intact. They'd also found six bronze cannons and two casts brimming with glistening jewels. An ongoing dispute broke out between Egypt and France after evidence on board confirmed that Napoleon's flagship, *The Orient,* was involved in a renewed salvage attempt by the Quebec Maritime Development Company.

"Don't let the Canadian reference fool you."

Rachel's spine stretched. *Finally.* She spun around to face Dr. Ying.

"Local divers were instrumental in that world-renowned project," he added. "And the photograph over there..." He gestured with the black attaché case in his grip. "That's a bronze breech-loader from a Spanish galleon off the Florida Keys, another remarkable find."

Fascinating, if she was in the mood for a tour. Which she wasn't. But at least her concern over his wellbeing was alleviated. As she'd sped through traffic to get there, her mind had played out all kinds of scenarios, including the possibility of a break-in.

"Professor," she prompted. "Your call...was there something—"

"As you can see, this museum celebrates worldwide explorations. That's why a local landmark opportunity of this magnitude shouldn't be ignored." His tone, coupled with his stiff posture, was that of an attorney defending his case. And that's when she noticed the wall of images behind him. It was as though he had strategically positioned himself to mount an assault. Every photograph featured a salvage crew with its arsenal of toys: tugs, cranes, pulleys, winches.

Anger simmered as she realized why he had chosen this particular spot to meet. Perhaps it even explained why he'd given her plenty of time to explore. But the emotions she struggled to hold in check reached a boiling point as she spotted Chase's unmistakable profile in nearly every frame.

"So *this* is the reason I'm here," she fumed. She wanted to storm out of the museum, leaving the professor in her wake. But not before clarifying that another manipulative stunt like this would prompt her to recommend that the foundation completely disassociate itself with the museum. "In the future, Dr. Ying, I would appreciate—"

"Rachel, please..." The professor stepped toward her. "I understand how unprofessional this all seems. If I've demonstrated any impropriety, I do apologize."

"Duly noted, but I really don't have time for this today." She stepped around Dr. Ying and headed for the closest exit, immune to his persistent appeal.

"Under usual circumstances, my actions would seem irrational," he called out. "But since your father died while working on this project, I thought it only right that I come straight out and tell you the truth."

She froze, stunned by his words. She twisted around and glared at him. Desperation was obviously making the man crazy. He'd use any tactic to get his own way. "My father died while salvaging the *Griffin* wreck," she shouted back. "He didn't know anything about your ship. How could he? Chase just found it."

"Well, that's not entirely true."

What wasn't true?

Rachel stormed back to confront him. "My father's crew told the police they'd been working the same grid for six months. They were pulling up cables, machinery...shell casings. Are you telling me they all *lied*?"

"Not technically," he corrected. "You see, after the *Griffin* had been abandoned by other diving operations, Sam's company acquired exclusive salvage rights for that site. His men sat on it for six months to validate their claim. But even though your father's salvage rights were legal, they weren't the same as ownership rights. He was going to face multiple claims on the ship's contents and would have been lucky to end up with 10 percent at best."

Doc wasn't telling her anything new. His recap was only adding weight to her discontent.

"With his funds running out, Sam was planning to call it quits," he said. "Then he came across two remarkable discoveries:

the anchor chain belonging to an ancient ship and a passage in the ocean floor."

Passage? What the hell was he talking about?

"Sam was convinced it led to the *Wanli*. But even Chase wasn't fully aware of his suspicions. Chase was going to serve as Sam's eyewitness...someone to validate his findings. But then we lost Sam, and the investigation brought everything to a screeching halt." Dr. Ying glanced at Chase's photograph on the wall. "After I authenticated the lacquered piece he'd found, your father fully intended to share everything with you. He just wanted to wait until he was absolutely certain. Until he could substantiate his claim and prove himself a credible explorer."

No, Rachel thought, *he wanted to wait until I believed in him.*

Even after four years, the final argument she'd had with her father tore at her conscience. They'd been at it for days, avoiding each other, speaking only when necessary. He'd been packing his bag for a weeklong trip when the morning mail arrived. A past-due phone bill was all it took to break the silence and send Rachel over the edge.

"Why don't you go back to chartering?" she'd said, glowering from the hallway. "They're cutting back my hours at the institute. I can't keep bailing you out."

"So don't. I never asked for your help in the first place," he'd snapped.

"Then how are you going to keep the lights on? Who's going to pay for your fuel? I don't understand why you insist on deluding yourself. You're never going to come out ahead."

He'd zipped up his bag and then faced her. "It's a good thing Chase has faith in me. That's more than I can say for you."

"Maybe you never gave me a reason." She had held her mug in both hands, anticipating his verbal assault, but it never came. He'd picked up his duffel bag and swept past her. Still feeling the fight, she'd followed him outside. She'd watched him climb into Chase's black truck. As they'd pulled out of the driveway, her father had leaned forward in his seat.

"One day you'll regret those words," he'd called out. Then he was gone.

Dr. Ying opened his briefcase, pulling Rachel back into the museum—back into the treasure hunters' sanctum. He extracted a file and showed her drawings of the *Wanli II's* figurehead: a fierce dragon covered in gold leaf and preserved in resin for all posterity.

"Somewhere on board the ship is the gift Mai Le intended for her lover," Dr. Ying said. "According to ancient scrolls handed down by my grandfather, it was hidden in a handcrafted box disguised as a Chinese betrothal chest. After a thorough examination of the wood fibers and inscribed markings, there's no doubt in my mind. The lid your father found belongs to this box. The heart of the dragon must be hidden in the wreckage or buried somewhere close by."

Speaking rapidly to keep Rachel's attention, Dr. Ying told an astonishing tale about Mai Le's treasure. Before he was through, he added a surprising twist. "Prophecy foretells of a lion rescuing the dragon's heart. This is your destiny, Rachel," he pleaded. "Your chance to turn your father's dream into reality."

She looked around, weighing her options. There was nothing she wanted more than to mend the past—to earn her father's forgiveness and respect. But Dr. Ying had lied before. Why should she believe him now?

"It's been four years, Dr. Ying. Why hasn't anyone gone after the *Wanli II,* if it's actually there like you say?"

"Sam kept it a secret. No one knew where he was headed or what he was up to. That's not to say divers and salvagers haven't been in the same waters. But there haven't been any reports or claims filed. It wasn't till Chase came back and discovered the plate that this adventure began again."

Rachel glanced away for a moment. "I still don't understand my part in all of this."

"Find the ship and your father will receive his long-overdue reward. The museum will fund a permanent exhibition to honor his memory," he assured her. "Bring back the heart and you'll earn *your* place in history."

Her eyes returned to the *Orient*, a treasure ship still buried in debate. What if he was right? The ship's rotting remains were sitting on the ocean floor, just waiting to be raided, dismantled, and ruined. Yet as selfish and unprincipled as it seemed, her decision could end all the nightmares—it could finally put her father's memory to rest.

She needed time to digest everything, to feel confident in her answer. "I'll get back to you as soon as I can," she said.

"Please keep in mind," he implored, "time and secrecy are of the essence. The foundation you represent would, of course, have the first right of refusal for acquired assets through its capital investment. But controversy lies in the fact that this historical ship technically belonged to China. Due to the crew's tarnished reputation, however, Emperor Wanli denied knowledge of this ship. Thus, if it's found, it becomes an abandoned shipwreck, entitling the finder to a sizeable reward. My contacts in Shanghai have provided me with records and documents affirming its existence. However, the greatest challenge is locating adequate proof to validate a salvager's claim in federal court. That's what your father was focused on, what he had hoped to accomplish. My concern is that once word of this discovery spreads, potential investors and raiders will surface. Security will become a greater problem."

Rachel heaved a deep sigh. "I understand."

With each departing step, she evaluated the burden of her decision. If she stood firm in her present position, she might not only jeopardize the recovery of valuable artifacts, but she could potentially eliminate a tremendous funding source that could greatly benefit both the museum and the foundation.

There was also the local economy to consider. Every week, jobs were being eliminated—businesses were closing. Income from tourism and agriculture was on a steady decline. Over the past four months, the very home she lived in had dropped considerably in market value. Although she'd be forced to curb her anger and forthright convictions, her verdict could potentially change lives, create jobs, and restore community pride. It could turn San Palo into a thriving destination location. Yet one question remained. Could she put aside pride and work with Chase Cohen on a daily basis?

That question would keep her up most of the night.

6

"What the *hell's* wrong with you?"

Selena's voice invaded Devon's sleep. His eyebrows pinched together against the unforgiving glare of morning sun. The sight of her naked body beside him refreshed his memory of their sweat-soaked night together.

"Morning." He smiled and reached for her waist.

She smacked his arm. "Get your hands off."

Cute. He reached for her again and found the softness of a thigh. "You didn't seem to mind where I put my hands a few hours ago."

"Grow up." She scrambled out of the sheets and started throwing on her clothes. Evidently, dawn had again turned the coach into a pumpkin.

Devon rolled over and buried his face in a pillow, too tired to dissect the female psyche. It was a wonder Mars and Venus hadn't collided by now, breaking into a million floating and thoroughly confused fragments in space.

"I should have known better than to stick my nose into whatever scheme you've got going," she muttered.

Her words—about Gabe Pollero, about the rocky deal—slowly seeped into his brain. Neither sleep nor sex was going to happen now. He groaned into the encased goose down. "I told you, it's nothing you need to worry about."

"Oh yeah?"

"Yeah."

"Then why am I getting text messages from Bo Novak, asking me if *I'm* involved?"

Devon turned his head and noted the small cell phone clasped in her hand. "Who's Bo Novak?"

"He's one of my brother's goons, you idiot. And he says you flat-out stole their money. You'd better get your ass out of bed, unless you'd like Bo to do it for you."

Haze thinning, he sat up. The full impact of her claims hit him, sending his gaze toward the window. No cars, no armed mobsters. Yet.

He scanned his bedroom for his robe. No, jeans. Jeans were better. He reached for a wad of denim from the floor and pulled on his pants. "Are they on their way?" He struggled with the zipper.

In her black, knit dress, Selena bent down to buckle the straps on her sandals. "Just great, Dev. You're in a shitload of trouble, and now you've pulled me into it too."

That didn't answer the question. "I asked you if they're coming here," he reiterated.

"I have no idea. But you wanna know what I *do* know?"

Uh-oh. Here it comes.

Selena pulled on her shoulder bag and marched over to face him. He prepared for a smack, a scolding, a shove to move him aside. Instead, her simmering eyes met his.

"You lied to me."

Her voice bordered on a whisper. The hurt sparked an ache in his chest. Time to tell her the truth.

His hand reached out and cradled her cheek. "Selena…I'm sorry. But I can explain."

She shook her head, her jaw set. Without a word, she pulled away and headed down the hall.

"Baby, wait…" He followed behind and caught her arm as she reached the front door. "Just look at me. Give me a chance."

Eyes down, she slowly turned toward him. She paused before raising her gaze, as if she had to muster the effort. "You had your chance and you blew it." She spoke with conviction. "So you might as well get out of town while you still can. Because I don't ever want to see you again."

Her fervent expression held him in place, speechless. Never had their bickering—a form of foreplay, in his mind—carried such weight or delivered such a sting.

"Good-bye, Devon."

She walked out. And he let her. What choice did he have? She was right. He had lied. And he was certainly in a shitload of trouble.

If Devon wanted any chance of getting her back, he had to clean up the mess into which he'd been suckered. Ironically, she was the only reason he was in this spot. By agreeing to launder her brother's drug money in a single transaction and line his pockets with inflated returns, he had hoped finally to gain Pollero's acceptance. To openly pursue Selena without fearing retaliation from her brother.

Devon inhaled her perfume, which still lingered in the air. He wasn't about to give up on that dream. He caught a glimpse of the clock on the fireplace mantel across the room. Half past eight. Plenty of time to straighten out his life, if he hurried.

Foregoing a shower, he pulled a gray sweatshirt over his head. He tossed some essentials into a blue sports bag. He wasn't sure exactly how far his hunt would take him, but he was determined not to come back until he had his missing boss by the nape of his neck.

7

Even though the sun was dipping on the horizon, Chase insisted on maintaining their position. He lowered his binoculars and spat the stub of his well-chewed cigar toward the vessel anchored two hundred yards out. *Legend.* The ninety-foot rig carried a regal name and top-of-the-line equipment, but her crew was an unscrupulous bunch. Five years earlier, while working on the *Dorchester* site with Sam, the same men took them to court over salvage rights, robbing them of their landmark discovery. Now the bandits were back—challenging *Alegria*, which was hovering over the *Wanli's* buried remains.

"Fuckin' pikeys," Ian cursed for the hundredth time. "We're gonna lose the whole lot." He gripped the wheel of Chase's boat with both hands, his knuckles whitening.

"They'd have their ROV down, if they had any clue," Chase assured him, hoping and praying he was right. The caged robotic vehicle was still harnessed on their competitor's massive afterdeck. But once the ROV hit the ocean floor, their chances of finding something substantial would multiply.

"Perhaps you're right, mate. But the longer we sit here twiddlin' our thumbs, the sooner they'll be finding our gold."

"And what exactly do you propose we do? Blow them up?"

Ian cocked a bushy brow.

"Don't even think about it."

"Well, it's a sight better than baby-sittin' that fuckwit."

Chase shot a glance aft. He had no idea how much time had elapsed since Blaine's last dive, but he was bound to surface soon. "Whether you like it or not, that *fuckwit* is keeping my boat in the water." The words had barely left his mouth when a hand reached the top rung on the ladder. A pair of fins slapped the afterdeck. Chase wasn't prepared for the scowl that followed. Apparently, Blaine hadn't appreciated his nickname.

As Ian lifted the tank off their meal ticket's back, Chase perpetuated his ruse.

"Did you see that enormous, rare, blue-spotted manta ray Ian was telling you about?"

Blaine jerked the towel out of Chase's hand. He wiped his face and replaced his round coke-bottle glasses. "Just take me back," he ordered.

"Are you sure? We still got a tank left. It's bound to show up sooner or later."

"I've been hungry for over two hours," Blaine complained. Actually, it hadn't been more than an hour and a half since he first grumbled about going back for lunch. But there was no point in Chase correcting him. "If you want to get paid anytime soon, I'd suggest turning this boat around." He tossed the towel in a heap and dropped into the khaki folding chair. With his back to them, he appeared to be staring at rolling waves in the distance.

Chase moaned inside. They'd agreed to bring the kid along only to get their equipment out of hock and to cover fuel costs for another round trip. If everything had gone according to plan, by now he and Ian would be floating filled goody bags instead of waiting for pirates to ransack their treasure. As he caught another glimpse of *Legend*, Chase found himself fighting the urge to use the pipsqueak as a negotiable hostage.

Once the anchor was raised, Chase turned over the engines. He was about to throw the transmission into gear when an unlikely solution dawned on him. Angling toward Blaine, he posed the two-hundred-thousand-dollar question—the question that could revive their slackened salvage operation. "Say, kid. How'd you like to be part of a treasure hunt?"

Ian nearly launched out of the copilot seat. But Chase's scowl silenced him in nothing flat. After sinking back into the white vinyl chair, Ian folded his arms over his chest.

"Mmm..." Blaine's gaze had found something over Chase's shoulder. When he smiled and nodded his head, it appeared that the genius was putting two and two together. "So, you want me to join your expedition?" he asked.

Ian's laugh morphed into an exaggerated chuckle. "That's right. Pirates of the Caribbean..."

Chase blanketed Ian's discouraging pun. "This isn't a joke, Blaine. What I'm talking about is *real.* We got ourselves a renegade merchant ship that was secretly carrying a fortune in gold."

"So what's *this* going cost me?" Blaine asked.

Chase glanced at Ian. "With fuel, repairs, equipment—"

"How much, Mr. Cohen?"

"We'll probably need around eighteen for starters."

"Eighteen hundred? Shit...no problem."

"Thousand," Chase corrected.

"You don't say. Now that's a lot of change."

"But you can manage it, right?"

A moment of silence. "I suppose. And just what kind of dividend would I earn in all this?" Blaine arched a brow. "I mean if I were to bail you out, then wouldn't I deserve a nice share of the booty you'd be stealing out from under that starboard ship?"

The kid was a fast learner—in a scary sort of way. "What do you have in mind?" Chase said, already regretting the question.

"I'll put up thirty thousand. In exchange, I tag along for a week. Whether I'm here or not, I get 40 percent. Way I see it, that's more than fair."

"Are you out of yer fuckin' mind?" The words flew out of Ian's mouth before Chase had the chance to block them.

"Only seems right if I'm covering the majority of your costs. Eventually, you're going to need new dive gear, hookahs, and a side scanner. And word has it you trashed your compressor, so your blowers are down. Might have to add an extra 10 percent to replace that." The kid had the same high-stakes poker smile that Chase had seen on the game show network. Their fish was quickly turning into a major asshole, a wheeling-and-dealing asshole. Still, 50 percent of something was better than nothing. Especially if it meant beating *Legend's* crew in a race to the federal courthouse.

Chase slid the throttle to full open and headed for the harbor. "Meet me at the dive shop tomorrow morning at seven and bring along your checkbook," he called out. "You're going to need it."

Ian's head dropped. He hugged his middle, as though he'd been socked in the gut. He did not relax his arms until they finally entered the harbor. "Can't believe you're doin' this," he huffed under his breath, out of Blaine's earshot.

"What choice do I have?" Chase's rhetorical question hung in the air. In reality, the "bail out" would cost closer to fifty thousand dollars. No one, including Blaine, was going to fork over that amount. He remained silent as he eased his boat into the first empty slip.

While Ian secured the lines to the dock, Blaine delved out six crisp one hundred dollar bills. "That takes care of today. See you tomorrow."

Chase stared at the cash in his palm. He was amazed how the kid had pulled the rolled stash out of his backpack as though it was chump change before walking away. With a long look at the now closed dive shop, Chase regretted not coming back sooner.

"You can always change yer mind, ya know," Ian offered.

Chase knew that wasn't the case. Without financial backers and a steady flow of greenbacks, they were only postponing the inevitable. And time was quickly becoming their greatest enemy. In two more weeks, if he didn't find something worthwhile, he might as well take up residence on the ocean floor.

"Hey, fish bait," Ian called out, just as Blaine rounded the last dock. "Where's yer plane?"

"Oh, that," he returned. "It was a charter. The pilot should be back in Bremerton by now."

Chase was in the midst of stowing his gear when he noticed Dr. Ying rapidly approaching along the dock. "Doc," he called out. "What are you doing here?"

The professor slowed, apparently searching for a clear path around yellow-bibbed fishermen battening down their hatches. He dodged plastic bait buckets, piled nets, and rope lines strewed across the walkway. Chase was about to commend Dr. Ying's sure-footedness, when his visitor stumbled and nearly fell on the dock's uneven planking.

"Mr. Cohen, I'm so glad I found you," he said. "I wanted to give this to you before it got too late."

Chase accepted the white envelope from the professor's wrinkled hand. He tore it open and read the contents. "I don't understand. Why are you giving this invitation to me?"

"I know you had no initial interest in the cocktail reception this evening, but under the circumstances, I think it's vital you attend."

"Circumstances?"

"Miss Lyons will be there. She's in the process of lending her support."

Chase widened his eyes. "She's giving us the grant money?"

"Not officially, but that could change after this evening. I need you to assure her that you're an honorable man."

In another lifetime, maybe. "Doc, if her decision to hand over free cash hinges on her impression of my honor, then you need to find a printing press…and fast."

"Are you telling me you can't be trusted?"

Under present conditions, the insinuation seemed to fit. Honesty had become a matter of degree.

"I'm telling you that no matter what I say to Rachel Lyons, she'll never believe me."

"Well, perhaps you need to find another voice. I'll expect to see you tonight, Mr. Cohen. That is, if you're still interested in finding the *Wanli II* before its whereabouts are disclosed to another salvage company."

Chase's jaw tightened. For a brief moment, he chewed on an unsavory thought. Had the professor already placed a call to the *Legend's* wheelhouse, providing the treasure ship's coordinates? The little bit of common sense he had left suddenly returned. After exchanging information with Doc for more than five years, he knew that a handshake was a binding contract. Still, he had no idea how the guy was going to take news of a third party being added to their agreement. Especially one whose hands were plunged deeply into both of their pockets.

"Hog-tied or not, he'll be there." Ian's voice came from behind. "I'll even loan him a clean shirt."

No way. The last person in the world he wanted to see tonight was Rachel. He didn't appreciate Ian's contribution—not in the least. Chase huffed a sign of frustration and scanned the invitation, seeking a justified out. "You have a monkey suit to go with that? 'Cause I sure as hell don't."

"Oh, I think we could manage to round one up," Ian replied.

"Thanks a lot," Chase mumbled. As he watched the professor weave his way toward the parking lot, he realized that he'd have to come up with a good excuse for blowing off the party. He flung the invitation at Ian. "What's got into you? Why would I ever go to this stupid thing? Rachel's never going to give in. At least I know where we stand with Blaine."

Ian's silence and furrowed forehead said it all: they were dealing with a kid who could very well take them for every cent, if they weren't paying close attention. But Chase had never been the kind of person who needed to sell himself to anyone, least of all a member of the female gender. They had always come willingly and with predictable expectations, and he'd never failed to deliver. Well, at least before Rachel Lyons screwed with his head.

"OK. I admit I shouldn't have gone along with boy wonder," Chase conceded. "But just how am I supposed to get Rachel to change her mind?"

Ian pulled his cap on backward and smiled. "You wouldn't be askin' yers truly for advice on talkin' to a fine lady, now would ya?"

Before Chase could reply, Ian smacked his back. "C'mon, Cap'n. We got work to do."

As Chase followed Ian down the dock, he rationalized. He *did* win her over once. Who's to say he couldn't do it again? Besides, by getting Rachel out of his system once and for all, he'd know for sure that leaving her wasn't the worst decision he'd ever made in his life...it was just an unavoidable one.

8

Rachel had been in her office since dawn, making calls and repeating her spiel to board members all over town. She double-checked her tally: four voting yes, four leaning toward no, and one undecided. Dear Megan Van Dozer. If Rachel didn't win the trenchant woman over by tomorrow's 10:30 a.m. meeting, she might as well kiss her father's potential honor and recognition goodbye.

Chase's history wasn't making the time-consuming process any easier, either. One scan of his file confirmed what Rachel had already surmised. Although he had an amazing gift for recovering the "unattainable," exorbitant expenses had nearly wiped out his amassed income. With full-time salaries for four crew members, workmen's comp insurance, busted equipment, and long-term legal battles, it was remarkable that his business had survived as long as it had.

Evidently, he was as thoughtless with his management dealings as he was with his personal relationships.

Rachel slipped out of her seat and walked into the next office. "Marcy, do we have any more information on Trident Ventures?"

The sturdy administrative assistant was an invaluable asset. She'd been with the firm since its inception. Although she now was spending a good portion of her time bringing the new president up to speed, she had the remarkable ability to pinpoint the exact location of virtually anything within the building's stone walls.

"Let me think," she replied, resting a hand on her desk. "If memory serves, there's another Trident folder in the storage room's file cabinet."

Oh, great. Rachel had no desire to wander past Tom Nash's open doorway. Over the last three weeks, he had seemed to materialize everywhere: at Starbuck's, Kinko's, and the San Palo Library. Yet with the founder's recent passing and his only heir's new promotion, she was hard-pressed to avoid the executive director. In order to pay off the loans she had cosigned for her father, she had no choice but to dig her heels into her job assiduously and disregard Nash's persistent advances.

"Is there any chance you could bail me out here?" Rachel asked Marcy. "I've got to get my report finished before tomorrow morning."

Marcy pointed at the volumes stacked on her desk. "Wish I could help you, but I don't know how I'm going to get through this as it is. Mr. Nash is leaving for Atlantic City in the morning and wants a summary of discretionary expenditures by the end of the day. Maybe Vern could help you. I think I saw him getting off the elevator on the third floor."

The combatant clerk from the mailroom would no doubt find Rachel's request absurd. He'd throw himself on top of his rolling cart to save it from an earthquake rather than abandon his deliveries.

Rachel took a moment to strategize her approach before half-sprinting down the long, carpeted hallway. The architectural renderings, cityscapes, and board members' photos lining the walls became an innocuous blur. She slowed as she neared Tom's office at the end of the corridor. Finding it empty, she blew out the breath she'd been holding and commended her excellent timing. However, her victory was short-lived. As she stepped around the corner, her stalker materialized inside the opening elevator doors.

You've got to be kidding me.

"Good morning, Rachel." Nash grinned and ran his hand over his wavy brown hair.

"Mr. Nash." She smiled politely and then continued on her way.

Why did the storage room have to be so far away? She passed three more doors before she realized that Tom was hurrying to catch up with her.

"That's a pretty outfit you have on today," he offered, now matching her stride.

Rachel glanced down at her ivory linen suit, forgetting she'd already dressed for the reception. "Thank you." She considered reciprocating with a compliment, but then dismissed the notion, realizing it would only encourage him. She sensed his dark eyes on her profile, but willed herself to concentrate on the beige-speckled carpeting stretching out before her.

Together, they veered down another passageway, and still she made no effort at small talk. Yet the man remained undaunted in his pursuit. "Are you going to the reception tonight?" he asked.

Rachel shrugged. "I was planning to, but I have a lot work to finish up before the meeting tomorrow."

"Well, if you don't mind, I'd really like you to be there."

She studied him for a moment, struggling to keep her eyes from narrowing. "Why's that?"

"I have a dinner meeting this evening and a flight early tomorrow morning. I need you to go in my place."

"But aren't there other board members attending?"

"Possibly...but it doesn't change the fact that you're the best person to represent the foundation. The mayor will be there, and Professor Ying would certainly appreciate your making the effort."

Rachel came to an abrupt stop before the open storage room.

"So, can I count on you?" he asked.

"Sure," she said, nodding. "I'll be here if you need anything else, Mr. Nash."

He took a few steps away and then halted. "And Rachel, if you don't mind, it's *Tom*. I've never been a big fan of formalities."

She held onto the doorknob and forced a weak smile. "Right." She waited for him to continue on his path before she ducked inside. "Phew."

After palming the wall for a switch, she flipped it, illuminating the stuffy space. A pair of lights illuminated an old portrait hanging on the wall: Warren Nash, the quirky Texas oil baron who had relocated to Los Angeles, bringing his millions with him. She'd never officially met Tom's grandfather, but shortly after she was hired, she received a handwritten letter from him encouraging her to spend his money wisely. Time would tell if his grandson intended to continue Warren Nash's conservative practices.

Well, as far as finalizing grants was concerned, anyway.

At the wall of metal file cabinets, she opened the S-T drawer and rifled through the crowded files. Trident's folder was nowhere in sight. She picked up the phone and was about to buzz Marcy when another option came to mind. She pulled out a closed-case drawer and discovered a file hand-labeled "Cohen." After tugging it free, Rachel considered returning to her office, however, that could mean another encounter with Tom. She opted for the bare wooden table and chair stationed beside her. Once settled, she spread out the contents of Chase's folder: information on his boat, endorsement letters, his personal resume, newspaper clippings in all shapes and sizes. After scanning them thoroughly and making notes about his misadventures for more than an hour, her heavy lids dropped.

She rested her chin on her arm, intending to close her eyes for only a few minutes. But the warmth in the room seduced her, drawing her back under the ocean. She was breathing on her own—without a mask or regulator. Completely weightless, with no sense of linear time. Through the murky water, an image came into view: a wet suit, rapidly approaching. But strangely, she felt no apprehension, no overwhelming fear. No need to escape. The second she recognized Chase, he reached for her face. His lips were on hers, soft yet demanding. They locked on hers in a passionate kiss. Although her mind told her that it was utterly impossible, that she should flee for her life, Rachel never wanted the sensation to end.

She never wanted to wake up.

"Rachel."

A man's deep voice startled her awake. Her clouded vision fell on the silver-haired man standing in the doorway.

"It's Uncle Paul. I was told you were in here."

As he stepped further into the room, she inwardly cringed. His resemblance to her father was uncanny. Disturbingly so.

"I haven't been able to reach you at home, so I thought I'd take a chance in coming here instead."

Rachel swallowed hard. *Why is he here?* She struggled to find her voice, but shame from avoiding him had stolen it. Gripping the top of the desk, she debated what to do. She wanted to get up and edge her way out of the room. Bolt from any remnants of her guilt-ridden past.

"This is a pretty big place," he continued, taking a seat in an adjacent chair. "You could get lost here."

"Unfortunately, I'm...just about to head out." She closed the file and rose to her feet. "Maybe we could do this another time?"

Paul Lyons reached out, placing his warm hand on her forearm. "This will only take a moment. I promise."

Rachel slowly lowered herself and lifted her chin. At the sight of his brown, soul-piercing eyes, she forced a dry swallow.

"I can't imagine how difficult this whole situation's been for you...with your dad and his accident. Not to mention the police investigation that went on for months. You would think after living in this community for so many years..."

She was painfully aware that he was hardly telling her anything new. When her father's financial shortfalls came to light, an investigative reporter from the *Gazette* saw an opportunity to make a name for himself. He stirred up the township with ridiculous theories ranging from foul play to suicide. The idea that insurance was a possible motive was nothing short of ludicrous, especially with her father's history of overdue bills and lapsed policies. But worst of all, the medical examiner had listed the cause of Sam's sudden cardiac arrest as equipment failure, and it had been Chase's job to make sure that the dive gear was working properly.

"Are you managing all right?" Paul's question invaded her thoughts. "Before I left for London, I know you insisted on handling your father's affairs, but there's no reason I couldn't pitch in now and—"

"I'm just fine. Really. There's no need to worry about me." She lowered her eyes to his conservative black suit. Belated bereavement attire.

"Yes, of course, you're right. Although I wasn't able to attend the funeral, your dad would never forgive me for not looking out for you now." He layered his arms across his chest, giving the impression he was preparing for a lengthy visit.

Too little, too late. She pressed her hands in her lap, willing him to walk out of her life, just like everyone else had. Just like her absentee mother, Allison Lyons, had years earlier. Even though the pretty former stewardess had had two young children at home, she'd grown disenchanted with her life. She'd cheated with a number of men before disappearing. Word had reached her father three months later that Allison was living in Alberta, Canada, with a corporate attorney who had three kids of his own. Although she'd continued to send birthday cards and impractical gifts over the years, she had never acknowledged the message Rachel left regarding Sam's death. She had never returned Rachel's phone call.

The bitter memory lifted Rachel's eyes. "Uncle…there's really no reason to keep you. I'm sure you've got more pressuring matters to attend to."

He angled a discerning look. "Well, I know you're busy. I suppose I should get to the point of why I'm here."

Finally.

He reached for Rachel's hand and placed a set of keys in her palm. "I had a time convincing the new owner to part with her, but I know this is what your dad would have wanted."

She drew her hand back and stared down at the gift, puzzled by his gesture.

"They're for *Stargazer*," he clarified.

Rachel stared at him in astonishment. Without question, he was talking about her father's106-foot motor yacht, outfitted with every possible amenity. Teak, polished brass, all the gauges and marine instruments her father could buy on credit. If it hadn't been repossessed years earlier and reclaimed from the auction block by her uncle, she wouldn't have hesitated to sell the grandiose toy that had come between them.

"When the time is right, you and Devon should take her out on the water. Spread your dad's ashes in the place he loved most."

Pressure was building behind her eyes. She struggled to stay focused, to keep her whirling emotions in check. "I…I don't know how to thank you. It's an incredible gesture, Uncle Paul, but it's just *way* too much and—"

"It's nothing. I'm just sorry it took me so long to get this handled. Between my trips abroad and personal obligations… anyway, she's back where she belongs. Maybe you can even put a crew together and come visit me sometime."

Rachel nodded appropriately. When her uncle stood, she pushed herself upright. She pressed her arms around him in response to his hug. After he disappeared through the open doorway, she blew out a guarded breath and looked down at the menacing metal warming her palm. Without hesitating, she tucked her anguish into a coat pocket.

For another time.

After returning Chase's file to the drawer, she collected her belongings and made her way back to her cramped office. She had just sat down at her desk when Marcy appeared in the open doorway.

"I hate to tell you this," she said, "but your undecided vote called and left a message. It seems that Mrs. Van Dozer plans to vote against your funding request tomorrow."

Rachel blew out a huff. *Great.* That's all she needed. Another complication. But never had she willingly backed down from a challenge, even a sizeable one. By her estimate, she had just enough time to assemble her notes and primp before cornering Megan at the reception. If she failed to sway the woman's decision, there was every reason to believe Dr. Ying's grant would be shelved permanently. All evidence would be tucked away and forgotten in the storage room's dusty file cabinet. With her obligation completed, the adventure into which she'd been involuntarily drawn would come to an abrupt, anticlimactic end.

9

By the time Chase arrived, the swanky party was in full swing. He snagged a sparkling flute from a passing tray and scoped out the museum's bustling arena. The floor was in perpetual motion. Tuxedos and cocktail dresses wove in and out, heads turned and bobbed, drinks flowed. Music wafted under the constant, respectable roar of conversation.

Chase approached a small gathering of jewel-encrusted matrons. His broad smile was met with blank questioning stares. After maneuvering around them and shaking a few hands, he glimpsed Dr. Ying in the crowd. He intended to assure Dr. Ying that Rachel's reluctance to work with him would be handled with his helmsman's capable assistance but, unfortunately, Ned Daniels intercepted him.

The stout, curly-haired waiter was balancing two trays while random hands reached around him, snatching assorted appetizers. "Man, never thought I'd see you here," Ned said.

"Me either." Chase took a sip from his champagne glass and instantly remembered how much he hated the stuff. He set it down and noted the growing line in front of the "gentleman's" bar. "So how'd *you* get roped into this?"

"My tight-ass aunt got me the job," Ned said. "Thinks everyone should earn their own way. Even if you're going to school and already got three jobs."

Chase was briefly distracted by a curvy blonde's inviting smile. "Sure glad she's your relative and not mine."

"You should be. She's a real bitch. Been barking orders all night, like she's in charge or something."

Know that feeling. Chase smiled. If not for Ian's bullying antics, he wouldn't have bothered to come. He stretched his neck, resuming his search for Ying. But Doc had already moved on—cornering a hot, Hispanic beauty. Or was it the other way around?

Chase relaxed his shoulders. He glanced back at his brooding friend. "Say, Ned, you wouldn't happen to know if Rachel Lyons is here, would you?"

"Actually, I do. She and my aunt have been in the main hall next to that Oriental picture for almost an hour." He tossed his head toward the bend in the room. "Can't image how she's managed to put up with Aunt Meg's crap as long as she has." His eyes dropped to the remaining cheese puffs on his tray. "Vultures," he grumbled. As soon as there was an opening, he squirreled out of sight.

Following his lead, Chase headed in the opposite direction. The farther he got from the bar, the louder the music grew. As he rounded a corner, the fresh view stopped him in his tracks. Overhead, the intricate ceiling was at least forty feet off the floor. Massive metal arches spanned the two hundred-foot span. The combination of metal and glass was ingenious, creating the overall effect of a domed amphitheater with an indoor terrarium and three winding, balcony floors.

On the main level, dozens of alcoves lined the walls, housing flickering candles, sculpted figurines, vases, and pottery—rare, exotic artifacts like the ones he'd seen in *Archeology Today*. His eyes traveled past the blaring quartet, above the bobbing dance floor to the enormous mural at the far end of the room. *The Great Wall of China.* The winding fortification had been impervious to attack, protecting anointed warlords for centuries. Even though Chase's extensive research had dispelled the myth that dying laborers had been added to the wall's mortar mix, the horrific possibility still captured his imagination.

As he glanced around, absorbing the soaring ceiling, the brilliant artwork, the bamboo floor, and the luminous architecture, it suddenly occurred to Chase that Doc's impressive renovation had to have been in the works for years. Perhaps Sam's initial discovery had inspired it.

Chase pulled the starched collar away from his neck. He pondered his enormous and arduous task. The job of filling this place truly belonged with a dozen fully equipped salvage teams, but his past association with the professor had afforded him the honor. He swallowed hard, his tongue thick. He noticed another bar close by and plunged deep into the heavy masses.

"Aren't you Chase Cohen?" a gray-haired gentleman in line asked.

Chase nodded. He wasn't up for idle conversation tonight.

"Word has it you found sunken treasure. That right?"

Suddenly, all eyes in the line were glued on him. The local gossip apparently had been spreading faster than he and Ian had anticipated. The last thing they needed were boatloads of treasure-seekers filling the harbor.

"Sure," he finally said. "About twenty dollars' worth of scrap metal and rusty pop cans so far."

There was nodding and a humming consensus before all of the heads turned away again. Everyone's except that of the pretty blonde he'd noticed earlier. Her smile grew with the intensity of her blue eyes. The slick guy at her side appeared to be entranced by the female bartender's micro skirt until he noticed the focus of his date's interest. His possessive paw clamped onto her arm, drawing her attention back. An angry, muffled backlash soon followed. In the past, Chase would have stepped in, but as he watched the couple exchange expletives, he realized that they were perfectly paired. They simply added color to the otherwise mundane crowd.

When the band's jazzy rendering came to an abrupt end, so did Chase's interest. Dancers dispersed in all directions, allowing him an unobstructed view of something far more appealing than anything else in the room.

Rachel. His heart skipped a beat. Her long, wavy, brown hair was twisted up in an elegant fashion, exposing the tempting curve of her neck. The tailored jacket she wore was molded to her sleek, athletic figure, and even though her midlength skirt concealed the best view of her long, trim legs, he had to admit that the beige stilettos rekindled his active imagination. She stood near the wall rigidly, with her arms crossed over her breasts, intense concentration narrowing her eyes. From the looks of it, Ned Daniel's aunt seemed to be doing most of the talking. No surprise, given her nephew's snide assessment.

Chase surrendered his place in line. He edged his way around the dance floor, shielding himself behind a curtain of faceless people. He waited a safe distance away for an opportune moment to interrupt, but witnessing a heated exchange hadn't been part of his plan.

"I *know* we keep going round and round." Rachel grumbled. "But for the last eight months, I've given away more than six million dollars to civic programs, charities...high-efficiency energy companies. I know Dr. Ying's new application doesn't meet our normal criteria. But Mr. Nash wanted us to use his money in a positive way. This project could bring life back into our community."

The rangy woman across from her snorted before rolling her dull eyes. "You above anyone should know what a losing venture this could turn out to be."

"What exactly is *that* supposed to mean?" Rachel's voice lifted. "If you're referring to my father again, then all I can say to you is—"

"Well, ladies," Chase cut in, "what a nice surprise. Might I add how beautiful you both look tonight?"

Rachel released an audible huff, but he paid her no mind. "Dr. Ying has sure out done himself, hasn't he?" he continued. "Never expected anything like this."

Apparently, idle conversation wasn't on Rachel's agenda. "If you would excuse me, there's something important I need to attend to." She stepped away, accepting a cocktail from a passing waiter.

Chase rubbed his jaw. *Important, huh?* He glimpsed the badly aged woman poised before him—a former actress whose expiration date had long passed. Her black, form-fitting dress begged for attention, but her beady brown eyes bore down on whoever drew near.

"Don't believe we've officially met. Chase Cohen." He offered a warm smile and his hand, but her lackluster reaction had him quickly retracting both.

"So *you're* Cohen." She sniffed and pulled a tissue from her small handbag. She dabbed it under her pointy nose before readdressing him. "I'm Megan Van Dozer. I've been hearing about you *all* night."

"Oh, really?" He spotted Rachel mingling with a group of partygoers a short distance away. When their eyes finally met, a tiny curl formed on the corner of her mouth. She was apparently enjoying his discomfort, and for some weird reason, he didn't mind.

Megan emptied her half-filled glass in one swallow. She waved it in the air at her encumbered nephew, as if summoning a lowly servant. Ned nodded his head while balancing his glass-filled tray, but the scowl on his face told Chase that he wouldn't be returning anytime soon.

"I'm going to tell you straight out, Mr. Cohen," she said. "I've been living here all my life. I don't believe in ridiculous fairy tales and I sure as hell don't appreciate folks in this town telling me what I should or shouldn't do." Her narrowed eyes were fixed on Rachel. "So if you've come here thinking you could sway my vote—"

"Do what?" Chase lifted a brow. "Mrs. Van Dozer, that honestly never occurred to me." Not until that moment at least. "I actually came over here to ask you to dance. But if you'd prefer that I just move on..."

"Dance? With me?" Her hand clutched the diamond necklace dangling from her leathery neck. "I...I haven't danced in years."

He could feel the weight of Rachel's eyes on him from across the room. "Then all the more reason." He hooked his arm through Megan's and steered her through the crowd to the edge of the dance floor.

"This is totally unnecessary," she said. "There's lots of other women here I'm sure you'd prefer spending time with."

He flashed a counterfeit smile. "If that was true, I would have asked one of them."

A smile lifted the corners of her plump red lips. "Well, I suppose one quick dance wouldn't hurt." She extended her right hand and draped her left arm over his shoulder.

Chase waited for dancers to pass by. He slipped between them, step-close-stepping. Swaying and whirling her about. Megan managed to keep up with him with surprisingly little effort. But then the music changed tempo. It picked up speed and morphed into a rollicking swing number.

Chase froze in place. He anticipated Megan's adamant protest, but instead, she smiled and nodded agreeably. She slipped her purse chain over one arm and reclaimed his hand.

You asked for it. Chase led her footwork, turning and spinning this way and that. With reckless abandon, he tested their limited boundaries, flinging Megan from one end of the dance floor to the other. Back and forth, they twirled and twisted. Kicking, sliding, jumping. Colliding into couples with every forward pitch. The open space around them grew larger as besieged performers surrendered their positions.

Megan's cackles and sweaty palms proved no detriment as he directed their unorthodox display. By the end of the lengthy number, a crowd had gathered and was enthusiastically clapping. Megan wobbled about, clutching her chest. Someone offered to fetch a glass of water, but she refused, preferring champagne. She gulped down two servings before signaling for a refill.

Meanwhile, Chase's interest stretched elsewhere. The only person he'd hoped to impress was now nowhere in sight. *Where the hell did she go*? Rachel had probably found some dark corner, convinced he'd come this evening to further humiliate her.

A persistent tap on his shoulder brought his attention back to the wild-eyed matron at his side.

"You're quite the dancer, aren't you?" Megan puffed. She drew another ragged breath and smoothed the side of her frizzy brown hair.

"Only with the right partner," he said, humoring her. He pulled at his sweaty collar and looked beyond her, longing for the right moment to escape.

"You know board members aren't supposed to fraternize with potential clients. Conflict of interest and all that," she claimed. "But I have to admit, it's a good thing we met this evening."

"And why's that?"

"You're an attractive young man. I have something you want. With a little imagination, we just might come up with a mutually beneficial arrangement."

His eyes swung back with astonishment. "Sorry…what did you say?"

Megan's hand gripped his forearm. "You know…a little prodding in all the right places." Her brow inched up a fraction.

Chase tendered a weak smile. "Sounds painful."

She snorted a laugh, drawing the attention of a nearby couple. With her senses restored, she leaned in closer and lowered her voice. "I don't mind helping my *special* friends." She looked up at him through heavily lashed eyes.

He could feel his dry throat constricting. *Are you kidding*? His vision dropped to the woman's glittery, gold shoes. They were as blaring and ostentatious as the woman herself was. He glanced up at her again, unsure of what to say.

"I have a room at the Ambassador," she persisted. "If you want my support, meet me there in twenty minutes."

His thoughts scrambled for a foothold. An escape route from the B-rated movie he'd fallen into.

She reached into her purse and extracted a plastic card. She held it out before him. "Take the green elevator to the penthouse," she instructed. "And make sure to park your car on one of the side streets."

The fog in his brain cleared. He took a step back and lifted his hand, rejecting her offer. "Sorry, but I have a previous engagement. Maybe we could do this another time?"

Her face scrunched. "Go fuck yourself," she hissed.

Whoa! Chase took a step back. The woman was obviously nuts. He turned away to escape and ran straight into a tall, distinguished stranger.

"Excuse me," Chase said.

"General Van Dozer. Don't believe we've met."

A multitude of ribbons and medals adorned the old soldier's uniform. A red-handled saber was strapped to his side. His sudden appearance left Chase stunned, intimidated, and grateful at the same time. He looked down at the man's meaty palm, extended in his direction, and realized that cooperation was the best policy.

"Chase Cohen. It's nice to meet you, sir," he said. A silent nod came in return.

Chase excused himself as quickly as possible and found a crowded, noisy corner. As a tray passed by, he snagged a drink and threw it back in seconds flat. He watched from a safe distance as the officer glowered and glared at Megan. By all appearances, she steadfastly refused to look his way. It wasn't long before he pressed his eccentric wife through the gathering, departing without so much as a backward glance.

With his dilemma now resolved, Chase resumed his search for Rachel. Off to his left, he caught sight of her ivory jacket. She was skirting around the crowd, making a beeline for the closest exit. He hurried after her and flung open the metal door. Soft moonlight illuminated the walkway and captured her near the top of the stairs, leading to the rear parking lot.

"Rachel, wait up! I need to talk to you." He reached out for her elbow, but she surprised him by spinning around. Her green eyes flashed, reminding him that this new unpredictable Rachel was easily angered and slow to forgive. "If this is about Mrs. Van Dozer, I can tell you—"

She shook her head and heaved an impatient sigh. "How long were you planning to keep your secret hidden?"

What? Devon was here? He chose tonight to tell her? Like a foul ball, her accusation came from out of nowhere, knocking Chase for a loop. After all this time, Devon had finally spilled the beans. He'd told her the real reason Chase had left town so suddenly after Sam died. No wonder she was so upset. It would take more than fancy footwork to get himself out of this mess. That was for sure.

"So, no explanation, huh?" she charged. "Honestly, Chase, do you realize whatever you find on this project can be confiscated? The state can take everything you own?"

He shook his head, trying to make sense of it all. Rachel was traveling on a different track. His challenge was in figuring out which one. "What are you talking about?"

"Your rights to the *Wanli*...or rather your *lack* of them."

How'd she find out? He considered asking that very question when his attention was drawn to a redheaded guy in the parking lot. *Skylar Zane.* He was revving the engine in his black Beemer. Chase had no idea *Legend's* captain had attended the event or why he would be here in the first place. For years, the cunning bastard had plagued Chase's life—dating the women he knew, buying up supplies he'd ordered, showing up in restaurants where he'd stopped to grab a bite. More than once, Chase had spotted him dropping anchor off his starboard bow, as if knowing the exact location of his dives. It was as if the man was trying to steal his life!

When their eyes met, Skylar's devil-may-care smile left Chase's stomach churning. At the creep's side sat the same flirtatious woman he'd seen in Doc's company an hour earlier. Only now, she was cuddling and nuzzling against Skylar's thick neck. Something smelled badly as they drove off, and it wasn't gas fumes or the drifting odor of day-old fish.

"Chase!" Rachel snapped.

He looked back at her and found her to be particularly annoyed. Her arms were crossed, her nostrils slightly flared. Her right hip was braced against the handrail. "Are you going to deny it's true?"

He remained silent, wondering if Zane and his female conspirator had come here to discredit him.

"Well?"

His eyes brushed over her lips. "No matter what you think, Rachel, I'm not stupid. I've already contacted a lawyer regarding our claim. But you can't get exclusive rights until you have valid proof."

"But what about the plate you found and the wooden lid Dr. Ying had analyzed?"

"Not enough. The plate has no markings and that piece of wood you're talking about came out of a junk shop."

"Really? Then how am I supposed to present your case when it's all based on conjecture?"

"I just need a little more time, is all."

"For what?" She huffed.

"To get in a few more dives."

"Oh, you'll have plenty of time for that after tomorrow."

"Just what is that supposed to mean?"

"The board approves grants twice a year," she said. "Tomorrow at 10:30 a.m., they're expecting me to defend your reputation, your credibility, and your legal rights. Even if you kiss Mrs. Van Dozer's backside a hundred times, it wouldn't matter. You can't claim to own something that doesn't belong to you."

Just like her. His eyes fell to the ground. Even though it had been the hardest decision he'd ever made, he'd had no choice but to leave town. It was the only way to keep his past hidden. To protect the love they shared. She never would have understood. Just like she didn't now.

"I don't know if my father was simply a dreamer," she said, recapturing his attention. "Or if given time, he would have found his fortune in gold. The only thing I do know for certain is that he always played by the rules."

Chase clenched his fists at his sides. "And you think I don't?" His voice rose. "We're talking about a stupid piece of paper. A claim that vultures like Zane couldn't care less about."

She looked away, shaking her head. She bounded down the stairs and then froze on the last step, as if having second thoughts.

"Rachel..."

She looked back up at him. "I don't even know why you're here. Maybe you should cut your losses and go back to wherever you came from."

Her callous words slammed into his gut. Scorched the last thread of hope he'd held out for her. He watched with blurred vision as she continued on her way, her heels clicking purposefully across the pavement. Heading toward her car at the end of the dark parking lot. Leaving him behind, more angry and frustrated than ever.

Damn it! What happened to the woman he loved? The spunky, fun-loving mermaid who never let anything stand in her way? Only the polished, hollow shell remained. He jerked the tie from his neck and shoved it into his coat pocket, knowing deep down inside that he was to blame.

As he rounded the corner of the museum, he heard Rachel's car peel off, and found himself wondering why he had bothered to come here. Why, given the chance, he hadn't lied to her about his admiralty claim. With one condemning look and one nullifying question, she had left him questioning his values, his beliefs. His self-worth.

Throughout his life, Chase had had to vie for approval. He had never measured up in school. He had paid his dues to earn respect from the men with whom he surrounded himself. Yet the opinion of one woman could topple his world and ruin the dream of a lifetime. Chase closed his eyes and shook his head. Rachel Lyons or not, he simply had too much on the line to walk away.

One moment Rachel was reaching for her car door handle, the next a damp cloth covered her nose and mouth. She kicked wildly, blasting muffled screams.

Still the stranger held tight. She twisted desperately trying to free herself, trying to see the face of her attacker. But the man's muscular arms tightened more firmly around her, pinning her thrashing body against his bulky frame.

Why is this happening?

A sweet, intoxicating scent filled her nostrils. She struggled to keep from inhaling, but the next breath turned her brain into mush. Strength drained from her arms. Her knees shook beneath her. She blinked repeatedly, trying to clear her blurred vision and keep her eyes from rolling back in her skull. She managed to steal a glance at the museum's lit landing. Chase was nowhere in sight.

Her assailant covered her mouth with duct tape and opened the car door. He flung her facedown onto the backseat.

"Tie her up," a deep, gruff voice ordered from the front.

In an instant, her hands were gathered and cinched behind her. The door was slammed shut, cramming her farther into the confined space. The engine turned over and the car sped away, swerving and rocking her from side to side. Within seconds, she felt nothing. She was numb, fuzzy, and disconnected. She was heading to a hellish place—that was the only thing she was sure of—and the two demons bickering in the front seats were on a mission to take her there.

10

Devon wrenched his bound wrists, hoping the drips on his palm were sweat. Across from him, Logan Tulles's battered body dangled from the warehouse ceiling. His financial partner's mutilated face was a bloody mess. His eyes were swollen; the bridge of his nose, flattened. Blood was oozing at an alarming rate.

"Unnngghhh..." Logan moaned softly.

An evil grin crossed Marcos's Latino face—it was the same menacing look he'd flashed before hurling Devon into the brick wall a week earlier. With his left hand holding Logan in place, Marcos sent his fist ripping into Logan's belly over and over again.

Shit! Devon's heart thumped wildly in his chest. Fear held his eyes wide open. He twisted in the chair, wanting to vomit, but his stomach was empty.

Marcos took one step back. He set himself like a boxer and delivered a savage uppercut, exploding under Logan's chin. The impact was so hard that Logan's head whipped over his shoulder, spraying an arc of sweat and blood across the concrete floor.

"Stop it!" Devon cried out. "You're killing him." He felt the sharp edge of Viktor's knife against his throat and immediately retracted his neck. Marcos's Ukrainian cohort was no doubt enjoying the show. In Devon's mind, he was the kind of guy who would shoot a neighbor's cat with a BB gun just to hear it screech.

"That's the whole idea, dumb ass," Viktor spat. He rolled a smelly wad around in his mouth and moved his blade up and down, dry shaving Devon's throat—a sadistic technique he had no doubt perfected on his own shiny scalp.

Marcos grabbed a handful of Logan's brown hair and jerked his head upright. After a quick survey, he let go, sending his bloody chin into his chest. He gave Logan's hammered body a shove, and smiled as Logan's listless form swung back and forth like a crumpled punching bag. Seconds later, he shifted his attention to Devon.

His ominous, black eyes narrowed. Moisture glistened on his dark forehead.

Devon stiffened in his seat. His breath caught. Every stabbing, nonspeaking moment tore at his nerves. Behind him, heavy footsteps approached and came to an abrupt stop.

"Back off," the unseen man warned. With only two charged words, Devon knew immediately who had spoken. *Gabe Pollero.*

The notorious hoodlum moved just beyond Devon's vision and engaged three of his men in a muffled exchange. Just beyond them, a collection of exotic sports cars waited. At first, when he'd awakened, Devon had thought he'd been taken to a chop shop—a remote place for storing and dismantling stolen vehicles. But then, as his throbbing brain cleared, he'd realized there were no tool chests in the warehouse. Only a chainsaw and a black, plastic tarp on the large workbench. The only implements necessary for dismembering bodies.

Pollero finished his conversation and stepped up to the plate in black slacks and a blue shirt, the sleeves of which were rolled up, revealing his formidable arms. Inside his open collar hung a rose-gold Saint Christopher medal. It twisted on a fine, gold chain, fighting a mass of wiry black hair.

"Hello, my friend," he said to Devon. A twisted smile lifted the small scar on his left cheek, mimicking the expression Devon had seen on the news two years ago. Pollero had been arrested for possession of cocaine and marijuana after driving his black Ferrari into a telephone pole in West Hollywood. His sister, Selena, had persuaded him to go to rehab. When she was interviewed for the story, she had claimed responsibility for helping Pollero sober up, sometimes drawing a knife and wielding a pistol in the process.

What a woman. Devon wished he had taken her advice and left town before everything went haywire. He could be across the border by now, enjoying an ocean view and a nice cold Corona. With a little gentle persuading, the love of his life might have agreed to come along.

Pollero blew out a toothpick. "My guys keepin' you comfortable? Wouldn't want ya to think we weren't hospitable or somethin'." He jerked his head to the right in an off-handed introduction.

Viktor took a few steps back and lowered his menacing knife. His thin lips curved downward, matching the discontent in his cold brown eyes.

"Nabbed your pal at the airport a few hours ago," Pollero continued. "Suppose he was looking for the money you owe me?"

He was obviously referring to Logan. From across the floor, Devon's friend could barely make eye contact, his lower lids red and sagging. The weight of his body pulled his bruised skin and broken bones even closer to the ground.

"Let me explain," Devon pleaded. "I'm not playing games... honest."

"Guys like you give me fuckin' ulcers. I'm telling you, there's nothing worse than a hole in your gut. Ya know?"

Marcos bumped Viktor. "Or in your head." The pair chuckled.

"Olivares, check on my package," Pollero barked. "I wanna hear what this goddamn liar has to say." He grabbed a chair from the floor and straddled it. Under fierce brows, his eyes took menacing aim.

Shit. Devon swallowed hard. He needed an answer. Something convincing to buy him more time. "I'll get the money I owe you. Even include interest. I just need to—"

"What? Give me another lame excuse? Here I'm thinkin' you gotta be laid up, as ya sure as hell wouldn't be that dumb. Then my guys turn up and tell me the freak you gave my money to fuckin' ran off. Were you plannin' to join him, Lyons? Is that what you were gonna do?"

The truth had been beaten out of Logan long before Pollero's guys had cornered Devon on the waterfront. Before he had been dragged there unconscious. He was sure of it. But Walter Moten had to turn up eventually. He had a wife, a mentally challenged kid, and a penchant for the finer things in life. Even after emptying five bank accounts and dummying-up returns to his shareholders, Devon's boss couldn't stay hidden for long.

"Just give me two weeks," Devon pleaded. "That's all I'm asking. I'll find him. I'll get all of it back."

From the self-satisfied look on his face, Pollero was enjoying this far too much. He pulled out a stick of gum and jammed it into his mouth. "Carla's gonna give me shit for messin' up another shirt," he claimed.

"Carla?" Viktor asked.

Pollero smirked. "New maid. Hot ass." He held out a hand. "Don't ya got anything smaller than that Crocodile Dundee knife?"

Viktor reached into the top of his boot and produced a switchblade.

Pollero flipped the knife open and snapped it back again. "Ah, that's better. By the way, Lyons, exactly how were you plannin' on fixing this?"

"I know everyone who's connected to Moten," Devon claimed. "I just need time to check his phone messages, search his records and e-mails. The guy isn't a genius. He's bound to have left a trail. Just let me go, Gabe. I'll do whatever it takes."

But that wasn't exactly true. Even with all the time in the world, Devon knew that it would take a miracle to find Moten with all the money he'd stolen. It had been close to a month since anyone had seen or heard from Devon's buttoned-up boss. Nosey reporters had been poking around for weeks. The firm's phones were ringing off the hook. As of four hours ago, half the staff on the twelfth floor had been called in for questioning by bank examiners and members of the Securities Exchange.

Pollero pursed his lips. "OK, just cause you done me some good in the past, I'll cut ya some slack."

Devon heaved a sigh of relief.

"One of my associates has been shuttling this creep all over the place," Pollero said. "Meetings, parties, you name it. The fool's got more money than brains, handing it out right and left. Looking down on the world from his fuckin' ivory tower. Lucky for you, he's got a hard-on for someone *real* close to you."

Devon racked his memory. Who could he possibly be talking about?

"Since you're not gonna cough up my mill anytime soon, you better hope she'll cover your ass."

Pollero motioned at Viktor, sending him running to the end of the warehouse. He returned a few minutes later with Marcos trailing behind. The jaw-crushing mobster stopped short, right in front of Devon. He lowered the large laundry bag that was slung over his shoulder. When his load hit the floor, a single high-heeled shoe escaped, confirming that a woman was concealed inside.

Selena? Surely, Pollero wouldn't use his own sister against him. Would he?

With one rough pull on the bag, the woman's disheveled clothes fell into place, covering her long, shapely legs. Her pale, wide-eyed face came into full view. For Devon, the only salvation rested in the fact that silver duct tape remained firmly attached to the hostage's chastising lips.

Rachel. If not for the dilemma he now found himself in, Devon would be laughing aloud. If they searched the world, they couldn't have found a more uncooperative person. Over the past four years, she'd assumed their mother's role, adding her own brand of criticism of Devon. Her disapproval extended to all aspects of his life, including all the women he'd chosen to love.

Even after making her own mistake with that loser, Chase Cohen.

As far as Devon was concerned, Rachel had inadvertently brought them to this impasse. If she'd accepted his advice and put her sentimental logic aside for one minute, they could have sold their old man's house six months ago when they received that reasonable offer. With Devon's share of the profits, he wouldn't have had the need to impress Gabe Pollero or be involved with his shady dealings.

"Why'd you bring *her* here?" Devon challenged. "This is between you and me."

Pollero's eyes swam between them. "Not anymore." He cracked the gum in his mouth and smoothed the side of his shiny black hair. "You know, my friend…terrible things can happen to beautiful women like your sister, here. Things a man like you could never imagine."

He reached out and stroked Rachel's cheek. She instantly pulled away. Fortunately for him, the tape muffled her rant. He motioned for her to stay back. When she complied, he circled around her and cut her cinched hands free. With her eyes still riveted on Devon, she reached up and jerked the tape off her mouth.

"Oh, my God," she blurted. "What have you done now?"

Rachel stared at Logan dangling from the warehouse ceiling. His battered head was slumped over. Blood dripped from the corner of his mouth and had pooled beneath him on the concrete floor. The pale color of his skin left her wondering if he was still alive.

Pollero waved a demanding hand in front of her face, capturing her attention. Her hands shook at her sides as she obediently followed him into an adjacent room. She lowered herself into the chair across from him and took a deep, calming breath before assessing her surroundings.

His office was decorated like a showroom with a stainless, ultra-modern floor lamp, a taupe leather sofa, a matching occasional chair, and a bronze-sculpted horse and rider clearing an equestrian post. All of his furnishings had no doubt fallen off the back of a delivery truck. Aside from the framed photos of his spearfishing buddies and of Pollero posing like Lorenzo Lamas behind the wheel of a red Lamborghini, the only insights into Pollero's "hobbies" were the bottle of Patrón tequila on top of his file cabinet and a spread-eagle centerfold taped to the wall above his mahogany desk.

"Your wife?" Sarcasm dripped from her words, which were braver than her cowardly manner.

Pollero grinned. "Only on Fridays." He pocketed his phone and stared openly at her cleavage. "Feeling better?"

She reluctantly nodded before looking away. There were plenty of rumors circulating about this thug. Whenever his name appeared in the news, it usually had something to do with drugs and criminal mischief, yet somehow he always managed to keep his freedom.

"My guys are useless," he claimed. "Haven't got a clue how to treat a lady." He pulled out a silver flask and offered her a drink. She declined, and he threw back a swig.

"Can you at least tell me why this is happening?" Her voice sounded small in her ears. "What is it you want, Pollero?"

"Well, miss," he started, "it seems your brother and I have a difference of opinion. See...he thinks he shouldn't be held accountable, and I think he needs to honor his commitments."

She shifted in her seat, studying the hood—memorizing every detail of him. Jet black eyes, expressive brows, prominent nose, thin lips. Coarse, irritating voice. She would need a frame of reference when she was called in to identify him in a lineup.

"What exactly did my brother promise you, Mr. Pollero?" she asked.

"Gabe," he corrected. The snake rattled off a sequence of events, touching on his missing investment and his pissed-off partners in Vegas who all expected to get a piece of the action. He stopped briefly to verify that she was following his tale of woe. That she understood the resulting damage to his credibility and the unfortunate necessity to detain her.

Pollero had just launched into his idea of a remedy when his cell phone rang. He flipped it open and tipped his head down, affording Rachel the opportunity to peer into the warehouse through the large, tinted window directly behind him. Logan's abusers had gathered in a dark corner like a band of nasty crows. Across from them, Devon remained slumped in his chair. He tilted his chin down and looked up at her through his blue-green eyes. The masked fear in his face was unmistakable. She'd seen it throughout his life. When he was ten and the lawnmower went up in flames. The time the police brought him home after joyriding and crashing their father's car. The day he returned from school and found out that his mother was never coming home again.

Recently, instinct had told her that Devon was in way over his head. His schemes always had a way of sounding too good to be true. As she looked down, contemplating her options, Rachel wished to hell she hadn't been right this time.

Pollero ran his finger under his nose and sniffed. "Yeah, yeah, yeah. Take a chill pill and relax, BOSS." He laughed and was still chatting away on the phone when the door opened. She turned to see a black man enter the room. He watched her with hooded brown eyes as he moved to a corner. At six foot five, with a dark leather coat and shoulder-length, braided hair, he cut an imposing figure. He pulled on a thin cigarette and blew a line of smoke to the side. Even though he stared at her for what seemed like an eternity, not a single word passed between them.

With his call completed, Pollero eased back in his chair. "Novak. It's about time you showed up," he said to the dark stranger. "Thought I told you to be here an hour ago."

A shrug was Novak's only reply.

"You deliver the goods like I told you to?"

"Yeah."

Pollero's eyes swung back to Rachel. "Like I was sayin', the only bargaining chip your brother has is for you to sweet-talk your boss into bailing him out. If Nash delivers and everyone keeps their mouths shut, we can all go about our business as usual, like nothin' happened. Right, Bo?"

Bo Novak. Rachel would make a point to remember his name.

"Sure," said the man of many words.

Novak and Pollero obviously didn't have a clue about the way a foundation operated or what safeguards Warren Nash had put into place. Even though his grandson maintained a comfortable lifestyle, Rachel knew full well that he didn't have access to the amount of money Pollero was talking about. Any sizeable payout from the nonprofit's account required bank authorization and the consent of every member on the board.

Pollero snapped his gum. "You ready to make that call?" He held his phone out to her, but she didn't take it.

"What if there's nothing he can do?" she asked.

His jaw stalled. "You don't want to know."

Rachel swung her eyes toward his captives beyond the windowpane. Tied up, bruised. One barely alive. For the sake of all of them, she had no choice. Not with a solution only fathoms away. She brought her eyes back to the scowling villain and drew a long, deep breath.

"Mr. Pollero…I mean Gabe," she began. "I'm assisting a team of divers involved in recovering a Chinese vessel and the valuable cargo she was carrying. One of the items on board is a priceless relic known as the heart of the dragon. Perhaps we could come to an agreement…"

11

Chase watched *Alegria's* blower work its magic on the ocean floor for nearly an hour. Sand disappeared in a vortex, replaced by shell and sandstone. He maintained his grip on the metal detector as a rock took shape before him. The particles continued to swirl, revealing the curved side of a blue-and-white porcelain jar. He freed it from the clinging soil and slipped it into his goody bag.

With two tugs on the air hose, Chase signaled a move and continued swinging the rod. He finished scanning another five-foot section where over twelve meters of silt already had been removed. He was close to calling it quits, when the detector blasted a melodious tune. He brushed the fine sand away, uncovering links in a heavy, iron chain. His heart thumped wildly in his chest, anticipating the discovery of Sam's elusive anchor. And there it was...covered in silt.

The ancient wooden structure described in Sam's book, just as he had envisioned it.

Chase feathered the sand in the opposite direction, following the chain's length. When he reached the end, the chain disappeared from view. Whatever had been attached to it was hidden on the other side of a mountainous outcropping. He smoothed his hand over the wall's jagged surface. A crack in the rock face caught his glove. He wedged his fingers between two loosened boulders and pivoted them in place. In domino procession, surrounding stones fell away, adding a blinding plume to the murky water. Anticipating a violent avalanche, he pushed off and waited. Remarkably, the hillside remained intact. He swam back and directed his flashlight into the dark portal leading to another world. The glowing beam moved across mossy rocks. On a second pass, he lit up a metal canister, tucked neatly into the undergrowth. A red-striped device crushed almost beyond recognition.

Sam's missing flashlight! Had his deceased partner made it this far? With unstable seismic activity in the region, perhaps falling rocks had struck Sam. If his air hose had been compromised and he panicked before freeing himself, there might be a reasonable explanation for his death—a cause that did not involve the dive gear Chase had personally checked.

Chase pushed the self-serving notions aside and continued his exploration. Within seconds, he realized that the water temperature had taken a sudden plunge. He glanced down at his fluctuating gauges. As it was, he'd be pushing his limits to reach the safety zone. He circled around and pointed his flashlight at the interior wall. A glimmer bounced back—a brilliant sparkle unlike anything he'd ever witnessed.

Yes! His heart leaped inside his wet suit. He slowed his ragged breathing and stole a few valuable minutes, extracting the weighty object. After one last look around, he exited the cave.

In the distance, sunlight filtered through the strong current—a beacon lighting his way home. He headed topside, allowing the necessary time for his stops. He broke through the surface with his fist raised high over his head and spat out his regulator.

"Gold!" he screamed.

Ian moved to the stern and reached out a hand to snatch Chase's shimmering discovery. "Yeeeoooo!" he hollered. He pranced about on one foot and then the other in an outlandish jig.

"Ian! Give me a hand!"

Chase's yell brought Ian back to the ladder. After passing off the metal detector, Chase hoisted himself onto the boarding platform and dropped his load. Still reeling with excitement, he untied his goody bag and followed Ian into *Alegria's* galley.

"Whatcha think?" Ian dangled the long chain in front of A. J. Hobbs, their newly acquired technician. AJ looked up from his notes. He slapped his archaeology book shut and cleared a space on the table before accepting Ian's offering. Then he began slowly unraveling it.

"Got to be near ten feet long. Definitely Spanish. Probably had a medallion of some sort attached." The technician's square spectacles rested near the end of his thin nose. He used a jeweler's pick to scrape away grains of sand and meticulously examined each link. "Quite a find you've got here," he said.

"Ya done good this time," Ian assured Chase. "'Tis a bit of a spoiler, me saying this and all, but we got us a fuckin' yeahootie on board. Ya know that kid's been in me wheelhouse all afternoon takin' readings with me sextant. Thinks he's Cap'n O'Neill or somethin'." Ian stared at the ceiling. "I tell ya it'd be a sight more peaceful if we jest fed 'im to the sharks. Save ourselves a whole lot of grief, it would."

Chase slipped his arms out of his wet suit. "We're a man short as it is, and from what I've seen, Blaine's been doing us a real service with that computer of his." He gestured toward the stack of papers on the sideboard. "Research, grid calculations, log postings…you name it. He's taken a load off of my mind." He noted Ian's furrowed brow and added, "Just find a way to mentally drown him, OK?"

Ian ambled away, leaving Chase with more pressing matters to address. "I don't want to get everyone's hopes up until I know for sure what we're dealing with," he told AJ. "I discovered a virgin cave at the end of an anchor. That's where the gold chain turned up."

Interest sparked in AJ's eyes. "You want me to go with you? I can be suited up in nothing flat."

"Not yet. Gonna grab some field lights and head down. But don't worry. I won't be long. While I'm gone, I want you to check on this, too."

The porcelain jar was in remarkably good condition. The faint bird design and embedded stamp on its base hinted at Chinese origins, adding excitement to Chase's discovery. "Only got two hours before we head in," he said. "I still need to verify the ship's name. If we're lucky, all the proof we need is in your hands." He smiled, exuding confidence. If everything panned out as he anticipated, come morning, he'd pick up his official papers and be back in the water claiming the ship and the treasure they'd been enlisted to find. He watched AJ flipping through one Asian antique book after another, sheer determination pleating his brows.

You're not getting away this time. Chase pulled the arms of his wet suit back on. He zipped up just as Ian returned, looking strangely perplexed.

"Was checkin' the blower and line anchors. There's somethin' ya need to see."

"Don't tell me the sea gulls have been heckling you again." Chase chuckled and followed Ian to the foredeck. His smile vanished in an instant when he grasped the cause of his helmsman's concern. Ten yards out, a long, moving gray sheen curled back on itself. A second dorsal fin trimmed the surface, moving in the opposite direction.

Sharks? Aloud, he asked, "What do you make of them?"

"Not sure yet. Been keepin' their distance."

The creatures swam in broad circles around the orange buoys marking the northwest quadrant dive zone. Suddenly, a third conical snout came into view.

"Whites!" Chase announced, his suspicion clearly vouched. The astounding sight was beyond his cognition. The clan leader appeared to be coming straight at them, systematically lifting its head as if spying its prey. By Chase's best estimate, the agitated creatures were between twelve and fourteen feet in length and more than curious.

Ian scratched his oily scalp before replacing his grungy cap. "Jaysus, I was only jokin' 'bout the pip."

Hunting grounds for Pacific sharks were a good six miles away, south of the jetty and near the dilapidated dock where harbor seals and sea lions were known to collect. The coast guard had cited the area as off-limits, and as a result, all the dive boats from San Palo kept their distance. All of them except Red Star Charters. Aaron Birch and his reckless crew made a practice of dumping chum to draw sharks for photo ops to earn larger tips from wealthy tourists—an illegal and highly dangerous practice.

The thought churned Chase's stomach. "You haven't seen Birch today, have you? Those idiots could be anywhere out here."

Ian shook his head. "Not even a dingy. No tellin' what's got 'em riled."

The sharks made another pass, skirting their hull, before diving and passing beneath them. As quickly as they appeared, they vanished from view, leaving only one explanation behind.

With no apparent food source or noticeable threat, the creatures had to have been drawn by the electrical fields *Alegria* was generating.

Chase raked his fingers through his hair and squeezed the back of his neck, debating how to proceed.

"Best be shuttin' her down," Ian suggested.

With nature at odds with them, Chase had to have faith in AJ's confirmation. He stared out to sea and offered a silent prayer. "Take her home," he told Ian.

With *Alegria's* aft anchors pulled, Ian made his way to the helm. Chase finished stowing his gear just as the winds kicked up. He snagged a shirt out of the master cabin and returned to the galley to look in on AJ.

"Any luck?" he asked.

Reference books were scattered on the small table and AJ appeared to be totally engrossed in the largest volume. His scribbled notes completely covered a pad of paper.

"Nothing firm," he reported. "No mistake it's Chinese, just can't pinpoint the province or exact date. It's unlike anything previously found. But don't worry, Captain. I have enough information here to get us a temporary claim."

"Not good enough," Chase said. "Temporary means nothing. Especially with the *Legend* breathing down our necks." He could feel the rise under the hull, the breeze pushing *Alegria* into a slow drift. Ian had already fired up the engines and was attempting to bring her about. Chase had to make a quick decision. Say something he wouldn't later regret. "We're not going anywhere," he announced.

Chase was on his way to the bridge to delay Ian's progress when Blaine appeared from above.

"According to Gotheborg.com," he said, "what you've got there is a Ming globular jar. It's dated somewhere between 1573 and 1620 and definitely an Imperial piece. Would have had an answer sooner, but that damn spicy fish Ian made for lunch and the constant rocking gave me the worst stomach ache I've ever had in my—" He covered his mouth and ran for the closest head.

"Yes!" Chase's fist punched the air. He bounded up the ladder to join his helmsman. "Full speed ahead," he charged.

Nothing was going to stop him now—not the *Legend*, the tight-ass bankers, or any of his bloodthirsty creditors. What's more, Rachel Lyons would soon regret insulting his integrity. That alone made finding the treasure worthwhile.

12

There it was, the Crow's Nest...home of the local commiserating club. A four-by-eight-foot sign sporting a squawking, black bird and red, hand-painted letters hung over the door of the worn, shack-like building. Rachel stepped inside, and the door slammed behind her, lifting her an inch off the floor. It took a full minute for her eyes to adjust to the dim light, but as soon as they did, she found a place at the end of the counter and dropped onto a padded barstool.

Naomi peeked out from the back room. "What a surprise finding you here."

Rachel offered a weak smile. It had been years since she'd been in the place, and her brief encounters with Naomi had been limited to occasional post office and grocery store visits.

"Put a fresh pot on an hour ago. Would you like a cup?" she asked.

"Sure," Rachel said.

On cue, an attractive Asian woman emerged with a black, steaming pot and an enormous, white mug. "Hi, I'm Mika Yamada. Naomi is finishing up in back. She'll be right with you."

She removed her stained apron and snatched a black coat from the hook. With a quick smile and a nod, she dashed out the door.

Cute. Must be related to the new family that moved into town, Rachel thought. She picked up the oversized cup and began blowing the heat from her coffee. She glanced around at the shiplap walls, recalling the day ten years earlier when she had found her father sitting on this very stool. He'd been buying rounds for half the town, foolishly accumulating a tab they could ill afford. When she'd attacked his rationality, he'd proclaimed his good fortune at having witnessed the destruction of his mortgaged-to-the-hilt boat and all of his leased gear.

Naomi had had to hold Rachel back to keep her from knocking him onto the floor. Luckily, the bartender had been quick to set Rachel straight. As it turned out, the owner of the largest shipbuilding company in the county had assumed full responsibility for the accident. In order to keep his juvenile-delinquent son out of jail and the only witness's mouth sealed, he'd presented Sam with the keys to one of his finest yachts.

Yet what good had it done him? Even though he'd converted *Stargazer* into a working ship by installing a ten-ton knuckle crane, an eight-ton auxiliary winch, and a full-time salvage crew, her father ended up with nothing more than a handful of coins and a shed filled with worthless junk.

Why did he have to be such a fool? Just like her brother Devon? Scheming all the time. Risking everything to get rich quick. Always testing her loyalty, her patience, her love. And now she'd been reduced to coming here—the most unsavory place in town—in an attempt to save Devon's unappreciative ass.

Tension stirred the anxiety in the pit of her stomach. She hadn't slept more than two hours the night before. Instead, she'd lain awake questioning every sound in the house. Every movement in the dense border shrubs.

She stared into her mug and considered adding a shot of whiskey to the steamy brew. But in her present state of mind, the reinforcement would simply leave her snoozing on the bar, not unlike the poor sap spread across the table in the room's darkest corner. He was a guy who'd been coming here for years, she realized.

Glimpsing her own image in the bar's age-spotted mirror, Rachel winced. The new trauma in her life had already taken its toll. She found some makeup in her clutch and set to work applying light foundation under her eyes and a fresh coat of pink lip gloss to her full lips. She leaned forward to reassess her appearance and was jolted by the reflection of Logan's face in the mirror. She clamped her eyes shut and willed the image to go away. When she lifted her lids, the gruesome portrait was gone. Yet the jarring impact remained. No matter what their differences were, she couldn't allow Devon to share Logan's fate.

Rachel drew a deep, ragged breath and released it slowly. She shifted her concentration to the adjacent window just as a boat neared the stony reef. The white, shimmering craft, capped with towering antennas of varying heights, was unlike any of the boats she'd seen in the past. Her current occupation, in a downtown corner office, provided no insight into the bustling activity on the waterfront, and for the past eight months, she'd preferred it that way.

Naomi returned from the kitchen lugging two crates in her arms. A shaggy white dog was following closely behind. "So what brings you out this way, Rachel?" she asked. After dropping her load of glasses on the back counter, she pulled the towel from her shoulder and began buffing the edge of the bar. The furry mongrel collapsed on the floor and looked up at Rachel with enormous, pitiful eyes. "Can't be my scorched gourmet coffee."

"Actually, I'm just waiting for someone," Rachel replied. As soon as she saw flashes of light behind Naomi's brown eyes, she wanted to take her words back. "It's a client of mine," she amended, and then wondered why she'd even bothered.

"Must be someone *real* important." Naomi snickered and returned to stacking glasses. After emptying one crate, she angled her head and tossed out a baited question. "Hey, you wouldn't by any chance be meeting Chase Cohen?"

For a brief moment, Rachel was impressed by Naomi's intuitiveness. Then she realized that word of Chase's return had probably blown across town. Her brief history with him was hardly a secret.

"So who's your friend?" Rachel asked, hoping to change the subject.

"Oh that's Yuki...Chase's dog. I keep an eye on him when he's out." A knowing smile formed on Naomi's lips. "That guy's pure eye candy, if you ask me."

"His *dog*?"

"No, Chase."

"Really? And here I thought you were happily married."

"*Were* is right, but happy had nothing to do with it. I'll tell you what...if I could keep that gorgeous man's attention for more than an hour, I'd take Chase home with me and keep him locked up for good."

Rachel remained silent, nursing her coffee. She had no interest in bringing Chase home or anywhere else. Just in recruiting his treasure-seeking skills.

"Well, would you look at that," Naomi said. "Seems we're both in luck. That's his boat pulling up outside right now."

Rachel's pulse quickened. She pushed her cup aside and slid off the stool. After rounding the bar in her black pumps, she joined Naomi at the window. Together, they watched the boat's slow approach. After it turned and docked in a nearby slip, several men scrambled from the upper to lower decks, most likely attending to their prescribed duties.

"They're in early today," Naomi announced.

Rachel's insides twisted. She didn't even bother to check her watch. The phone call she'd made to the dive shop's owner had provided her with *Alegria's* estimated arrival time. "So *that's* his boat," she muttered to herself.

"Are you two on again?" Naomi's gaze scoped Rachel's face.

"Hardly," she said.

"Hmmm...well, that can change." A soft smile lifted the corners of Naomi's lips. She sashayed toward the bar, appearing confident in her assessment.

Noisy sea gulls pulled Rachel's attention back outside. Chase had finished tying off his boat and was collecting his tanks. Although she had no intention of acknowledging his trim physique, she couldn't stop herself. Like a sketch artist's pencil, her gaze traced his broad shoulders; the ripples in his bronze, sculpted abs; and the edge of his low-rise jeans.

Chase's chin suddenly lifted. A fortuitous look in her direction trapped her in an invasive stare. With their eyes still locked, she read her name on his moving lips. All sound evaporated from the air. The distance folded into itself like a collapsing spyglass, leaving no barrier between them. But then, Chase's face suddenly darkened. He tugged a T-shirt over his head and leaped onto the dock. With his pained expression tacked firmly in place, he strode briskly toward the entrance of the Crow's Nest Bar.

Rachel distanced herself from the window. She waited against the wall, fingernails pressed into her palm. He pushed the door wide open and stepped inside. Barely ten feet away, he stood eyeing her from head to toe, not uttering a word. Yuki sprang to his feet and bounced around trying to get his owner's attention. But aside from a quick pat on the head, Chase didn't seem to notice.

"Hey, sweetheart," came from behind the bar. "Want your regular?"

"Later." His light-blue eyes never left Rachel. "So, what are you doing here?" he asked.

Her heart skipped.

She should have anticipated his irritability, especially after their most recent exchange and her suggestion that he leave town. At that moment, more than anything, she wanted to flee. But her dire circumstances prevented an escape. Prevented a full explanation. "I came here to tell you that the board—" she began.

Ian blew in through the door carrying a sizeable box. "Matey, yer gonna need this." His gaze found Rachel. "Darlin'! What a nice surprise." He handed his load to Chase and crossed the floor to take hold of her hand. "Yer still the prettiest thing that ever was."

Rachel couldn't help but smile. The gentle giant had always been one of her favorite people. It had been hard to see him leave town after her father's funeral. But after three months, there had been no work to be found—at least nothing that suited Ian's disposition.

"I heard you were back," she said. "Sure hope you're managing to stay out of trouble."

Ian guffawed. "Course not. What fun would that be?"

From the corner of her eye, Rachel spied Chase's downturned mouth. It seemed he didn't appreciate their friendly exchange.

"Isn't there somewhere you need to be?" he tossed at Ian.

The Irishman winked at Rachel. "Don't' fret, darlin'. Everything's got a way of workin' out." He did an about-face and waved at Naomi. "Come on, Yuki." The dog charged, leading Ian through the open doorway.

Chase shook his head and released a weighty breath. "What were you saying?" he asked.

It took a few seconds for Rachel's thoughts to reconnect. To plot a more receptive approach. "I thought you might like to know about your funding before—"

"Oh, that," he interrupted. "So you came here to gloat. To tell me I got turned down…just like you expected."

"Actually, that's not the case. I got up early this morning to make phone calls. The board agreed to hold off on its decision for forty-eight hours. You know…to buy you some time."

His brow raised a fraction of an inch. "Now, exactly why would you do that? If memory serves me, you said there was nothing keeping me here and that I needed to go back to wherever I came from."

Naomi suddenly coughed—a reminder that they weren't alone. Before Rachel could react, Chase snatched her elbow and led her to an empty corner. He stepped back and rested his weight on one hip, waiting for an explanation.

Stay calm. Her nail traced a seam on the edge of her blouse. "This is purely business," she said. "I've had time to reevaluate my decision. From what Dr. Ying has told me, the foundation would be greatly remiss by not participating. The last thing I would want to do is interfere if there was a chance—"

Chase laughed aloud, leaving her speechless. When he finally regained control of himself, he motioned for her to take a seat.

She adamantly refused.

"No doubt about it…you're as mystifying as ever," he jested. "Twelve hours ago, I was your worst enemy. Now you want to help me out in the worst way possible. So, what's going on, Rachel? There's got to be a catch in all this."

Guilt weighed heavily on her heart. She braced her hand on the back of the chair, steadying herself. "Don't be silly," she said. "If you turn up evidence identifying the wreckage as the *Wanli II*, everyone would benefit. And if something of value is found, I'd make sure the news reached them…I mean *him*…the professor. You'd go down in history as the hero who saved our town."

Complete silence. Chase's scowl was back. Distrust narrowed his penetrating eyes.

She swallowed hard and measured her words, battling the overwhelming urge to look away. "I'm only trying to be professional here. With Mrs. Van Dozer's cooperation and the additional information I have, everyone will lend their support. You'll have the money you need within hours."

Chase shook his head. "There's *still* something you're not telling me, but no matter. I don't have time right now. I've got an attorney and a federal judge waiting with my petition to salvage. When you decide to fill me in, give me a call. Naomi knows my number." Chase picked up the box and headed for the exit. Without a backward glance, he pushed his way clear and disappeared from view.

Shit! Rachel stared after him. She never considered the possibility of being rejected. Of being humiliated in front of the town gossip. She looked down at the chair in her grip, longing to pitch it across the room. She squeezed her eyes shut and willed herself to remain calm.

What do I do now? She ran through her short list, settling on Dr. Ying. No one had been more insistent about her involvement than he, and at that hour, he'd no doubt be in his office. Although unaware of her dire predicament, he'd be ecstatic about her change of heart.

Rachel rifled through her purse and pulled out a five-dollar bill. She left it on the bar and made her way toward the same door through which Chase had vanished.

"What about your change?" Naomi called after her.

"Keep it."

Rachel maintained a steady pace as she crossed the parking lot. She climbed into her car and drove the back roads at a breakneck speed, avoiding patrol cars along the way. After arriving at the museum, she ran up the stairs to the main doors, but a padlock and thick chain barred her entry. At her wit's end, Rachel considered soliciting help from the approaching guard—a foolish notion, according to Pollero. One that would expedite her brother's death.

"Miss Lyons? I thought that was you." Roger Dailey's long strides shortened the distance between them. "Did you just come through the north entrance? I must've forgot to secure that gate."

She assessed the near-empty parking lot. Only a service vehicle and the professor's ratty Volvo remained. Had she overlooked a national holiday? A reason for everyone to stay home?

"What's going on?" she asked Dailey. "Why is the museum closed in the middle of the day?"

"Oh, I guess you haven't heard, then." He hooked his thumbs on his black belt. "Doc's twin brother was killed trying to free his dogs from an electrified fence. Freaky accident, if you ask me. Seems his eighty-year-old neighbor failed to install the regulator, and instead of sending a pulsating current like it should have, the wire hit him nonstop with 110 volts."

"That's terrible."

"Yeah. Doc took it real hard, too. After the police told him what happened and how that old guy was arrested for manslaughter, he keeled over on the spot."

Rachel covered her mouth. *Oh my, God. Is he dead?*

"He's all right, ma'am. Had a minor heart attack, is all."

Her hand fell away. "Where is he?"

"The paramedics took him to Saint Vincent's Hospital." He glanced past her to the posted "closed" sign. "With school kids running up and down the hallways and Miss Briggs all keyed up, the fire chief thought it best to shut down early and send everyone home. I'll tell ya, though," he said, shaking his head, "between Moten emptying bank accounts, my wife's hardware store laying off workers, and the body they found in the dump this morning, this town's going straight to hell."

Rachel grasped the handrail. "Body?"

"Just came over the radio. The SPPD thinks it might've been a homeless guy, but they're not sure yet. It wasn't bad enough that the poor sap was beaten to a pulp. Whoever did it finished him off with a point-blank shot in the face. It'll take days before they ID him."

13

Forty-eight hours had slowly passed as they waited in the sleazy hotel room. Marcos was slouched in his chair, thumbing through a smut magazine, his white, sleeveless T-shirt exposing his huge chest and biceps—a physique built, in all probability, by bench-pressing up to five hundred pounds a day. His black tattoos looked like a roadmap to his time spent in prison and covered his brown skin with no rhyme or reason. On the opposite side of the table, Viktor shuffled cards, preparing for another round of poker. He wore his usual, tight-fitting, black shirt and loved touching his small muscles, which probably "arrived" with good genes and not through hard work. His cocky demeanor reminded Devon of a guy he'd met once who didn't realize that people were bigger and stronger than he was, and if someone told him that he was small, he simply didn't believe it. Besides idly flicking his knife, Vik had a peculiar habit of rubbing his bare head and flexing his right shoulder every time Pollero was around—it was like a nervous itch he couldn't scratch. When he smirked, which was often, it came with a nasty curled lip and a showed off the scarred dent in his chin. Between phone calls from Pollero and bathroom breaks, the slimy duo flipped through old-movie channels, and bragged about their guns, their female conquests, and the size of their dicks.

Devon tried his best to remain unaffected, to follow the rules for survival. Unless he was in immediate danger, he needed to bide his time. To wait for a slipup, and then use the opportunity to escape. But patience was never his strong suit. He stood up and resumed his ritual, pacing back and forth in front of the curtains, consumed with Rachel and Selena's safety.

Whomp! A brown-plaid pillow hit him square in the chest.

One look at Marcos's snarl and he knew exactly where it came from. "Keep it up, and I'll snap your fuckin' neck," he promised.

Asshole. Devon dropped his shoulder against the wall. He remained silent, measuring the validity of the man's threat. Without a doubt, Marcos's endurance was wearing thin, but not on his account. Without asking, Viktor had drunk the last beer in the fridge while Devon watched him. Then he filled the ash-tray with his smelly, hand-rolled cigarettes. And now, with his poker losses piling up before Marcos, his open blade was resting on the table only inches away. He dealt another hand and peered over the top of his cards. He anted up the last of his wadded bills and waited like a flea-bitten alley cat for his rat to move.

After witnessing their verbal jabs for the past two hours, Devon was convinced that a fight would break out any minute—especially if Marcos delivered the final winning hand. On cue, Marcos's cheek began twitching. His nostrils flared. He picked up a handful of bills and matched Viktor's bet. He laid down two jacks and a pair of tens, and then boasted, "Beat that." Confident in his win, he leaned forward to collect his money.

Viktor's face tensed, adding furor to his demented stare. He grabbed his knife and plunged it into the table.

Marcos shot out of his seat. "Are you crazy?" he yelled.

The Russian psycho waved his four kings in the air. "I win. Read 'em 'n die."

"*Weep*, you fuckin' idiot."

"Why I do that?"

"Forget it!"

Viktor scooped up his cash, keeping a wary eye on his partner.

"Deal again, *socio*," Marcos demanded. "I'll prove you were lucky."

Shit! Devon kicked a pile of dirty clothes out of his way. He dropped down onto the foot of the bed. Close quarters and empty food cartons had turned the air into boiled sweat socks.

"It's hot in here," Devon complained. "Can't you crack a window or something?"

Marcos twisted in his seat. "How bout I crack your head, amigo?"

His partner flicked his lighter, igniting the cigarette dangling from his lower lip. He drew in a short breath and blew out a stream. "Do it, Marcos," he said. "Snuff him out...just like friend."

Friend? Devon swallowed hard. "What are you talking about? Pollero told me that Logan is—"

"What?" Marcos sniped. "Kissing nurses? Eating strawberry Jell-O?"

Devon's hands were now balled into fists.

"What is Jell-O?" Viktor asked.

Marcos rolled his eyes. He snatched the bag of Doritos from the floor and jammed the remaining chips into his mouth. He crumpled up the bag and tossed it aside. "When's the pizza coming?" he grumbled.

Devon silently fumed. Why had he allowed himself to be taken in? To believe Logan had actually survived? With reckless abandon, he reached down and picked up the phone receiver. "I'll call and find out."

Marcos's black eyes narrowed. His nostrils flared. "Just try it, smart ass."

He ignored the threat and began punching numbers. "9-1-1, right?"

"Put it down!" Marcos yelled. He stood up and shoved the table, dumping everything on it. Devon pitched the phone at his head, but Marcos blocked it with his forearm, sending it flying. Before he had a chance to deliver a bone-shattering blow, Devon swung a powerful uppercut into Marcos's gut, slamming him into the wall.

"Omph," came from his mouth.

Devon threw another punch with all his might, snapping Marcos's head hard to the right. He followed with a kick to his midsection, sending him spinning and bouncing off the adjacent wall. With a blank look on his face, Marcos collapsed onto his knees.

Blind rage drove Devon on. He charged at Vik, ducking just as his fist hit the air. With precise aim, Devon landed a punch, lifting the Ukrainian and smashing him into the floor on his back. He straddled his chest and drew back his fist to deliver another blow. But Marcos caught Devon's arm, blocking his punch. He wrenched Devon's elbow behind his back, forcing him off Vik. Then, with a quick jab to Devon's ribs, Marcos dropped him to his knees.

"You're dead," he yelled. Blood seeped from the corner of his mouth. He grabbed the knife from the floor and brought it tight against Devon's throat.

"What the fuck's going on here?" Pollero's voice blasted across the room. He stood in the open doorway, his frowning bodyguard at his side. "Get off the floor...all of you," he ordered.

Viktor jerked Devon to his feet. He shoved him toward the bed and then crossed the room to right the table and toppled chair.

Marcos's frown deepened. Sweat trickled down the side of his face. He glared at Devon, massaging his bruised chin. "It wasn't my fault," he growled.

"It *never* is," Pollero scolded. "And why the fuck is it so hot in here? Open a goddamn window."

Marcos moved to the window and jerked the curtains back, nearly ripping them off the rod. He flipped a lever and shoved open the glass pane. Pollero joined him and murmured something that seemed to calm his tirade. All the while, his slick sidekick stood in the doorway, his narrow black eyes fixed firmly on Devon's face.

The phone on the nightstand suddenly came to life.

"Pick it up," Pollero said.

Marcos moved quickly, grabbing the receiver. After a brief, indecipherable exchange, he hung up. He faced his boss and launched into a Spanish explanation. Although Devon's comprehension was limited, "crystal meth" and "courier" transcended any language.

Viktor ran a hand over his smooth scalp before piping up. "I go this time. We can handle it. Right, Bo?"

Pollero's bodyguard lowered his layered arms. A question mark resonated on his face.

"Forget it," Pollero answered. "She's got it handled, just like always."

Devon was lost. Who the hell was he talking about?

"Just do the job you're paid to do and—"

Boom! The explosion outside rattled the window in its frame. From where Devon stood, he could see flames shooting high into the night sky. Fire was encompassing a vessel in the harbor. Perhaps a sailboat, a tour boat, or maybe a fishing charter. In the street below, spectators flowed from buildings and parked vehicles. They collected in masses on the docks and waterfront, watching and waiting like sharks for the first sign of blood.

Marcos turned from the window. "Nice..."

Pollero's eyes gleamed. He faced Devon and flashed his perfect white smile. "I heard that pretty sister of yours is working with Chase Cohen. Be a real shame if she was on that boat."

14

Chase never understood the purpose of wearing a little noose around his neck. It just wasn't his style. While parked in the federal courthouse parking lot, he pulled off his Tommy Bahamas T-shirt and tossed it onto the seat next to him. He slipped on a stiff, white shirt, buttoned it to the neck, and tucked it into his jeans. Then, pushing aside his resistance, he tied his purple, happy-dot tie with a four-in-hand knot and cinched it tightly against his throat.

As it turned out, his attire was the least of his problems. All afternoon as he sat in the courtroom, his thoughts wrapped around Rachel's unpredictable mood swings and strange behavior. His preoccupation with her left him appearing mindless, uninvolved, and, in general, bored stiff. By day's end, Chase's attorney had to call his name three times before he finally answered, leaving the judge hesitant to grant his exclusive salvage rights.

Rachel. What was he going to do with that woman?

He returned to his truck with papers in hand, unbuttoned his shirt, and pulled off his strangling tie. As he waited for the traffic light to change, two blaring emergency vehicles and a fire engine whizzed by. They were traveling due west through the center of town. Chase edged his truck closer to the vehicle ahead of him and watched them weave with precision through the congested intersection.

What's going on? His gaze lifted toward the skyline in the distance. Just beyond the towering rooftops, gray smoke was billowing and darkening the early evening sky. Trepidation seeped into his soul. When the light changed, he searched for a gap in traffic and then pulled out and accelerated, following the deafening procession toward the marina. When he arrived, cops were everywhere, pressing through hordes of onlookers and blocking off access to the marina. Local reporters with their camera crews in tow appeared to be negotiating for prime locations. Off to his left, an ambulance waited as paramedics checked for possible survivors. And just beyond the man-made reef, hoses from coast guard boats were running full bore, saturating a blazing hull.

With no place to park, Chase abandoned his truck beside a Dumpster in an alleyway. Like a man possessed, he scrambled down the walkway between two waterfront shops. He squeezed through an opening in the security fence. Forty to fifty boats, ranging from decades-old motor cruisers to sail-driven skiffs, bobbed on anchor lines in the north harbor. Nothing seemed odd or out of place. Once he reached the first row of docks, he picked up speed, visually scanning the vessels moored there. When he reached the final section of occupied slips, he was stopped dead in his tracks. Number forty-nine was empty. His gaze claimed the south harbor, where his boat was now fully engulfed in flames.

Alegria! His part-time home and only possession. His sole means of survival. Why would anyone do this? A sickening punched-in-the-gut sensation weakened his knees. He wrapped an arm around the wooden post at the end of the dock to keep from toppling over.

A young police officer approached and stopped a short distance away, balancing his rocking stance. "Excuse me, sir. No one's allowed down here."

Chase turned around. He had no interest in addressing the rookie's remarks. Not with venom gathering in his heart.

The officer's face softened. "Oh, it's you, Mr. Cohen. I'm Gary Saunders. My dad's the publisher of the *Examiner.* I've been reading about you for some time now. Treasure hunting…wow! Must be an exciting way to live. Anyway, I just wanted to assure you that we'll get to the bottom of this, sir."

Two more cops joined them, but their sympathies and exchanges were muted in Chase's ears. He lowered himself onto the edge of the dock and watched his dreams go up in smoke. As time ebbed away, the culmination of four years of work slowly sank into the bay.

An ambitious reporter appeared from out of nowhere. "Mr. Cohen, is that your boat? Were any of your men onboard? What do you think happened to it?" He spouted half a dozen unanswered questions before the cops finally escorted him away. Members of the coast guard and fire department arrived shortly thereafter. They all assured him that a thorough investigation would ensue, his men would be called in for questioning, and no stone would be left unturned. But the only thing Chase could do was stare at the destruction—at the drifting, heart-wrenching debris.

A tall man came up behind him. "One leaky propane canister, a faulty electrical box, and a nice insurance policy. Put them together, and a man's problems would virtually go up in smoke."

The false accusation brought Chase to his feet and back to his senses. It was a known fact that the harbor master had had a huge crush on Rachel throughout high school. Any respect the belligerent man might have had for Chase evaporated the day Chase left town.

"If what you say is true, then how the hell did I do it?" Chase asked. "How did I get *Alegria* into the channel and out in the bay if I spent half the day in court on the other side of town?"

"You could have hired someone."

"With what?"

"My point exactly."

"So what are you telling me? You're going to ride my ass instead of trying to find out who really did this?"

The harbor master's tight mouth told him all that he needed to know. No assistance would be forthcoming. No justice would be served. If the guy had his way, it would take weeks—maybe months—before an official determination was made. By that time, the *Wanli* claim would be long gone.

Chase was left alone to mourn his loss. He used the silence to steal a glance toward the Crow's Nest Bar. In the crowd, a copper-haired hustler with a sinister face seized his attention. Their blue eyes locked, and in that undefined moment, Chase knew without doubt who was responsible. *Skylar Zane.* No one had more to gain from Chase's complete ruination. With his boat out of the way, the scavenger would have free access to the *Wanli* and everything she contained.

Chase charged down the gangway, hell-bent on breaking the man's neck. With less than thirty feet between them, Ian swooped in, blocking Chase's determined path.

"How'd it happen?" Ian asked. "Were there witnesses?"

Chase shoved him aside, but to no avail. His nemesis had already slipped away.

"Shit!" Chase bellowed. "Zane was standing right there, grinning like a goddamn possum…watching *Alegria* burn and sink. I know it was him! I *know* he did it!"

Ian followed Chase's line of vision before turning back. "There's nothin' to be gained by going after him. 'Tis a matter of words and no proof ta back 'em. Rest assured, mate, when the time's right, I'll pay him a little visit."

The ice in Ian's steel eyes told Chase that his faithful friend would follow through on his promise—even if it meant chaining the creep's ass to a two-hundred-pound anchor and lobbing it into the bay.

"I'm so sorry."

Chase heard Rachel's voice. He looked down and was surprised to see her warm hand resting on his forearm.

"I heard all about the fire on the news. I can't imagine how this could have happened."

His vision brushed over her snug jeans, her white, half-buttoned blouse. Her beautiful parted lips. Somehow, her presence at the worst moment in his life soothed him and lessened the pain of his loss.

"If there's anything at all I can do..." Rachel's voice trailed off. Her hand slipped away.

"Ah, jeez...the chain!" Ian erupted. "Tell me it wasn't aboard."

Crap! Chase squeezed his eyes shut, praying it was all a horrible mistake. A bad dream from which he'd suddenly awaken. The day before, he'd been so distracted by Rachel that he'd foolishly left the treasure behind.

"Chase?" Rachel's voice tugged at his ear.

"We had our first taste of gold yesterday," he explained. "An incredible find. Now that's gone, too."

"Jaysus," Ian moaned. "Ya gotta be kidding me."

Chase heaved a heavy breath. "I'm cursed. You'd be wise to get as far away from me as you can." He reached into his pocket. He looked down at his boat keys and pitched them as far as he could into the ocean.

Ian layered his arms and angled his head. "Yer not cursed, mate. Don't ya be thinkin' that way. If Zane's got a hand in this, there won't be a safe place in this world." He heaved a sigh. "For now, let's grab us a wet one, toast *Alegria*, and figure out where we go from here."

Chase laughed sarcastically. "Exactly where is that? If it hasn't soaked into that thick brain of yours yet, we're salvage divers without a boat. We're finished, Ian."

The helmsman's meaty hand landed on Chase's shoulder. He stared into his face. "Miss Lyons and her foundation offered to help us out. What's ta say we can't accept? Get us a brand new boat and finish the job we started."

Chase looked down. He was still mourning the loss of *Alegria*. Replacing her so quickly seemed callous and disloyal.

"Don't be forgettin' what's important here," Ian added.

Chase lifted his eyes, glimpsing the charred remains floating in the distance. There was more at risk than he was willing to admit. He looked back at Rachel and swallowed his pride. "Can you still help me out?"

Her hesitance told him otherwise. "I don't know what to say. The trustees are under the impression that your company's stable and fully equipped. They would never cover the cost of a new boat."

He snorted a laugh and shook his head. "Of course not. Why would they?"

Rachel stared at the ground. When her gaze met his, she appeared to be mulling something over. "There *is* another way," she said. "But I'd have to be directly involved."

"In *what*?" he asked. "Selling pencils?"

"No, Chase. With all the relics and treasures discovered during your six-day expedition. At that time, you'd return to San Palo, where I'd prep, document, and store them. We'd work independently with the understanding that this is a business arrangement and nothing more."

He almost laughed, but the look in her eyes told him that she was deadly serious. "And just how do you propose that we find these relics and treasures?" he asked.

"My uncle came to see me," she explained. "He tracked down *Stargazer* and convinced the new owner to sell her back. She's being brought out of dry dock as we speak. You'll have complete say-so on how she's run, just as long as you stick to our agreement."

Stargazer? It was too good to be true, but what about Rachel? "You wouldn't be coming along?"

She shook her head.

"I'm still not clear. What do you expect to get out of this?" he asked.

"I'd be working on behalf of the foundation and museum, ensuring that all of our obligations are met."

Our obligations? Her words puzzled him. "And what about payment? Surely, you'll be expecting a percentage out of this."

"Not at all. My salary takes care of me. My only concern is how quickly you can get this job done."

Really? Her extraordinary generosity and timing should have set off warning signals, but the opportunity to man *Stargazer* overshadowed any doubts and concerns. Sam's yacht was a salvager's wet dream. Four cabins, eight berths, fly bridge, twenty-six-mile-per-hour cruise speed, twenty-foot beam, five-and-a-half-foot draft hull, and fifty-ton displacement. She'd been outfitted with every possible amenity: a Zodiac raft with an Evinrude motor, hydraulic hoists, a MAXAir compressor. A fifty-four-hundred-liter fuel tank. Anyone would be a fool to refuse such an offer. Better yet, with the foundation now covering his costs, Blaine's investment would no longer be needed. Should he choose to come along as a member of the crew, Blaine would pocket 10 percent, just like the rest of his men.

"OK," Chase said. "You've got a deal." He held out his palm for a handshake, only to have it pressed with a set of keys.

"I'll handle the necessary calls," she said. "You'll find her fully stocked and ready to go at the end of pier thirty-two at 7 a.m. And one more thing, Chase. There's a satellite phone on board. Make sure you use it for my daily reports." With that, she turned and walked away.

Chase hadn't done anything to deserve her kindness, her generosity. Her sudden change of heart. So what had spurred it? As he watched her gorgeous backside sashay down Main Street until it vanished from view, he found himself wondering if he'd missed a swagger or a contemptuous note in her voice.

Ian's joviality cut into his thoughts. "Can ya believe that? What an amazing woman."

Chase massaged his jaw. "Yeah, isn't she something?" Regret had become a constant in his life. For more than four years, not a single day had passed that Chase didn't wish he'd made other choices. Now, in his darkest hour, the woman whom he'd discarded and whose father he was responsible for killing had had the perfect opportunity to revel in his despair. Instead, she had thrown him a lifeline. *Inconceivable.*

Even with his helmsman bursting at the seams with enthusiasm, Chase's instincts told him something was wrong. This "arrangement" had the potential to overshadow everything on his list of regrets. He glanced at the entrance to the Crow's Nest Bar and then back at Ian.

"About that drink…make it a double and you've got a deal."

Rachel wove around pedestrians emptying into the streets and vehicles parked at the curb. Having seen the news report on television, she'd immediately suspected that Pollero was involved in the explosion. But after studying the scene and digesting Chase's full account, she realized that the gangster had nothing to gain by destroying *Alegria.* In all probability, her newly acquired partner had an enemy of which he wasn't even aware.

It suddenly dawned on her that by providing Pollero with a censored update, she might be allowed to speak with Devon. Just the sound of her brother's voice would lessen the stress; she'd know that he was still breathing, at least. With renewed purpose, she continued on her path, heading north on First Street toward Howard's Hardware. Her silver Kia would be waiting at the far end of the lot, where she'd parked it. Absentmindedly, she'd left her cell phone in the car.

A look to her left made her heart skip a beat. She spotted a black leather trench coat and an all-too-familiar head of hair traveling on the opposite side of the street. *Bo Novak.* What was he doing here? Did he know where Devon was being held? If she could find out, there might be a possibility of rescuing him—once she knew what he was up against.

Pollero's errand boy crossed in front of a moving car and continued north on Fifth Street with long, enthusiastic strides. Rachel narrowly missed being seen when he cast a backward glance in her direction. Even though she feared a physical confrontation, Bo's caginess pulled her along. When he reached the light at Callow Street, he turned right and detoured down the alleyway between Macy's Café and the All-Night Market.

Rachel glanced around before slipping into the alley behind him. With brick walls blocking the light, she stepped carefully around trash cans and a discarded appliance box, where a bum had taken up residence.

Bo veered left toward the small parking lot behind Gordy's Pawn Shop. She continued to trail him, maintaining a safe distance. He finally came to a screeching halt under the O'Neill

Street sign. His quick glance around sent her lunging for cover between two Dumpsters.

"Over here," Bo called out in a loud whisper. The sound of heavy footsteps left her crouching behind the smelly mountain of trash. She waited with bated breath. After a few seconds, she ventured a peek. A man dressed in a light-gray suit stood beside Bo, his square jaw vaguely familiar. When his deep-rooted chuckle reached her ears, Rachel knew without a doubt who Bo was meeting. *Detective Brennan.* The cop had been a close friend of her father's for more than ten years.

From her vantage point, it was impossible to hear their guarded conversation—an exchange that might have come in handy at some point. But what she did witness made an indelible impression.

Brennan reached out a hand and accepted a stuffed envelope from Bo with the precision of a practiced crook. He slipped it inside his breast pocket. They shook hands and then parted ways in a casual manner, leaving individually. The thirty-second incident told her more than any words that she might've overheard could have revealed: Gabe Pollero had her brother squirreled away and the police in his pocket, just as he had claimed.

15

Rachel stood before the cottage's picture window, transfixed by the flickering lights in the harbor. She tossed back her wine, draining the glass along with her remaining trust in humanity. As in a Hollywood horror flick, evil had crept out of the deep, wrapping greed around the hearts of everyone in her life. She closed her eyes, longing for a tranquil world—a place where corruption and deception did not exist. Where threats didn't multiply by the hour.

The doorbell rang, jarring her upright.

Now what? She crossed the room and peered through the peephole. The local florist was waiting on the front porch with an enormous bouquet in her hands. Rachel paused briefly before opening the door. "You sure you didn't make a mistake?"

"Says your name right here on the envelope. Either you have a secret admirer or a love interest is trying to make points." The rotund, curly haired blonde grinned from ear to ear. She'd been a close friend of Rachel's throughout high school, before their lives veered off in different directions. Now, years later, while Rachel filled her days with Starbuck lattés, gym memberships, and foundation business, her friend was raising five boys, running a flower shop, caring for a sick mother, and presiding over the local Rotary club.

"Care to come in?" Rachel asked. "I have a bottle of wine open."

"Wish I could but I have two more stops before I pick up the boys at school, attend basketball practice, and take the youngest to a dental appointment. What I wouldn't give for a day of leisure or a man with a sizeable checkbook."

They both giggled.

"Can I get a rain check?" her friend asked.

"Absolutely."

"Then I'll be back to collect in twenty years."

The florist snickered as she hurried across the wet pavement to her waiting delivery van. As soon as she was gone, Rachel kicked the door shut behind her and set the heavy glass vase down on the dining room table. She tore the tissue free and leaned down to inhale the heady fragrance emanating from three dozen, perfect, lavender roses.

Beautiful. She extracted the envelope from its plastic stand and smiled, anticipating a thank-you note from Chase. It seemed that he was more considerate than she originally believed.

> *My heart has no defense for itself. My mind, no escape from the constant desire to think of you. Without trying...without thought...I would give myself for you. That's why I know it's true love. Why my eyes fill with tears when I let myself think of all you are to me. I am truly smitten. My whole being captured by all that you are. With your strengths...and what you perceive as weaknesses. I will protect you with my life. With all I am.*
>
> *Love,*
> *Tom*

Tom Nash? "Unbelievable!" Rachel stared down at the note, reading it a second time. Apparently, her boss was more enamored of her than she thought. Although sweet in his intent, his obsession had become disturbing. How could she ever face him again knowing the scope of his feelings?

A knock at the door sounded, setting her teeth on edge. She peered through the peephole, dreading the possibility of Tom Nash making a personal appearance.

Fortunately, that wasn't the case.

Dr. Ying's assistant stood in the rain, her shoulders hunched more than usual. Without hesitation, Rachel opened the door and encouraged the frail woman's advance.

"It's nice to see you," Rachel said. "I had no idea you knew where I lived."

Eleanor tapped the dampness from her closed umbrella and leaned it against the wall. When she lifted her head, worried bags darkened her spectacles. "I'm sorry, Miss Lyons. I just need a few minutes of your time. Would that be all right?"

"Of course. Please make yourself at home."

Eleanor wandered inside. Still clutching a manila folder, she lowered herself onto the living room's orange, overstuffed chair.

"I stopped by the hospital to check on Dr. Ying this afternoon," Rachel volunteered. "But no one would give me any information regarding his condition."

Eleanor's hands were shaking. "Are you alone?"

"Yes. What is it? Did something happen to Dr. Ying?" The woman appeared dazed and confused, adding angst to Rachel's contentious mood.

"He's resting comfortably at the moment," she divulged, "but I'm actually here for another reason."

Rachel held her breath, waiting for the other shoe to drop.

"There's something I desperately need to share with you—something that Lao's kept hidden for years." She peeled the folder away from her body and held it out before Rachel.

"What's this?" Rachel glanced at the brown, elasticized folder and back at the woman's cinched brow.

"It's...rather complicated. I'm not sure where to begin."

Rachel looked at her wineglass and considered filling it to the brim. The world was getting bleaker by the minute. "Would you like me to make you some hot tea and you can—"

"No, I'd rather you didn't, dear. I need to get back to the hospital as soon as possible. I'd like to be there when Lao wakes up."

"Oh, sure. I understand." But she didn't. Not really.

Eleanor remained fixed on the edge of her seat, a timid bird teetering on despair. Emotion stole her voice, leaving it tight and uneven. "Lao told me he wanted to be left alone. That he had private matters to attend to. I returned to my desk and finished filing his papers. Then a policeman called to report a horrible incident involving Lao's twin brother. After he hung up, I knocked on the professor's door, but he didn't answer. When I opened it, I found him slumped over his desk, clutching his chest. Complaining of terrible pains. I dialed 9-1-1, and while we waited for the ambulance to arrive, he told me it was most urgent that I give you that file. He said to tell you that his time is running out."

For what? Rachel unstrapped the file, freeing its contents. She flipped through scrawled notes, postmarked envelopes, and aged newspaper clippings. Memorabilia providing more questions than answers. On closer inspection, she realized they were funeral announcements—printed and handwritten accounts involving the mysterious deaths of various members of the Ying family. A chronological history of tragedy spanning more than two hundred years.

"I don't understand," Rachel professed. "What does all this mean?"

"It's the curse," Eleanor answered. "A terrible plague against the captain of the *Wanli II.* Four hundred years ago, he stole a Chinese concubine's gift intended for her lover. Lao's convinced that the gods sought their revenge by driving the ship and everyone aboard under the sea."

"But what does any of that have to do with Dr. Ying and his family?"

"Lao is a direct descendent of Captain Zao Qing. As it turns out, the captain died aboard his ship at the age of sixty-nine, a prescient number, according to the professor. Since the captain's death, none of the men in Lao's family has outlived him. With the professor's sixty-ninth birthday only one week away and his twin brother's sudden death, he's convinced he'll be next."

"But I don't understand. What can *I* do?"

"There's only one solution," Eleanor replied. "The heart of the dragon. Lao said that if it's found and returned to the rightful owner, the gods would be appeased. All will be forgiven and his grandsons will have the opportunity to live a long life."

Why the big secret?

Eleanor answered, as if reading her mind. "The professor had intended to tell you himself. But since this is a private matter, he didn't want to overwhelm you. Especially after all the information he'd already provided."

Rachel nodded thoughtfully. "I understand."

She pulled a hand-scripted note from the file. The writing was instantly familiar.

Lao,
Chase and I agreed to help you, believing we would all benefit in the end. But lately I've been having second thoughts. I wake up in cold sweats. I've been seeing

strange visions under the ocean and even aboard my ship. Half the time, I don't know if I'm losing my mind or if we're all cursed in this unholy mission. But wherever the truth lies, I need you to promise me one thing. If for some reason I don't return next week, you'll watch out for Rachel and make sure she's happy and safe. She'll always be my proudest accomplishment...all I care about in this world. Nothing, not even the dragon, is worth losing her.

Sam

Rachel held her breath for an endless moment. What was he afraid of? How did he know he was going to die? She could feel the pressure of unshed tears behind her eyes.

Why couldn't he just tell her the truth? If only she'd known...

"I know this is difficult," Eleanor explained. "I wrote dozens of letters for the professor asking for assistance from exploration groups all over the world. As we expected, they all declined. Everyone except Mr. Cohen, that is. When he returned to San Palo, Lao's hopes were resurrected along with this project. I felt it important to assure you, dear, there's *no one* he trusts more than you."

Rachel gathered the papers and clippings. She set her father's note on top. *Prophecy foretold a lion would save the heart of the dragon.* That's what Dr. Ying had said. Perhaps in his own way, he'd alluded to the fact that the old dragon she'd been asked to rescue was none other than the professor himself.

She closed the file and took a weighted breath. "Tell Dr. Ying I'll do whatever I can to help him."

Eleanor smiled and ardently nodded. "You're a remarkable person for doing this," she said. After walking to the door and collecting her umbrella, she turned back. "Oh, there's one more thing I really should mention. It's about the dragon's heart, dear.

You might notice a few letters in the file from a psychic in China. According to him, Mai Le's ghost still guards her treasure. The mere sight of her can stop a man's heart."

Rachel's mouth sagged. *Stop a heart?* Like in her father's case? "And you don't think this is something I should be concerned about?"

"Oh, no, dear. That's a silly old superstition. Nothing to trouble yourself over."

"OK…if you say so."

Rachel paused a moment before standing. She opened the door and waited as Eleanor made her way down the sidewalk. With the wave of a hand, the well-meaning woman climbed into her car. After she drove away, Rachel fell back against the doorjamb.

By providing Chase with the means to find Mai Le's treasure, was she putting his life at risk? Was she being foolish to give credence to Eleanor's haphazard warning and her father's strange accounts? No matter, it was time to take control of her life. To push aside residual doubts, protect her brother, and honor her father's promise.

She walked over to the end table, picked up the receiver, and redialed the last number she'd called on her phone. If she timed it right, she could catch the dive shop owner before he headed home for the night.

A man's gravelly voice came on the line. "Hello."

"Walt, it's me…Rachel Lyons. I know it's late, but I need you to do me a favor. Can you throw together some dive gear for me? Looks like I'll be joining Cohen's crew after all."

Hours later, she curled up on her bed, troubled by her impulsive decision. She drifted off to sleep, and once again she found herself under the ocean—holding her breath, struggling, about to burst at any moment. But this time, her lungs gave out. Beaten and exhausted, she resigned herself to her fate. Opening her mouth, she allowed the water to rush in, knowing full well she would drown. Miraculously, when she inhaled, she discovered that she could breathe! The oxygen flowed from the water into her lungs, leaving her with the extraordinary feeling of weightlessness. A tap on her shoulder turned her around and left her staring at an inconceivable sight.

Dad?

Sam Lyons, framed in a saintly, white glow, drifted before her. She should have been panic-stricken or at least stunned with disbelief. But seeing him again, so handsome and happy, warmed her heart. She wanted to touch him—to know for sure that he was real and not a figment of her imagination. But Sam withdrew, just out of reach. He swam a short distance away and motioned for her to follow. She eagerly complied, swimming beside a colorful school of fish. He came to an abrupt stop before a dark, vast cavern and pointed inside.

She peered into the blackness and asked, "What is this?"

He shook his head and sliced his hand across his throat. But she aligned herself with temptation and discarded his warning. She crossed into the cave, kicking a stone loose along the way. Immediately, enormous rocks began falling, blocking her only means of escape. She reached down and tried to move them, but the weight was insurmountable. She was trapped, buried alive, with no one—not even her father—able to help her.

Why didn't she heed his caution? Listen when she had the chance?

She awoke suddenly, damp with perspiration…exhausted from her battle to survive. Whether a warning from the grave or the result of her built-up anxieties, the message was clear: death was waiting for her at the bottom of the ocean.

16

Devon awoke strapped to a chair in the empty hotel room, dizzy and sick to his stomach. He attributed the pounding ache in the back of his head to a minor concussion. Using most of his willpower, he stretched out his muscles, igniting pain in his arms. He struggled frantically, pulling at his bound wrists. But sweat was causing the ropes to stick to his body, and he was rubbing his skin raw. About a half hour later, he resigned himself to his predicament; he just hoped that he wouldn't suffer the same fate as his partner had.

A woman's voice came through the wall, reconnecting the circuits in his brain. "It's Selena," she called out. "Are you in there?"

Devon couldn't believe his ears. *How'd she find me?* His dull mind searched for answers, but they were lost in his senseless situation. Once again, she stood outside, but this time he couldn't respond. Not with a sock jammed in his mouth and his body hog-tied to a chair. He squirmed excitedly, rocking back and forth. Trying anything to draw her attention.

"Mmmphh!" he yelled under his gag. He tugged at the knot on his ankle, but the binding became tighter. The unbalanced chair rocked on two legs and toppled over, slamming him into the floor.

Fuck! Pain skyrocketed into his shoulder. He lay on his side with his hands almost reaching the soles of his feet. But the rope became so tight that Devon didn't dare move for fear it would tighten more. Then his hand touched something in the brown shag carpeting—a metal object. His fingers identified it as a key. Rolling it around until he could fix a strong grip on it, he applied pressure and began sawing back and forth on the coarse binding with blind determination, praying it would actually work.

Snap! The binding broke. The rope fell away. He freed his whole body and tore the gag out of his mouth. Seconds later, the sound of approaching footsteps traveled through of the walls.

"Marcos!" Selena called out. "What are you doing here?"

"Working. How 'bout you?"

"I'm looking for my brother. Have you seen him?"

"Not today. But he's on his way. While we wait, we could go to my place, *hermosa mujer*," Marcos purred. "Got a nice bed we could share."

"In your dreams."

Marcos exploded in laughter. "*Ah, que cosa dulce.* One day I'll show you what a *real* man can do."

"You haven't got a clue," she retorted.

Devon could hear Marcos snickering and imagined the ugly smile on his face.

"Tell him to call me when he shows up," Selena said.

Although Devon admired her tenacity, he was grateful when the hall grew quiet. When he could make a run for it without jeopardizing Selena's safety. As soon as Marcos stepped inside, he launched himself into the man's midsection, pitching him onto an end table, which shattered under his weight. While the creep rolled around, moaning and grabbing himself, Devon scrambled to his feet. He ran through the open doorway, bumping into a drunken hooker in the hallway and spinning her around.

"*Que pasa?*"

She swayed back and forth in her thigh-high boots, blocking Devon's one chance for escape. Marcos's fist came from out of nowhere, slamming into his back, throwing him full force into the wall.

"Shit!" the woman screamed. A neighbor cracked her door open and peeked into the hallway, only to be pushed aside by the hooker. The door slammed shut, hiding them both inside.

Devon managed to get back on his feet. He braced himself against another impact just as a second punch landed. He bounced off the wall and doubled over. As soon as he raised his head, Marcos swung a right hook, but Devon ducked just in time. Marcos's knuckles swished past his nose, throwing the guy completely off balance. Seeing an opening, Devon darted forward and delivered a jaw-crunching blow. Then, filled with a rush of adrenaline, he wove left, anticipating Marcos's next move.

"Not so easy to hit a moving target, is it?" Devon taunted.

Marcos swept his right foot, but Devon jumped back out of reach. He kept his gaze leveled on his staggering opponent, preparing for his line of attack. Marcos charged like a raging bull, and Devon responded, jamming an uppercut into his middle. Devon felt his fist connect with muscled flesh, leaving his assailant buckling in pain.

"Motherfucker!" Marcos yelled, as he dropped to the floor, clutching his gut.

Devon wanted to beat the shit out of him, leave a permanent impression. But as Marcos had said, Pollero would be back any minute now. There was every reason to believe that Pollero would vent his anger on Rachel when he discovered the empty hotel room.

Devon had to get to his sister before word of his escape got out.

"Adios, amigo," he tossed at Marcos. He raced down the hallway toward the elevator. Just as he reached it, the doors parted, and a new threat came into view.

"Going somewhere?" Viktor snarled from inside the elevator. He drew his knife from its sheath and shoved aside the elderly woman standing between him and the opening. She flew into a rage, preventing him from leaving, and a shoving match ensued. They were still wrestling for the doors as they closed, sealing them both inside.

Devon bolted in the opposite direction, searching for an alternative route out of the building. He found an exit at the end of the winding corridor and slammed the metal door open. With his heart racing, he clambered down the stairwell, clearing two flights in a matter of seconds. When he reached the seventh floor, he heard the sound of pounding footsteps descending from above.

"I got 'im!" a man's voice shouted.

Pollero?

Devon noted the exit sign directing guests to the parking garage. He quickened his pace. Only five more floors to go. He rounded another corner. He spotted an exit door and twisted the handle. Locked. *Damn it!*

Fut! Something zipped past his ear. It ricocheted off the door and left a dent. Devon glanced at his hand, still hovering above the knob. *Oh, my God!* The chilling image left him stunned and amazed at the same time. The slug had passed clean through his hand. A fine red line grew into a thick stream, dripping down the length of his arm. He gripped his wrist, stemming the flow, and hurled himself around another corner.

Pollero's shoes pounded the concrete steps above him; he was growing closer by the second. Devon willed himself downward.

Just a little farther, just a few more steps. As he neared the next landing, he stumbled and fell to his knee. A hand snatched his shoulder, bringing him back to his feet. Pollero's fist smacked his jaw, hurling him into the wall. Devon shoved him away, but the guy charged right back, slamming him harder this time. Devon latched onto the bastard's middle.

"Ahhh!" Pollero cried out. He reeled, sending them careening into the opposite wall.

Devon gritted his teeth and slipped his blood-soaked arm around his assailant's neck. But Pollero retaliated, jabbing his elbow repeatedly into Devon's ribs. With survival foremost in his mind, Devon pushed back with all his might. Somehow Pollero managed to hold on. Then his heel slipped over the edge of a stair, sending both of them crashing down the concrete steps. Devon heard the sound of a crack when they hit the wall on the landing below. He released his hold, and Pollero's head flopped sickeningly to the side.

For a timeless moment, Devon just looked at his face. Pollero's black eyes stared into space. Blood collected in the corner of his slack mouth. Without checking his pulse, Devon knew he was dead. The horrific sight ratcheted his stomach. He forced himself upright, grasping the handrail to steady himself. He slid along the wall, hugging his throbbing side. Pinning his wrist against his chest. He reached the basement and held onto the stairwell door. Gasping, he pulled himself around the doorframe and threw himself into the room. Around him, the concrete walls tilted. He closed his eyes to still the spinning motion. To control his uneven breathing.

Ding! Devon looked up just as the service elevator door opened. Inside, three snarling faces stared out at him, and then they blurred into one monstrous mask. Devon felt his knees buckle. His head hit the floor. His nightmare dimmed to the darkest shade of black.

17

Naomi met Rachel on the dock with a mug of hot coffee. The barkeeper's unruly curls were mostly hidden beneath the triangular, green scarf tied at the back of her neck. "Figured you could use a jolt before losing your land legs." She held her jacket close to her body, fending off the morning chill.

Rachel remained puzzled, as she sipped the hot brew. "How'd you know I was coming?"

"Chase told me you called this morning. Had a change of heart or something. Personally, I'm kinda surprised he didn't show up to greet you. But then, Ian's comment about women not belonging on ships might have slowed him up."

"He actually said that?"

"Yeah, but don't take it personally. That old fart says a lot things he shouldn't."

Actually, it was Chase who had given her an earful...telling her she'd be more effective staying in town, conducting research, and waiting for his calls. But she'd already convinced herself that her presence was essential. Whether he wanted to hear it or not, she was determined to go along. It was the only way she could ensure that the expedition would go according to plan and her brother would be set free.

With a quick nod to Naomi, Rachel boarded *Stargazer* and made her way belowdecks. She passed two doors in the companionway before arriving at her destination. After setting her bags down in the midship cabin, she bent her knees to test the queen-size bed and then surveyed her surroundings, familiarizing herself again with every detail. On the port side, the room featured a polished teak wardrobe and small bureau with adequate storage space. In the stern, an unlatched door was open, exposing a compact head, complete with white towels, a shower stall, a stool with a flushing bidet, and a tiny sink. Her eyes traveled to the starboard side, where a flat-screen television and DVD/VCR player were mounted. Although the accommodations were slightly outdated, she had to admit that the yacht was clean and well appointed.

A sudden surge in the ship's momentum brought Rachel's attention back to the porthole. She watched the shoreline disappear as *Stargazer* trudged through the harbor and into the gentle swells of the Pacific Ocean. With no assigned duties to perform, she renewed her commitment to stay out from underfoot. She unloaded her T-shirts, jeans, jacket, swimsuit, and deck shoes and laid them neatly on the wardrobe's built-in shelves. After placing her toiletries and sleeping pills on the bathroom counter, she reached into her backpack and pulled out Dr. Ying's mysterious file. She climbed onto the bed and propped herself against the padded headboard. She thumbed through the documents: a stack of aged and illegible letters, copies of manifest records, an envelope containing a strange lock, and pages torn from a Chinese reference book. Beneath them, the handwritten translations from Dr. Ying's personal journal captured her attention. She began reading and was instantly transported to another time and place.

In the late sixteenth century, Father Matteo Ricci, a Jesuit priest from Rome, presented Emperor Wanli with a chiming clock. As a result, he was allowed to present himself at the imperial court and was given free access to the Forbidden City. Mai Le, one of the emperor's loveliest concubines, possessed an amazing ability to learn languages and was permitted to have exchanges with Father Ricci. In this way, she often informed the emperor of unsavory activities in the outer world. During one of his many visits, the priest introduced Mai Le to an Italian sea captain, Vito Brunelli. She instantly took a liking to the handsome stranger and looked forward to his seasonal visits.

Emperor Wanli was known to regularly use opium and morphine and was often preoccupied with Empress Xiaoduan or Empress Xiaojing, his wife and his favorite concubine, respectively. As a result, Mai Le's visits with Captain Brunelli would go virtually unnoticed, as the Jesuit priest, who conversed fluently in Chinese, focused on converting important officials and members of the imperial family to Christianity.

After Captain Brunelli's final visit, Mai Le obtained the assistance of an imperial eunuch to commission a bronze sculpture encased in a lacquered box under the guise that it would be given to Father Ricci as a goodwill gesture. However, in actuality, her gift of affection was intended for Brunelli. With the aid of a talented artist and Chinese shaman, this remarkable creation incorporated the couple's Chinese horoscope signs—the dragon and snake—bringing them together before the next lunar eclipse. Zao Qing, the new captain of the Wanli II, *assured Mai Le that her prized token would safely reach her beloved captain in Lisbon in four months' time, following his trade mission to Fusang. However, shortly after Captain Qing's departure, Father Ricci visited the Forbidden City and informed Mai Le of Brunelli's death from tuberculosis three weeks earlier. Realizing that her fate was now sealed by mournful loss, Mai Le secretly left the walled city clothed in servant's attire and dove to her death in the China Sea.*

Meanwhile, Captain Qing encountered dozens of trade vessels destined for Portugal and Malaysia. One night, his crew spotted lamps from a distressed ship. Twenty men, led by Qing, boarded her and discovered half the crew belowdecks, suffering from scurvy. One of the delirious men raved about the gold they were carrying aboard, and by night's end, the distressed ship was ablaze and the Wanli *was heading west with full sails and a king's ransom in gold in the hold.*

For eight months, the captain and his band of cutthroats exchanged cannon fire with other merchant ships, destroying the vessels and killing thousands to add gold to their bounty. By late November, with their supplies running low, they sailed farther west, seeking safe harbor. However, they were also entering a draconic month, which is the average interval between two successive transits of the moon through its ascending node. As a result of retribution by the ancient gods, Mai Le's treasured gift became a curse to everyone aboard. Her ghost, languishing at the bottom of the sea, had been waiting for an opportunity to enact her revenge and it finally happened on December 1. A tremendous storm broke out and reliable rumor confirmed the last sighting of the Wanli II *at eight bells, when gale winds hit the coast, and the sky went black eighty nautical miles northwest of Manzanillo, Mexico.*

Reliable rumor? The double entendre made Rachel smile. She closed the file and stood up to stretch. The history lesson had left her hungry for fresh air and an update on the ship's progress. She left her room and traveled back down the companionway. She climbed the ladder through the open double hatch and entered the main salon. In the helm station, Chase and his sidekick, Ian, were busy at work, steering and talking boat language over the drone of engines and voice traffic on the VHF marine radio. Nearby, a third man sat before a display screen and an extensive instrument panel. The port-mounted electrical panel had breaker switches to power a multitude of operations, including controls that allowed the helmsman to sweep the bank of spotlights on *Stargazer's* hull from side to side and vertically. Absolutely nothing was lacking in the ship's treasure-seeking capability.

Rachel was so intrigued by the sonar's pulsating readings that she didn't hear a man's footsteps behind her.

"Excuse me," he said, announcing his presence.

"Oh, sorry." She moved aside so the young crew member could enter the bustling room.

The brief interruption pulled Chase's attention away from Ian. "Welcome aboard," he called out to her.

"Didn't mean to intrude." She hesitated before looking him in the eye.

"No chance of that. This *is* your ship."

The words ratcheted up the anxiety that she had managed to temper. Although Chase had been led to believe that their expedition was being funded solely by the foundation, the night before their departure, Rachel had called in a favor. To safeguard her brother and Dr. Ying, she had pledged the *Stargazer* and her father's house as security for a short-term loan from Merchant's Trust. Like a bet at a gambler's table, everything Rachel owned was now at stake.

Ian tightened his grip on the ship's chrome throttle. "I never thought I'd miss this beauty, but I sure did."

Chase smiled. "He's talking about the ship, you know."

"Is that right?" Ian said. He tossed a wink at Rachel. "Yer both beauties in me book."

"You haven't changed at all, Mr. Lowe," she said.

"Not so, darlin'. Thicker round the middle, thinner on top. Though I still appreciate the company of a fine lady now and then." He flashed a cheeky grin.

"So, you all settled in?" Chase asked, detouring around that subject. "I don't mind moving my stuff if you'd prefer the captain's quarters."

"Not necessary. You're *Stargazer's* captain. I'm just along for the ride."

"Oh, I see…that's how it is." He shoved hair out of his eyes, drawing attention to the gleaming silver bracelet on his wrist.

"Never noticed that before," she said.

He glanced at his arm nonchalantly. "Gift from a friend." He returned his concentration to the windshield—a cool reminder that he was occupied with more important matters.

Right. Rachel gave Ian a quick salute before returning to the afterdeck. She climbed the companion ladder on the port side and arrived at the fly bridge. After a quick look around, she sat down on the smooth leather seat and leaned her head back. Closing her eyes, she tasted the salt in the wind. She relished the warm rays on her face and the sound of the ship plowing through the waves. Why had she shut herself off from the ocean? Deprived herself of such beauty? Ignored the pleasure that vacationing tourists enjoyed?

In the emerald water ahead of them, dolphins shimmered just beneath the surface, leading the way. She smiled at the sight, having forgotten the rush that came from being on the open sea—the sense of freedom it unleashed. She'd barred it from her life since her father died.

Ian suddenly cut *Stargazer's* engine, jolting Rachel. Within seconds, feet were scurrying in all directions. Marker weights fell, buoys were tossed. Anchors fore and aft hit the ocean floor.

"All hands inside," Chase called out.

With the anchor lines secured, *Stargazer's* crew joined the captain in the helm station. Around them, refinished teak gleamed and polished brass shimmered. The aroma of fresh-brewed coffee wafted from the galley below in the warm morning air. They settled on the refurbished white-leather sofa that stretched from the aft portside door to the starboard wing door. Outfitted in low-slung jeans and a gaping green shirt, Chase collected his charts and assumed his directorial position before them.

Rachel leaned a hip against the paneled wall and layered her arms over her starched linen blouse. *Doesn't he know what a button is?* Her focus shifted from Chase's sun-bronzed chest to the four men seated before him. Varying degrees of apprehension lined their faces. Young, middle-aged, various ethnicities. They were an odd, disjointed lot brought together by a common goal: stealing cargo from the carcass of a four-hundred-year-old ship. Yet as reckless and self-serving as they might be, their sins would soon pale in comparison to her own.

"All right," Chase said, "now that we're all here, let's run through our drill one more time. I want to make sure everyone's on the same page before we—" He stopped midstream, apparently assuming the disquiet on Rachel's face was due to his lack of decorum. Before she had time to object, he launched into introductions, briefly touching on her qualifications. His blue eyes dropped from her eyes to her lips, jacking up the temperature in the room a few degrees. "We're fortunate to have Miss Lyons along."

Right. Rachel smiled and glanced around the table, making a full assessment. Blaine McKenzie was a computer whiz kid who had flown in from Seattle. A. J. Hobbs was a dive technician who had studied in Boston. Ian Lowe, the Irish helmsman, was her father's old pro. The fourth member of their crew was a Native American warrior by the name of Wade Hawkins. His coal-black hair reached his shoulder blades and was swept back, exposing a wide forehead, high cheekbones, and chiseled, straight nose. Although extremely quiet, he was Herculean in size.

"Excuse me." A woman's lilting voice turned everyone's head. "Would anyone like more coffee?"

Here was the Asian beauty Rachel had seen at the Crow's Nest Bar—the twentyish waitress who had handed her a cup of coffee before rushing out the door a few days ago. Now she was standing in the adjacent salon with a sweet smile and a coffee pot in her hand. Short, black hair framed her round, petite face and accentuated her large, catlike eyes. Her snug-fitting, pink T-shirt and frayed micro shorts left little to the imagination. A quick glance at the grinning men told Rachel that none of them had overlooked the woman's sex appeal.

"Would love some," Chase piped up.

Mika hurried to his side and filled his cup to the brim, while everyone looked on.

"Thank you," he said faintly, as if he was hard at work concentrating on some difficult mental task. "By the way, this is our chef, Mika Yamada. Her father's the new pastor at Westbury Foursquare, and I have to tell you...this girl makes the best *yakisoba* I've ever had in my life."

How nice.

Mika tilted her head to one side and gave a coy, cutesy smile. "Then you should *love* dinner."

Rachel wondered how the pastor would feel about his daughter flirting and flashing her hot pants at a bunch of horny men. Her speculation must have translated into a scowl. After one look in her direction, Mika scurried around the room, collecting empty cups, and then vanished from the room.

Chase resumed his command. "If any boats or ships come into the area, as far as anyone's concerned, we're working the *Griffin*...the WWI commodity wreck you've all been briefed on."

The deception continues. Her father must have uttered the same words before his run ended, demanding the same mindless loyalty from his crew.

"But the copper and shell casings are completely tapped out," Blaine interrupted.

Ian grumbled, "Ya think?" He jerked his thumb left. "Good thing we got Genius on board." His remark deepened the scowl on Blaine's face but failed to silence him.

"I still don't understand why we're being so secretive. We've got every right to be here, don't we?"

Before Chase could explain that their salvage rights in fact had been granted, Ian spoke up, heightening the drama in the room. "Scavengers and scourges don't care. They'll walk on water ta add coin to their pocket. One flick of their blade, and yer a shark's noon delight."

Blaine smirked. "Scourges...like in pirates and cutlasses? That's absolutely ridiculous. Next, you'll be claiming we're cursed for coming here."

"Ah...not so," Ian cajoled. "Was cursed the moment ya stepped on board."

Blaine was visibly angry. "Are you serious? How do you expect me to work with this moron?"

Ian pivoted in his seat. "Moron, ya say? Ya mangy cur. Open yer mouth one more time and I'll toss you over the side me self."

Egad. Rachel looked back at Chase. What had she gotten herself into? There seemed to be an ongoing dispute between Blaine, an American version of Harry Potter; and Ian, an abasing Richard Harris. If not for their intrusive timing, the men's interactions could have been an entertaining distraction.

"OK, enough already," Chase admonished.

Blaine sank back in his seat. He shoved his glasses up on his nose with a downturned glare.

Chase threw a warning glare to Ian. "Hopefully, you all remember why we're here..."

AJ added his two cents. "The *Wanli.*" He tipped his head back, taking another sip from his cup. Although his brown, close-cropped hair and rectangular, wireless spectacles could place him unnoticed in any corporate office, there was something inherently familiar about him. Was it possible he'd been a member of Sam's former crew? A recent visitor at the foundation office? No...but Rachel had definitely seen him somewhere.

Chase began unfurling his treasure map and anchoring it with stones on the newly varnished table. "Like I was saying, there are modern-day pirates all over these waters. We're traveling fully armed, so stay alert and keep calm. I'm not looking to spend the next five years in jail."

Armed? As in guns? Rachel stared at him, completely dumbfounded.

"This is our position," he pointed out. Everyone's attention was drawn back to his triangulated diagram. "We're going to finish laying the grids and going about our business as usual."

AJ scribbled notes on his pad as Chase dictated coordinates and varying field degrees. Meanwhile, Wade remained propped on his elbow at the far edge of the sofa, casting disparaging looks at Rachel.

"As you all know," Chase continued, "Sam Lyons played an important role in this project. What set him apart from other salvagers were his instincts...his willingness to search outside the box. Although he's no longer with us, he put us on the right path. Twenty kilometers beyond *Griffin's* perimeter, porcelain shards turned up. We've since discovered a virtual trail leading to the Nimbus jetty, where the *Wanli's* anchor was found. In sector twelve, we might be looking at cannons, which according to Doc, the smugglers used to protect their hoard. So keep your eyes peeled and stay on target. We're after china and jewelry here, but any relics you come across are a bonus in our pockets. And one more thing," he added. "Don't take any unnecessary risks. I intend to bring everyone home safe and sound."

As he reviewed hand signals and safety issues, Rachel's mind slid to a dark, ominous place: the concrete building where she'd last seen her bother. She reminded herself that after four days—five days max—she'd be gone. After amassing whatever she could to satisfy Pollero, she'd find an excuse to get off the ship, collect Devon, and hightail it out of town before anyone was the wiser.

Chase cleared his throat, drawing Rachel's attention. "One last thing," he said. "We're a team here. Everyone watches each other's back. And follow the orders you're given. I don't want any heroics on or off this ship."

Although his directives seemed to be leveled at her, she saw no point in them. Much to Chase's apparent chagrin, neither did AJ.

"Any objections if I make the first dive? Got some great hits on the sonar and if my theory's correct—"

"Cap'n," Ian broke in, "thought we agreed...Hawkins and I go first."

From the tightness in his voice, Chase's patience appeared to be running on fumes. "Listen! We're all diving. Check the schedule. Right now this is how it's gonna run. AJ, I need you to double-check your readings. And let me know if any unauthorized boats or ships turn up...especially the *Legend*. Wade, as soon as you finish helping with the dive gear, set up a cleaning station for Rachel. And make damn sure no one trips over any lines." He jotted down numbers on a sheet of paper and then handed it to Blaine. "Get our log up to speed," he told him. "Is everyone clear on their assignments?"

"Aye, Captain," the crew bellowed. They all began sliding out of their seats. AJ looked up in time to catch Rachel's stare.

"So what's AJ stand for?" she asked.

"Alexander Jackson. Sort of an old family name," he said matter-of-factly.

Ian snickered. "And here I thought it was short for arse-weed jackass."

AJ smiled back, but behind his square-framed glasses, his eyes remained cool and calculating.

Alexander Jackson Hobbs. Rachel looked away. His name didn't register.

"One last thing," Chase announced. "The first person to hit pay dirt cracks open that bottle of Hennigans scotch that Naomi gave me."

"Kiss it good-bye, mates," Ian boomed. He charged through the doorway with Blaine following closely behind. Wade, on the other hand, was slow to leave.

"Interesting group," she said.

Chase's eyes were trained on his map. "They'll get the job done."

"So, I guess all your dreams are about to come true." As soon as the words left her mouth, she regretted uttering them.

"Are you offering something, Rachel?"

"I was referring to the wreck."

"Yeah, figured as much." He tossed her a quick sideways glance. "Anyhow, after that 5.9-magnitude earthquake hit the Pacific Ocean about 120 miles off the Oregon coast last week, there's no telling what we're looking at. We'll either get lucky today or end up like the *Olympic*."

"The *Olympic*?" she echoed.

"Ian and I worked that project awhile back. A ton of sand buried our markers. Set us back weeks. We had to bring in a barge and go a hell of a lot deeper than we originally planned. The total recovery ran way over budget and ended up taking six months to complete."

Six months? Her heart skipped a beat. "But what about *this* project? You're only days away from finding treasure in the *Wanli* wreck. Right?"

"Hopeful thinking, I'm afraid. But in any event, the porcelain we've collected so far should be worth something." He treated her to one of his boyish grins. "We'll be striking it rich before you know it."

Shit! Pollero and his thugs would never settle for a Chinese tea service. Rachel was fuming. It was all big talk. Nothing more. Just like her father's incredible claims were.

"It was just a lie?" she tossed. "How could you do that, Chase? After everything that's happened?"

He cocked his head to the side. "What are you talking about? I didn't lie to you. If memory serves me, I told you we were close to finding something. I never said *how* close."

Rachel looked down, shaking her head. Trying to make sense of it all. The professor had been so convincing, so *sure*. She'd used his hopes and fantastic dreams as leverage to save her brother. If anyone was to blame for this mess, it was she.

The revelation closed her eyes.

"Come on, Rachel, relax," Chase chided. "We're just getting started. I assure you we're not leaving here empty-handed."

"I can't take that risk," she murmured. Knowing Devon's temperament, Rachel knew that he would be hard-pressed to sit back and cooperate with his abductors. The more time they wasted at sea, the greater his chances of being killed were.

Chase tilted his head. "Why not?"

"It's a long story. You just have to trust me."

"Ah…I see. That's awfully convenient, isn't it? Especially since you don't have an ounce of trust when it comes to me."

"Chase—"

"You provided this ship and insisted on coming along. As far as I'm concerned, you're stuck out here with the rest of us. No one's leaving without a damn good reason. And since you're not willing to provide one, maybe you can find something better to do." He turned his back on her. "Hawkins!" he yelled. The silent warrior sprang to attention. "Escort Miss Lyons back to her room. I believe she has some research to finish."

He was dismissing her? Like a child? How could he do that?

Wade Hawkins was at her side. By her estimate, his six-foot frame weighed in at a solid 220 pounds. His tree-trunk arms poked out of his gaping black vest, adding girth to his sculptured appearance. He lifted one hand in the air, presenting a demanding, unyielding signpost.

"This way," he said in a deep, guttural voice.

Rachel looked to her insensitive protector. "This is ridiculous. You have to listen to me, Chase. We're wasting time."

"Totally agree with you there." His eyes never left his nautical charts.

"It wouldn't be any problem for me to pilot the Zodiac myself, you know."

His blue eyes swung back to her, ferocity filling their depths. "As long as I'm in command, you don't leave this ship without my authority. Is that clear?"

"Aye, aye, Captain," she huffed.

Wade took another step forward, forcing her to back up. "Come with me," he said.

He moved stealthily past her, barely clearing the exit. Rachel joined him, trailing closely behind. They descended the stairwell and followed the passageway to the forward cabins.

"Here," he announced. He lowered the brass door handle on her designated room.

"I know," she grumbled, edging past him. One look at his morose expression and her voice softened. "I'm fine," she said. "You can go now."

He angled his dark, deep-set eyes. "You don't remember me, do you?"

She paused for a moment before answering. "Should I?"

"You must have been ten the first time I saw you. Your brother was sitting on the Santa Monica pier with a line in the water. You were hanging off the bow of your father's boat, yelling at the top of your lungs…doing everything you could to scare off the fish."

The fuzzy memory drew a brief smile.

"My dad was a longshoreman in Redondo," he continued. "Everyone knew him as McCoy, but his true name was Running Elk."

Mac? The image of a gentle, tawny face formed in her mind. "Of course! He was one of my father's dearest friends. I wore the moccasins he gave me on my twelfth birthday until the soles wore out. And your mother...Theresa, right?" When Wade solemnly nodded his head, Rachel continued. "She had the most beautiful long, black hair. I remember going on a camping trip and she made this amazing Indian bread. I must've eaten ten pounds and gained just as many."

A soft chuckle rose from his chest.

With each flashback, her smile grew along with the speed of her words. "Didn't we go skinny-dipping one night in a rocky ravine? If I remember right, there was this amazing waterfall. We hid directly behind it. It was incredible. Everyone was calling out our names, trying to find us."

His gaze slipped from her eyes to her lips. "I kissed you there," he said.

Rachel cringed internally. Her cheeks warmed. Of all people, how was it possible she'd forgotten him? She'd dreamed about that kiss—his warm gentle touch—for years. "I...I'm sorry, Wade. I don't know why I would—"

"It was no big deal, really. We were just kids."

She smiled at the memory, thinking back to when things were simpler—when she wasn't confined to her quarters with the lives of two men depending on her.

Thundering sounds lifted her eyes to the overhead vent. Men were running fore and aft. Shouts were coming from the upper deck. Somehow, Wade didn't seem to notice.

"I was a lumberjack in southern Oregon for about six years," he continued. "Came home to visit my folks. That's when I ran into your dad. He told me what you'd been up to and convinced me to try diving. I ended up spending five years in Florida, learning the ropes. When I got word that the *Stargazer* was going back out and the captain needed a crew fast, nothing was going to keep me from signing on. He's sort of a legend, you know."

Rachel had only been half listening. "Who?"

"Captain Cohen." He squared his shoulders. "He called me last night. Told me about this adventure you're on. I have to tell you, I wouldn't have missed this for a lifetime."

Great. "Do you have any influence on this ship?" she asked.

"Not really. Excuse the pun, but I'm kinda the low man on the totem pole."

She sniffed a laugh. "Of course."

It was suddenly silent on the upper deck. Her gaze was riveted to the ceiling.

"So…you married?" Wade asked.

"No, I'm not."

"Then you're available. For some reason, I thought you and the captain were an item—"

"Hell, *no*!" She astonished herself with her fervent reaction.

Creak. There was a fresh sound from the floorboards in the hallway. Her ardent admirer stepped aside. Chase stood in the open doorway with his wet suit dangling low on his hips.

Rachel's breath caught. She never would have hurt him deliberately, but it was evident by his heated complexion and disparaging scowl that she had done just that.

"Chase, I…I'm sorry," she stammered. "I didn't see you there."

"So, you're mad at me. Just tell me what I've done now."

"If you don't know, I can't help you."

"Well, for whatever it's worth, I'm sorry. OK?"

"Fine. Apology accepted."

"So, we're good then."

"Uh-huh."

"All right. I'll see you back on deck, OK?"

She lowered her voice to a whisper. "No problem, jerk."

Wade's brow quirked.

"All right!" Chase retorted. "We can't keep this up. Not while we're both on this ship. We have to put our differences aside… figure out a way to get along."

"Got it."

"If we're going to work together, we have to forget all the negative stuff between us."

Rachel rolled her eyes and looked away.

"Wait a minute. I thought you agreed."

"About working with you? Sure. But I'm still mad at you. I'm just sorry about embarrassing you, is all."

Chase looked at Wade, shaking his head. "Women," he grumbled. "Come on, let's go." They were both out the door with Chase leading when Wade suddenly paused. He glanced back with a spreading smile.

"Hell, no, huh?" he teased.

Rachel smirked before shutting the door between them.

Twenty minutes later, Rachel pushed her books aside and ventured from her room to observe the crew in action. She climbed the closest ladder and arrived on the afterdeck. Wade was in the lower compartment handing scuba tanks, regulators, and buoyancy vests to Ian. Weight belts, fins, masks, and snorkels soon followed. Chase slipped into his double, eighty-cubic-foot tanks and waited while the Irishman wedged a small pony tank containing emergency air in between them. With three regulators now dangling securely under his chin, he faced Rachel.

"Guess you're hoping I'll drown, huh?"

"How did you know?"

The wry smile on his face proved her sarcasm had been taken lightly. No matter how irritating Chase might be, she had no desire to see him harmed.

He finished adjusting the dive computer on his wrist—an aid for his bottom time, ascent depths, and decompression timing. In his vest pocket, he added a slate with the stops and requisite times penciled in. He checked his wristwatch and noted the time. Just when she thought he was fully equipped, he tethered a primary light to his right wrist and latched a strobe to his vest. Chase Cohen was diving alone and leaving no margin for error.

Ian nodded at Rachel. "Got yer skin right here," he said.

"What?" Her stomach lurched. He held up the Camaro wet suit she'd left on a hook below, next to the lockers that were all full.

"Cap'n says yer his good luck charm."

"He needs to find another one," she mumbled.

"So you coming or not?" Chase asked.

She glanced around the ship. Everyone had a duty to perform—an assignment keeping him busy. Through an adjacent cabin window, she spotted the young software genius pecking away.

"I'm helping Blaine today…with financial statements and an updated report for the foundation."

"That's really going to take two of you?"

She nodded quickly.

Frustration marred Chase's forehead. "Well, I suppose the trustees won't mind when we pull up with drained tanks and an empty hold. Just as long as my books are in order."

Rachel could feel her pulse racing as her buried fears rose inside. Every nightmare had left her panicked, screaming. Dying. Whatever was out there had been waiting for four years, anticipating the day she'd be back.

"Come on," Chase persisted. "Here's your chance to show me up. Who knows, you might even steal that bottle of scotch from Ian."

"I thought AJ wanted to go. Can't you ask him?"

Chase grumbled under his breath. "Never mind. Ian, suit up. You're going with me."

"But Cap'n, remember? Ya had me checkin' the rudder. It's been runnin' a bit off, ya know."

"Are you serious? We're anchored. Can't that wait?"

"Not if ya don't mind goin' round in circles."

"Honestly. Am I the only one on this ship interested in finding treasure?" Chase's frown returned to Rachel.

"OK, OK! I'll go with you, but only on one condition," she said. "If we strike out and there's nothing down there, you'll arrange to have someone take me back in the launch."

Chase huffed and shook his head. "I've never met anyone so anxious to jump ship, but if that's what you want, Rachel, I'll take you myself."

18

Downstairs in her isolated quarters, Rachel yanked off her pants and blouse and struggled into a black Speedo bathing suit that molded itself to every curve in her body. A few minutes later, she returned to the afterdeck and dragged on the wet suit Ian held out to her. She strapped a rubber-handled Bowie knife to her calf, attached a wide-beam light to her wrist, and latched two goody bags to her BC vest. She waited while Ian assisted with the balance of her gear. Then she secured her video strap and picked up the metal detector.

All the while, Chase stood near the gunwale, silently watching her with unreadable thoughts on his face.

Her nerves were making her edgy. "Go," she snapped at him.

After testing each regulator, Chase gave Ian the thumbs up and tumbled over *Stargazer's* side.

I can do this. I can do this, she assured herself. Ian and Wade hovered nearby as she slid on her mask and adjusted her regulator. After one last look around, she dropped into the icy underworld, joining Chase in his weightless descent.

As soon as their bubbles dispersed, she took her bearings. She deflated her vest and dove deeper, following his strong kicks.

She remained close enough to feel the churning water from his scissoring motion, to trace the lines of his taut, muscular thighs. They passed mossy, green boulders on the sandy ocean floor and rounded a cliff, where the ground vanished into a dark, shadowy chasm. Without Rachel's awareness, her instincts had taken over. A sense of well-being seeped into her soul.

After skirting one of *Stargazer's* anchors, they paused to purge their masks and ended up observing an inquisitive rock cod. To Rachel's surprise, a diamond stingray arrived on the scene. She reached out and trailed her gloved hand over its back. It circled around and swooped downward, vanishing into the ocean's depths. The brief encounter reminded her of the first dive she'd ever made. Having been mesmerized by Hawaii's colorful marine life, she'd settled in a single coral head and hardly moved for almost an hour.

Chase beckoned her onward. He halted before a mountainous outcropping and signaled his intention to enter its ruptured mantle.

No. Rachel shook her head from side to side. Cooler water bled through the wall's opening. It was an ominous reminder of Sam's dream message.

Chase moved his fist from his face to his chest. He exposed his palm and pointed a single digit at his heart. *Trust me,* he was saying in the sign language they'd shared at a dinner table years earlier.

Ironic. In another place, Rachel might have shoved Chase and walked away. Now she had no choice but to depend on him. She nodded slowly and trailed after him, ever mindful of their growing distance from the cave's jagged mouth. Once inside, he turned on the blaring light and motioned for her to lift the camera. Directly in front of them, microscopic bits of sediment and algae danced in the yellowish-gold light. Rachel strained her eyes to peer into the shadowy recesses. To cut through the murk blanketing the cavernous floor. And there it took shape in all its ghostly wonder: the *Wanli.*

Impossible. The beam of light panned over the tilted illusion, a sight that left her gasping for air. Beside her, Chase remained stationary, staring for an eternal minute, perhaps as mesmerized as she was.

He turned and signaled, "OK?"

She nodded, but the shock had barely worn off. Below them rested a vision beyond her comprehension. Beyond the dreams her father had so ardently shared. Instead of the few rotten timbers or rusted pieces of metal she had imagined they'd find, this was a complete ship. It rested on its side, half-buried in silt on the ocean floor, and it extended beyond her field of vision. By her best estimate, it had to be over 300 feet long and 160 feet wide. According to her research, this had been an extraordinary merchant vessel...one of the largest in the Chinese fleet.

She glanced overhead and studied the igneous rock formations surrounding them. Somehow, the ship had settled inside of a volcanic crater. Over time, a microcosm had been created. With seismic activity in the region causing underwater rockslides, the *Wanli* had become totally encased while miraculously remaining unscathed. Lost and forgotten in the earth's inner core, she'd been protected from the sea's damaging wave action and had managed to survive the ravages of time.

Amazing! Even though sand blanketed a third of her hull, slowing the inevitable decay, nature had found its way into the ship's catacomb. Algae hung from her two remaining masts, waving as if caught in a gentle breeze. Sea anemones covered the ship, and in every dark corner, schools of iridescent fish flittered about, reacting to the invaders' slightest movements.

The spike in AJ's readings had been a clear indication that the ship's cargo far exceeded their original expectations. Once located, they could begin the arduous task of floating their finds to the surface with lift bags and air from a spare tank. With Blaine's help, her real work would begin: cleaning, identifying, and tagging each piece. Finding the heart of the dragon and taking it to Pollero without anyone being the wiser.

Although the *Wanli II* was not a simple merchant ship as her father originally believed, the bow of the massive, sixteenth-century junk was exactly as Dr. Ying had described it. The prow's brilliant figurehead had broken off, leaving a large, gaping hole in the ship's hull.

Chase motioned with two fingers, signaling their entry. She waited as he attached a penetration line. He finned through the opening and disappeared from view. She glanced at her computer and noted the depth readout of eighty feet. After a few seconds, his flickering light pierced the wooden slats. She glanced back at the cave's entrance and mentally measured the distance.

With her camera secured, she swam through the gap with her light leading the way. The cone-like beam bounced off a school of marble-eyed fish. They dispersed above stacked crates, broken planks, and smashed porcelain that littered the surface. She reached down and picked up a green shard, stirring a cloud of black sediment. She dropped it back into the dissipating cloud before joining Chase.

He'd found a barrel and had wedged a piece of wood under its cracked top. She instinctively wanted to halt his actions. Urge him to leave his discovery untouched. But then she reminded herself of her new role as a salvager. From now on, discovery took priority over preservation.

When the rotten lid gave way, they both peered down into the barrel's demolished contents. Chase reached inside and extracted the single plate that remained remarkably intact. He slipped it into his mesh bag before moving on.

Rachel kicked up silt as she followed behind him. She held out the detector and waved it in a broad arc. The shrill alarm sounded. She picked up a large, elongated rock and turned it over in her gloved hand. It appeared to be a calcified artifact—perhaps some type of carving. She pulled a blue bag from her stash and secured it inside. She snapped it onto the lower section of her harness to keep it from dragging.

Up ahead, Chase motioned for her to hurry. She continued after him, waving her directional beam from side to side. An interesting rock took shape before her eyes. She stopped long enough to pick it up and realized she was looking into an empty eye socket. *Shit!* Her heart leaped into her throat. She dropped the skull, watched it disappear into a cloud of blackness, and then looked around for Chase.

He was nowhere in sight.

No doubt wanting to be the first to find treasure, Rachel assumed he had swum ahead to gain access to the cargo hold. Aside from an appealing reward, his success would set him apart from the crew members who were anxiously waiting above.

Rachel proceeded along the route where she'd last seen him. Seamen, caught unaware, had been interred in a common grave for all eternity. She could feel their presence in the murky shadows of the godforsaken wreck. She increased the speed of her fins to escape the ship's dark, eerie vastness.

Her flashlight flickered several times and then died. Rachel drifted in place, shaking it hard. She banged on the lens, but to no avail.

Damn it! She peered into the blackness, trying to determine which way to go. Wishing Chase would wake up and discover that he'd left her alone.

That's when she saw it out of the corner of her eye: the white glow of a bioluminescent light form. Almost simultaneously, a buzzing sensation seized her brain. Her muscles locked up and her chest constricted. She watched as the illusion glided across the top of the ship's broken rail. Remote. Drifting. Ghostly. The image hung in the current for an eternal moment, studying Rachel and all her myriad flaws. Then it turned and folded into itself, disappearing like a magician's silk handkerchief.

On cue, Rachel's lungs filled. The tingling in her nerves passed. The flashlight on her wrist sprang to life, sending the beam toward the vanishing object's portal. But other than shimmering particles dancing in the light, the gunwale appeared vacant.

What was that? Had her mind been playing tricks? Serving up the side effects of nerves and an overactive imagination?

Plunk. A sound spun her around. Chase had come back to find her.

Did you see it? she signed quickly. He looked about before shrugging, and she realized that she'd have to share her experience with him another time. Preferably after a strong drink on *Stargazer's* warm foredeck—after her nerves had calmed and her thoughts had congealed. The story would give his crew all the elements they needed for a fantastical tale—Chase rescuing her from Mai Le just as they were about to claim her priceless possession and a fortune in gold. It would be an inconceivable yarn to anyone who hadn't witnessed the ghost firsthand.

They continued with Chase in the lead. The motion of their fins turned the powdery sediment into a billowing cloud of dust. Below them lay a jumble of decaying timbers and the massive bulk of a broken mast. In the midst of the wooden debris, Rachel spotted an opening in the middeck—a gateway into the vessel's vast underworld. She pointed before letting out a few short bursts of air from her BC vest. She slowly descended onto the ship with the intent of venturing inside. But Chase tapped her arm. It seemed that he had another plan in mind.

She followed him toward the bow and entered the gaping hole left by the disemboweled figurehead. Decaying remains and barrels lined the cramped, inner hull. Their fins dusted the floor, exposing piles of green and blue porcelain dishes strewn across the floor.

Nearby, an open hatch led to the floor below. Chase dove even deeper into the hold. He turned back and seemed to be searching Rachel's eyes for any sign of apprehension before continuing. They were now in the bowels of the cursed ship, one hundred feet below the surface and an unnerving distance from their entry point. The cargo hold extended beyond the scope of their lights in both directions.

Rachel released more air from her vest. She turned off the metal detector's blaring alarm before setting it down. She fanned her hand across the floor's surface. A corroded iron band came into view. She dusted more sediment away and realized she'd uncovered the top of a chest. Nearby were three, possibly four, more chests, all buried in the blinding murk. Chase joined her and pulled one of his knives free. He jammed it under a single latch, forcing the lid open.

Gold! It couldn't be! The sight sucked the air from her lungs. The gleaming metal danced before her eyes: a stockpile beyond imagination. She picked up a single coin, amazed by its unblemished appearance. She turned it over and studied its unusual markings. She held it out for Chase's inspection, but his dark, wild gaze had already found the stronghold's alluring treasure. He reached down and scooped up a handful. He dumped a flurry of coins into his goody bag. He tucked the coins into the neck and sleeves of his suit and motioned for her to join in the plunder. Following his example, she filled her empty green bag with blind abandon. No wonder her father was hooked. It was so easy, so exhilarating…this treasure-seeking business.

The adrenaline rush warmed her heart and drove her blindly into Chase's arms. She was still locked in his embrace when the buzzing started. When the approaching entity filled the shadowy exit. Had she come back? The ghost who guarded the ship's secret treasure? Rachel dislodged herself from Chase's grip.

Who are you? At first glance, the distorted vision appeared to be a school of barracuda. But then, as the murky water cleared, her gaze traced a familiar outline. Dread gripped her, reminding her to guard every movement, control every breath. She signed "danger," and just as Chase turned, *a huge shark* escaped the swirling cloud, confirming her worst nightmare.

By her estimate, the creature was twelve feet long and weighed close to 230 pounds, making it considerably *bigger* than they were. She counted seven gills on each side of its pectoral fins as it swam by. With its claspers visible, it was unmistakably male. Rachel noted its brown-spotted underbelly and the jagged teeth arranged comb-like in its bottom jaw.

Notorynchus cepedianus. She relaxed a bit, having experienced this species before. Although the creature fed on virtually anything, it wasn't typically a threat to humans. It generally dwelled in more temperate waters and at much greater depths than this. What the hell was it doing here? She was still debating that question as the shark circled around them in a figure eight, keeping its back toward the dark, deeper water.

Chase seemed to be taking no chances. He unsheathed his knife. *Ball up,* he motioned.

Rachel waved off his warning. She pulled out her slate. *OK, seven gill,* she scribbled. But as she continued watching the creature's guarded behavior, she realized that something was off. The shark cruised above them a second time, and once again disappeared into the murky shadows. Rachel drew up her legs, all the while assuring herself that the shark's constant eye contact was purely an act of self-preservation. It was searching for an escape route. Its nearness had nothing to do with a desire to devour them. Their size, smell, and vibrations didn't fit into the large shark's spectrum of prey. But after a third pass, its inquisitive dance ended. It charged unprovoked, bumping into Chase, spinning him around. Rachel grabbed hold of his elbow and stared into his mask.

"Are you hurt?" she signed. He shook his head from side to side. She watched him adjust the knife in his hand in preparation for the next assault. In an instant, the shark was back. But this time, Rachel's reflexes took hold. She blocked Chase's avenging arm, and with a well-placed kick, she thumped their attacker's nose with her fin. The menacing fish stole out of sight, seeking a safe refuge.

Amazing! Rachel smiled, still caught up in the exhilaration. But Chase bristled at her side.

Up, he motioned repeatedly. She recognized his apprehension and reluctantly followed him as he backtracked through the ship and out of the cave. With minutes cut off their stops, they burst through the surface. They pulled off their masks simultaneously.

"What the hell were you doing down there?" he bellowed.

Rachel reached the ladder. "Saving your ass," she replied. She handed her gear and the calcified artifact she'd found up to Ian.

Chase stole in behind her and passed off his load. Before she cleared the second rung, however, he caught her elbow and pulled her back down into the water. His body pressed into hers, crushing her resistance. His breath was on her face now, and his bright eyes were inescapable. "No matter how you feel about me, I'm still the captain of this ship. When I give you an order, follow it!"

She jerked her arm free, completely baffled by his behavior. "I'm not a complete idiot. I knew what I was doing."

"Oh, really? You knew that shark was going attack."

"No, but I—"

"We could have been killed. Do you understand the danger you put us in?"

His argument was completely illogical. As far as she could tell, he hadn't been hurt. And any experienced diver knew a good thump on the nose was the best line of defense against a shark. So what was he so worked up about? A bruised ego?

"Where's your green goody bag, Rachel?"

Her hand brushed the empty metal clip on the back of her buoyancy compensator.

"That's right. You lost a fortune in gold. And here you were worrying about *me* delivering the goods."

Rachel felt like a child being admonished—scolded by the same man who had wrecked her life. She dropped back into the water, distancing herself.

"I should have left you down there to fight it out like the Neanderthal you are," she yelled as he climbed the ladder to the ship.

He unhitched his weight belt and dropped his gear on the deck before handing off the porcelain artifact to Wade. Then he leaned back against the rail, unzipping his wet suit. Watching her out of the corner of his eyes.

Rachel's irritability escalated. *Bastard.* She climbed the ladder, rejecting the helmsman's assistance. With her back turned to everyone on board, she removed her tanks and unhooked her belt, letting it fall. She scooped up a towel from the bench and wrapped it around herself without bothering to remove her vest.

She eyed Chase from behind the edge of the nubby cloth, anticipating his self-promoting announcement.

Ian's brushy brows quirked. "That's all you found, Cap'n?"

"Afraid so." He glanced at Rachel before stepping up to the glass tank and upending his goody bag. Gold coins rained down, raising the water level. He pulled half a dozen more coins out of his sleeves and added them to the glowing collection.

"What the..." Ian grabbed the handrail. "Is that fuckin' real?"

Chase held up a single coin. Stamped on the front of the doubloon was the Hapsburg Shield. "The *Wanli* treasure," Chase announced. "And there's a lot more where this came from."

Ian rushed over and snatched the doubloon from Chase's fingertips. He weighed it in his palm before flipping it over and eyeing the crusader's cross and lion stamped on the coin's reverse. He was still biting down on its edge when Blaine and AJ suddenly appeared out of nowhere. They joined in the merriment, gathering coins, examining them. Laughing and punching each other.

"Wait a minute," Ian said. "Why aren't the two of you screaming? Cap'n, you jest found a fortune in gold. What's more, you get first crack at that twenty-year-old."

Chase nodded in Rachel's direction. "That honor goes to Miss Lyons. *She* found the chest, not me."

"No kiddin'?" The helmsman's lips curled into an easy smile. "Well done, darlin'. Yer da would be right proud of you."

"Thanks." She brushed her chin with the back of her hand, feeling cheated by her inability to share in the excitement—to fully appreciate the historical significance of their find. She looked to Chase, who was now leaning over a lounge chair, fishing something out of his shirt, which was hanging there.

"That's not all." He pulled out a cigar, bit off the end, and spat it to the side. "Her quick thinking saved my skin, too."

Ian's gaze swam between them. "Ya don't say."

Under the protection of her towel, Rachel dropped her yellow BC vest. "It was no big deal," she murmured.

"I beg to differ." Chase lit up and tipped his head back. He sent a gray cloud into the air. "Ran into a real monster down there."

"A seven-gill," she corrected. "But more important than that, the *Wanli's* been found. Ian, it's unbelievable! It's as if she's been sitting there for hundreds of years...just waiting for us to find her."

The Irishman patted Chase on the back. "Long time comin'. Aye, mate?"

"*Too* long." He drew another pull on his cigar.

"Jaysus...Allie's gonna go freakin' nuts!"

Chase coughed and choked. He practically doubled over, piquing Rachel's interest.

"Who's Allie?" she asked both of them.

"Ah..." Ian raked his grizzly chin. "Jest a gal I know."

"A girlfriend?" Rachel persisted.

"Somethin' like that."

"Does she live in San Palo?"

Chase's blue eyes flashed an unspoken warning, instantly silencing Ian.

Odd. Maybe this Allie wasn't *Ian's* true love at all. Maybe she was involved with Chase.

Before Rachel could delve further, Chase moved to the platform and picked up Ian's tanks. "Let's get going," he ordered. "We're losing daylight."

Beside them, Wade finished suiting up, apprehension etched on his face. As his last straps were fastened, a thought registered in Rachel's mind. She realized she couldn't let the divers go without issuing a fair warning. No matter how silly it might sound.

"There's something you both need to know," she announced. Mika appeared on the afterdeck and stood by quietly. "While Chase and I were down there, I got the distinct feeling I was being watched and—"

"Pirates?" Wade erupted. He looked to Ian. "What are we waiting for? They could be stealing our claim right now."

"Before ya shit yer pants, let's hear what she has to say."

Rachel glanced around. Everyone's attention was now on her. "I only saw it for a minute," she explained. "But I'm telling you, there's a ghost on that ship, and it knows we're all here."

AJ exploded in laughter. "I suppose you saw aliens, too?"

"No, a ghost," she insisted. She looked to Chase for support but got his annoying, crooked smile instead.

Mika stepped forward. "Listen to her. She's trying to warn you."

"Really?" AJ taunted. "And we should believe her because..."

"I've heard stories like this before. My grandfather owned a photography shop in Kyoto, Japan. One night while he was working late in his darkroom, his shop door opened and closed. He heard footsteps and yelled that he'd be right out. But when he stepped into the room, no one was there, and the hands on the wall clock were running backward."

"OK...I admit that's a little spooky," AJ conceded. "But what does that have to do with us and the ship we're after?"

Blaine stood next to AJ. "An earthquake opened the crack in the ocean floor, right? Who knows what that means? You said yourself that finding the ship in its location and condition was an anomaly. By diving down there, bringing up treasure, we could end up with more than we bargained for."

"All right, this has gone on long enough," Chase said. "We have a job to do."

Once stirred, there was no detouring Ian's imagination. "Jest think about it, mate. Don't ya think the gold was too easy to find? Someone could be temptin' us. They want us to come back. Maybe they're lonely and longing for company. Wantin' to add souls to their hell and back ship."

AJ snorted. "What kind of crazy shit is this? You're reacting to the word of a woman who, up until yesterday, wouldn't put her damn face in the water."

Rachel stared at the insolent bug, wishing someone would squash him into oblivion.

"Enough!" Chase yelled. "Everyone get back to work. It was just a particle cloud...nothing more."

Rachel gritted her teeth and swallowed her retort. As soon as his back was turned, she bolted for her quarters, still clutching her towel. She reached for the doorknob just as AJ's voice rang out.

"Rachel, wait up."

Are you kidding? She watched his rapid approach. His white polo shirt, tan Bermuda shorts, and matching deck shoes, were as bland and unimpressive as the man was himself.

"I'm sorry. I don't usually go out of my way to be rude," he said. "It's just that after a history of bad luck, no one's been able to dive this site until now. We need to stay on target if we want to get done any time soon."

"*Bad* luck?" she quizzed.

"The regular stuff: equipment failures, shark attacks, missing divers. It sounds worse than it really is." He angled his head in a condescending manner. "You know as well as I do there's always risk involved."

Her mind snagged on his words. "Just how many deaths are we talking about here?"

He hesitated before answering. "Four in three years."

"And you don't find that excessive?"

"Not with strong currents and unstable conditions. I suppose you read about the attorney general's son drowning in this area eight months ago. Anyway, the coast guard conducted a thorough investigation and ruled out foul play. There's always a logical explanation."

"Really? What about my father? According to Chase and my dad's crew, his dive gear was in good working order."

AJ cleared his throat. "Look, I know this must be difficult for you, but from what I understand, he had a heart condition. He shouldn't have been down there in the first place."

Rachel shook her head. "You have *no* idea what you're talking about."

He looked down for a moment. When he spoke again, his voice softened. "You're right. I was totally out of line. I wasn't there when it happened." His blinking increased. "All the same, I've done my homework. I understand you've been put in charge of all our discoveries. It's not my place to question the captain, but I honestly—"

"You're right. It's not." She surprised herself with how much she sounded like her father. How strong she'd suddenly become.

A nerve jumped in his temple. "Wait a minute...I was prepared to broker this deal. But Cohen didn't want a partner. At least not until *you* came along. Now he's got a foundation board and a museum to answer to. Talk about getting screwed—"

"We're done here."

AJ moved to grasp her arm but she pulled away, shaking her head.

"Come on," he said. "Try to see this from my point of view. I spent months researching that ship. There's nothing I don't know about the *Wanli II*...where she was built, what she was carrying, what brought her down. Let me be your right hand...your assistant, if you will."

Years ago, her brother had expressed his philosophy on life. *Keep your friends close but your enemies closer.* It had backfired on him. She'd have to be extra careful to make sure the same thing didn't happen to her.

"Fine," she finally said. "Blaine's been assigned to help investigate whatever turns up. I'll let him know you've offered your assistance."

AJ took a few steps back, enthusiastically nodding his head. His lips stretched into a pencil-thin smile. "You won't regret this."

"Yeah, right. Now, if you don't mind..." She waved him away, alluding to her need for privacy. After slipping inside her room, she fell back against the closed door and blew out a shaky breath. She waited until the only sound was the ocean slapping against the side of the ship. When she felt safe, she released her firm grip on the towel. If her calculations were correct, the goody bag she'd kept hidden beneath it held at least twenty gold coins. At this rate, in four days she'd have plenty with which to bargain for her brother's freedom. There would be no need to recover the heart of the dragon, if it even existed. But then, there was Professor Ying's dilemma to consider. According to Eleanor, only five days remained before his deadly prophecy would come true. If Rachel ignored her promise to him, there would be no escaping the guilt or regret she'd most certainly endure.

It was time to make calls. To deliver news where it was needed. Rachel glanced at the business card she'd been given before dialing the number on the ship's satellite phone. "We found the *Wanli II* and have been bringing up her load on a steady basis. As far as Mai Le's treasure goes—"

Eleanor cut her off before she could finish. "The gold dragon! Oh, Lao. She found the treasure just like she promised."

"I don't think you understand, Eleanor. We found the *ship*."

"I know...I know," she persisted. "Dr. Ying opened his eyes this morning. It's a miracle, isn't it? He's still quite tired, mind you. But his color is back, and as far as I'm concerned, he's never looked better. Oh, Miss Lyons, I don't know how we'll *ever* be able to thank you."

There was no point in correcting the woman or in crushing their delusional dreams. As long as Dr. Ying's health was improving, Rachel would let him believe whatever he liked and maybe even remind him of his obligation.

"Just tell the professor to get well soon. He'll need his strength to help fill the museum wing he's naming after my father."

"Yes, dear," Eleanor assured her.

With Rachel's call completed, she dialed another number—the seven digits that were now ingrained in her memory. Gabe Pollero's phone rang repeatedly before his coarse voice came on the recorder. "You know the routine," he said.

"It's me, Rachel. I still haven't found Mai Le's treasure. But I do have something substantial to bargain with, provided my brother is still alive. When I call back at this time tomorrow, I want to hear Devon's voice. If I don't, our deal's off, Pollero. I'll bring in the FBI or whoever I have to if anything happens to him." With that, she hung up the phone feeling more anxious than ever.

Chase stripped off his clothes and climbed onto his bed, innately aware of the short distance to Rachel's room. There was something unnerving about having her so close and so far-removed at the same time. It was easier to battle his feelings when his mind was occupied and Rachel was hundreds of miles away. But here, on this ship, he could smell her in his sleep, visualize her tantalizing expressions, the color of her eyes, the warmth of her touch. It was a miracle that he could sleep at all, and sleep was only possible when his mind and body were exhausted. Yet even in his dreams, she was a vivid reminder of what he had lost. His craving for her had become an obsession, a longing that slowly was wearing him down. He could relieve himself sexually, as he'd done on other nights, or drop to the floor and pump out fifty push-ups to battle his frustrations. Tonight, neither alternative appealed to him.

"Shit," he growled, raking his fingers through his hair. Before shoving off, Rachel had made of a point of reminding him not to smoke in closed compartments or rooms. For the past three days, he had complied, indulging in his vice only on the open upper decks. But tonight, his foul mood urged defiance.

As the sea gently rocked the ship, he stared at the ceiling and finished off his cigar. When he crushed the smoldering stub in a glass ashtray he'd stolen from the galley, the hands of his alarm clock pointed straight up. In six hours, his routine would begin: breakfast in the galley, updates from AJ and Ian, supply and equipment checks. The dives would commence promptly at seven, just as they had every morning.

"Damn it! I've gotta get some rest." He lay flat on his back with one arm thrown over his eyes and settled his head deeper into the pillow. After tossing and turning, struggling to still his thoughts for endless minutes, Chase's body finally relaxed. But no sooner had he fallen asleep than an urgent knock at his door brought him upright in bed.

Mika's soft voice pierced the sealed doorway. "Mr. Cohen… Sir, are you awake?" Her knocks came in rapid succession, followed by his name.

What the hell? He stepped to the doorway and cracked the door. Mika stood outside in the muted light of the hallway, a pink robe cinched around her waist. Her large brown eyes and messy hair reminded him of a shaken doll. Mindful of the hour, he kept his voice low. "Yeah, what is it?"

"Didn't you hear her? Rachel's been crying out in her sleep. Maybe *you* should check on her this time."

"She's at it again?"

Mika's hands found her hips. She pursed her lips, obviously irritated. "Well, aren't you going to do something?"

Chase glanced down. Sleeping in the nude had its disadvantages. "I'll take care of it," he grumbled out of the corner of his mouth. "Go back to bed."

He stepped away from the door long enough to pull on some jeans. Then he trod the passageway in his bare feet, stopping outside Rachel's room. An ear pressed against the door revealed nothing. He rapped lightly on her door. No answer. He waited a few seconds, debating what to do next. If he saw that she was resting comfortably, he might be able to return to his cabin and do the same.

With apprehension, Chase turned the door handle and leaned into the room. "Rachel…" he called softly. Still no answer. He stepped fully inside and noticed that the bedcover had been tossed to one side, exposing the rumpled, white sheets beneath. The contents of a file were strewn across the desk, and a low-wattage lamp was on. But Rachel was nowhere in sight.

"What are you doing here?" her voice came from behind, startling him.

"Geez! Don't sneak up on someone like that." His gaze slid from her face to her snug blue T-shirt and plaid boxers—sleepwear capable of making any man come to attention.

God, she could look sexy in anything.

Rachel eyed him suspiciously. "You still haven't answered me. You get lost or something?"

His defense was immediate. "Mika heard you…I was just checking to make sure you were all right."

"Oh, sorry if I disturbed anyone."

"Don't worry about it."

"I went to the galley to get some hot milk." She held out a steaming glass to validate her claim.

"Great. That should help you relax." *Dumb.* Chase looked away, feeling like a kid with a crush.

"Was there anything else?"

Chase smiled and shook his head.

"In that case…" She took a step aside, leaving a clear path to the open door. "I think we all could use some sleep, don't you?"

"Sure. Good night, Rachel." More than anything, he wanted to throw her down on the bed and make love to her, but her dispassionate expression held him back. He swept past her, inhaling the scent of her lilac body lotion, and forced himself to keep moving. With only five hours till daybreak, this night would remain one of the longest in Chase's sex-deprived life.

19

Even though the sun was beating down hotter than ever, recovery operations were going incredibly smoothly. The team had recovered spears, swords, a bronze crane, dozens of trinkets, four chests filled with gold coins, and six crates of porcelain in miraculous condition, all of which had been stored below. Two more chests were still partially buried in the *Wanli's* tangled remains. But aside from the strange silver lock Dr. Ying had provided and the lacquer-ware lid her father had found, there was no evidence suggesting that Mai Le's treasure was on board.

Following the scheduled dive rotations, Wade and Ian rolled over the side while AJ and Chase remained at the helm. Rachel wandered into the galley and spotted Blaine bent over the table, sound asleep. She opened the refrigerator and stood there for a moment, bathing her legs in the cool downdraft. She took out a tray of ice cubes and dumped the contents into the metal sink, creating a resounding clatter.

Blaine jerked his head up, dropping his book on the floor. He cast a disparaging glare at her while he leaned down to retrieve his crumpled pages. "Jeez, Rachel."

"Jeez what?" She picked up a cube and began rubbing it against the back of her neck.

"Was hoping to have some peace and quiet while I was reading."

She smiled wryly. "Must be reading through your eyelids, then." She dropped into the booth beside him. "Won't be disturbing you for long. Got plenty to keep me busy." She added a pained expression for good measure. "How hot is it out there, anyway?"

"Over ninety last time I checked. Looking forward to my dive this afternoon." He fanned himself with the paperback.

She caught his hand and glanced at the cover. *Treachery at Sea.* How fitting.

As she released his hand, he said, "Just finished a novel about a hundred-million dollar gold recovery from the HMS *Edinburgh* in the Arctic Ocean."

"No kidding? At least it was colder there."

"Oh…so, you didn't hear?"

"Hear what?"

"There's a 50 percent chance of thundershowers tonight."

Great. More nightmares on the way. At the age of eight, Rachel had sat at the top of the stairs hugging her brother as they witnessed a screaming match between her parents that rivaled the explosive drumfire outside. When the storm had passed and the house was quiet again, she'd stood beside the living room window with the curtain drawn back, watching her mother climb into a cab and disappear from their lives. For years, memories of that night would come rushing back at the sound of thunder.

"Was there something you needed?" Blaine asked, pulling her attention back.

"I just finished checking the cleaning tank and couldn't help noticing the coins are gone. Do know happen to know where they are?"

"Yep. Chase secured them down below after I did some research and discovered they're worth about four thousand dollars each."

"No kidding." A fresh bead of sweat slid down her back. By her best estimate, that meant she now had close to eighty thousand dollars stashed away in her room. The thought was unnerving.

"Got a question for you, too," he said. "With your dad being in the business for so many years, any chance he knew a guy by the name of Mitch Harper?"

"No, not that I recall. Why?"

"Turns out he discovered a sunken ship in the South China Sea and ended up with an amazing haul. Planned on keeping all the money it brought at auction at Christie's, but then officials from the Chinese government caught on." He flipped through the book until he found the page he sought.

"They took Harper to court, convinced that they held preferential rights, but since the ship was built in the Netherlands, Law of the Sea rules didn't apply, and the Chinese officials weren't able to claim the assets. They had to buy them, just like anyone else. Problem was, the Chinese archaeologists couldn't afford to buy them at the time, and as a result, Harper became one of the richest salvagers of all time. Put a real bad taste in the Chinese government's mouth, too. But if that wasn't bad enough, Harper found a seventeenth-century junk two years later and brought up about a million pieces of porcelain. Knowing full well that the rarer the item, the more it brings, he had half of it smashed and still pocketed over thirty million dollars. Unreal, huh?"

Rachel swallowed hard. "Tell me, Blaine, what do you know about our legal rights here? Chase assured me that his papers were in order, but if the Chinese government gets wind of what we're up to, can it shut us down and confiscate everything we've recovered?"

Blaine closed his book and smiled. "Oh, you don't have to worry about that. According to Chinese historians, the *Wanli II* doesn't exist. Even though she was modeled after the original ship, there are virtually no records of where she was built or her true country of origin. I guess you could say she's kind of a ghost ship, which makes the manifest records the captain acquired from Professor Ying a real mystery. In any event, they have a signed personal agreement between them. You know... to make sure we get a nice finder's fee for all the porcelain and relics we bring up. I even checked it out myself to make sure. I'm just grateful we're not tied to a self-serving thief like Harper, is all."

"Right," she said, offering a weak smile.

Blaine rose to his feet. "Think I'll grab something to eat. You want anything?"

"Maybe later." She watched him disappear into the pantry before slipping out of the booth. On her way to the afterdeck, she spotted Mika spread out on a lounge chair, singing to an eighties version of "Louie Louie" playing on her iPod.

"Loowee loowhy ono sadday we gowgow, yeh yeh yeh yeh yeh," On seeing Rachel, Mika smiled and pulled out her ear-plugs. "Hey, didn't see you there."

In Rachel's opinion, being raised in an Evangelical house-hold had left the girl emanating too much joy to be real. "Damn it, girl, how can you stand this heat?" she complained.

"It's mild compared to Tokyo summers. With 90 percent humidity, you sweat all the time. Some people even take showers twice a day."

"Sounds awful. So is that why you moved here...to California, I mean?"

"My eight-year-old brother became ill two years ago and one of the best teaching hospitals is in San Palo. After I graduated from UCLA, my father accepted his church position with my brother's full-time care in mind."

Rachel regretted her invasive questions. Mika's life was her own affair. "I'm sorry. I didn't mean to pry."

"It's all right. We can't control everything in our lives. My father believes that God has a plan for all of us. Sometimes we're blessed and don't even know it. A good example is the fact that I wouldn't have this job if I hadn't met Mr. Cohen at the hospital. And I wouldn't have met you if you weren't involved with Mr. Cohen."

"That's nice and all," Rachel said, "but Chase and I aren't exactly involved."

"Really?" Mika's eyebrows twisted. "Then how do you explain the way he looks at you…especially when you're not watching?"

"Oh, that's nothing," Rachel claimed. "Just history."

Mika's eyes twinkled. "Looks like a current affair to me." She slid out of her chair and replaced her earplugs, amplifying her music. Then she smiled and danced away, humming.

Rachel caught herself smiling, too—something she hadn't done in a while. As soon as Mika was out of sight, she took up her post at the cleaning station. She opened her goody bag and pulled out the eight-inch, black, calcified artifact she'd found the day before. It felt strangely warm in her hands, a phenomenon she attributed to its cupreous alloy or metallic core. She flipped it over and examined it thoroughly. Although it was heavily coated with marine crustaceans, from all angles it appeared to be some kind of creature—a serpent or maybe an elongated dragon.

Was it possible that this was the dragon they'd been searching for?

Her research book on spectroscopic techniques suggested a quasi-monochromatic x-ray for analyzing the patina on ancient metal relics. It also recommended a careful, supervised examination to preserve the archeological significance of a relic. *So much for integrity.* She picked up a sharp, metal tool and set to work scraping and chipping away the coating. After twenty minutes, she used the compressor to blow away the gritty residue. Then she reexamined her find.

"Interesting." It appeared that she had unearthed an upright cobra with its hood fully exposed. The blue coloration hinted that the relic was bronze, but it would take another twenty-four hours to know for sure. She filled the glass tank with water, ethanol, and a solution of BTA before laying the strange object inside. Although the water's greenish tint would confirm her suspicions, it would ultimately crush her hopes.

In the meantime, she cleared her workspace and picked up the first plate Chase had recovered. Running a bath was the quickest way to remove the soluble salts that had been absorbed in the porcelain, but she didn't have the vats necessary to keep the water moving. She carried the mesh bag, along with its contents, into the closest head. With no one in sight, she opened the customized, gray-water reservoir and deposited the bag inside. Since it was essential to put nothing toxic down the drain—no bleaches, bath salts, artificial dyes, or cleaners—this was the best undrinkable water source on board, and it came with its own electronic flushing system. *Particle dust, huh?* With every toilet flush, hand washing, or shower, the crew would unknowingly assist in cleaning the captain's prized china. She couldn't help but smile.

Thump, thump, thump. The sound of running footsteps overhead drew her up to the deck. Chase was leaning over the rail, scanning the surface for bubbles. Three minutes passed...five... then eight. His face suddenly reddened.

"What is it?" she finally asked.

He zipped up, wide-eyed, and cried, "Something's gone wrong!"

At ten meters, Chase saw Ian emerge through the bubble screen. He was ascending rapidly, his BC vest full and his eyes large as saucers.

He grabbed Ian and signaled, "OK?"

Ian was physically shaking. He didn't respond to the question but seemed to be breathing fine. Chase released him, allowing his continued ascent. Then his thoughts shifted to Ian's absent partner.

Hawkins! Chase's mind screamed. Chase continued his dark descent through the murky water, scanning in all directions. With each dead end, his pulse quickened. His mind raced. He anticipated the worst-case scenario: facing another death like the one that almost destroyed him.

Wade broke through a cloud, nearly colliding with Chase. He seemed confused, perhaps disoriented, but fully intact. He signaled that he was fine and then vigorously motioned below.

After Rachel's dubious warning, Chase could only guess what the two men believed they'd seen. He continued on, looking in nooks and crannies. Keeping an eye peeled for eels and sharks. But the only thing he spotted at the end of their anchor line was a set of dive tables. He returned to the surface and found Ian coughing and gasping. Fortunately, he was none the worse for wear.

"So, what happened?" Chase asked. "You run into Casper, the angry ghost?"

It was then that Ian found his voice. "Wasn't me fault," he claimed. "I only tried to kill it."

"Kill what? Casper?"

Ian laughed and choked at the same time.

"We were down in the hull when a great white came charging from out of nowhere," Wade explained. "Ian pulled me through a crack he found in the ship's side just in time. When we cleared the cave, he signaled to hurry up, so I added a shot of air with my power inflator. Somehow, it got stuck. The only thing I could think of was to grab hold of him."

"From behind," Ian added. "Shocked the bijous outta me."

Wade chuckled. "Anyway, we were both bumping around in the dark. At about seventy feet, he reached down, pulled out his knife, and stabbed me a half dozen times in the chest."

"Oh, my God!" Rachel yelped.

"Hey...was tryin' to dump air," Ian said indignantly. "How'd I know he was wearing fuckin' armor?"

Unbelievable. Chase shook his head. "Why didn't you just disconnect the hose?"

Ian sulked. "Ah, sure. Easy for you to say."

Chase turned back to Wade. "I'm afraid to ask, but why did you signal down?"

"I was pointing at the ledge that Ian stuffed me under to keep me from shooting up."

Their story was getting wilder by the minute. "So how'd you get loose?"

"He shoved me free."

Ian arched his neck in their direction. "And jest how did I manage that when I was headin' up to get help, ya nitwit?"

"But I...I felt your hands." The slice between his brows suddenly deepened.

Ian shook his head. "Weren't mine."

Rachel pressed closer. "Then whose were they?"

Chase surveyed the perplexed expressions surrounding him. Although he wanted to squelch the ghostly notions that had been circulating all morning, Wade's close call had the earmarks of the far-fetched tale he'd overhead recently at the Crow's Nest. It seemed that a craggy fisherman from up north had ventured into the area two months ago and witnessed inexplicable visions in the fog one night. The next evening, he heard voices calling out warnings. He wrote both experiences off to lack of sleep and too much beer. However, hours later, a wild storm struck, sending him flying into the ocean, and someone pulled him to safety aboard a rubber dingy just before his ship went down. It was pure coincidence in some minds, but the truly disturbing part of the man's tale came at the end. It seemed that before the fisherman had a chance to thank him, his guardian angel vanished into thin air.

Chase blew out an exasperated sigh. He needed to put this silly episode to rest quickly. "Wade, let it go. You panicked, is all."

"Yeah, you probably wiggled free and didn't even realize it," AJ added.

After a thoughtful silence, the tension in Wade's face vanished. "I suppose you're right," he said.

Off to his left, Rachel scorned their logic. "Oh, really? And what about the hands he felt?"

From the determined look on her face, she wasn't about to let the matter die. She dropped down on one knee and rested her hand on Wade's forearm.

"I think there might be another explanation," she said. "Did you see a flash of light, a sudden movement just beyond your line of vision?"

Damn it! Chase was losing control again. Any minute now, Rachel would have Wade believing that spooks were taking over their claim. His whole crew could be rendered useless if they bought into the woman's delirium. "Back to work," he growled.

"Aye, aye, Cap'n." The response resounded around him, but Wade didn't answer. He didn't move from his hunkered-down position next to Rachel. The two of them shook their heads, blatantly ignoring Chase's order.

Chase had reached the end of his rope. "Enough of this. Grab a fresh tank," he demanded. He smacked Wade's shoulder harder than he actually intended.

The warrior's gaze shot up. His hateful snarl matched his cool reply. "I'll put my time in on board from now on."

It was a directive, not a request. The beginning of the end, in Chase's mind.

"The hell you will! If you can't handle the job you were hired to do, you better start packing now!"

Wade remained silent, brooding, as if contemplating his dead-end future. "Sorry, captain. Got a little carried away. I'll get right on that." The enormous man slunk away, looking a few inches shorter than he normally did.

With his command restored once again, Chase drew a cleansing breath. He glanced at Rachel as she pushed herself upright and noticed the disapproval in her eyes. "You got a problem *too*?" he tossed at her. "I can have the launch ready in ten minutes."

"I'll be ready in five."

She spun on her heel just as Ian emerged from the galley, a bottle of liquor locked in his fist. He dropped a meaty arm over Rachel's shoulder and, despite her protests, steered her toward the inside cabin.

"A deal is deal, darlin'. But I'm sure hopin' yer the generous sort." He cast a dark look in Chase's direction. It was a silent warning to back off. "With yer help, we jest might warm up this motley crew," he told her. "By all accounts, they could damn well use it."

Chase turned back toward the open sea. Years earlier, after a heated exchange with Rachel, he'd stood on this very spot with a half-empty bottle of scotch, wallowing in self-pity. Sam had wandered outside to join him under the pretense of taking in the view. When the sun finally touched down, setting the horizon ablaze, Sam had tossed his cigar aside and stolen Chase's bottle. He gulped down the last swallow before reaching into his pocket and handing Chase a folded paper. "My wife copied that out of a book," he explained. "She left it on my nightstand the day she moved out. Been keeping it in my wallet, hoping to pass it on to the right person one day." He slapped Chase on the back lightheartedly and disappeared inside the ship.

Chase had been left standing there alone and confused, just like he was now. He reached into his back pocket and pulled out his wallet, extracting the same folded page. He'd read the treasured quote numerous times over the past four years.

> Love is patient, love is kind. It does not envy, it does not boast, it is not proud. It is not rude, it is not self-seeking, it is not easily angered; it keeps no record of wrongs. Love does not delight in evil but rejoices with the truth. It always protects, always trusts, always hopes, always perseveres.
> -1 Corinthians 13:4-7

Wise words. Chase glanced at the glowing cabin where his crew had gathered. Rachel stood among them, laughing and filling their shot glasses with her well-earned reward. He longed to be the man in her life—her loving, devoted hero. To be the leader among men Sam had always been.

"Treat them like Thoroughbreds," Sam had once told him. "Jab 'em with strong words, if necessary, but always keep a carrot in your pocket."

Chase chuckled at the memory. It was a classic Sam colloquialism. A self-serving anecdote that could bring a blush to his daughter's face and a snappy retort to her beautiful lips. How he wished Sam were here now. Standing beside him, handing out his fatherly advice. Keeping him and his crew in line and their ambitions fixed on Neptune's prize.

Ian cracked the cabin door, releasing the noise in the room. "Aye, mate…you plannin' on joining us anytime soon?"

20

Boom! In the distance, thunder clapped and the heavens lit up. A cloudburst erupted, sending rain slamming into *Stargazer*. The ship rocked to and fro with the swells of the sea. Aside from Mika, who had the good sense to go to bed early, the crew was fully secured in the galley where beer and scotch had been flowing for hours. The storm's intensity unnerved Rachel, but it did little to detour AJ from his fixation on maritime history. He managed to hijack every conversation that circled the dinner table and turn it into another sunken-treasure story. She'd had her fill of both for the night, but being jammed between Ian and Wade in the white leather booth left no avenue for escape.

"Yesterday, while reviewing *Wanli's* manifest records," AJ was saying, "I came across this article about the *Soleil D'Orient*, which belonged to the French East India Company. In 1681, it set sail with three ambassadors and twenty valets, who were assigned to look after sixty crates of presents sent by the king of Siam to French royalty and the pope. Among these tokens were hundreds of diamonds from the king of Bantam. Most accounts say she hit land and broke up near the southeast tip of Madagascar, so the wreckage may be in shallow water. The first to find her could end up with a thousand-piece gold dinner set from the emperor of Japan and a shitload of silver."

Rachel glanced at Chase, who was seated across the table from her. His cool blue eyes remained faintly amused. As if prompted by her chafed look, he lifted his drink in salute. "Sounds like a job for our fair maiden."

Get a life. She was blanketed in warm fuzziness—the result of three shots of Hennigans scotch, the finder's reward she gladly would have forfeited.

Wade tapped her arm. "I understand you know a lot about the Mai Le treasure. I'd like to hear about that."

Chase peered at him over the rim of his glass. "What are you talking about, Hawkins? We combed every inch of that ship. Get it through your head: it doesn't exist."

"But Captain, Doc was right about the *Wanli.* Maybe we're not looking in the right place."

"We need to focus on bringing up what we've already found."

Rachel glared at Blaine, curled up like an innocent kitten on the floor, his soft snores the only indication he was breathing. She was still angry with him for breaking her trust by spreading rumors about the letter from the professor's file, which she'd been foolish enough to share with him. If she wasn't careful, Chase could change his mind and issue a bounty for finding the heart of the dragon next.

Ian snickered. "Hey, I've got one for ya. An old salt was sittin' at a pub when a young lady sits down and announces to one and all, 'I'm a lesbian. I don't care a bit for men. I love women! I love everything about the female body—lips, tits, and ass. I jest can't get enough of 'em.' She tosses back her whiskey and leaves. Ten minutes later, a tourist couple enters the fine establishment and sits down next to the old salt. 'We're jest wondering,' they say, 'are ya a real ol' time sailor?' The old salt tosses back another one, stands, and replies, 'I thought I was but I jest found out I'm a lesbian.'"

The room roared with drunken laughter, the loudest coming from Ian. When it quieted down, Wade reclaimed the floor. "It's Rachel's turn," he insisted. "She's the ship's official historian. Come on, Rachel. Tell us what you know about Mai Le."

"I know something better," AJ claimed. He started to spill his third story of the night as fast as he could get the words out. "Three hundred years ago, there was this British, seven-mast schooner equipped with—"

"Yes, Rachel," Chase interrupted. "We're up for a nice bed-time story. Huh, guys?"

While the men around her elbowed one another, Chase reached across the table to collect her glass. He filled it a fourth time and set it before her.

She shook her head in protest. "I don't want any more."

A mischievous smile spread across his lips. "Oh, really? Guess I didn't hear you right then. You know, when you told Ian you wanted to be treated like one of the guys."

His challenge left her biting her lip. The man was a rounder—willing her to knuckle under. Daring her to embarrass herself in front of his men. But she was Sam Lyons's daughter. Stubborn to the end. She wasn't about to back down. Not when her endurance was being put to the test.

She looked down at the fried chicken and hashbrowns still sitting on her plate in their own grease. A lard-coagulating heart attack in the making. "All right," she finally said. "But this is the last one. *Understand*?" She lifted the amber fuel and hesitated before tossing it back. She choked, coughed, and teared up as it blazed a fresh path down her throat, igniting in her chest.

Shouts and guffaws erupted in the room.

"And ya thought she didn't have it in her," Ian said to Chase. They shared a mutual smile, confirming her suspicion of a malign plot.

"Now what about that story?" Wade asked.

"Yeah, lass," Ian prompted. "If yer still able, that is."

Chase winked before empting his glass.

Would this never end? All eyes were now on fixed her, waiting for her to deliver an incredible yarn to best the dozen or more she'd heard over the past few nights. With the challenge made, she had no choice but to deliver. Especially if she hoped to maintain the respect she'd earned from her fellow crew members. She leaned back against the cushion and stared in a daze at the oil lamp's orange flame. Flickering and dancing…tempting and taunting. Urging her to divulge the secret tale.

"Mai Le was one of many wives and concubines in Emperor Wanli's court," she began. "Although appreciated for her beauty, intelligence, and grace, she was treated like a swan in a pond, untouched and isolated from the world. She often thought of herself as a tiny, insignificant gnat in the Qinghui Garden, the place where a mere glance from a handsome Italian sea captain had set the stage for her ruin."

Wade braced his head on his elbow and gazed expectantly at her. "*This* should be good."

"With each of his biannual visits, their smiles, hidden touches, and secret meetings shifted her devotion away from the emperor to Captain Vito Brunelli. And for these treasonous acts, for her veiled betrayal, the gods bound her soul in despair. In the wake of the foreigner's final departure, she endured months of melancholy. Her silence and loss of appetite resulted in an order that she be confined to her chamber. For days on end, the disapproving murmurs of fellow concubines permeated the suffocating prison of her room and spiraled into the hollow shells of her ears. She pounded on the carved elm doors and clawed at decorative scrolls and silk-covered walls, fruitlessly demanding her release.

Early one morning, a eunuch's whisper carried news that due to consumption, her dear captain would never return. The imperial doctors, with their herbal potions and bloodletting, could find no cure for the anguish that plagued the young woman's broken heart. However, in her delirium, she revealed her love for Brunelli to her handmaid. Realizing that come morning, the cause of her despair would be known, Mai Le avoided execution by taking fate into her own hands.

Dressed in a young boy's attire, she made her way to through the mountains to a sheltered bay. The glowing lanterns of distant fishing boats glistened on the water's surface as she stepped into the sea. The waves wrapped higher and higher around her legs and then around her breasts before slamming into the shore."

Chase retrieved his cigar from the ashtray. "Nice imagery."

"Shhh!" Ian hissed.

Rachel remained undaunted. "Mai Le wasn't chilled by the autumn breeze or the Yellow Sea's frigid temperature. Instead, she felt the warmth of the sea's tempting pull. It cradled her and rocked her. Moved like silk across her skin. When she eventually lost her footing, she relaxed and laid her head back, allowing her long, black mane to sway in the current like a painter's brush. As she gazed high into the heavens, every twinkling star was a painful reminder of the price she'd paid for the captain's love. Despite his promise, he would never return. And the fact that she had trusted the gods to bring him home safely – to reunite them for all eternity – had turned her into a senseless, naïve fool."

Chase looked away. His reaction to her thoughtless jibe gave Rachel pause.

"Go on," Wade encouraged. "What happened next?"

She forged a smile before continuing. "Mai Le's only means of escape and redemption rested in the ocean's depths. As her tears mingled with the salty water, the last of her anger drained away. No longer would she damn the priest who had brought the outside world into the Forbidden City or the captain to whom she'd so willingly given her heart. She would forgive them both—forgive their lack of compassion and life's cruel reward. 'I will love you for all eternity,' she whispered into the night. Then with a final exhaled breath, she sank into her watery grave."

The room was still for a long moment. Ian finally broke the silence. "Ah...what a forlorn tale it is."

AJ harrumphed. "You didn't say anything about her treasure. How do we know what we're looking for?"

Rachel looked at Chase. "Like the captain said, it's only a fairy tale."

With his golden tan, five o'clock shadow, and the cigar between his teeth, Chase resembled Leonardo DiCaprio—a twisted thought when Rachel remembered that the actor had starred in *Titanic.*

"She wins it," Ian announced.

Rachel was puzzled. "Wins what?"

Chase faced her. "Prize for best story, of course."

"But I already won the bottle of scotch. I honestly can't handle anything else."

"You won't be drinking this." He pulled a jade pendant from his pocket and laid it on the table before her. It was an ancient trinket that Chase had pulled from his goody bag earlier that day—one she had secretly coveted.

"I...I don't deserve that," she said.

"Then call it a gift for the use of your ship. For everything you've done to make this adventure possible. I think all of us would agree to that." He blew a thin stream of smoke heavenward and fanned it with his hand. "It's nothing compared to what you've done for us."

He was suddenly on his feet, moving toward the open doorway. "Rain stopped. Think I'll grab some fresh air before turning in. Wanna join me?"

"No." She looked down at the moving floor, willing it to swallow her up.

He snorted a laugh. "Why doesn't that surprise me?"

Rachel shoved herself upright and then realized too late the mistake she'd made. The ship's constant rocking added angst to the room's acute tilt. Everything around her began swirling. She gripped the edge of the table and squeezed her eyes shut, trying to still the queasy sensation.

Chase had left the door open. The cool ocean air was drifting inside, lifting the fine hairs on her arms. The thought of drawing a fresh, sobering breath pulled her outside. She gripped the cold rail with both hands, closed her eyes, and leaned her head back. The gentle breeze moved through her hair and had an ethereal, calming effect. She drew several more deep breaths before hearing Chase's soft voice, which had a nurturing gentleness she never expected from him.

"Honey, it'll pass. You're going to be all right, I promise." He moved closer and slipped his arm around her shoulder. A shiver escaped down her spine. "Are you cold?" he asked.

Before she could answer, he tugged a blue towel from a nearby chair and draped it over her thin T-shirt and bare arms. Then he pulled her against his body, protecting her in a warm embrace.

"I don't know what gets into me sometimes…acting all crazy and macho. It's hard being at sea, needing to be in charge—to have all the answers. I think I have it all figured out and then I look at you and the past comes rushing back. I remember that place in the middle of your thumb. That spot halfway up I'd rub between my fingers when I ran out of things to say. You would hold my hand when you were afraid and, although I wanted to help, I could never fully understand."

Rachel pressed her head against his chest, listening to his heart speak.

"I remember the first time you leaned in to kiss me," he said, "and I swear not a single force on earth could stop my hands from trembling. I remember how you smiled through the smoke in a crowded little pub and laughed at all my stupid jokes. And God, I'll never forget the way you dressed for New Year's Eve and how we got wasted in alcohol and sweat. Maybe that's why I was pouring that bottle tonight, Rachel. To rekindle those memories again."

Rachel enjoyed the deep hum of his voice. Precious moments like this. She understood that life changes, people grow up and grow apart, and you're forced to accept the inevitable. But somewhere, deep down inside, she recalled how good it used to be, and a single tear slipped away. She was afraid she'd never experience love again—afraid she'd already lived the dream and lost it.

Tipping her head back, she met his perfect blue eyes and for or a timeless moment, they were back. They were that fun-loving couple again. The one everyone in town envied—the one that was destined to be together. Then, just when she thought Chase would surrender and meet her lips with a kiss, he leaned down and slipped his arms under her knees, lifting her from the deck. With her hands looped around his neck and her face buried in his shoulder, he carried her back to her room. After setting her down carefully on the bed, he secured a heavy blanket from the closet.

Rachel stretched out her legs and made room in the bed for him to join her. But instead, he covered her and tucked in the sides of the blanket, leaving her cocooned and slightly amused. As if bidding a child good night, his lips brushed her forehead in a fleeting kiss. Then he stepped away and closed the door, leaving her befuddled.

What just happened? If she'd been in her right mind, Rachel might have resented his invasion, his nearness. His touch. She would have ordered him out of her room and blamed him for causing her inebriation in the first place. Then she realized that Chase hadn't uttered a single admonishing word. He wasn't the rogue and conniving blackheart she imagined him to be or the culprit who stole into her dreams to disrupt her life. This man had been nothing but kind, gentle, and caring. When angered, he was quick to apologize and willing to forgive. In his role as chief authority on the ship, he'd honored their business relationship and treated her with utmost respect. So why the hell was it bothering her that he hadn't made a pass? That he hadn't taken advantage of their nearness when given the chance?

As she drifted into a hazy, sleep-deprived slumber, her analytical thoughts tumbled one over the over, knocking off points of contention, pushing aside Chase's imperfections, discarding her years of resentment, cultivating a neglected resolve that would grow her tolerance and understanding. Without her knowledge, a seed had been planted. Rachel Lyons was falling in love again.

21

Devon cracked one eye open, and then the other. Although his mind told him it was morning, the streetlight blaring through the window confirmed it was nighttime. He could hear the gray droning of cars from the street or perhaps the parking lot at the back of the building. His body ached with the slightest movement, as if he'd been hit by a Mack truck. He tried to get up and realized that his arms and legs were secured once again, this time to iron bedposts.

"Damn it!"

Marcos and Viktor were gone, but there was no telling when they'd be back. He tugged at his bindings, trying to free himself, but it was no use. He noticed bruises and cuts all over his arms and chest. A stained white bandage bound his right hand. He could see brownish-red blotches on the carpet and walls where a struggle apparently took place. But any memory made after the lights went out had been permanently erased.

Only the image of Pollero's lifeless face remained constant.

The door suddenly creaked. Viktor stood in the opening, silhouetted by the light behind him. "He's awake. We dope him up again or get rid of him now?"

The red welts on Devon's arms now made sense. They'd been sedating him...possibly for days. Keeping him quiet and under control.

Marcos sniffed. "Dunno. Whatever the boss says."

Boss? As in Gabe Pollero? Maybe he'd made a mistake. Maybe he dreamed up the whole fight, and Pollero was still alive. But how would that explain his injured hand, which was beginning to hurt like hell?

"Why don't you put me out of my misery once and for all?" Devon asked.

Marcos closed the distance to the bed. "No chance. When we get the order, we're gonna take our time with you, asshole."

"How did I know you'd say that?"

Viktor snorted a laugh. "Won't have to wait long. Boss just showed up."

Devon could hear footsteps in the hallway. Someone rapidly approached the room. When the sound stopped and the door opened wide, he couldn't believe his eyes.

His beautiful angel of mercy had come to rescue him.

"Selena!" he called out.

Her gaze dusted his face and body and then returned to the two hoodlums at her side. "Why is he awake?" she asked. "I told you to keep him out until his sister showed up. Why can't you follow simple directions?"

Devon's jaw slacked. There had to be a mistake. He had to have misheard. "Selena...what's going on?"

Marcos's lips twisted. "You think that fuckin' bastard you killed is our boss? Shit no! Selena's in charge."

No. It isn't possible. Devon stared at her, refusing to believe the truth, even as it played out before him.

She patted Marcos on the shoulder and then glanced at Viktor. "Call for an update, Dubov."

The Ukrainian grinned. "Sure…no problem." He flipped Devon off and disappeared with Marcos through the room's only exit. Selena secured the door with a click.

She turned on the bedside lamp and moved silently around the bed. She pulled the curtain away from the corner of the window and for an endless moment remained silent.

"I gave you every opportunity," she finally said. "Why the hell didn't you leave town like I told you to?" She waited for an answer. When none came, she faced him straight on.

Devon was lost. His gaze traced her flawless face—searching for any sign of deception, the slightest hint of ruthlessness. None existed.

"Are you deaf or something?" Agitation registered in her voice, but still he refused to believe the obvious. He'd been duped and used, and there was simply no getting around it.

"I don't understand any of this," he said. "I thought we had something special between us. That we were planning our future together. When did…*how* did this happen? Your brother…the money…Logan?"

She dropped the desk chair next to the bed. "I guess you deserve some kind of explanation." She sat down and crossed her shapely legs. The hem of her snug, black dress inched slowly upward, exposing her perfect thighs.

"I hooked up with Walter Moten," she continued. "Had my flight to Paris confirmed and my suitcase packed. Then you showed up at that hideous cocktail party…the one his wife insisted on throwing. You were just a fun distraction, Dev. Nothing more. All flirty and sweet. Following me around all night like a lost puppy."

She tilted her head, scrutinizing him. "You just wouldn't take no for an answer, would you? Just kept showing up all over town. Calling me, leaving notes. Sending those damn flowers. I tried to get rid of you so many times. Even told my guys to do whatever was necessary to scare you off."

Devon looked away, disbelieving his ears.

"But I have to admit… there were times when you were just too tempting to resist."

"Lucky me. So, if all you cared about was the money, why didn't you and Moten just run off? He's already stolen enough to live on for ten lifetimes."

Her smile waned. "Moten's wife caught on and threatened to expose us. Then that stupid cop got wind of what was happening. He thought he'd do me a *big* favor by gettin' rid of both of them. Trouble is, with the Motens out of the picture, I had no access to his overseas accounts. That's where I was hoping you'd help out. With all your poking around, I was sure something would turn up. When nothing did, I figured I'd head to Vegas, soak up some rays, and cut my losses." She pushed loose strands of hair off her forehead. "Then an old friend called. After a few late-night dinners on his boat, he told me all about your sister and the treasure her boyfriend was after. With all the gold they're collecting, it's just a matter of time before we have all the money we'll ever need."

Devon glared at her. "So you steal whatever you want, no matter who gets hurt."

She shifted in her seat. "What can I say, Dev? You should have kept your distance when you had the chance."

"I still don't believe you, Selena. You can't be this cruel."

"You're wrong; I can be. Only a few more obstacles to get rid of and we're off to South America."

"Really? And those obstacles you're talking about…they wouldn't happen to be my sister and me?"

Her smile twisted. "What can I say?"

She's lying. It had to be an act. She loved him. She *still* did. He searched her eyes for a sliver of truth. "You know I would do anything for you, Selena."

Her frown spoke volumes.

"We still have a chance to be together. I *know* it," he said.

She shook her head. "No, we don't. You don't know anything about me. What I've done. What I'm capable of doing. There's no future for us, Devon. There never was."

He wanted to grab her by the shoulders and shake some sense into her, but his bindings made it impossible. "Just tell me you never felt anything," he pleaded. "Not when I was touching you, kissing you...holding you in my arms. Convince me that you never cared about me and I'll shut up forever."

Her gaze slid to the floor and then back to his face, raising his hopes with each passing second. Suddenly she stood and walked into the bathroom.

I knew it! Devon was sure he'd gotten through. Reached inside her heart and turned it around.

Minutes dragged. Sickeningly sweet smoke seeped under the door, reminding Devon of the pot he'd enjoyed during his college days. He was thinking how odd it was to smell it here when Selena suddenly reappeared. They mystery was solved with one look. Her expression remained stoic—cold and detached. Uninvolved in whatever plan she had in mind.

Devon's gaze dropped to the hypodermic needle clenched in her hand: death in a vial. She lifted her stony-eyed stare.

"I have no choice," she said. She set the needle down on the nightstand and began rolling up his shirtsleeve.

Panic heightened his plea. "Selena, I beg you. Don't do this!"

No answer. Her focus was locked on his inner arm. She was scanning for a willing vein, an easy target to still his troubled heart.

"Honey, please. Listen to me!"

She picked up the implement. Tension was building on her twitching brow and at the corners of her downturned mouth.

Devon closed his eyes and waited, his fate resting in her hands. Time stretched. Seconds became a full minute. Still nothing happened. He ventured a peek, only to discover that her eyes were closed. He watched her solemn face, her meditative breaths, trying to determine what was going on in her head.

This was his Selena. The woman he loved. It wasn't in her to be a murderer.

He just knew it.

Boom, boom, boom! His gaze flew to the door.

"Who is it?" Selena called out.

"It's Bo Novak. Let me in. I need to talk to you right now."

Devon's gaze came back to her. "So, what's the hold up?" he asked. "Here's your chance to finally get rid of me."

"Listen. If I wait until Marcos and Vik get back—" Her voice cracked. "I know what they'll do to you."

"Selena!" Bo yelled louder. "Open the door."

Devon knew her troubled expressions all too well. A war was ranging inside of her, pulling her between right and wrong. Life and death.

She slipped the needle back into her purse and shook her head. "You're right. I could never hurt you." She leaned down to kiss his cheek, but Devon turned away. When he looked back, her brown eyes were pleading for understanding. "I need you to get out of here. Just consider my car yours. It's parked on the ground floor, space forty-two." She untied the rope binding his bandaged hand. She moved to the foot of the bed and freed his ankles.

"But what about you?" he asked.

She reached into her purse and extracted a set of keys. "I'll be fine. As far as anyone's concerned, I let you go the bathroom and you bolted. With your history, they'll believe me."

Devon rolled onto his right side and loosened the knot still securing his hand to the iron headboard.

Wham! The door's wooden frame exploded. Bo filled the open space, his gun drawn and his stance low, as though he were a cop in a *Law and Order* episode. Behind him, six state troopers were crowded in the hallway. "Police! Put your hands up!"

Devon stared in total disbelief. *Bo Novak...a cop?*

Everything seemed to move in slow motion and at the same time, incredibly quickly. Selena pulling out a revolver, yelling for him to stay down. Dropping to the floor at the side of the bed.

"No!" Devon screamed. "Don't do it!"

He curled into a ball to avoid being hit.

Bang! Bang, bang, bang!

Bullets flew in all directions—knocking over lamps, shattering glass, sending the room into total darkness. The ear-shattering blasts left him burying his face in the pillow, praying that he wouldn't die in this seedy hotel room.

22

Rachel stared up at the wobbly ceiling fan, watching it rotate for what seemed like an eternity. She got up to take another pill and then climbed back into bed. She pulled the covers under her chin and longed to be lulled to sleep by the ship's rocking motion—to be transported to a peaceful place. However, whether her nightmares were triggered by being aboard *Stargazer* or in the proximity of the place where he had met his untimely death, they had grown in intensity. They had become so horrifying and real with each passing night that she got little or no sleep at all. She closed her eyes and concentrated on the sound in the room.

Click. Knock. Click. Knock. Click. Knock. The ceiling fan became wipers on her car, keeping a steady rhythm. Sweeping back and forth like a metronome. She peered through the moist windshield at the glistening harbor lights in the distance. According to the notebook on her passenger seat, she'd been at work all day, protecting the ocean sanctuaries off the California coast. She had no desire to question her good fortune. The tranquilizers had worked their magic, smoothing out the wrinkles. Filling her soul with bliss. She sank back in her seat and smiled at the world outside, which was passing by in a Technicolor blur.

A chance look in the rearview mirror stole her peace. Two of Pollero's thugs were following her in a menacing-looking black Corvette. Even though her foot was jammed to the floor, they matched her speed. They pulled up beside her in the left lane, bumping her car repeatedly. She swerved on and off the shoulder of the highway, desperate to stay alive.

A bicyclist suddenly appeared in the road, causing her to slam on the brakes. The Corvette plowed into the rear of her car, sending her careening off the hillside and into the black ocean below.

When she opened her eyes again, she found herself encased in a watery grave. The windows wouldn't open. Darkness was everywhere, and the ocean was seeping into the car. She tried to open the door, but it wouldn't budge. She pressed her back against the front seat and kicked at the windows with all her might. Yet it was useless. She was trapped, and her life was passing before her eyes!

"Ah!" She screamed as loud as she could, over and over again. No one could hear her. No one could see her. No one was going to rescue her.

"Help me! Oh, Daddy, *please*," she sobbed. "Don't let me die like this!"

That's when she saw it. The light drifting outside in the ocean. Growing brighter as it drew nearer. Blanketing the left side of the car with its blinding glow. Was it a flashlight? A diver, risking his life to save hers? She pressed her palm against the cold glass and met someone else's on the other side. The connection was electric, but it lasted only an instant. Without warning, the door opened. She swam free, clawing every inch of the way. She cut through the surface, gasping, choking on her first breath of air. She laid her head back in the water, trying to calm her racing heart. Trying to collect her thoughts. Overhead, a multitude of stars filled the heavens. She was alone, floating with the current. Moving gently with the evening tide. There was no rescue boat. No diver who might have interceded on her behalf.

Who was he? Like a sponge in a tub of water, reality sank in. Sam had been her angel of mercy. He was there when she needed him most, just as he had always been in the past. She needed to make peace with her father and help him to find his peace.

23

"No! No! No!" Rachel's blood-curdling screams woke Chase from a sound sleep.

He hopped out of his bed, still groggy, and glanced at the clock. It was barely 2:00 a.m. and for all he knew, her nightmares had been going on for hours. He flew down the passageway, nearly colliding with Wade and Blaine.

"It's none of your business! Get back to bed!" he yelled at his men.

Just like obedient children, they solemnly turned and disappeared behind their doors.

Ian charged down the ladder, abandoning his post, yelling nearly as loud as Rachel was. "What's happenin'? It sounds like bloody hell in there."

"She's getting worse," Chase whispered. "Go back up. I'll take care of this myself."

He waited until the soles of Ian's shoes left the last rung, and then he cursed under his breath. The nearer he got to her screams, the higher his temper soared. He felt mean and nasty by the time he reached her door. He shoved it open and rushed across the room to verbally attack her—to bring an end to her night terrors once and for all.

"Stop it!" he almost shouted. "Snap out of it! You're driving everyone nuts!" An obliging and sympathetic man would neither think nor say such things. But Rachel had subjected his crew to two long nights of hysteria, and Chase thought that hearing some stern words might snap her out of her paranoia and bring her back to reality…to being the woman he once loved.

After all, kindness hadn't helped. The night before, he'd gone running into her room with the intent of comforting her, of throwing his arms around her and assuring her that he still cared and that her dreams weren't real. Yet what good had that done? She'd all but driven him out of her room, barking at him like a crazy woman. Treating him like a villain who was intent on doing her harm. He'd never experienced anything so baffling. So totally beyond his control.

"Don't come near me! Someone stop him! Someone keep him away!" she'd cried out.

Now he stood at the foot of her bed, prepared to yell back, to remind her who was truly in charge. But as he stared down at her, his heart softened. He became deeply involved and transfixed by what he saw.

Rachel was lying facedown, tangled in her sheets. Sobbing and screaming, her words muffled by her pillow. "Help…*please*… Daddy…don't die…"

After all these years, she was dreaming about her father's death? He shook his head, hardly believing his ears. He sat down on the edge of her bed, trying to wrap his mind around the damage he'd caused—the torment buried in her dreams. He was the one who deserved the blame…who never should have let Sam out of his sight.

"Rachel…honey, wake up," he murmured.

She almost jumped out of bed at the sound of his voice. Her flushed and swollen face looked heartrending. She was gasping and choking. Struggling to catch her breath. She flung her arms around his neck and hugged him with all her might. But he felt undeserving. He felt felonious inside.

He pulled away quickly and stood up. He backed away, seeing the pain in her eyes. He needed to keep his distance, no matter how much it hurt. "I'm sorry," he said. "You shouldn't have come on this trip."

She stared up at him, appearing dazed and confused.

"I'll have one of the guys take you back," he told her.

She reached out and gripped his forearm. Her sorrowful eyes tore at his heart. "Please, Chase," she begged. "Don't send me away. I need to be here…with you."

24

Selena had stopped breathing, but Devon wasn't about to let her go. He frantically attempted CPR—arching her neck, lifting her chin, covering her mouth with his own.

Two quick breaths, he told himself. Just as he'd been taught in the first aid class he'd been hesitant to take years earlier. *One, two, three, four...*

He pumped her breastbone with thirty compressions and repeated the cycle over and over again. *Live, damn it, live*! Nothing was going to stop him from saving her life. Nothing.

Ten minutes ticked by, then fifteen. And still he persisted, gauging each rise and fall of her chest. It seemed an eternity before the paramedics finally arrived. Before one of them checked her vitals, looked up, and officially pronounced her dead on the scene.

"I'm sorry, sir," the ambulance driver said.

Devon's mind dulled at those words. Faces around him blurred into hideous kaleidoscopes. He felt detached and oddly fascinated.

"Got everything you need?" Novak asked the coroner. At the old man's nod, the sea of white uniforms parted. They exited one by one through the open doorway.

Devon suddenly came to his senses. "Wait!" He approached the gurney and gazed down at Selena's flawless face framed by her auburn hair. The sleeping angel about whom he had dreamed night after night. With whom he had shared his bed… for whom he had counted his blessings. The woman who had spoiled the sight of every other woman for him.

He touched the bullet hole in her chest, affirming that it was real. He clenched his teeth, struggling to control his emotions. *This can't be happening,* he told himself. *It's just a bad dream.* But there was no denying the truth. Not when his eyes were wide open. The woman he had loved with all his heart, who'd had him beaten repeatedly, was dead. She was the gang's mastermind, the manipulator behind the scenes. She had made it clear that she'd intended to kill him and his sister. So why in hell was he feeling such remorse? How was it possible that he still loved someone who had never been the person that she seemed to be?

The air in the room was perfectly still. No one approached him, comforted him, or assured him that the woman he had loved was in a far better place. They were busy snapping photos, making notes. Removing the small bottle of Dilaudid and bag of weed from the bathroom.

"Sorry, man." An enormous hand fell on his shoulder. He lifted his chin and met Bo Novak's soulful eyes. "Gotta let her go," he said.

Devon noticed the team of DEA agents standing in the doorway, talking to the silver-haired medical examiner. All the while, federal agents and state troopers streamed in and out of the hotel room. Even though his body quaked from frayed nerves and residual drugs, he wasn't about to let her go. Not yet.

"Heard the craziest story yesterday," said Matt Brennan, the short, boxy detective he remembered from his childhood. "Some pissed-off guy in Wisconsin called 9-1-1 to report that he'd been ripped off. Turns out a pair of strippers promised him freebies in his hotel room after he spent a thousand bucks on lap dances at a gentleman's club. When they didn't show, this wacko calls the cops at 1:00 a.m. to file a complaint."

The medical examiner sniffed a laugh. "You know, they might have turned up when the police were there and decided not to stay. Now *that* would've been funny."

Devon was amazed by the pair's callous exchange. *Where are their hearts*? Did they forget there was a dead woman in the room?

"Yeah...which reminds me," Brennan continued, "where's the DOA's brother? Probably skipped town after he heard we were on to him."

"The Forty-Second got a 3:00 a.m. call," Novak answered over his shoulder. "Turns out his body washed up in Oceanside. The county coroner confirmed it."

"No kidding?" Brennan said with a smile. "Wow...somebody did us a *real* favor."

"It seems."

Brennan pulled his sunglasses from his breast pocket and covered his eyes. "By the way, Novak, make sure you get your story straight before you file your report."

Devon watched the two men with detached interest. From what he gathered, Novak would need Devon's corroborating statement in order to clear himself, but Devon had a self-defense matter of his own to worry about. He swallowed the lump in his throat. It would only be a matter of time before his role in Gabe Pollero's death came out.

Brennan blew out an audible breath. "Lyons, I know this is tough, but we need your cooperation. Pollero's guys are still on the loose, and on top of that, you've got your sister's safety to think about. You *do* care about her, don't ya?"

Devon sniffed. "Of course, I do." He wiped his face with the back of his bloody sleeve.

"Then how 'bout getting that hand looked after? Novak!"

"Yes, sir."

"Escort this gentleman to the hospital. When you're done, bring him by the station to answer a few questions. I want this case wrapped up as soon as possible."

The coroner slipped Selena's body into a black bag and hid her face with the pull of a zipper. He rolled gurney through the hallway and into the waiting elevator.

Devon accompanied them, and then silently watched as Selena's body was loaded into the coroner's van. Like a stone statue, Devon remained fixed in place as the van's taillights retreated and darkness enveloped him. After a short while, he noticed a dark figure skulking under a glowing lamppost.

Novak.

The DEA agent ground out his thin cigar beneath his heel before joining him. "Are you ready to go?" he asked.

Devon averted his eyes. What was he expecting to hear? Accolades for a job well done?

"You know...this isn't easy for any of us," Novak insisted.

Devon's attention remained embedded in the cracked pavement at his feet. It was broken, crumbling, and uneven—a reflection of his disintegrating life. He ventured a sidelong glance and asked, "Did you really have to kill her?"

Novak's black nostrils flared. "Don't you get it? I had no choice. I don't know what kind of delusion you're under, man, but that chick was out to get you all along. You obviously had feelings for her, but she's gone and you're not. Now why don't you do the right thing and let me get you to the hospital?"

Devon rubbed his pulsing hand. The dope he'd been given had finally worn off. Blood was seeping through his bandages once again. But he didn't care. *Pain is good,* he told himself. The sting of severed skin, the throb of ruptured vessels, the burning ache of open flesh. In some kind of weird, maniacal way, it reminded him that he was still alive when everything inside was dead.

25

Rachel shut off the faucet and stared up at the dripping showerhead. The thought of stealing from anyone, especially from the hard-working men on board, left a bitter taste in her mouth. It had been her plan to treat this experience as a business venture—to avoid becoming personally involved. But after five long days and nights, she'd become a valued member of *Stargazer's* crew. Everyone aboard sought her advice, applauded her accomplishments. Showed her respect. Their gibes left her laughing. Their endless stories captured her imagination. The only salvation on this expedition had been her ability to maintain a cool demeanor when it came to Chase Cohen. However, even that had become increasingly difficult. Every smile, every passing glance left her stomach churning, her pulse quickening. She had to get off this ship fast, before her resistance completely gave out.

A sudden knock at the door arrested her thoughts.

"Just a minute," she called out. She grabbed her white robe from the hook and secured it around her waist before cracking the door open. Chase stood in the hallway in his usual snug-fitting jeans and unbuttoned white shirt. His expression was stern.

Now what?

"So, I hear you're leaving first thing in the morning," he said.

"That's right. AJ offered to take me back."

"But we've still got two days to go. I thought you wanted to stick around and finish your job."

"Of course, I do. It's just that I've got some pressing matters at home that need my attention."

"Oh, I see." He nodded thoughtfully. "Anything I can help you with?"

"No…I don't think so."

Rachel followed Chase's gaze to the opening in her robe. She gathered her collar in one hand, covering her exposed cleavage. "Was there something else?" she asked.

He averted her stare and muttered something about "hot."

"What did you say?"

He looked her straight in the eyes, and the steadfastness with which he held her gaze left her stomach fluttering. He spoke clearly this time. "I said you look hot."

She swallowed hard, not sure how to react. She felt herself blushing, her heart racing in her chest. She wanted to distance herself from him as quickly as possible. "It was the shower. The water's warmer than usual. If you don't mind, I need to get dressed now."

She watched him take a step back, allowing her the space needed to close the door. Believing him gone, she moved to the alcove where her pajama bottoms and T-shirt were waiting. As she bent to pick them up, she heard Chase walk up behind her. She straightened abruptly, turned, and found him inches away.

How did he get in?

With Chase nearly a foot taller than she was, she suddenly felt incredibly vulnerable. "I need to get dressed and..." Her voice was breathless, uncertain.

The residual heat from the shower caused new sweat beads to form on her skin. He reached out and touched one, trailing his finger along her throat. She shivered.

Chase, no. Her clothes were in her hands. But he just stood there, considering her face. He shifted, slowly bending his head toward hers.

"Don't do this..."

He paused, but still she could feel the heat of his breath on her lips, the moisture between her thighs collecting. This was the moment of decision. He was close, too close. All she had to do was say "leave" and it would end forever.

"You're so...beautiful," he said with wonder. "Just one kiss, then I'll go."

He gave her no chance to answer as he closed the space between their lips, touching his softly to hers. His lips were warm and moist as they covered hers, and she shuddered as his tongue pushed its way into her mouth. The taste was unexpected. Warm bourbon, strong but not unpleasant. His tongue tentatively touched hers and then began making a hungry exploration. First tasting, and then practically drinking.

Her clothes fell from her hands. She moaned softly, her mind and body at war with each other. Her anger, her convictions, her sense of everything that was right told her that she couldn't let this happen. But then he touched a thumb to her left breast, pushing away the terry cloth fabric until it found the fleshy nipple beneath, and all sensible thoughts ceased. His finger moved over the sensitive peak, circling and stroking, causing her nerve endings to scream. He moved his body into hers, their shapes molding effortlessly into one. She could feel his tumescence, his desire. His thighs were hard as they pressed into hers. His free arm slipped around her waist. He moaned in her mouth as his exploring hand kneaded her ass. He backed up just enough to pull her garment free, and the cool draft lifted tiny hairs on her skin, restoring some of her common sense.

No! She pushed him away. "We can't...do this." Her voice was breathless, as though she'd just run a three-mile race.

His blue eyes were glazed and hooded, and for a moment, she thought she'd never seen anything so sensuous. He was practically panting.

"You don't want me to go. You know you don't." He tried to close the space between them again, but she held out her hands, keeping him at bay.

She shook her head. "We've already gone too far."

"You won't feel that way when I'm inside you."

"Don't say that," she pleaded.

He pushed his chest against her hands, and on their own, her fingers spread against his taut muscles. Her body involuntarily trembled. In one motion, he reached out and grabbed her, pulling her roughly against him.

"Tell me," he breathed in her ear. "Tell me you don't love me." He claimed her lips again, devouring them like a starving man. His warm tongue slipped between her lips and into her mouth. But this time, she allowed it to happen.

She worked the top button of his jeans and pulled down his zipper. She pressed him into the mattress, covering his body with her own. A soft groan escaped his mouth, as she brushed her lips softly against his neck. In one swift movement, he rolled them over and then kicked off his pants.

"So I guess you want me after all," he murmured.

Rachel's head lolled back when his hungry mouth found the mounds of her breasts. She sighed with exquisite pleasure as he gently stoked the wet, slippery nub of her clitoris.

"Mmmm..." she moaned as his determined fingers moved even faster. As his tongue traced her neck and found one of her nipples. He continued his simultaneous assault until she was left gasping for breath. Until his bulging penis pressed hard against her thigh.

"Oh, baby," he whispered, sliding down her body. "I want you so bad."

Her body shuddered as his eager lips latched onto her labia and began sucking away.

"Chase, ooohhh," she moaned, encouraged, capitulated.

His tongue continued where his fingers left off. In and out, in and out, his tongue invaded and withdrew. She cried out and realized actual tears were flowing.

He climbed back onto the bed, straddling her body. "Do you want me?" His warm, rapid breaths washed over her skin.

She gazed into his craving eyes and trembled with excitement, but didn't answer with words. Instead, she crashed their mouths together in a passionate gesture of lust, tasting herself on his lips.

"I love you," he murmured.

He slid his swollen cock into her depths, causing her body to arch in response. She wrapped her legs around him and gripped his shoulders. His slow, steady tempo began. The padded headboard banged the wall relentlessly as he pounded his rigid staff into her yielding flesh. Driving her to the peak of pleasure, then down and up again.

"Chase!" she cried out.

He found her fingers and locked them tightly, pinning her hands to the bed. She could feel his heart pounding wildly in his chest. Hear the low moans in his throat as his body bucked and jerked above her. As though her body were an electric blanket that had been switched on high, heat began building in the soles of her feet and traveling slowly up her legs to her inner thighs. She could feel the delicious sensation growing, spreading throughout her lower extremities. She impulsively lifted her hips to meet each of his thrusts.

"Aaahhh!"

A groan tore from his throat, and a hot current ignited in her ankles. She arched her back as it shot up both of her legs and met at the core of her being. Her toes curled as moans escaped her mouth.

"Yes!" Spasms gripped her, constricting and relaxing, over and over again, leaving her scorched nerves tingling. She dared not breathe—dared not move. She wanted the bliss to last forever. How was it possible to feel so complete, so incredibly spent, and alive at the same time?

Rachel didn't realize that she'd fallen asleep and had a dreamless night until she opened her eyes and felt Chase's strong arm tucked under her neck. She angled her head to the right to study his profile—his prominent cheekbones, the defined brow, and the slightly square jawline. She wanted to hold his face in her hands, memorizing every detail, and then kiss his gorgeous mouth and thank him for giving her a wonderful night of peaceful slumber. He continued sleeping soundly, drawing soft, even breaths. Leaving her captivated and marginally amused. Then, just as quickly as the fantasy came, it faded. Common sense took hold, overshadowing her rose-colored world.

What the hell have I done? She moved gingerly away from Chase and attempted to rise from the bed without waking him. But Chase must have felt her stir, as he instantly rolled onto his side. He wrapped his other arm around her and drew her back against his chest.

"Good morning, beautiful," he breathed into her ear.

His rough whiskers brushed against her neck with each kiss, tickling her skin and reminding her of his masculinity. He folded his right leg over hers, pinning her in place. His throaty moans were an instant reminder of the hours they'd spent making love, entwined in each other's arms.

She angled her face toward him. "Aren't there chores you need to attend to?"

His hand found her left breast and held on possessively. "I think I can come up with a few." A brush against her inner thigh guaranteed that every inch of him was fully engaged.

She tensed. "You've got to be kidding. Are you trying to set some kind of record?"

"Mmmm...just warming up, sweetheart," he purred.

He molded her shoulders into the mattress and rolled on top of her. He leaned down, kissing her lips—leaving her no opportunity for escape. Then he propped himself on one elbow and gazed down at her.

"Now, tell me...why are you in such a hurry to get rid of me?"

Rachel considered her options. Maintain her angry facade and keep her predicament a secret. Or throw caution to the wind and tell Chase everything. Seeking his help would make it possible to end her troubling deception. And after the night they'd shared, she needed to believe he was worthy of her trust... even if her heart told her otherwise.

"It's about my brother, Devon," she began. "He's gotten himself into some serious trouble and—"

"Cap'n," a voice called from behind the door. "You're needed on deck, pronto."

"Be right there. Sorry, honey. Can we take this up later?" He stared into her face with his intoxicating blue eyes, waiting for an agreeable answer.

"Sure." What else could she say?

He grabbed his pants and shirt from the floor and dragged them on. Then he covered the few steps to her. "I swear those guys would sink this ship without me." He leaned down and brushed his lips against her temple, rekindling the warmth in her heart.

She was tempted to say the words he longed to hear just to keep him from leaving. And yet confusion over her true feelings kept her silent.

As soon as the door closed, she fell back into her pillow. She took a deep breath, hardly believing any of this had happened. There was no doubt in her mind…Chase Cohen would always be her weakness. But she needed to be strong. She needed to depend on no one except herself.

She slipped out of bed and opened her black carry-on. She pulled out the purple Crown Royal bag that had come in handy, and mentally calculated the value of the treasure she'd hidden in it. In a matter of hours, she'd be in San Palo, bargaining with Gabe Pollero and his band of cutthroat thieves. She alone had taken on Devon's debt. Guilt or no guilt, it would be up to her to settle his losses.

26

Whomp!

Rachel's heavy duffel bag hit the afterdeck. She glanced up at the second-tier deck and realized that the Zodiac was missing. She ran from stern to bow, listening for the sound of the raft's rumbling motor, looking for AJ. But to no avail. Her navigator and only means of escape had vanished.

What the hell? Her eyes shot daggers into the ocean's churning waves. She checked the storage locker next to the compressor. Two air tanks were gone. Apparently, Wade and Ian hadn't returned from their second dive of the day. According to her watch, Chase and Blaine were due to follow them in less than fifteen minutes. They *had* to be aboard.

Determined to get a full explanation, Rachel set off in search of Chase. She found his bed and room neat and tidy—a far cry from the bunks of the rest of the crew. She ducked through the open hatch, passing though the lounge and galley. She climbed the ladder to the bridge deck and passed the empty chart room.

Where is everyone?

Static was coming from the wheelhouse. She peered inside and found Blaine completely absorbed on the radio transceiver.

"I already contacted CBC about the new Ion," he said anxiously. "The PDF functionality we've incorporated will allow them to convert their files. They've also elected to reunify the compilers GCC and EGC, and make the EGC the new base compiler to coordinate all their work." He twisted around in the captain's chair and bristled at the sight of Rachel in the open doorway.

Her gaze skimmed the navigation desk. An open briefcase, stacks of files, cluttered papers. "Where's Chase?" she asked.

Blaine spoke over the VHF marine radio. "Gotta go. Call you when we get in." He jumped to his feet and stood before the console like an awkward schoolboy, a skinny, red-faced kid tugging on his green Sasquatch shirt.

The transmitting receiver was still in his hand, and he slipped it back on its hook before facing her again. "I…umm… was just taking care of some business issues that came up and…" His brows lifted, as if he suddenly remembered something. He reached into his back pocket and extracted a note. "The captain left this before shoving off with AJ and Mika." He closed the distance between them, and then waited silently as she read.

> *Honey:*
> *Sit tight until I get back. There's something important I need to tell you.*
>
> *Love, Chase*

She flipped the page over. Finding it blank, she glared at Blaine. "That's it? Two scribbled sentences?"

He pushed his glasses up a notch. "I guess you were indisposed or something. Anyway, there was this radio call. Some kind of emergency in San Palo. AJ said they'd be back in a few hours."

Emergency? What did that mean? Had Professor Ying taken a turn for the worse? Expired before she could tell him about the bronze snake she had found? "Blaine, please tell me what happened."

"It was the hospital. Some patient the captain knows who's in intensive care and—"

"Dr. Ying!" Oh, God. It was true.

"No, no...nothing like that. It's some chick the captain knows."

"*Excuse* me?" she said, her voice a full octave higher.

"I'm trying to remember her name. I think it was Annie or Amy. Or maybe—"

"Allie?" Rachel finished.

Blaine's brown shaggy head bounced up and down. "That's it! Do you know her?"

Unbelievable! Chase's reaction to the woman's name days earlier suddenly made sense. Ian's faltering answers had puzzled her for days, but now they made sense. Rachel's heart sank. No matter the circumstances, the fact that Chase had a secret woman tucked away was more than she could bear. She looked down at her hands, wanting to run to her room, climb into a shower, and scrub her skin until every trace of him flowed down the drain. How could she have been so foolish? Completely blindsided by his manipulative charm? She collapsed on the sofa, her head filled with venomous thoughts.

"Miss Lyons!" Blaine's raised voice captured her attention. "There's something I've been wanting to share with you all morning. I found it on my last dive." He laid the towel-wrapped object on the table before her, and then stood back, waiting for praise.

Rachel sat up and shoved aside her resentment. Glimpsing Blaine's hopeful expression, she peeled the soiled cloth away and exposed his discovery. She stared at the item and then back at him, completely dumbfounded.

"I don't get it," she said doubtfully.

"From Internet research, I was able to determine that the item you're looking at is a Chinese dowry box. Now, if you look inside, you'll notice it was stamped with the same imperial seal as the lid your father found. Handcrafted boxes like this were very rare. They were created solely to hold items of substantial value. As it turns out, the heart of the dragon might be a porcelain teapot, a jewel-embedded relic, or some type of religious rendering. Anyway, I'm convinced that if we go back and search Sector Ten again, we just might find—"

Rachel jumped to her feet. "Stay here," she said excitedly. She carried the box down two flights of stairs and ran through the passageway to retrieve the snake she'd been researching. As she lifted it from her desk, she was instantly reminded of its warmth—of the indescribable sensation she'd attributed to its molecular composition rather than to whatever celestial power it might possess.

She carefully inserted the snake into the dowry box. To her amazement, it fit perfectly, turning a fantastic legend into an undeniable truth. The heart of the dragon wasn't a dragon at all. It was an eight-inch, bronze cobra, poised for attack. Rachel chuckled and shook her head. Although the long-sought treasure might end the Ying family curse, its value rested primarily in its romantic allure.

She opened her desk drawer and removed the lid with its square spring lock and silver key. She tucked the lid's wooden edges into the box's grooves and slid it back in place, encasing the cobra. She flipped the lid's silver hinge, aligning the center metal eyelet between the two matching eyelets on the box. Then she took the heavily etched square lock and shoved the key forward, releasing its hidden catch. Matching the notched opening in the lock, she placed it over the eyelets and used her index finger to shove the square catch back into place. The small, tubular key elongated once more, but no matter how she tried, she couldn't pull the key free. It was simply a clever tool designed to open the sliding lock.

"*That's* the heart of the dragon?" Blaine asked. He stood in the open doorway with a quizzical expression on his face.

"Yeah...sorry to disappoint you, champ, but the emperor's jewels must've been on loan."

"And here AJ was convinced that we were looking for something grander than the almighty grail. What an idiot."

Rachel smiled. "It's nice to know two of us agree."

"Hey, I've got an idea. Let's hide the snake in his bed and see what happens. It'll be just like *The Godfather*." They both laughed. Although highly unlikely, the sight of AJ screaming at the top of his lungs would be worth the admission ticket.

The sudden change in *Stargazer's* rhythmic motion stilled Rachel's humor. Instinctively, she peered through a porthole and was stunned by an alarming sight.

"What's wrong?" Blaine asked.

"We're not alone anymore."

He stepped around her, following her line of vision. Ten degrees off their starboard, a white boat bobbed from its tethered anchor. In the midst of their merrymaking, a foreign invader had arrived.

With no time to secure the boxed cobra below, Rachel knelt down and jammed it under the bed. She came to her feet quickly. "Topside!" she yelled. "Now!"

She ran ahead of Blaine, scrambling up the ladder. She kept her eyes peeled on the surrounding water and arrived in the helm station breathlessly. Blaine was trailing closely behind. At first, she couldn't tell if the boat was a pleasure craft or simply a local fishing vessel. All she could see was the high, white prow and pitched roof. She snatched the binoculars from the console and adjusted the lenses. Immediately, a grizzly old man came into focus. He was standing at the bow with a rope looped in his hands. An additional line vanished below the surface. The air compressor in the aft was running full throttle and gear was strewed across the deck. She looked up and realized that the man's attention was fixed on their northeast buoy—just a short distance from where Wade and Ian would soon be surfacing.

They must have seen the Zodiac leave. Or intercepted Chase's radio transmission. Either way, they had to have known that *Stargazer's* captain was gone. She looked away, her mind reeling. She lifted the field glasses again, this time tracing the distant horizon.

"You've got to be kidding." She couldn't believe her eyes. *Legend.* The enormous scavenger loomed like a black vulture waiting to devour its prey. Somehow, the appearance of both vessels was related.

She was sure of it.

Rachel turned back to Blaine. "We've got divers off our starboard bow. You have to get a message to Chase and notify the coast guard right away. With Wade and Ian still down, we might be in a fight for our lives."

A heavy thud drew their attention to the lower deck. Rachel ventured a look through the wheelhouse's rear window. She spotted an air tank and fins on the dive platform. A modern-day pirate soon followed. She remembered the guns Chase had stowed in the locked cabinet on the lower level. If they could reach the galley without being spotted, they just might stand a chance against the invading marauder.

"Blaine," she whispered over her shoulder. "Where's the key for the gun cabinet?"

When he didn't answer, she turned. He wasn't on the radio, as she'd asked, or assuming his usual role of mild-mannered nerd. Instead, he stared back at her with knitted brows and a four-inch fillet knife clutched in his hand.

"What...what are you doing?" she asked.

"Taking care of business."

She would have laughed if the situation weren't so dire. A skinny kid with a saltwater bait knife, thinking he was Indiana Jones. "Where's the key?" she asked again.

"On the captain's neck."

"Great." A lot of good that was going to do them. "What about the coast guard?"

"No time." Blaine stepped past her with one finger pressed to his lips. He made his way stealthily down the ladder. Rachel trailed close behind. Reaching the main level, they continued to mimic one another, plastering themselves against the ship's wall, scoping out the interloper from a safe distance. By now, the diver had removed his hood and scuba mask, revealing a bald head, a beak-like nose, and beady eyes.

Viktor? What was *he* doing here? She leaned in close to whisper in Blaine's ear. "Believe me, you don't want to tangle with this guy."

Blaine remained silent for another minute as if contemplating her warning. Then he sprang into action, charging from his hiding place—the tiny, serrated sword outstretched before him. "Who are you and what do you want?" he yelled.

Rachel stepped out of the shadows, anticipating Viktor's answers. But the brazen gangster held his tongue. He regarded them without curiosity.

She looked toward Blaine and realized the futility of keeping her secret any longer. "He's one of Gabe Pollero's men," she told him. "One of the creeps that's been keeping my brother hostage. I don't know what's going on or how he found me, but I have a feeling something's gone terribly wrong or he wouldn't be here."

"Hostage? Why didn't you say something? Why didn't you notify the police?"

"It's a long story," she said, shaking her head. "You don't want to be involved, believe me."

"Enough!" Viktor snapped. "I know you have it."

She stared back, hating him more than ever. "I don't know what you're talking about."

He leered at her, threatening. "This not game. Give to me or go to hell with Polleros."

Polleros? "What are you saying? Are Gabe and Selena—"

The ferret ran his hand over his smooth scalp and hitched a shoulder. "Dead, broken neck. Bullet through heart…thanks to brother."

"*My* brother? I don't believe you. Devon wouldn't kill anyone. Especially Selena."

"Really?" Viktor freed his arms and left his wet suit dangling from his waist. When his hand slid into his waistband, Blaine crouched into a fullback position, brandishing his weapon before him.

"Drop whatever you've got!" he ordered.

Instead of a weapon, the villain pulled out a rose-gold Saint Christopher metal on a fine gold chain. Blaine snatched it from his fingers and motioned Rachel over. With one glance, she knew right away. The necklace belonged to Gabe Pollero.

Viktor waited until she looked up. "Now you know truth. Polleros no more."

"What about my brother?" she asked, her voice rising. "Is he all right?" A half dozen more questions immediately came to mind, but the insolent man looked away. He obviously had no intention of cooperating.

"Answer her!" Blaine demanded.

"Maybe." He glanced around and then smiled at Rachel. "Only two of you on big boat, eh? Tell me where treasure is and you live, too."

Blaine angled his head. "Hey, *I'm* the one with the knife, pal." He faced Rachel, appearing more assured than the situation allowed. "Hand me the rope from the locker and call the police," he demanded. "We'll let them handle this maggot."

She was about to step away when another set of fins slapped the afterdeck.

Ian, please tell me that's you. She held her breath, waiting for his dripping, white-blond head to appear above the rail. Instead, cropped black hair and a broad, tawny face appeared.

Marcos. He dropped his gear before joining his partner in crime.

"What do we have here, Vik?" he asked. "A little gringo and our favorite señorita?"

A ghost of a smile, evil and snide, formed on his lips. He pulled a six-inch knife from the strap around his leg. Like a character straight out of *West Side Story,* he tossed it from one hand to the other. Blaine was clearly out of his league. The hoodlum beckoned him forward. Perhaps thinking better of it, Boy Wonder relinquished his weapon, dropping it to the floor with a clank.

Marcos immediately scooped it up. He grabbed Blaine's shoulder, spinning him around so that he now faced Rachel. He pressed the knife's jagged edge against his throat, threatening to slash it with one deadly draw.

His black eyes narrowed into slits. Flecks of spit collected at the corners of his mouth as he spoke. "So, Miss Lyons, you tell me where to find the dragon heart you promised Pollero or your friend will die…now," he threatened.

"It…it doesn't exist."

"Neither do you, if you don't tell us where it is."

"Listen to me. The shipwreck's been searched from top to bottom. The treasure I told Pollero about isn't there."

"You *lie*!"

"I'm telling you the truth!"

She watched a fine line of blood suddenly appear beneath the knife's sharp edge. Her breath caught. She swallowed hard. She couldn't be responsible for anything happening to Blaine. He had no part in any of this. But she also knew that if she surrendered the cobra, there would be no reason for Marcos and Viktor to keep them alive.

"I'll get it," she promised.

Marcos stared at her, impatience evident in his narrow eyes. "So, now it's real?"

Rachel remained silent.

"Where is it?" he demanded.

"Inside the crater, eighty feet down. I know exactly where to find it."

Blaine flashed a questioning look. Fortunately, both of the other men missed it.

"*Si.* That's what I want to hear," Marcos said. "I don't want to kill you. But as for your little friend here—"

"You don't have to kill either one of us," she insisted. "I'm telling you the God-honest truth. The dragon is down below. You only have to follow me to see for yourself."

Marcos stared at her for an endless moment and then shifted his attention to Blaine. "She better not be lying, amigo…for your sake."

He lowered the knife and Blaine crumpled to the floor. Marcos's leering eyes swung back to Rachel.

"So, you go like *that*?" he asked.

She looked down at her blouse and jeans and then scanned the afterdeck for her carry-on. She spotted it near the dive platform, exactly where she'd left it. "I need to put on my suit," she said with visible tension. She waited for Marcos's approving nod before moving toward the bag. However, Viktor stopped her.

"It's in my duffel, right there," she assured him. "Just let me get it."

Viktor wasted no time in claiming the bag himself. He carried it back to her and was about hand it over when an "ah-ha" look came over his face. Without a word, he immediately set to work unzipping it, rummaging through her clothes, tossing pants, shoes, and shirts right and left. After a few minutes, he looked up.

"Nice," he said, displaying a pair of sheer, white panties.

Marcos's lips curled. "Throw 'em here. I'll keep those."

Rachel remembered the Crown Royal sack still tucked in the bottom of her bag. She cringed at the thought of him finding it—at how he and his friend would react. She knew that demands would get her nowhere, so she spoke as pleasantly as she could manage. "Please, if you don't mind, let me do that."

"You want *this*?" Viktor asked, dangling her black swimsuit in the air. He tossed it at her before she could answer. "Get ready."

"Not here," she said. "Let me go down below."

"You've got something to hide?" His greedy eyes slid over her body, assuring her that treasure wasn't all he was after.

"Please. I won't be long."

Marcos wrinkled his beak. "No need, *socio*. We got her friend, eh?"

Rachel released a closely held breath. She glanced at her carry-on, relieved that her secret trove was still hidden. She hesitated before asking, "Can I have that, too?"

Viktor lifted the bag and for a brief moment, he seemed to be weighing his load. He dumped it upside down, emptying its remaining contents. He untied the sleeves of her balled-up windbreaker and exposed the bulging purple sack. "What we have here?"

No, no, no! Rachel's hand found her throat.

Viktor loosened the drawstrings. His nimble fingers slid inside. He withdrew a single gold coin and waved it in front of her face. "So…you lie. You have gold and don't tell us. I knew it!"

She gulped hard and then looked down at Blaine. Surprise and then disappointment registered on his face. *I can explain,* she wanted to say. *I had no choice.* But there was no point. The damage had already been done.

Marcos joined his accomplice. He examined her loot, counting and then recounting the coins. It didn't take long for him to lose interest in the tidy sum. "Where's the rest?" he asked.

"That's all the gold we found," she claimed. "There isn't any more."

"So you say. But I don't trust you no more."

"Please…you have to believe me. I'll help you find the heart of the dragon. That's what you came here for, isn't it?"

"I hope you're not lying again, señorita. You *do* know what happens to liars, don't you?"

She slowly shook her head.

Viktor wagged his tongue back and forth. He looked at his partner with a conspiratorial smile. "We cut tongues out. Feed them to sharks."

Rachel looked away, shielding her disgust.

"Search below!" Marcos shouted.

Her plea had proved utterly useless. Blaine was escorted back up the ladder and into the wheelhouse while the bald-headed ferret pushed her in the opposite direction. He followed her down below and scoured the forward cabins. He emptied closets, dumped drawers, cleared tabletops. He filled a large, empty basket with pilfered iPhones, watches, computer disks, Blaine's laptop—whatever caught his fancy. Fortunately, unbeknownst to him or his partner, the crew's cache was stowed in the ship's belly, beneath floor planks in the galley. The secret compartment, which her father had included in the ship's alterations, had seemed frivolous at the time. But it didn't now.

As soon as Viktor left the first cabin, Rachel tore off her clothes and changed quickly into her Speedo suit. She passed through the main salon and was heading toward the ladder to the chart room when a man's arm circled her waist. He pulled her into a dark alcove and covered her mouth with his meaty palm.

Not again! She delivered a swift elbow jab to the man's midsection, loosening his grip. She twisted free and spun around, primed and ready to deliver a fisted blow. In the nick of time, recognition dawned. "Wade?"

The mountainous man was still grabbing his gut and biting his lip. He nodded in affirmation.

"Sorry," she whispered. "Some creep grabbed me like that before and—" His hand sealed her words.

Marcos looked down from the open hatch. He moved to the ladder's third rung, displaying his newly claimed flare gun. His beady eyes scanned the entire area. After a few minutes, he grunted and climbed back inside.

Wade's hand fell away. "We saw their boat and dive gear," he whispered. "Do you know how many divers there are?"

"Two, maybe more." With Marcos now controlling the wheelhouse and radio transceiver, there was no telling how many villains would eventually surface.

"Ian's waiting for me at the bottom of the dive platform. We'll swim over to their boat and get some answers. Wait here out of sight until we get back."

Rachel eagerly agreed. She watched from behind the ladder as Wade skirted the afterdeck. He successfully eluded the villain in the wheelhouse and vanished from sight. When he reappeared, he had his trusty spear gun in hand. Without making a sound, he slipped over the side—a warrior on a deadly mission.

Meanwhile, the racket in *Stargazer's* lower level came to an abrupt halt, a sure sign that Viktor had finished ransacking all the cabins and forward storage compartments. He climbed up the ladder and called out to Rachel in a ludicrous, singsong voice. "*Kraseevah,* where *are* you?"

Against her better judgment, she ventured from her safe haven to see what the obstinate thief was up to. He tossed the basket of stolen items overboard, and then turned to see if she'd been watching.

What was the point of that? If the man had a half a brain, he would have realized that they'd been logging all of their discoveries on the computer he'd just discarded. With the tap of a few keys, he could have revealed the contents of the load buried in their hull.

"You forget to tell me something?" he quizzed.

She shook her head, more puzzled than ever.

"*This*!" He held out the jade pendant Chase had given her. The reward she'd left sitting on her nightstand. "Hmm..." he persisted. "Gift from boyfriend, maybe?"

She glared at him. It wasn't a priceless keepsake, but to Rachel it held sentimental value—something this villain would never understand.

He moved closer to the rail and dangled the pendant over the side. "Maybe you understand now."

"Stop it! Give that to me before you drop it." She ran at him, reaching for it, but he instantly whipped around. He held it tightly against her chest, pinning her in place, and breathed in her ear, "Tell me...what you do for it?"

"Dubov!" came from above. "We're wasting time."

Viktor slid his wet tongue along her neck, leaving Rachel cringing. "Get treasure, maybe I give back," he murmured in her ear.

She bit her lip, willing herself not to respond to anything he said—anything he might do.

He released his hold and looked up at Marcos, grinning. "If we no come back, you kill boy. *Poinyal?*"

"No problem," Marcos called down.

Rachel scowled as she collected her dive gear. She headed for the dive platform and cast a backward glance. Viktor was tucking the pendant inside his wet suit, claiming ownership.

Moron. If all went according to plan, she would never see it again—not in this lifetime.

After donning her equipment, she opened her pack to check her tools: hammer, goody bag, chisel. Dive knife. It would come in handy when she needed it.

Viktor picked up his mask and tank. He was in the midst of tightening his straps when she slipped the knife into the strap around her leg.

"Give that to me," he ordered, pointing at her thigh. The black-hearted pirate had been paying more attention than she realized.

"What about sharks?" she asked. "I have to protect myself, don't I?"

"My job. Take it off!"

She peered up at the helm station, to the place where Blaine now stood watching. She hesitated before obliging. Viktor snatched the knife from her fingers and added it to his arsenal.

Creep. She glimpsed her wrist. Thanks to Marcos's stupid cohort, her dive computer was now at the bottom of the ocean. She would have to depend solely on her gauges and years of diving experience. Once she entered the *Wanli's* hull, she'd have less than fifteen minutes to trap Viktor in the cargo hold and even less time to make it back safely. She looked at the white boat, still bobbing in the distance. Where the hell were Ian and Wade? How could they not know she was about to risk her life?

Viktor tapped her arm. "What's plan?"

"We're making a forty-five-minute dive and then stopping for three minutes at five meters before surfacing. Understand?"

"Yes."

With her tank and vest fully secured, she pulled the mask down over her face. Though not of any consequence to her, she noticed that Viktor lacked a depth gauge. He hadn't even bothered to check the air pressure in his used tank. She'd be cleared of all charges should there be an investigation into his self-induced death.

"Let's go!" he barked.

She stuck the regulator into her mouth. With one last look around, she dropped over the side and into the ocean's deep-blue coliseum.

27

Viktor followed Rachel in her rapid descent, hugging the cave's steep wall. As they approached the *Wanli*, she pointed out the dragon's gold, decapitated figurehead, half buried in rock. She smiled, having delivered exactly what she had promised. But the irony was totally lost on Viktor. He withdrew his knife and motioned her onward.

They swam in a westerly direction for five more minutes before arriving at the merchant ship's hindquarters. Rachel's companion stalled instantly—perhaps as much in awe as she'd originally been by the *Wanli's* vast and inconceivable presence. After a few seconds, he finned up beside her and signaled, "Go!" He waited for her to proceed and then resumed his position.

She shimmied through an open window on the third level and entered a small cabin, where the greatest collection of dishware had been found. She aimed her flashlight into the room's dark interior and shadowy alcoves to verify its vacancy. Fortunately, the only sign of life was the shimmering particulate reflected in the light's beam. The moray eel she'd encountered on a previous dive was nowhere in sight.

She swam half the circumference of the room before coming to a partially open doorway. The passage beyond led downward to the ship's main cargo hold, where the shark had taken up residence. By all accounts, it wouldn't be long before the illusive creature transformed into a vicious predator and disposed of the belligerent fool who trailed her.

Rachel slowed her approach. Except for the broad mast slanting through the dark, the huge space appeared empty. A cloud of silt was wafting down from the upper floor, obscuring the view before them. The quickest exit was in the ship's darkest corner—the camouflaged crack that had provided Ian and Wade with an alternate escape route.

Rachel concentrated on their pitch-black surroundings, primed for any sudden movement. But a sudden flash from an enormous school of glistening fish startled her and nearly cost her the beacon of light leading the way. When she regained her composure, she continued. But Viktor stalled more than once in obvious protest.

"Where are we going?" he signed repeatedly.

She motioned downward. "Just five more minutes," she assured him.

When they reached the bottom of the hull, the visibility had diminished to ten feet. She was also keenly aware that a cloud of fine silt now rose in her wake, completely obscuring Viktor's vision. His hand signals were reduced to indiscernible complaints and no longer warranted response from her. She glanced over her shoulder as they swam on and was reassured by the growing distance between them. Her lips curled around her regulator, as she delighted in the perverse pleasure. Viktor would soon be trapped in the *Wanli's* tangled maze with his dimming flashlight, empty air tank, and no one to lead the way out.

She increased her speed and seized the opportunity to change course. She ducked under rotting timbers and headed south, increasing her depth as she left Viktor far behind. She entered the last compartment in the *Wanli's* vast cargo hold and kept her eyes peeled for the crack in the ship's outer hull. But it didn't take long to realize that something was terribly wrong. The escape route she'd been counting on was now blocked by rocks.

What the hell! The unstable volcanic sediment had shifted, causing huge chunks of basanite to break through the *Wanli's* underbelly. Nature's resolve had foiled any possibility of escape. She carefully pushed away rocks, but after ten minutes, she realized that it was suicidal to keep looking for the opening. Her air level was getting dangerously low. She'd already disregarded every rule, every ounce of common sense, and by her calculations, she was one hundred feet down with only ten minutes of air left. The quotient was disturbing. Without the aid of a pony tank, her own life was now on the line.

She doubled back, slowing her steady breathing. By now, Viktor's tank had to be close to empty. He would be coming after her in a panic. She wasted no time working her way out of the ship's cargo hold, pushing the BC rig ahead of her. Even though she hadn't passed any intersecting vents, she maintained contact with the monofilament line Chase had attached to the Penn reel leading to the *Stargazer.* Wrapping it inch by inch over her right wrist, she retraced her path until she sensed the *Wanli's* open hatch ahead of her.

Upon entering the blackness of the open ocean, Rachael sensed that she wasn't alone. She scanned the watery space surrounding her, half-expecting Viktor to materialize. But that wasn't the case. The luminous creature Chase had angrily dismissed and the crew had disannulled was back! Her attempt to erase its presence from her mind only made the image grow stronger. It was more apparent than ever and inescapably real. Before her eyes, the specter took shape, becoming a glowing orb. From its center, the face of an angel slowly emerged. She was surrounded in streams of white gossamer that floated around her like fluid, shimmering silk. Her black hair framed her angelic face, flowing aimlessly in the ocean's current.

Rachael stared at the woman's astonishing face, transfixed by her gentle smile. She felt blissfully content, foolishly light-headed. She smiled back, giddy over the vision's kind, whole-some goodness. But then in an instant, the woman's brown eyes became black. They darted to the right, compelling Rachel's eyes to follow.

A great white was charging, preparing to devour her in one bite. Its dull, lifeless eyes were fixed. Its mouth was stretched open, exposing white, limb-ripping teeth. Instinctively, Rachel reached for her knife. Then she remembered that it was gone. Miraculously, the shark passed by, coming within inches of her.

Oh, my God! Rachel's eyes followed its fast-moving tail. The shark had been attracted to something larger, more threatening. Far more appealing than she was. A black wet suit was rapidly approaching from the opposite direction. Viktor Dubov's knife was extended before him. After discovering he'd been duped, he obviously had been intent on doing her harm. But the villain wasn't prepared for a head-on collision with an angry, 400-pound shark.

The creature slammed into Viktor full force. Viktor's eyes bulged as the big fish whipped away. Behind his mouthpiece, his voice remained a hostage.

Rachel had no intention of sharing his fate. She swam closer, focused on reclaiming her knife. But Viktor panicked. He grabbed her, wrapped his arms around her, and held her help-lessly in place.

No! She squirmed and twisted, trying to free herself. Yet the fool held fast. The shark returned and attacked from below, latching onto Viktor's left leg. She could feel the terrific jolt as the shark shook his body, demanding ownership of its prey.

Then suddenly, there was blood everywhere. Viktor was aghast, stunned.

Use the knife! Use the knife! Rachel pointed repeatedly at his weapon.

He released his hold and brought the knife into view. She grabbed it from his hand just as he was pulled down beneath her. The shark swept by in a deep, methodical circle. On its second pass, the great white brushed her shoulder. Viktor was firmly locked in its jaws.

Stunned, Rachel watched as the monster took the villain away.

28

Rachel could still feel the pressure of Ian's hands under her arms, lifting her out of the ocean. Setting her down on the seat. She stared mindlessly at the men in uniform staring back and surmised she'd been deposited on the deck of a coast guard cutter following the shark's vicious attack.

"Where's the man who was with ya?" Ian asked, concern stitching his brow.

Rachel closed her eyes again, trying to still her jangled nerves, her quivering lips. But her bent knees wouldn't stop shaking. "Great white took him," she mumbled.

"Was no fault of yers. Ya let it go now." His arm was draped over her shoulder, pinning the warm, gray blanket in place. She glanced to her left where a coast guard officer was cross-examining Wade. From the look on his face, her exuberant protector was anxious for the clipper to shove off and let them to get back to business as usual.

She looked out at the rolling waves extending far beyond their starboard side. "She was there." The words fell out of her mouth.

"Who's that?"

Rachel lifted her chin, meeting Ian's gaze. "Mai Le. I saw her."

"The ghost of that dead Chinese girl?" At Ian's question, two coast guard officers turned. "Jaysus," Ian bellowed. "She offed herself four hundred years ago. We're not jawin' bout that again, are we?"

Rachel recognized the stress in his eyes. She shook her head and looked away.

"That's me, girl. As it is, Cap'n's gonna have a conniption when he hears what's gone on."

Wade's voice suddenly grew louder. "Why isn't anyone listening to me? I'm telling you she needs a *real* doctor."

The coast guard paramedic glared at him. "Like I told you, she's pinking up. She's obviously shaken, but under the circumstances, her pulse appears fine. She doesn't show any sign of nausea, and somehow, despite everything she went through, she made all her stops. I can call and arrange for an ambulance, if you'd like...just to put your mind at ease."

Rachel's head snapped to the right. "I'm fine. I just want to be left alone."

"I think it would be a good idea to have a doctor look at you anyway, ma'am."

Two more uniforms approached. The first officer, a clean-cut, middle-aged man, eased himself onto the padded seat beside her. Off to his right, the prim young woman with short brown hair simply observed.

"I'm Lieutenant Commander Phillips and this is Petty Officer Nelson," he said. "San Palo sheriff's deputies are still searching the area for the man who went down with you and the diver who escaped before we arrived. We're also trying to piece together exactly what happened here. According to Blaine McKenzie, who's waiting on board your ship, you were boarded and accosted by these men, and one of them managed to get away with some of your personal effects. Their boat was rented from the San Palo marina. Assisting officers are currently towing it back to the harbor. But there seems to be some confusion with regard to the third individual who was manning that craft. He was fished out of the ocean twenty minutes ago and claims he was brutally attacked without provocation by members of your crew. I know that's unlikely, given their story. However, since your captain is unavailable at this time, I'm hoping that as the owner of this vessel, you're willing to answer a few questions."

Petty Officer Nelson stepped away to answer a call.

Rachel glanced at Ian and then at Wade, who was leaning against the rail. She hoped for a hint as to what they'd told the coast guard. Their lax postures and bland stares revealed nothing. She looked back at the lieutenant and cleared her throat. "I'll try," she said doubtfully.

He opened his small binder and reviewed his notes. Then he looked up. "Mr. Olivares claims you have a Chinese relic belonging to him and his associates. Is there any possibility this is true?"

Rachel almost laughed aloud. The question brought obsolete airline security questions to mind. *Has anyone unknown to you asked you to carry an item on this flight? Have any of the items you're traveling with been out of your immediate control since the time you packed them*? No wonder those questions were scrapped years ago.

"Let me ask you something, Lieutenant," she said cynically. "If I had this item in my possession, what makes you think it would belong to *any* of these men?"

"I just ask the questions, Miss Lyons."

Ian's left brow lifted a fraction. Wade's eyes returned to the sea.

"Sir," she added, "I don't mean to be crass, but they're pirates. They ransacked our boat and threatened our lives. They'd say anything to keep from going to jail, wouldn't they?"

"Normally, I would completely agree with you. But given Mr. Rodriguez's claim and his relationship to the mayor of San Palo—"

"Relationship?"

"Turns out they're brothers. But in any event, if your ship's log and dive journal are in order, you should have no problem clearing all this up. Otherwise, it becomes a matter for the courts."

Rachel swallowed hard. Disclosing the fact that all their records were now at the bottom of the ocean would be the right thing to do. The only sensible thing to do. Still, even in her mind, the account sounded preposterous and extremely convenient. "Just out of curiosity, did Mr. Rodriguez provide you with a description or name of the piece in question?"

"He wasn't real clear, but I believe it was a dragon."

The *Wanli* immediately came to mind. "Then I assure you, Lieutenant, our documents are in complete order. The only dragon in these waters is a four hundred-year-old ship that I'm sure everyone's going to be hearing about."

Phillips got to his feet smiling. "Well, congratulations, Miss Lyons. We heard rumors, but it's nice to know Sam's prediction finally came true."

"You knew my father?"

"Oh, sure. We'd run into him occasionally out here. He was always boasting about finding his treasure ship one day."

She smiled and looked around for Ian. He was still huddled near the rail, deep in conversation with Wade. The stolen looks over their shoulders convinced her that Blaine had already revealed her part in the fiasco. She cringed, realizing she'd foolishly put all their lives at risk.

Should I tell the lieutenant about Devon's kidnapping? Pollero hadn't said anything about not involving the coast guard.

"And Miss Lyons," the lieutenant commander continued, "stop by the hospital and get yourself looked at, OK?"

"All right. Thank you." Rachel pushed herself upright and drew the towel around her shoulders. She glanced out at the waves and then looked back at Phillips, just as Petty Officer Nelson returned with a note in her hand.

"Sir, two issues have just been brought to my attention," she told him. "It seems Red Star Charters is dropping chum again. We're getting complaints from dive boats in Scoria Bay."

"Get ahold of Commander Harris," he instructed. "Those guys are complete idiots. He'll shut them down once and for all. Now, what was the other matter?"

"We also received a radio dispatch from a gentleman who claims that Miss Lyons works for him. Apparently, the San Palo sheriff's office has been trying to reach her all morning with regard to her brother, Devon. Apparently there was an altercation involving a shooting, and he was admitted to San Palo General with a severe wound."

Rachel felt the air leave her lungs. Her heart leaped into her throat. *Oh, my God. Devon*! Her shaking knees buckled, and she dropped to the deck.

The lieutenant commander rushed over and leaned down. "Miss Lyons…Miss Lyons, are you all right?"

29

Rachel looked up at the San Palo General Hospital sign, confused as to why she'd been brought there in the back of ambulance.

"I'll take her from here," Wade told the driver. Without waiting for a response, he assumed control of her wheelchair and waved the man on his way. The taillights were barely out of the driveway when Rachel got to her feet. She pinned the towel she'd been given around her waist with one hand to shield her bathing suit. With her other hand, she clutched her black duffel bag.

"I need to find my brother," she insisted.

"Down," Wade growled. He pushed her back into the chair, forcing her to sit.

"This is ridiculous," she grumbled. "I'm fully capable of walking."

He chuckled humorously. "That's why you collapsed on the boat and passed out."

"I was a little dizzy, but I'm all right now."

He set the bag on her lap and stepped behind the wheelchair. "Like it or not, you're getting checked out." He steered them through the hospital's rear emergency entrance and into a room filled with waiting patients.

"There should be a doctor with you shortly," said a woman passing by with a clipboard in her hand. She repeated the same words to everyone in the room.

Rachel looked around, scanning strange faces, searching for any sign of Devon. "Can you ask where we can find Devon?"

"We're here about you. After we get you taken care of, I'll find out where they've got him stowed."

His answer wasn't good enough. She needed to know if her brother was critical…if he was going to survive his wound. "Wade, I need to see him right now."

He patted her arm. "Calm down. Let me ask, OK?" He was gone for a few minutes, and then he returned, still looking solemn. "I couldn't get any information, not being the next of kin and all, but one of the nurses told me he'd most likely be in surgery or in recovery on the fourth floor."

Rachel looked up at him with pleading eyes. "Wade…"

"OK, OK. But you're not moving an inch unless I take you there."

She agreed, and he directed them through the door. As they waited for the elevator, the smell of chemicals, deodorizers, and disinfectant assaulted her senses, churning her stomach once more. The doors parted and closed several times, allowing passengers to crowd into the packed elevator.

She glanced up past her shoulder. "How do we know where to look?"

Wade leaned down and whispered near her ear. "Trust me. I'll find him."

When they reached the fourth floor, an elderly man came to their aid, holding the door open wide. Wade veered around him and curved around a few corners before coming to an abrupt stop in front of a reception desk. No one was there. The medical clerk's chair was empty.

Rachel felt the weight of Wade's hand on her shoulder. "Stay put. I'll get someone," he said.

She sighed as he approached two conferring doctors. From the stale look of their faces, she was the least of their concerns. As she continued to wait, she glimpsed a white-sheeted gurney against a wall and recalled her last visit to San Palo General Hospital. She'd come here to meet with Dr. Walters, the morgue coroner. She had listened to his inane explanation of her father's death and stood back, waiting for the sheet to be lifted. Chills had run up and down her arms. She'd held her breath, imagining the worst, and then looked down at her father's finely chiseled face. It was difficult to look at him. He wasn't the man she knew and loved. His eyes had bulged out slightly from his bloated face, conjuring up thoughts of a surreal, scary mask. She had willed herself to remain calm—to appear subdued and unaffected. She'd been brought there to witness something. But what was it? An opportunity to heighten her sensibility about life and death? To somehow engage her critical, emotive, and human response, and to act on that outrage?

She blew out a shaky breath and glanced to her right. A stout, middle-aged woman had returned to the desk and resumed her authoritative position. She rolled forward in her executive chair, mumbled a few words, and then collected the pen that she'd tucked above her ear.

Rachel glanced around. Wade was nowhere in sight. She spotted a restroom sign a few yards away. She pushed herself out of the chair and scurried barefoot across the floor with her bag in tow. Once inside, she locked the door and dropped her towel. She changed out of her Speedo and into a pair of jeans, flip-flops, and a fuzzy, blue sweater. She splashed cold water on her face and found a brush in the bag's outer pocket. After a half dozen long strokes, her hair was restored to a presentable state.

She rolled her suit up and was about to tuck it into her duffel bag when she spotted the corner of a white towel peeking out from under her windbreaker. She dumped her clothes and shoes onto the floor and was astounded to find Mai Le's box hidden among them. Taped to the top was a scribbled note from Blaine.

Let me know what Doc says.

Rachel shoved everything into her bag and zipped it up. She unlocked the bathroom door and wandered back into the hospital corridor. The wheelchair she'd vacated was nowhere in sight, and neither was Wade.

Still anxious to find her brother, she approached the counter and addressed the medical clerk's down-turned head. "Excuse me..."

"Yes, I'm listening," she answered.

"I was told that my brother, Devon Lyons, might be here."

"He's consulting with Dr. Canzler."

"I'm sorry. Who was that?"

"No. He's a general practitioner at the Roberts Street Clinic."

She was stumped by the clerk's strange response until she realized the woman had been speaking into the tiny headset attached to her ear. Rachel's cheeks warmed. She tucked a long brown strand behind her ear and adjusted her hold on the bag.

"Is there something I can do for you?" A young nurse's voice came from behind. Her shiny, blond hair was coiled in a bun. Her light-brown eyes sparkled with interest.

"I couldn't help overhearing you," she explained calmly. "We haven't officially met but I'm Judi Swift. I feel like I already know you. My next-door neighbor, Mrs. Van Dozer, is on the seventh floor having a procedure."

"I hope it's nothing serious."

"Just a little nip and tuck. She's being very hush-hush this time…wants everyone to believe she's lost weight. She's never been shy about her fake boobs and Botox injections, so I don't get what the big deal is." She snickered and then drew closer. "I'm totally convinced she's been shooting up her lips, too. Have you noticed how's she's beginning to look like a bad Jessica Rabbit? But then, it could be those *amazing* makeup tricks she's using."

Rachel found herself giggling. Judi's humor was truly a dose of good medicine. Although Megan Van Dozer had been the butt of Judi's jokes, most of the rich Betties in town were equally obsessed with their looks. Judi could accumulate enough material to headline at the local comedy club.

"Devon Lyons?" Rachel reminded her.

"Oh, yeah…your brother." She pulled Rachel aside and spoke in a hushed tone. "The basket case behind the counter had a regular meltdown last night. She got all bent out of shape when he refused to supply an emergency contact. Security got called in and she ended up claiming he'd verbally assaulted her."

Rachel glanced away, shaking her head. It was a good thing the clerk had been too busy to answer her question. Her reaction would have been anything but pleasant.

"Soon as he was treated for the bullet wound in his hand, he up and left. Dr. Rosenstein was totally pissed." Judi rolled her eyes. "Anyway, no big deal. That guy's a complete asshole. Even the seventy-year-old orderly hates him…and Melvin loves *everyone*."

Rachel cringed. Although Devon had left a virtual storm in his wake, one question still remained. "Was my brother alone when he arrived?"

"Nope, and that's one man I'll *never* forget. Dark, long braids, black leather jacket. The soft-spoken, mysterious type. Sort of looked like that character in *The Matrix*. You know what I mean?"

Rachel drew in her lips and nodded. Unfortunately, she did.

"Anyway, they had this heated argument and as soon as the guy's back was turned, your brother took off."

Great. "Did he leave a clue as to where he might be headed?"

Judi pursed her lips as if weighing her options. "Not exactly. When I mentioned he'd lost a lot of blood and needed to take it easy, he smiled and said something about getting a transfusion. I assumed that he meant at the local bar."

Are you kidding? While Devon had been off drowning his sorrows, she could have been eaten alive. So much for brotherly love.

"Oh, and Miss Lyons…Mrs. Van Dozer tells me that you've been working with Chase Cohen. I just saw him walk by a few minutes ago. He's absolutely gorgeous, isn't he? All the women on this floor practically wilt every time he shows up."

Every time? The comment perked up her ears. Had she heard correctly?

Judi's smile blossomed. "I don't make a habit of handing out my phone number, especially when I'm not asked. However, in *his* case, I'd certainly make an exception."

Rachel snorted. "He'd probably make one, too."

"You think so?"

"No doubt in my mind. Can you tell me where I can find him?"

"Sure. Room 310. She held out her hand like a directional signpost. "Go down to the end of the hall, turn right, and then left. It's straight across from the elevator. I'm taking a patient to physical therapy in a few minutes, but if you'd like, I can show you—"

"No, please don't bother. I can find my way." She waited until the nurse turned and walked away before resuming her objective. What was Chase thinking…dropping everything to come here? And just who was this woman? What hold did *she* have over him?

Rachel strode down the long hallway fuming. Ultimately, she'd have her own share of explaining to do, but his trust-breaking actions surpassed hers. No matter how charming and persuasive Chase might be, she would never forgive him. Not this time.

Then she saw him coming off the elevator. Heading into room 310. By all appearances, he was unaware of her presence. She heaved a deep breath and mentally counted before charging through the open doorway.

"Chase, for crying out loud..."

Rachel's mouth instantly dropped. Directly across from her was a little girl, half buried under the white bed sheet. Her enormous blue eyes blinked repeatedly. Two ebony pigtails sprang from the sides of her head. A tube inserted into her tiny nose was taped to her left cheek, securing it firmly in place.

Rachel couldn't stop staring. *She's just a baby...can't be more than six years old.*

"Did my daddy make you mad?" she asked. Her words were barely audible above the sound of the beeping monitor.

Daddy? Rachel shook her head slowly. There had to be a mistake. She'd obviously entered the wrong room. "I...I'm sorry. I didn't mean to disturb you." She took a step back and immediately bumped into Chase coming out of the adjacent bathroom. He grasped his filled-to-the-brim Styrofoam cup with both hands, somehow managing not to spill a drop. He showed no sign of alarm or surprise at finding her there. In fact, he smiled.

"It's about time you two met," he said. "Allie...this is Miss Lyons. She's the friend I've been telling you about."

Oh, my God! Rachel rounded her shoulders. *A daughter? He has a daughter*?

Her heart skipped a beat. The air thickened. She considered high-tailing it out of the room—out of the hospital. But the sight of the little girl's glistening blue eyes and down-turned mouth cemented her heels to the floor.

"Honey?" Chase said to his daughter.

Her tiny, dry voice broke the silence. "Nice to meet you, Miss Lyons."

"Likewise," she answered, still in shock.

The pixie-faced girl watched her from beneath her lowered lids. "I had friends at school. But I don't go no more."

What could Rachel say? She glanced at the monitor next to the bed, at the crude cutout of a turkey and the drawings taped to the wall, and then back at the cherub's tiny face. A strange sensation washed over her. She wanted to reach out, gather this innocent creature in her arms, and assure her that she'd get well soon. But how could she? Until thirty seconds ago, she didn't even know Allie existed.

Unbelievable! Why hadn't he told her? What other secrets did he have? And what about Allie's mother…his *wife*?

Allie's moist eyes forced Rachel to bury her bubbling hostility. She smiled and tried her best to remain calm. "My goodness, what a lovely name you have," she ventured.

The little girl brightened. "My real name is Alegria. My mama named me after my Grandma Craven. They live in heaven with Papa Cristo."

Rachel glimpsed Chase at the foot of the bed, staring into his cup. Remorse, if he felt it, was hidden beneath his heavy lids. Whether due to concern or lack of sleep, dark circles had formed under his eyes, drawing presentiment and incidental sympathy from her.

"I'm sorry to hear that, sweetheart," she said. "But you're one lucky girl. You've got a daddy who loves you very much."

"I know," she chimed. "Nurse Marcia says that all the time." The corners of her tiny lips curled. "Do you have a daddy?"

"I did. But he's in heaven, too."

"Just like my mommy."

Rachel nodded. She battled with her emotions—her confusion and frustration. Her relief that Allie's mom was no longer in the picture. The whole situation was perplexing. But this wasn't the right time or place to vent. Not with Allie in the room.

"Do you have any brothers or sisters?" Rachel asked.

Chase snorted a laugh. "Not that I'm aware of." He turned the green upholstered chair and offered it to Rachel. She hesitated a moment and then quickly sat down. She set her duffel bag on the floor and nestled her hands in her lap. Then she glanced at her watch: it was 4:40 p.m. She'd stay for five minutes. No more.

"Isn't it nice that Miss Lyons came to visit?" Chase prompted.

"Uh huh," Allie said. "You're very pretty."

"Why, thank you."

Apparently, the child's cruel dilemma hadn't tarnished her sweet disposition.

"Don't you think so, Daddy?"

"Absolutely," he said, smiling.

Rachel could feel his eyes on her, adding heat to the room. As she focused on the box of crayons and *Pirates of the Caribbean* coloring book waiting on the bedside table, everything fell into place. Tucked under the sheets was the reason for Chase's sudden disappearance and his financial shortfalls. His obsession with finding treasure. Whatever his daughter's needs and condition might be, he'd obviously been dealing with exorbitant medical bills in addition to his salvage company's expenditures.

For the next fifteen minutes, she became the silent observer—watching Chase's coltish exchanges with his daughter. Listening to his wild, seafaring story and her cute, spontaneous giggles. She measured their matching blue eyes and realized there was something remarkable about their bond. The playful bantering she'd missed growing up with her own father. But she also noticed that something was blatantly absent from this sweet, heart-warming scene. There were no photos, no get-well cards or personal mementos. Only the bare necessities for a sick child. And where were the flowers and stuffed animals one would expect from the family for whom Chase had left Rachel?

"Hello, Allie." A distinguished-looking man in green medical scrubs stood in the open doorway. He crossed the room, arriving at his patient's bedside. A semicircular fringe of white hair surrounded his bald crown like a broken halo. A stethoscope hung from his thick neck. A very serious, middle-aged nurse followed him.

The physician turned to Rachel and smiled. "I'm Ted Bailey, but the kids on the floor call me Dr. Baldy. It's sure a beautiful day outside. Did you get an opportunity to visit our terrarium? It's really quite nice." Throughout their superficial conversation, he kept a watchful eye on his assistant as she checked the monitor and Allie's vital signs.

"Can Yuki come visit?" Allie asked him.

"Not right now, baby," Chase answered in his place. "They don't allow dogs. But I'll ask Ian to bring him by in the next few days. You'd be able to see Yuki and say hello right through the window over there."

Disappointment darkened her brow, and Chase was quick to respond. "You know what? I saw your friend, Shishi, in the hallway a few minutes ago. If memory serves me, he said something about an ice cream sundae cart coming this way. But he wasn't sure anyone in here would want one."

"Oh, yes, Daddy. Please, please..." Allie's shimmering eyes captured Rachel. "You want one too, don't you? There's strawberry and vanilla with orange...and chocolate fudge, too. That's my favorite."

"How bout I ask Shishi to keep you company while Rachel and I track down some of that yummy ice cream?"

Allie nodded enthusiastically.

"Be right back," he told the nurse.

Rachel rose and followed Chase out of the room. She gnawed on her bottom lip, feeling like a tabloid reader...needing to know the whole story.

"So who looks after Allie when you're working?" she asked, as they strode down the hall.

Chase answered with an easy smile. "They've got an amazing team of nurses here. Real sweethearts. And Naomi McKenzie stops by to check on Allie whenever she can."

Really? Rachel looked away, mentally shaking her head. Was she the only one in town who didn't know about Allie? Without knowing it, Rachel had crawled into a bubble and cut herself off from the world.

The thought was unsettling.

"And, of course, there's Uncle Ian. He calls her Gator and tells her all kinds of crazy stories...although I've had to censor him a few times."

Near the elevator, they met up with a doll-faced Asian boy. He was sitting cross-legged next to the wall, engrossed in a *Kung Fu Panda* comic book.

"Hi, Shishi," Chase said, bringing the young boy's head up. "I'd like you to meet my friend, Rachel."

His eyes and mouth bent into rainbows and exuded contagious happiness. He jumped to his feet, bowed, and then extended a small bronze hand.

"It's very nice to meet you," he said, his manners befitting a much older child.

"I believe you know his sister, Mika," Chase added. "The great chef that I hired..."

Rachel smiled at the young boy. "Mika's your sister? Oh, of course...silly me.," she said. "You look just like her...and are equally charming, I'm sure."

Chase leaned closer, commanding the boy's full attention. "Would you mind visiting Allie for a little while? She'd really enjoy your company."

Without another word, the tiny gentleman ran down the corridor and vanished into Allie's room.

Rachel and Chase continued to the cafeteria. While she stood by, he found a food server willing to deliver a chocolate sundae to Allie and two vanilla scoops to their table. As soon as they were both seated and the ice cream arrived, he launched into a lengthy explanation, obviously attempting to answer all of her questions.

"Allie's mother and I first met at an orphanage in Redlands, California. We became best friends and grew up sharing everything. Homework, secrets, hopes, and fears. After we graduated from high school, I had this crazy notion about traveling the world. I wanted to backpack, bicycle across America...see it all. But Helen wasn't interested. She wanted to put down roots, and raise horses and a houseful of kids. We tried to make it work and even got married. But after four years, we just couldn't see eye to eye anymore and ended up going our separate ways. Six years later, she was diagnosed with stage-four lymphoma."

Rachel's mouth sagged. "Wait a minute. You were *married*? Why didn't you say something? Why did you let me believe—"

"It wasn't a real marriage, Rachel...at least, not in the true sense of the word. I got a fishing job in Alaska and was gone four months out of the year. Helen had her own interests and friends. I'd call once in a while and send checks home to pay bills. But we were nothing more than roommates."

Beneath the table, Rachel's dangling foot rocked with nervous energy. "So when you came to San Palo, were you still with her?"

As he spoke, Chase smoothed his thumb over the silver bracelet on his wrist. "No, I'd filed for divorce two months earlier. She got scared when I told her it was over, and we ended up spending one night together. In the morning, we both realized that the feelings weren't there. We were friends—just kids—that never should have gotten married. The day I left Fort Lauderdale to come work for your dad, she signed the papers and sincerely wished me good luck. She wanted to get on with her life, just like I did."

"And the bracelet? She gave it to you, didn't she?"

Chase dropped his hand immediately. "It was a gift before she died…at the hospital. A reminder of the past we shared. I can take it off if it bothers you."

Rachel didn't know how to answer that. The connection he felt to his wife was apparent, but she was no longer part of his life. Or was she? "I just have one question," Rachel said. "All this time…why did you keep this a secret? Was it because you still loved her? Maybe even still do?"

"I'm not going to lie to you. I cared about her, but I didn't know what real love was until I met you. I didn't want you to think less of me because of a mistake I made when I was young. Because that's what it was. A mistake."

Rachel closed her eyes and breathed for a moment.

"Honey, I just want you to know," he said, "I had a valid reason for disappearing after Sam's death. You see, I didn't have a clue about Allie or why Helen chose not to tell me about her for six years. I didn't even know she was dying until your brother intercepted an urgent call from the hospital in Denver and relayed the message to me."

Rachel snorted a sarcastic laugh. "Devon. Well, that explains a lot. But the fact remains, you left to be with her and said nothing to me about it....not until you had no choice but to come clean." Indignation brought her to her feet.

Chase immediately reached for her hand. "Please...just listen." He stood and touched her on the shoulder, urging her to sit down.

She resumed her seat and stared down at her melting ice cream. She felt angry, hurt, bewildered. Betrayed. "No wonder Devon had me believing you were a heartless bastard. Turns out you were."

Chase cracked a smile to shield his embarrassment and nodded at a couple seated nearby. His gaze returned and he asked, "Are you sure you want to hear the rest of this?"

"Why stop now?"

He leaned in on his elbows and looked her square in the face. "The first time your father invited me to dinner and you walked in the door, my heart jumped out of my chest. We spent that night talking for hours and I knew I'd met the girl of my dreams. The two years we spent together were the *best* of my life, Rachel. And when I got that call and left you after your father died, I honestly thought I was doing the right thing...for everyone."

Rachel shifted in her seat. She glanced at the neighboring table, wondering if the elderly couple was hearing to this, too.

"For the past four years, instead of holding you, I was holding out. I should've come back. I should've let you into my life, but instead all I did was let you down. I'm asking now...no, I'm begging...give me a second chance, Rachel."

She peered into his crystal-blue eyes, searching for a reason to believe—a reason to have faith in the man she once loved. "You're the first person that broke my heart," she told him. "For the rest of my life, you'll always be the one who hurt me most. Don't ever forget that."

Chase wagged his head. "Never." He took her hand and kissed it, and somehow the hurt began to fade. Yet it would take time for trust to grow.

Rachel stirred her ice cream and placed a spoonful of the creamy mixture on her tongue. Staring down at the bracelet on his arm, she thought of a woman dying in her bed with a sick child to care for and decided it was time to be the bigger person—to find the compassion buried in her soul.

"So, tell me about your daughter," she said. "What do the doctors think?"

"Allie needs a bone marrow transplant and has a severely weakened immune system. Dr. Bailey mentioned the possibility of putting her in an experimental antibody program. As it turns out, she's the perfect candidate. Being so ill and young, her lungs, liver, and stomach would be severely damaged by intense chemotherapy."

Rachel remained silent, trying to absorb his words and the severity of his poor daughter's condition. She realized that fate had brought Chase and Allie into her life. If she could set aside her doubts and fears, and forgive the past, there would be more than enough room in her heart for both of them.

As they made their way back to room 310, Rachel noticed an ominous-looking man standing at the far end of the corridor. He was watching them with pointed interest. She wasn't sure if she would've recognized him if she'd met somewhere else. But whom was she fooling? She'd recognize Pollero's bodyguard anywhere.

"Miss Lyons," Bo called out.

Click. Click. Click. With each approaching step, she could feel a new surge of adrenaline in her veins. Her anxieties multiplied.

She glanced at Chase and realized his eyes had already found the source of her concern.

"Who is he?" Chase asked, vexation tilting his brows.

Bo halted a few feet away. "I need to talk to your brother. Do you know where he is?"

She narrowed her eyes, annoyed by his bold manner. "From what I've heard, your business is through. I think you need to leave us alone."

Confusion resonated in Chase's face. "Rachel, what's going on?"

Before she could answer, Bo pulled out a leather wallet and flashed his ID.

"The name's Bo Novak. I'm a DEA agent. Miss Lyons and I met while I was working on an undercover investigation."

DEA? Rachel stared at Bo in disbelief. "You're a narcotics officer?"

"That's right."

"Since when?"

"Miss Lyons, I'm sorry, but I need your cooperation. Especially with one of your brother's captors now on the loose."

Chase's hand tightened on her forearm. "*Captors*? Is that what you were trying to tell me? Devon was kidnapped?"

Novak had turned into a fountain of knowledge, spouting more than Rachel wanted revealed. "His name's Marcos Olivares. He's wanted on suspicion of murder, drug smuggling, theft, assault, and the list goes on. According to your crew member, Blaine McKenzie, he was on your ship this afternoon and made off with a small fortune. My mission is to—"

"Holly shit! You're saying I was *robbed*? Why didn't anyone tell me?"

Rachel cut in. "Listen to me, Chase. This man isn't at all who he claims to be."

Bo snorted. "Then who am I, Miss Lyons?"

She folded her arms over her chest. "You're the creep who stood by while my brother's partner was beaten to death. The same lowlife who did nothing while a mobster threatened my life. What kind of a cop does that, Mr. Novak? If that's who you really are."

"I know this is hard for you to understand, but I didn't witness Logan Tulles's murder. Your brother did. I assure you that if I'd known what was going to happen, I would've taken measures to prevent it."

She shook her head, still unconvinced.

"I was under orders to bring down a drug lord by whatever means necessary. If your brother's willing to testify about the shooting and murder that took place, then I just might be able to bring down the *real* criminal behind the Polleros."

"You don't say. Well, you know what? Far as I'm concerned, you're the one who needs to go to jail."

Chase cast an admonishing look at her while Novak pulled out a card.

"Here's my number, Mr. Cohen. When your girlfriend wakes up and realizes the danger she and her brother are in, give me a call." He walked across the hallway and bent down over the water fountain. He remained there, cooling his thirst for what seemed like an eternity.

Chase turned to her. "I don't understand any of this. Why didn't you tell me? Why didn't you ask for my help?"

"I know it sounds bad, but you don't know the whole story." She glanced in Novak's direction. "There were really bad people involved. Guns, knives, death threats. I didn't know who I could trust. I wanted to tell you, but there just wasn't the right—"

"Time? Or maybe you didn't care enough to confide in me."

Even with hurt showing in his eyes, her indignation won out.

"Wait a minute…how did I become the bad guy here?" she spouted. "You know, on second thought, this matter doesn't have to involve you at all. You've got your daughter to think about. Just let me grab my bag, and I'll be on my way."

Bo straightened. He wiped his mouth with the back of his hand. He stepped into the closest elevator, still watching her as the doors closed. Assuring her with a downturned look that he wouldn't be far away.

Chase touched Rachel's cheek, bringing her troubled thoughts back to him. "Listen to me. I love you…unconditionally. How could I *not* be involved? But, honey, you've got to tell me everything and you need to start by explaining what happened on the ship."

Rachel closed her eyes, realizing she had no right to be angry with him for keeping secrets when she had so many, herself.

"Excuse me," the nurse said from Allie's doorway. "I'm sorry to interrupt you, Mr. Cohen, but Dr. Bailey would like to speak to you right away."

Chase nodded. He reached for Rachel's hand and gazed down at her. "Don't go anywhere. If you care about anyone… including yourself, you'll be here waiting when I come out."

After the door closed behind him, Rachel stood in the hallway, measuring the distance to the closest elevator, dreading the thorough interrogation that was sure to come.

30

Devon's upper body was out spread across the table. His forehead rested lifelessly on his layered arms. After three beers and four shots of tequila, he was blissfully numb and intended to stay that way for as long as possible.

"Wake up!" Naomi snapped.

She hovered like a dog looking at a patch of grass. Even in the bar's dark corner, with one eye cracked, he could see the phone in her hand. He pushed himself upright in his seat and belched. His eyes mindlessly traveled over Naomi's voluminous breasts, eventually landing on her delicious, downturned lips.

"Want me to call you a cab?" she asked.

He pinned on a smile. "Been called worse."

"Cute."

"Yep, that's me."

"Old joke."

"Getting older by the minute. Just bring me a cup of coffee, OK?"

She huffed. "Straighten up, Lyons. You're not going anywhere until you sober up." She sashayed behind the bar looking more perturbed than usual. She turned on the faucet full force, and in a matter of seconds the glass coffee pot was full. She dropped it on a burner.

Devon looked to his right. There were half a dozen patrons in the room, all well lubricated despite the fact that it was barely 6:00 p.m. A stubbly hustler walked in, trying to sell concert tickets, but a noisy, vulgar blonde shouted him down. At the end of the bar, an acne-scarred kid hugged a beer bottle, scoping his hopeless options. Devon ventured a look in the opposite direction. Two men were huddled in the opposite corner, throwing back shots, unaware that their voices could be heard over the high-pitched theatrics in the room.

My kind of place. Devon was barely twenty-one when his old man offered to buy him a drink in this seedy establishment. Somehow, Sam had managed to keep his anger hidden after discovering that his son was planning to drop out of college and sacrifice his hard-earned scholarship.

"Get your life together or you'll end up like the rest of these bums," Sam had warned.

Sam's disappointment in him and the drunks staggering out of the place had made a memorable impression. Two months later, Devon was back at school and eventually graduated with honors. Yet here he was, eight years later, a loser. Just like the rest of them.

He leaned on his elbows and stared into the corner, subconsciously seeking the shadows.

A vociferous character on his left suddenly stood up, knocking his chair over.

"I didn't sign on for this," he yelled. There was something oddly familiar about the respectable-looking guy with the specs. But Devon couldn't place him. His companion, on the other hand, was easily recognized. *Skylar Zane.* Devon had spotted him days earlier in the warehouse with Gabe Pollero. But it wasn't the first time he had seen him. The smooth-talking character with the buzz-cut red hair had been making his rounds in town. Selena had called Devon's office on the first of the month, only a few days after he first showed up. She had bragged about the guy's net worth, claiming he had a lucrative salvage company with multiple government contracts and was extremely interested in buying stock in Mesoblast Limited, a biotech highflier, and Brambles Limited. Following their introduction, Devon sat back and listened, and was impressed by Zane's confidence and knowledge of the market. However, as it turned out, the fast-talking con artist had no interest in investing. Not even a dime. He never returned any of Devon's calls, but he had a private meeting with Walter Moten two days before his boss turned up missing. Or, more accurately, was killed.

Zane had obviously been scheming on the Polleros' behalf for quite a while. The crazy thing about it was that apparently nobody knew to what extent. Not even Selena.

"Sit down," Zane snapped.

Devon continued to watch the two men from the corner of his eye, amazed at how his ears could pick out their voices from the room's constant drone, and by the fact that these two idiots had picked such a public place to meet.

Zane's companion dragged his chair upright. He dropped back into his seat. "We had a deal. I pass on information, you cut me in. Nothing was said about drowning anyone."

"I told you to fix a tank...same as you did when you were working in the dive shop. No one's going to suspect nitrogen narcosis or your part in this. Just like they didn't four years ago."

"Yeah, but I did that gradually. After a month, the guy was walking around half stoned. It's not going to be so easy this time. We're dealing with the same ship, same coordinates, and same helmsman. You don't think the police are going to come asking?"

Wham! Another woman blew in through the door, turning the heads of the devious conspirators. She took a seat directly behind Devon and smiled. He ducked down and pulled up his collar. When the men resumed their conversation, he breathed a long sigh of relief.

"Like you said," Zane continued. "There's loose rocks, hazards, dozens of drownings. Who's going to freak over one careless diver? Especially Chase Cohen? Everyone knows he takes stupid risks."

The mystery guy shook his head. "I can't do it. Not this time." He glanced nervously around the room.

"Goddamn it, Jeremy," Zane huffed. "Just tell me what I need to know. I'll take care of him myself. But your share's getting cut in half."

"If you weren't my brother, I wouldn't be doing this at all."

"And if Lyons had admitted that we were his sons, he wouldn't be dead."

Sons? *Dead*? Devon's mouth sagged. He felt the air go out of his lungs. Zane had to be lying. It just wasn't possible. They couldn't be talking about his father. He leaned closer, trying not to miss a word.

"Cohen's still at the hospital looking after his sick kid," Jeremy continued. "With it getting dark soon, he'll be staying in San Palo for the night. Hawkins came in with Rachel, so there's only Ian and Blaine to contend with. Ian has the first watch. Blaine takes over at midnight. He always falls asleep after a few hours. You'll find the storage locker where Cohen keeps his gear below the aft deck. It's easy to find and well-marked. You shouldn't have any problem switching his tanks. Like I told you, all the gold's being stored in the *Stargazer's* hull under the midship hatch. But you'll need the key, which Cohen wears around his neck, and at least three guys to transfer the gold to the *Legend*. Also, Cohen dives every day at 10:00 a.m. sharp, but you'll still have to deal with the Indian, that damn Irishman, and the computer nerd. So, what are you planning to do with them?"

"Slit their throats. Toss them over the side. Cohen said there's pirates in these waters, right?"

"Yeah." He looked down.

"With all their records destroyed and Cohen finally gone, the *Wanli* and whatever's left of his claim will be up for grabs. I'll simply be at the right place at the right time." Zane leaned back and took another drink from his glass. "Even though Pollero's bumbling hoods fucked up and didn't kill Rachel like they were supposed to, after her close call and stealing anything she could get her hands on to save our dear brother, she'll be keeping a low profile."

Devon clenched his jaw. Rachel was back in town, safe and sound—that's what Novak had claimed. *Shit*! Right now, she was probably thinking he was a self-absorbed asshole.

Zane smiled. "When the time's right, collect from her, too."

No! Devon's pulse quickened. In the worst way possible, he wanted to jump out of his seat, slam his fist into Zane's contemptuous face, and beat the shit out of his gutless brother. But where would that leave him? How could he prove they were murderers? They were plotting against his sister, Cohen, and his men. As he weighed his objections, Zane's chair suddenly scraped the floor. His brother stood and left a few bills on the table. Then they filed by, one after the other, exiting through the barroom's heavy wooden door.

Devon waited a few seconds before crossing the room. He found Naomi mixing drinks behind the bar. "I need to make a call right away," he insisted.

"Don't know," she teased. "Depends on who you're calling."

The kid seated at the bar flashed his pathetic, lopsided grin, leaving Devon wondering what he found so humorous.

"How about my sister and the police?"

Naomi faced him, concern etching her brow. She set the bottle down and reached for the house phone. "Anything I can help you with?"

"A cup of coffee. Fast!"

"No problem, doll. Let me get that for you."

Devon punched 9-1-1 on the keypad and stood beside her, waiting for the dispatcher to answer.

Bam! The front door slammed. Jeremy was back, standing ten feet away. Devon turned away quickly and waited.

"Forgot my coat," he told Naomi.

Devon could feel Jeremy's cold, dark eyes on the back of his neck, on the phone resting against his ear. Time stood still until the door slammed again. Until he ventured a look over his shoulder. The blue jacket on the wall hook was gone, and so was Jeremy, but Devon had every reason to believe he'd been seen.

31

Rachel shifted her position on the seat in the hospital hallway for the umpteenth time. Twenty minutes had passed, feeling like forever, and she was struggling to stay awake. More than anything, she wanted to go home, crawl into her bed, and forget the last two weeks had ever happened. It wasn't bad enough spending every waking hour worrying about her brother. Now she'd become the self-imposed guardian of the cobra in her bag.

The door to room 310 finally opened, amplifying Dr. Bailey's voice. "Look forward to hearing more about your great adventure." He passed his assistant, bringing Rachel to her feet. "That's quite a man you've got there," he said.

"Thank you, but actually, we just work together."

"Oh, I see. Somehow I got a different impression."

A quick diversion. "So, is she doing better...Allie, I mean?"

"Like I was explaining to Chase, it's all about faith. Today, I operated on an eight-year-old girl who was in a car accident. She desperately needed type O negative blood, which is a bit rare. We didn't have any available, but her twin brother had the right type.

I explained to him that it was a matter of life and death—that his sister desperately needed his blood. He sat quietly for a moment before saying good-bye to his parents. I didn't think anything of it until after we took the blood we needed, and he asked, 'So when will I die?' You see, he thought he was giving his life for hers. Thankfully, they'll both be fine."

Rachel met his gaze and smiled. She wasn't clear about the message he was sharing, but the story was cute.

He waved a hand in the air as he strolled down the long corridor with his nurse trailing behind. A slow-moving, aging orderly soon fell in behind them. Rachel remained still, watching the odd procession. When they were finally out of sight, she pushed open the door that Bailey had left ajar and stepped into Allie's room. Chase was hunched over in the green chair, watching his daughter sleep. Her tiny hand held two of his fingers, as if clinging to the life source within him.

Sweet. Rachel swallowed hard and drew closer. "Hi," she whispered. "Is everything all right?"

He angled a doleful look. "She's amazing. Never complains. Not even when they poke her with needles."

She looked down at his daughter, who was breathing silently. Her long, dark eyelashes rested on her round, chubby cheeks. Her uneven bangs naively covered one brow. In many ways, she represented a younger, unsullied version of Chase.

"I can handle her hospital bills and occasional disappointments," he said, "but I have no control over Allie becoming a test patient."

"There isn't a way to add her name to the list?"

"Not unless someone falls off of it."

Or the hospital received the right incentive. Her gaze dropped to her bag. "Wish there was something I could do."

"Believe me...you being here is enough."

But in reality, it wasn't. Not when she had a chance to make a *real* difference. She glanced up at the ceiling, suddenly conscience-stricken.

"What is it?" he demanded.

"I need to tell you something."

He stood slowly, allowing Allie's fingers to slip away. "Outside," he breathed, motioning with his head.

Rachel collected her bag and headed toward the hallway.

As soon as the door was closed, Chase turned to her and asked, "What's wrong?"

She deliberated on how to apologize. On how to explain her dilemma. "About the gold Marcos took…" she began.

"How much do you think he made off with?"

"According to Blaine, a quarter million."

"Wow. That much?" He quirked a smile. "Have to admit, you were a better thief than I thought."

She stared at him, perplexed, until his words sank in. "You *knew*?"

"Not for sure. Suspected a few of the guys when the counts came up short. Then I realized that aside from myself, you were the only one with complete access. Knowing how you feel about honesty, I knew you had to have a good reason."

"That's it? No questions asked? You're not pissed off or anything?"

Chase shook his head. A smile softened his face, making him look more charming than ever.

"But what you said in front of Novak…"

"That was purely for his benefit, not yours, sweetheart. There's no reason for him to know we're working together."

"We *are*?"

He took her face in his hands, framing it so that he could look into her eyes. "I'm not about to risk losing you…not again."

They shared a deep drowning gaze and a kiss that turned her knees to rubber. When they separated, the secret was searing her brain.

"There's something else," she said.

"Oh, yeah…your brother. You should probably check on him." He pulled out his phone and handed it to her.

Rachel called her service and ran through her list of thirty-plus messages. There was still no word from Devon.

"No luck?" Chase asked.

She shook her head.

"How about the Crow's Nest? I know it's a last resort, but he might have gone there."

Rachel doubted the idea, but after a brief exchange with Naomi on the phone, she was quick to admit her mistake. "Turns out you were right. Naomi said Devon was there for a couple hours. He stuck around long enough to make a few calls. Then he took off in a hurry. There's no telling where he might be."

"Your brother sure isn't making this easy."

"No, he isn't." The stress of the past few hours came crashing down on her. She ran a hand through her hair and heaved a weary sigh. Chase smoothed his thumb against the tired lines under her eyes. He wrapped his arm around her shoulders and squeezed tightly.

"Let's get out of here. We'll have better luck finding Devon in the morning." He reached down and picked up her duffel bag, adding speed to her racing heart. He led the way to the lobby and was instructing her to wait, while he retrieved his truck, when a voice called out.

"Rachel!" Wade was standing next to Judi, looking particularly annoyed. "I've been all over this hospital looking for you. If you didn't turn up soon, I was going to call security."

Chase laughed. "When did you become her bodyguard?"

"Since she nearly died." Wade's direful words hung in the air.

"Go on," Chase coaxed.

Wade leaned in closer. "Tried my best to keep an eye on her, like you asked. But after the pirates stole onto our ship, she went over the side with the worst one of them. Ended up witnessing a shark attack and almost getting killed herself before we pulled her out."

"Wow!" Judi said. "It's amazing you survived."

Rachel's close call hadn't seemed real to her—not at the time. She glanced away as the image of Viktor's body being torn apart replayed in her mind. Although she preferred to keep that experience buried for the rest of her life, the gruesome scene would be ingrained forever in her memory.

"They were after Mai Le's treasure," Wade continued. "Haven't got a clue how they found out about it, but they were sure we had it on board."

Chase's anger was visible. "I want you back aboard as soon as possible. Here's the key for the Zodiac. Use the spotlight if you need it. Just make sure you get there in one piece. I'll try calling AJ again. If he doesn't show up at the dock in fifteen minutes, head back anyway. I'll rent a skiff and bring him back with me first thing in the morning."

"What about Rachel?" Wade asked, as though she weren't there. "The guy who got away knows she can identify him."

"I'll look after her."

The scowl on Wade's face told her that he wasn't pleased with this arrangement. "Personally, I think you should call the police. Rachel should have some kind of protection. Someone with her at all times."

Chase's eyes narrowed; his lips thinned. "She's got me."

32

Rachel hesitated before climbing into the cab of Chase's truck. She watched him slam the heavy door and round the grill before seating himself beside her. As they drove across town, she answered his questions, telling him as much as she could remember about her harrowing experiences and brief encounter with Gabe Pollero.

"Just wish I'd known," he said before becoming uncomfortably quiet.

After ten minutes, they turned into Hillcrest, an older residential neighborhood of 1940s bungalows and condos. They veered left and passed a corner drug store before turning right on Cobbler Way. The street was buzzing with activity. Rachel stared through the passenger window at Chase's neighbors, who were collecting mail, turning on lights, walking dogs on the winding sidewalk. Nothing seemed odd or out of the ordinary. But retelling her story had set off a mental warning. She couldn't dismiss the nagging feeling that Marcos was close by, watching their every move.

As they slowed down, nearing his driveway, a sports car pulled out of a narrow alleyway between two buildings and passed them, going the opposite direction. The tinted windows made it impossible to see the driver, but there was no doubt in Rachel's mind…it was a candy-apple-red Lamborghini. Just like the one in the photograph in Pollero's office in the warehouse.

"Did you see that car?" she asked.

"Where?"

"The red one that just went by."

Chase glanced in his rearview mirror, catching its taillights before it sped away. "Nice."

"Gabe Pollero had a car like that."

He shrugged nonchalantly. "He's gone. Isn't that what you said?"

"I know…but how do you explain—"

"This is California, sweetheart. Exotic cars are all over the place. Just because one looks like his, doesn't mean it is."

Although her first instinct was to climb out of the truck and storm away, she closed her eyes and drew a deep breath. Chase's condescending tone obviously was due to his lack of sleep. She deserved a degree of impatience from him, even though it was testing her own patience. She slammed the truck door and trudged after him through the maze of inside hallways leading to his apartment. She waited behind him while he unlocked his front door.

"Maid's day off," he said. "No complaints, OK?" He stepped aside, opening himself up to silent ridicule. "There's a couch in the living room, if you want to lie down. Just need to make a few calls, and then I'll fix us something to eat. You want anything to drink?"

Rachel shook her head. She watched him disappear in the kitchen. To her left, in the makeshift dining room, she couldn't help noticing crayon drawings taped to the wall above the folding card table. There were sailboats, sparkling treasure chests, and pirates wielding swords. Assorted artistic renderings in a spectrum of colors.

"Nice pictures," she called out.

"Allie's. Claims she's going to be a sea captain like her old man one day."

"With no influence from you."

"Course not."

When she heard Chase's muffled voice on the phone in the kitchen, she stepped down into his sunken living room and took advantage of the opportunity to inspect his simple abode. Her gaze brushed the textured, cream walls and traveled to the brass chandelier in the center of the room. It hung slightly off kilter and just begged to be straightened. She crossed the oak-veneer floor, reached up, and tugged on the chain, attempting to right the fixture. But it swung right back into place, more catawampus than before.

She rolled her eyes and shifted her attention to Chase's odd assortment of knickknacks and worn furnishings. She'd never seen such an eclectic ensemble: painted decoy ducks; fishing reels; two mismatched winged-back chairs; and an oversized, flat-slatted trunk for a makeshift coffee table. A bent-willow rocker with a blue-plaid throw sat in front of the slate fireplace. Hobo Americana at its best. Although his acquisitions resembled bargain-basement items, there was something remarkably charming about their multiversity.

She kicked aside a well-chewed tennis ball and remembered Yuki—the white, furry mop she'd met during her visit with Naomi. She waited until Chase's voice grew quiet and then asked, "So, is Ian taking care of your dog?"

Chase turned off the faucet in the kitchen. "We sorta share him," he called back. "I found him wandering around the docks with no collar, all skin and bones. Gave him some scraps. Next thing I knew, he was living here part time."

Rachel continued her dual mission—milling about, prying into his life. She relocated a denim shirt and sat down in the middle of the lumpy, brown couch. A nautical map was anchored to the top of the trunk with a SPC coffee mug, books, and a glass starfish paperweight.

"Are you charting the course to another ship?" she asked.

She leaned forward to study the chart when Chase suddenly appeared. He was shirtless. A blue dish towel was draped over one shoulder. Her gaze slid down his ripped abs to the top of his low-slung jeans. She could feel his eyes on her, adding heat to the room. Instead of meeting his stare, she looked back at the map.

"Here, let me get rid of that." He confiscated the ocean blueprint and stowed it on top of a walnut wardrobe chest resting against the wall. He collected a crushed Domino's pizza box from the floor and snagged his discarded shirt from the back of the sofa. After briefly disappearing down the short hallway, he resumed housekeeping chores—gathering newspapers, collecting empty beer bottles, and returning books to the bookcase. The chime from the microwave timer pulled him back into the kitchen. He quickly returned with two steaming bowls of clam chowder and a bottle of beer tucked under his arm.

Rachel took the bowls and set them on the table before her. She slid over to the next cushion, allowing him room on the sofa. But he stayed on his feet. He took a swig from his bottle and stepped over to the window. Above the neighboring rooftops, the night sky was fiery red and brilliant orange, reflecting on the simmering ocean.

"*Stargazer's* safe for the time being," he assured her. "But with all that gold in her hull, I regret not bringing her home." He turned back and caught her idly stirring her soup. A look of concern furrowed his brow.

"Guess my cooking's not that great, huh?" he asked. "Campbell's soup, TV dinners, and peanut butter sandwiches. That's the extent of my culinary skills."

"It's fine, really." She took a mouthful and hummed her approval.

"A guy on the second floor gave me a cookbook after smelling the macaroni and cheese I burned. Haven't cracked the cover yet. Just don't see the need when I'm cooking for one…at least until Allie comes home." Chase ran his hand over his jaw. "You sure I can't get you something to drink? I've got a bottle of white wine open, if you'd like."

She looked up from her bowl. "Maybe a small glass…as long as it doesn't come with scotch."

"Right." The reference brought a smile. He returned from the kitchen with a half-filled wineglass. "The woman next door gave it to me for letting her borrow my truck. Said something about having a lot of points…whatever that means."

Rachel took a generous sip and smiled. "That was nice of her."

"No threat, I assure you. Virginia's eighty-two. She's had four husbands and I don't think she's looking for number five. At least not in this neighborhood." He walked to the corner of the room smiling and then bent down and turned on the pilot light in the gas fireplace. With the strike of a match, the fireplace erupted in amber flames. "There's a blanket on the chair if you get cold."

His nervousness was perplexing. Totally uncharacteristic of the man she knew. But then, she'd never been in his new apartment, and social skills had never been his strong suit.

"Stop worrying about me," she said. "I'm all right, honest. Come sit down and finish this nice soup before it gets cold."

His mind seemed to be elsewhere. He dropped into the winged-back chair across from her and hung one leg over its arm. He took another pull on his beer and continued to watch her eat until her bowl was nearly empty.

"So what do you think of my place?" he asked.

Rachel shrugged. "Looks good to me, although you might rethink the Budweiser sign with Allie living here."

Chase glanced over his shoulder at the wall. "Yeah, I know. Ian gave that to me. He's a generous guy and all, but he's got no sense when it comes to handing out gifts. He actually gave Allie a makeup kit for Christmas. She'll be thirty before she cracks that open."

Seemed he had faith that Allie would beat her illness after all. "Hate to disappoint you," Rachel said. "Kids grow up fast nowadays. She'll be using it by the time she's ten."

He smirked. "Not if I have my way. How's that glass of wine, by the way?"

There was something odd about the way she was feeling. She wasn't sure if she was experiencing symptoms of the bends or if the wine she'd consumed was having an overt effect. Whatever it was, focusing on Chase's face had become a chore. Her tongue was thick and dry. The light in the room was dimming, and her lids were fighting gravity. She laid her head down on the arm of the sofa and drew her legs up beneath her. She stared at the crooked chandelier on the ceiling, which now seemed to be hanging straight.

"Sorry," she mumbled, her voice echoing in her own ears. "Must be tired."

Chase leaned down and scooped her up into his arms. He carried her to his bedroom at the end of the hallway. She felt the bed give way as he laid her down. He covered her with a furry blanket and stepped back.

"Chase..." she murmured. "Where are you going?"

"I'll be right outside. Close your eyes, sweetheart. You've had a full day. You really need some rest."

She obeyed his orders and snuggled into his pillow. His lingering scent warmed her heart. In the next room, she heard the sound of the front door opening, muted footsteps entering. A man's muffled voice. *What are they saying? Who's he talking to?*

Chase's voice was distant...disconnected. "Gave her something to sleep."

For a brief moment, she thought she saw a shadow in the bedroom doorway, but then it was gone. The world was slowly fading away...turning into oblique darkness. She was floating soundlessly in the sky, drifting toward the heavens and the galaxy beyond.

The smell of fresh coffee invaded Rachel's senses and rekindled her memory of the previous night. With everything that had gone on, there hadn't been time to share her good news—to reveal the discovery she'd been carrying in her bag. In the light of day, she realized that after everything that they'd been through and Chase's open profession of love, she needed to end her deception, forgo her excuses. Learn to trust him again.

"Chase..." she called out. No answer. She climbed out of bed and wandered down the hallway, imagining him half-nude with a mug in his hand, leaning against the sink with his ankles crossed. The thought made her smile. "What...no coffee for me?" she said, as she entered the kitchen.

Devon was seated at the table, scanning the *Gazette.* "Help yourself," he said in a cavalier tone.

"Jeez! You scared me! When did you...*how* did you get here?" She stared at him in stunned disbelief.

He set the paper down. "No welcome home? Thought you'd be glad to see me, at least."

"Are you crazy? Of course, I am! Do you have any idea how frightened I was for you?"

He shrugged a shoulder. "Yeah...I do. But I also learned something the hard way."

"What's that?"

"There's only one person I can depend on."

"Who? Yourself?"

The look in his eyes was that of a man crestfallen by the torment he'd endured. By a hard-earned life lesson that had taken a toll. He held his arms out and offered a sweet, crooked smile. "No. You, silly."

She went willingly—wrapping her arms around his neck, resting her cheek against his broad chest. Relief washed over her in waves. "I was so afraid of losing you," she said, her voice cracking. "Of finding out you were dead."

"I know, honey. I'm sorry."

After a while, she calmed down, and Devon held her at arms' length, his strong hands gripping her elbows. "Hey, we're Sam's kids, right?" he said. "Can't get rid of us that easily."

"Right," she conceded. "But you still haven't answered my questions."

He motioned for her to take a seat across from him. She plopped down in the chair, and he began, speaking slowly. "I showed up last night while you were sleeping. Naomi gave me these shitty directions and, believe it or not, my car died in the parking lot. I ended up using Selena's car and parked it down the street…knocking on doors until someone was finally willing to help me." A flash of anguish crossed his hazel eyes.

She lowered her head. "I'm sorry about Selena. I know she meant a lot to you."

"Yeah, well…turns out you were right after all."

"I honestly didn't want to be."

"I know that now."

"Devon, I wish we could move on…just forget what happened to both of us. But something tells me this thing's not over yet." She looked out the kitchen window at the rustling yellow leaves on the trees. White clouds raced against light blue. "Novak's looking for you," she said, "and Marcos is out there somewhere. He knows I'm responsible for Viktor's death…that we've been bringing up gold. I'm convinced he's not working alone, but I have no idea who's involved."

"I do. Did some nosing around. Turns out AJ Hobbs is really Jeremy Zane."

How is it possible? Rachel stared at him, not truly believing her ears.

"He's an academic who flunked out of Harvard and worked at the dive shop for three years. Anyway, this guy and his brother, Skylar, somehow got it in their heads that our dad was their father. He wouldn't accept them and…" Devon paused, acknowledging her wide eyes. "Long story short, they're responsible for killing him."

Her breath caught. "*Dad*? Are you sure?"

Devon nodded. "No doubt about it. I heard everything… including their confessions. I'm telling you, these guys are worse than Pollero and his gang. In fact, I have every reason to believe they were behind the scenes, directing everything…if you can believe that."

"Where's Chase? Does he know about this?"

"After I told him what they had in mind for him and the rest of his crew, he made a few calls and flew out of here around 6:00 a.m. He's probably back on board *Stargazer* by now."

"Jeez, Devon. Shouldn't we involve the police? I mean Novak—is he someone you can trust?"

"Already called him. He should be here any minute. I promised to give him a statement. I'm sure he'll want yours, too."

Rachel glanced at the floor. "I don't know what I'm supposed to say. I was pretty rude to him the last time I saw him."

"He'll get over it. Just relax and be a sister instead of a mother, OK?"

She smacked him playfully on the arm just as a knock sounded on the door. She remembered the secured entrance at the front of the building and the kind neighbors Chase had mentioned.

"Someone must have let him in," she said. This was one instance when a peephole would have come in handy. She leaned close to the door and asked, "Who is it?"

Wham! The doorframe shattered from the impact of Marcos's body. Rachel fell backward and banged her head against the floor. When she lifted her eyes, his snarling face was pointed at her along with the barrel of a .44 Magnum revolver.

33

Rachel rifled through her duffel bag, tossing clothes to the floor. "I don't understand. I'm telling you it was in here."

Marcos rested the gun against Devon's forehead. "We're not doing this again," he growled. "Give me the fuckin' treasure or you're both dead."

"I know you don't believe me," she said, "but you can see for yourself." She shoved the empty bag toward him.

"You got ten seconds…then I'm pulling the trigger." He cocked the gun and began counting. "One…two…three…"

"Stop!" Rachel yelled.

"Four…five…"

"Listen to me!"

"Six…seven…"

"Chase has it," Devon said, halting his progress.

Marcos was silent for only a moment. "How do you know this?" he asked.

"He's a treasure hunter, isn't he? If the cobra is as valuable as Rachel believes it is, he probably took it and ran off. He's skipped town before."

Rachel shook her head, rejecting Devon's assumption. "You're wrong. Chase wouldn't do that. Not to me."

"Really? Then how else do you explain it?" he said. "You had pills in your bag. He gave you something to sleep. And now the box is missing."

"How could you say that?" she asked. "He went back to rescue his men. He didn't even know I had it."

"How can you be so sure?"

Marcos lowered his weapon slowly, watching their debate.

"I don't know," Rachel whimpered. She pushed her hair back with her fingers and exhaled loudly. As doubt crept in, a solitary tear trickled down her cheek. With Chase missing, there was no one to stop it. No one to assure her that she hadn't been duped.

"Think about it," Devon demanded. "When was the last time you saw it?"

She gnawed on her bottom lip, blocking the emotional turmoil in her brain. She looked up at the ceiling, trying her best to recall everything that had happened the previous day. "On the ship…in my cabin. Blaine saw the cobra. He put the box that held it into my bag. But I didn't open it again…not until now. It's possible he might still have it."

Devon motioned to the side with his head, warning her that he was going to make a grab for the lowered gun. She attempted to hide her look of discovery. But her trailing gaze and telltale expression must have registered on her face. Marcos snapped the gun back into place. His finger was on the trigger. He resumed his countdown, more determined than ever to kill both of them.

"Eight…nine…"

"Chase has millions of dollars in gold coins," she said quickly. "Just like the ones you already have."

Marcos stared into her face, gauging the validity of her story. "Where?"

"In the ship's hull…where it's been all along. Now put the gun down and let my brother go."

He stalled briefly. Then he shoved Devon aside and grabbed Rachel's arm, spinning her around. "There's one way to find out," he told Devon. "Give me the keys."

Devon fished in his back pocket and produced a set. The villain snatched them away. His nostrils flared, as though he were a bull preparing to charge. "I *knew* it was you in Selena's car," he hissed.

Before Devon had a chance to react, Marcos delivered a blow to the side of Devon's head with his gun, knocking him down to one knee. The .44's barrel met Devon's fiery glare. If Rachel didn't act quickly, her brother would be joining Selena, Gabe, Logan, and who knew how many others.

"Listen," she said. "If you fire your weapon, the neighbors will hear it. You won't make it out of here without being seen."

"So tell me, señorita. What would you have me do with this… *cabronazo*? This worthless piece of shit?"

"Let me tie him up. I'll take you to *Stargazer.* There's no need for anyone to get hurt. I'll explain to Chase that we have a special arrangement. That you have the right to claim 50 percent of the gold. As for the cobra, it's yours alone."

"This man, Chase, he would just give these to me?"

"He'll do whatever I ask. If he doesn't, you can shoot him along with the rest of his men."

Devon's mouth dropped open. "I know Chase screwed up royally, but do you really want to see him dead?"

She paused only for a moment. "If he doesn't cooperate, what choice is there?"

Her eyes were on Marcos as he glanced around the room. At the adjacent bedroom, the closed bathroom door, and the wardrobe closet leaning against the wall. He reclaimed her arm and moved across the living room, arriving in front of the canvas-covered trunk.

"Open it," he demanded.

She lifted the latch and raised the lid.

"Now empty it."

She pulled out the heavy Pendleton blanket and laid it aside, and then waited. Marcos motioned for her brother to join them.

"Get in," he barked.

"I can't," Devon protested. "It's too small."

"Then I shoot and stuff you inside."

Devon threw Rachel an apprehensive look before relinquishing his stand. He tucked in his arms and legs and curled into a ball. Marcos placed the gun at the back his head. The maligning expression on his face was a clear indication that he had planned all along to kill Devon.

"Don't…please," she pleaded. "He did what you asked. He's going to suffocate in there anyway."

Marcos's mouth twisted into a wicked smile. "Huh…I didn't think of that."

He slammed the top of the trunk shut. Then he slid his knife into the lock and snapped it off, trapping Devon inside. His calls for help would remain silent to anyone living nearby.

"Just you and me now," Marcos told Rachel. He tucked his gun in his belt and gave her a little shove toward the open doorway. "Time to go. My treasure is getting lonely."

The guy was either the stupidest criminal he'd ever met or hungry for a death sentence. Either way, Devon was grateful that Marcos hadn't detected the phone in his breast pocket. He was also grateful that he knew exactly where Marcos was headed.

Having gained access with the superintendent's passkey, Novak arrived five minutes after Devon's muffled call. It took him another fifteen minutes to break open the trunk, be he'd had the foresight to call his partner and alert patrol cars in the area.

As they drove to the marina, Devon answered every question, bringing Novak completely up to speed. When he finished, the seasoned agent snorted his disapproval. "This wouldn't have happened if you'd listened to me in the first place."

Devon wasn't about to be criticized. "*None* of this would have happened if you hadn't used me...or my sister."

"I had no way of knowing she was going to be involved."

"But you knew about me."

Novak stole a sidelong glance. "Not right off. Pollero liked having everyone think I was his bodyguard, but in reality, I was part of a sting—posing as a launderer, picking up his drug money, making deposits in legitimate banks, and then wiring funds to traffickers in Mexico. His guys would tell me they were bringing me two hundred-fifty grand and show up with a cool million. In a matter of months, Pollero was climbing the ladder, approaching Class One. You know...one of the big moneymakers. I was told to do whatever was necessary to gain his trust."

Devon massaged his aching hand while Novak continued.

"We'd coordinated a major bust at a pickup point. But they got tipped, or Pollero got nervous. Either way, no one was at the location, and our plans got scrapped. Marcos showed up at my place an hour later and took me to the warehouse. That's when I discovered you and your partner. I had no way to get word out without Viktor getting suspicious."

As they wove around cars, Devon studied the passing streets, keeping a watchful eye out for the red Lamborghini.

"Anyway, no one anticipated Selena going rogue," Novak added. "Guess she got a charge out of laundering her brother's money through your firm. With you promising to double his earnings, it turned into a vicious game of cat and mouse. Only this time, Selena was guarding the cheese."

"So, I'm still asking. Was it worth it? Did you get what you were after?"

"We'll know that for sure after we grab Zane and his brother. If our theory proves right, he's a big link in their chain—helping traffickers, smuggling dope. Selling off stolen goods from dive expeditions to pad their pockets." Novak pulled into the gravel parking lot at the marina. "Got yourself tangled up in a nasty sharks' nest."

"Sharks don't have nests."

"These guys do. Stay here." Novak was out of the car, charging into the crowd of officers from every department in a twenty-mile radius. Moments later, he returned with a scowl on his face. "State troopers found Jeremy Zane floating facedown with a rope tied around his neck. He was hooked to the bollard on Fifty-Seven—the same slipway Cohen checked a boat out of this morning. Unfortunately, the only witness we have is the drunk who was sleeping in the neighboring skiff. Right now, my partner's in the Crow's Nest pouring coffee down the poor sap's throat…hoping to give the detectives on this case a lead."

"What about my sister?" Devon asked. "Where is she?"

Novak hesitated before answering. "The SPPD thinks Olivares might have spotted a patrol car near the marina before detouring west on 107. They figured he had to be going close to eighty when an oncoming truck clipped him and sent his car sailing over the side and straight into the Pacific." Novak shook his head and lowered his voice. "Sorry, man, but I have to tell ya. If your sister was with him, it'll be a miracle if she survived."

34

Chase hated leaving Rachel alone, but with the lives of his crew at risk, he knew she would've insisted on coming along. After the phone message he received from Devon, a muffled return call from his kitchen was all it took to ensure that Rachel would be looked after. No one, in Chase's opinion, was better suited for the job than the brother she'd risked her life to protect.

After arriving on *Stargazer,* Chase sat with his men and hashed out a battle plan. When the time was right, Ian would stay on board to protect their ship. As soon as *Legacy* divers crossed their threshold, he would contact the coast guard for assistance. Until then, it would be Zane's word against Chase's; catching them red-handed would be far more persuasive.

Wade and Blaine dropped over the side. Chase soon followed and swam toward the open hatch where the last chest of gold waited. He signaled to Blaine and Wade to hide and hold their breaths to prevent two unknown divers from seeing their bubbles too early. Following his orders, Blaine and Wade hid behind the *Wanli's* hull and waited as the invading divers swam closer.

When the marauders were only five meters away, it happened. Blaine couldn't hold his breath any longer and blew out a stream of bubbles. The invading divers abruptly turned. Blaine and Wade reached down and pulled out their knives. The triangular gold logo on the first diver's wet suit was all the proof they needed. It matched the insignia on the *Legacy*. They were, indeed, members of *Legacy's* crew. The invading divers were expecting to claim their unjust rewards.

Chase released a flare, signaling Ian.

As the third *Legacy* diver approached, Chase doubled back and came up behind him. While he struggled, trying to pin his opponent, Wade's assailant pulled out his knife. But Wade reacted quickly, catching his thrusting arm. Chase watched from a distance as they spun round and round, turning upside down and back up again, each trying to overpower the other. Although enmeshed in his own battle, from Chase's perspective, both men had nearly the same strength. Neither one could get an advantage.

A quick look to his left told Chase that Blaine wasn't so lucky. When he sprang on his opponent, the diver was able to hit him in the arm with his knife. While still grasping his wound, Blaine flipped his fins toward the diver's face in an obvious attempt to dislodge his mask and regulator.

Chase wanted desperately to go to Blaine's aid, but his challenger had pinned him against the *Wanli's* hull and was holding a blade to his throat. He growled into his regulator and pushed hard, managing to free himself. But his opponent struck again. Chase diverted the knife, which was aimed at his stomach. However, the knife grazed his left shoulder. When he used his right hand to press the wound, he left himself open for attack. Realizing his folly, he raised his hand in time to catch the diver's plunging arm. He twisted around in aikido fashion and drove the weapon back into the man's lower body. Looking down, he realized that his hand was still on the end of the knife, buried in his opponent's black wet suit. After a moment, he extracted the knife. The man lost his mouthpiece in the midst of a scream and swam away in a panic.

Meanwhile, it appeared that Wade was in big trouble. The *Legacy* diver he'd been fighting was now holding his shoulder down, preparing to stab him. In an instant, Wade grabbed a second knife from the left side of the man's air tank and shoved it into his midsection. The diver halted his attack. He slowly began to fall to the left. Wade pulled the knife out of the diver and pushed him away. As Chase watched in morbid fascination, the diver sank, landing on his air tank and then sprawling onto the ground.

With Wade now safe, Chase scanned their surroundings, looking for Blaine. He spotted him on the ocean floor—his arms limp and his head tipped back, touching the ground. Bubbles escaped from his mouth as the rapture sought to claim to him. Chase swam with all his might to help him.

As blood seeped from Blaine's body, Chase became painfully aware of the damage that had been inflicted. He forced the regulator back into Blaine's mouth, wishing he had told Blaine to guard the ship instead of Ian. He motioned Wade to take Blaine back to the surface as quickly as possible. As they both swam off, he looked around for Blaine's attacker, determined to even the score.

At first, Chase saw nothing. Then he saw bubbles rising from below. As he swam closer, the *Legacy* diver reached for his knife, but Chase was fast in the water. He grabbed the man's shoulders and threw him to the rock-covered ground, causing him to lose his knife. Chase waited for nearly a minute, but the man remained motionless, as if knocked unconscious. Given time, he eventually would drown.

Movement overhead activated Chase's defense mode. Another diver remained in the area, and Chase was on guard. He swam several meters away, stopped, and turned. To his surprise, the first diver was gone. There were no bubbles. No indication of the direction in which he'd gone. Chase circled the ship and then concluded that the man was either holding his breath or hiding inside the ship. No matter...his air would soon run out.

After two minutes, the first possibility became reality. Chase saw bubbles coming from an open hatch. He swam there, ready to fight, and charged with his knife. But this time, the diver was able to stop his attack. Using a discarded pulley, he knocked the knife out of Chase's hand. But Chase's instant reflexes kicked in. He grabbed his assailant's mask and ripped it from his face.

The *Legacy* diver struggled to restore his mask. When it was finally in place, Chase was there, too. He grabbed the diver's arm, pulling him forward, and delivered a powerful thrust, connecting serrated metal to the man's shoulder bone. Chase pushed away, withdrawing his knife, leaving the diver writhing. Before Chase could confront him again, the coward retreated, swimming for home with all his might.

The second diver suddenly reappeared overhead. As he drew closer, his fair complexion and close-cropped red hair were a clear giveaway. *Skylar Zane.* What was he doing here? It appeared that the marauder's greed had blinded his judgment and led him straight into the lion's den.

Chase circled around and came up behind him. He was waiting for the right moment to strike. With a flick of his blade, he cut Zane's air hose. A squall of bubbles escaped instantaneously. Panic grew in Zane's face as he looked up and discovered that Chase was holding him down. By his best estimate, Zane had no more than one minute to break free and rise from a depth of thirty meters. Otherwise, he would drown.

As Zane struggled to get free, he clawed at Chase's regulator. But Chase held his regulator firmly in hand, anticipating that move. Within seconds, Zane began to weaken. In a last-ditch attempt to save his own life, Zane managed to push Chase away and tried to swim to the surface. He took his reserve regulator into his mouth and sucked hard, trying to get air. But as Chase was well aware, after one hose is cut, the reserve no longer functions.

Chase drifted, watching from a distance, while Zane's strength weakened. Finally, Zane surrendered to his fate, slowly sinking to the ground. He looked up a final time to see if anyone would help him, but Chase's heart had turned to stone. Without looking back, he swam away, confident that there was one less murderer in the world.

35

Rachel was hanging from the edge of the cliff by her fingertips.

"Hold on!"

She lifted her eyes to verify that it truly was Tom Nash—her self-declared knight in shining armor—kneeling down to rescue her from sheer disaster. She lowered her chin slowly and caught sight of the waves crashing against the shore. Jagged rocks pointed straight up at her from fifty feet below. Waiting for her with open arms. Her heart raced, her body shuddered. Loosened gravel fell. She squeezed her eyes shut tightly, waiting for the inevitable drop.

"Rachel, look at me," Tom demanded.

She looked up toward the sky and squinted. The sun was shining brightly from behind his head.

"Give me your hand and I'll pull you up," he said.

Her arms were getting tired. Gravity was adding weight to her dangling body. Her hands were growing wet with sweat. "I can't…I can't do it."

"Listen to my voice," he said softly. "It's going to be all right. Just take your time. When you're ready, I want you to let go with your right hand and give it to me. Then you're going to reach up with your left hand."

She stared up into his gray-blue eyes, truly seeing him for the first time. Realizing how handsome, compassionate, and remarkable he was. No matter how cruel she'd been, how many times she'd deliberately snubbed him, he had always come back, loving her in spite of her faults. Now he was here, a guardian angel, risking his life to save hers. Yet, no matter how much she wanted to, she just couldn't let go. Not when her fingertips were her only means of survival. Not when she lacked faith in all of mankind.

"Trust me," he said. "I won't let you fall. I wouldn't let *anything* happen to you."

She closed her eyes for a moment and then took a chance. She reached up. Tom snatched her wrist instantly and held it tightly. She drew a deep breath and threw up her other hand, and he grabbed that wrist as well. As he continued pulling, her feet frantically searched for footholds. But then something went terribly wrong. Her footing slipped, and Tom was jerked forward. He was now hanging halfway over the cliff, still clinging to her. They were both going to die if she didn't act fast.

"Let me go!" she screamed.

"You'll die."

"I…I know." She stared up at him with wide, pleading eyes. "So will you if you don't…"

"No chance, honey. We're doing this together." He pulled with all his might and managed to edge himself back onto the cliff, pulling Rachel behind him. The second they were both on solid ground, they collapsed in a heap. Rachel's head rested in his lap. As her hero panted for breath, they stayed there unmoving for what seemed like an eternity.

Finally, she broke the silence. "How did you find me?"

Tom sat up, causing Rachel to move her head and sit up as well. "I believe the words you're looking for are 'thank you.'" He took a few moments to compose himself before standing. He seemed to be stalling on answering her question.

"How'd you know where to look?" she asked again, rising to her feet.

"I was driving into town and spotted you in the passenger seat of a passing vehicle. You had this frightened look on your face, and the driver wasn't anyone I recognized. I turned my car around and followed closely behind. Fortunately, I saw you open the car door, tumble out, and roll over the side just before the car sped away. My heart stopped when I thought you were gone."

Rachel bowed her face to the ground. "Why'd you save me, Tom? You could have been killed, too."

"You already know the answer to that." He gripped her shoulders in his hands and looked deep into her eyes. "I love you, Rachel. I knew it the moment I first laid eyes on you. I would give up my life to save yours. Don't you know that?"

Her stomach clenched. His words struck her mute.

Tom leaned down and took her mouth with his own. He wrapped his arms around her, drawing her into a tight embrace.

Rachel's befuddled mind sobered. Using both hands, she shoved him away and took several steps back. She closed her eyes briefly and cursed herself for allowing this to happen. For not acting sooner. With her hands clenched at her sides, she drew a shaky breath. "Tom…I'm sorry, but I don't feel…that way."

Her face warmed beneath his troubled stare.

"I don't love you," she said.

They stood across from each other at a silent impasse—trapped in the awkwardness of their situation.

The sound of crunching gravel turned their heads. Devon was peering through the windshield of Novak's car with a shocked look on his face. It was as though he couldn't believe she was actually there.

"Rachel!" he yelled. He ran from the car and threw his arms around her waist, lifting her off the ground. As soon as he set her down, he studied her face and asked, "Are you all right?"

Although her heart was still racing, she nodded and glanced back at Tom. His hands were jammed in his pockets. His eyes were fixed on the ground. No matter what had gone on between them, she still owed him her life.

"Thank God," Devon lamented. "When I heard that Marcos drove Selena's car into the ocean, I honestly thought I'd lost you."

"Tom saved me from going over the edge," Rachel explained. "He's a hero…the real McCoy."

At the mention of his name, Tom lifted his eyes and smiled.

Devon extended a hand. "I can't thank you enough. My God, I don't know what would have happened if you hadn't been here." He was still listening to Tom's full account when Rachel happened to glance at Novak.

The man stood with his arms crossed, looking more intense than usual. And there was something about his eyes that made Rachel believe he wasn't buying Tom's story. After a few minutes, he stepped closer and identified himself as a federal agent.

Tom's jaw went slack. A look resembling panic flashed across his face.

"It's amazing how you arrived here just in the nick of the time," Novak said, skepticism edging his voice. "I'm real glad everything worked out all right, but I have to ask you, Mr. Nash, why didn't you call the police if you suspected something was wrong?"

Tom blew out a breath. "Just wasn't enough time."

"Yeah...had a feeling you'd say that."

"Is there a problem, sir?"

"Not with me. But since there's a death involved, I'll need you to answer a few questions."

Just then, a San Palo patrol car pulled up. After a brief exchange between Novak and the two uniformed officers, Tom Nash was put in the back of the car and escorted to the nearest police station. As soon as he was gone, Rachel slipped into the rear seat of Novak's vehicle. She waited until Devon was settled in the front before leaning forward and speaking to the back of Novak's head.

"I don't understand," she said. "Is Tom involved?"

Novak pulled onto the road and looked into his rearview mirror. "More than you know," he said.

36

Chase kicked with all his might until his last ounce of air was gone. Then he switched to his pony tank. After a few deep breaths, he relaxed as the world took on a whole new flavor. The *Wanli* was suddenly alive with brilliant crustaceans—a virtual rainbow of jewels covered her sides. Each fish that darted in his direction battled the others for Chase's attention. Particles danced in the beam of his flashlight. Never in his life had he been more intrigued. More in awe of the ocean.

With each stroke, Chase's sense of well-being grew. Nothing was going to keep him from impressing the world. From delivering his showcase of ancient Chinese treasures. Doc would be overwhelmed by the miracles Chase produced. By the gold coins filling twenty-two white buckets. His name would be known in every museum; his accomplishments shared aboard every ship. He laughed as he thought about the grief he'd needlessly endured...the worries that had left him paralyzed and mentally incompetent.

He spotted a small, red-speckled eel, unlike any he'd ever seen. Its fringed gill collar and jaw structure were reminiscent of a fish that dated back over one hundred million years.

Rachel should see this, he told himself, as he reached out to touch it. But as it darted away, he realized that something was terribly wrong. He'd taken chances before and knew the signs of nitrogen narcosis—the euphoria that could render a man fearless and prompt him to drift aimlessly as the last ounce of air was spent. He shook his head and tapped his tanks, but to no avail. He could feel the onslaught of dizziness, the disorientation take hold. No longer could he discern the ocean's dark floor below. Oddly, he didn't care. He could live here forever, he told himself. Enjoy the amazing wonders of this aquatic world without a care or concern. Yet somewhere in the distant recesses of his mind, he saw Rachel's stunning face and, for brief moment, he felt a sense of sadness at not seeing her again. For not telling her how much he adored her. How, more than anything, he longed to share the rest of his life with her.

Suddenly, something flickered in the distance, leaving him smiling and completely fascinated. The shimmering light grew in intensity as it rapidly approached. Chase marveled at the remarkable sight: a beautiful woman surrounded by flowing, white fabric was staring endearingly into his eyes. Angling her sweet, Asian face as if to say, "What are you doing here?"

Mai Le?

She pressed her hand to his chest and nodded in empathetic understanding. She touched the bracelet on his wrist—the gift from Allie's mother. She held out an open palm and smiled, inviting his touch. When their hands met, her fingers folded over his. His eyes closed of their own volition. As she held his hand tightly, a surge of energy shot through him from head to foot. He was propelled through the water at an amazing speed. It was as if Mai Le were physically pushing him up from the bottom of the ocean without actually being there.

When Chase opened his eyes again, he was floating on the surface, taking long-drawn-out breaths without the aid of his regulator. Drifting painlessly toward the side of a forty-seven-foot boat.

Wade's panic-stricken face was gazing down at him. He was screaming at the top of his lungs, "Captain! Over here!" He reached over the side and pulled Chase out.

Chase was amazed to see tears in his crew member's eyes.

"Are you all right?" Wade asked repeatedly, panic evident in his voice.

Chase wanted to respond—wanted to ask questions about the vision he'd seen. About Blaine's injuries and the coast guard boat secured to the side of their ship. But a paramedic had an oxygen mask over his face in a matter of seconds.

"Rachel," he choked. His quick ascent had taken its toll. His teeth were chattering so violently that even without the aid of the mask he could barely speak.

"I'll let her know you're safe," Wade assured him.

Ian was suddenly at his side. "Look at me, mate," he demanded. "Are ya hurt anywhere?"

Chase shook his head back and forth, relaxing the crease in Ian's brow. He drew several deep breaths before pulling the mask away from his face. "The heart of the dragon...she just saved my life."

37

Rachel's stomach twisted as she followed Devon into the Crow's Nest Bar. Detective Brennan was sitting alone in the far corner with a Padre's baseball cap on, looking up at a photo of Sam and his boat on the wall. Her last encounter with the detective had been at her father's funeral, which had taken place only four days after Brennan's wife had committed suicide. Under the circumstances, Rachel never expected him to show up at the church. His loyalty to her family, even during the worst possible time in his life, had left her amazed and truly grateful. Now, four years later, he had a ruddy complexion, an extra thirty pounds wrapped around his middle, and Rachel had watched him accept a bribe. She couldn't wait to see him destroyed.

"Come over here," Brennan said, his deep, gruff voice a stark reminder of the night she was kidnapped. He motioned at the two empty chairs across from him.

Rachel and Devon stared at him.

"I said come here," he repeated more loudly.

Rachel studied her brother's profile, gauging his temperament by the tense look on his face. She followed him, weaving between tables with chairs on top of them. Arriving at the same table where the town drunk normally sat. She eased herself into the chair next to Devon and swallowed hard before glancing up at the waitress, who had suddenly joined them.

"Coffee," Mika said. She held two mugs and a half-filled pot. Rachel bit her lip, curbing her temptation to speak.

"Won't be staying that long," Devon said. He reached for Rachel's hand and squeezed it to reassure her. He glared at Brennan and spoke more bluntly than she'd ever thought possible. "OK, we're here. What do you want?"

Brennan's bloodshot eyes narrowed. It was only 1:00 p.m. and he reeked of alcohol. "You really think I'm going to sit back and do nothing after Novak calls my department and tries to discredit me?" he slurred. "None of you have a clue who you're dealing with."

"I have an idea," Devon said.

"Really? You're still breathing only because I've allowed it. Believe me…that can change."

Devon glanced at Rachel. "That's why you wanted to meet? To threaten us?"

Brennan's evil smile looked out of place on his amiable features. A nearly empty bottle of vodka sat next to his glass. "Was just curious to know what you think you've got on me. It doesn't take a great stretch of the imagination to figure out that Skylar Zane and AJ Hobbs are my sons. At least, that's what my wife told me before I found out she was fuckin' your old man." He shifted his gaze from Devon to Rachel and back again. "Trained those boys real well to keep their mouths shut. Sent them to separate schools, changed their names. Planned my revenge for a long, long time. Now that they've both served their purpose, there's nothing to connect me to anything they've done or to anyone else in this town."

Rachel looked down at Devon's hand resting on hers. She wished more than anything she hadn't promised to keep her mouth shut.

"I can sit here all day, telling you tons of shit," Brennan boasted, pouring another shot. "How I spent years planning my revenge...turning those pea brains against your greater-than-thou family. How I celebrated for months after Claire and Sam turned up dead." He downed another glassful. "How I convinced Pollero and his hoodlum pals to take you both down. And guess what? There's not a fuckin' thing you can do about it. No matter what you claim or whom you try to convince, no one's going to care. No one will take the word of a blubbering idiot and his nursemaid sister over a highly respected, decorated cop's."

"If that's the case, Brennan, why did you insist on seeing us? Why did your partner frisk us outside if you've got nothing to worry about?"

He huffed. "Don't go giving yourself undue credit, Lyons. I play it safe, that's all."

"Yeah, right," Devon muttered under his breath.

Brennan leaned forward on his elbows. He lowered his voice. "You haven't got a thing on me, understand? I know for a fact no one saw me put a bullet in your partner's head. No one heard me on the phone changing the drop site or can ever link me to the Polleros. So take a free piece of advice while I'm still willing to give it: Keep your mouths shut and move out of town, or you'll find yourselves buried next to the rest of your kin."

Rachel jumped to her feet. "I heard you in the car the night I was kidnapped. I saw you take a bribe from Novak when you thought he was on the take. And your partner was seen dumping Logan's body. What's more, there's a man who saw you fighting with your son, Jeremy, just before he was killed."

Brennan guffawed. "Who's going to believe the town drunk? Like I said, you've got nothing."

"Except your word," Devon said.

"Yeah…mine against yours."

Rachel banged her fist on the table. "Exactly! Now that I know you were behind my father's death, I'll do whatever it takes to put you behind bars. I'll stand up in court to make sure you rot there."

The detective snorted. "Good luck," he said, reaching for the bottle.

Devon stared at him—his aggravation apparent. "No, your bad luck," he snapped. "This bar has ears and you just filled all of them."

Brennan glanced around nervously. Spotting Novak in the doorway, he rummaged under the table and pulled out a gun. Devon swung a backhanded fist, knocking his gun from his hand. Before Brennan had time to react, Mika rushed over and snatched it from the floor. She pointed her weapon at the detective's throat, daring him to move. Within seconds, uniformed officers, led by Novak and the chief of police, rushed through the door. As soon as Brennan was handcuffed, Mika recited his Miranda rights. All the while, Rachel leaned back in her seat watching. She was stunned and exhilarated. She was still amazed by the discovery that Mika was an undercover officer. Although Novak explained that she'd been recruited to join *Stargazer's* crew to insure everyone's safety, Rachel had a hard time believing it was true until she actually witnessed her in action.

Ultimately, Brennan and his partner were handcuffed, loaded into the backseats of two patrol cars, and driven away. One of the detectives removed Sam Lyons's photo from the wall and lifted the bug from its frame before handing the picture back to Devon.

"I still can't get over the fact that Brennan was behind everything," Devon said. "Even when his name kept coming up, I didn't have a clue."

A soft smile came to Rachel's lips. She laced her fingers through his, and together they looked down at their father's smiling face. "It's a good thing Lyons look out for one another," she said.

Novak had just finished his phone call when Rachel approached. "I can't thank you enough for letting us be involved," she told him. "With Brennan put away, Devon and I can finally get on with our lives and put our father's memory to rest."

"Of course, you understand this was far from normal procedure. Your brother was determined to make this happen. But all the same, you both had me worried for a while there."

Her lips curled. "Guess my brother's kind of used to getting his own way," she said. "Anyway, there's still something I've been meaning to ask you. What about Tom Nash? Your cryptic comment had me wondering about him all morning. I was honestly half-expecting Brennan to incriminate him as part of his drug-smuggling ring."

"Sorry. Should've been clearer about that. Especially with the guy having his own set of issues."

Rachel glimpsed Devon outside with Mika. They were deep in conversation. "*What* issues?" she asked Novak.

"Remember when I said he was involved more than you know?"

She nodded.

"I was referring to you. Far as we can tell, he never meant you any harm, but there was good reason to believe he'd been stalking you for months. The guy came clean when we accused him of running Olivares off the road. Turned out that his greatest fear wasn't getting arrested for manslaughter. It was that his wife might find out about you."

"*His wife*? I didn't even know he was married."

"Separated, actually. The guy decided to move on…literally. Back to Texas, where his family's originally from. You won't have to worry about him bothering you anymore. Just the same, you're one lucky woman. If he hadn't been breaking the law at the time, he wouldn't have been there to save your life."

Rachel looked away, shaking her head. When Chase returned, she'd have another crazy story to share. One that would leave him lecturing her for weeks. She'd end up having a battle on her hands trying to convince him that she didn't need his full-time protection. A soft smile came to her lips at the thought. She imagined his hands on her shoulders. His sky-blue eyes peering into her soul. Although she hated to admit it, Chase had definitely wormed his way into her heart again. Having him around, looking after her, wouldn't be such a bad thing. Would it?

"Novak!" a police officer yelled from the open doorway. "Have you seen the chief?"

"Not recently, why?"

"The coast guard just received an emergency call from the *Stargazer*. Turns out we have another dead captain on our hands."

"What…what did he just say?" Rachel stared at Novak, disbelieving her ears. The debilitated look in his eyes. It couldn't be Chase. It just couldn't be! Her breath caught. Her heart skipped a beat. There had to be a mistake. *Oh, God, please…it has to be a mistake*!

Suddenly, Devon was there, folding her in his arms, keeping a world filled with heartache at bay.

38

As he leaned in the bedroom doorway, Chase couldn't imagine a more exciting homecoming. The only things lacking were the words Rachel refused to speak—the words that came so easily to him. He pushed his hair out of his eyes and stared at her naked body, which was positioned like a teenage boy's wet dream in the middle of his bed. Even though a trail of clothing provided evidence of the passionate exchange that had led them there, he had to blink to assure himself that the vision before him was real—to verify that she hadn't turned and bolted just when he found her again.

Rachel lowered her chin. "Stop looking at me like that."

Her arousing feminine scent overcame him. Just the thought of straddling her made him tremble. "In a minute," he murmured. He scanned every inch of her body before moving closer. A soft blush crept into her cheeks and flowed down the curve of her neck. It reached the rigid nipples on her perfect breasts. As she shifted her shoulders, long, chestnut tendrils interrupted his heart-racing appraisal.

"Maybe this wasn't such a good idea," Rachel said. She reached for her shirt at the foot of the bed.

Chase snatched it and tossed it aside. He smiled as he lowered himself onto the bed. "No...it was a *great* one." He grasped her knees and kissed them before pressing them apart. He stared down into her face as he slid his hand along the silky skin lining her thighs. "Been dreaming about this for far too long." He blazed a path of kisses to the soft, brown mound between her legs, stopping briefly when a moan escaped her lips. He stole an upward glance and watched her breasts rise and fall with rapid breaths.

"Don't stop," she murmured.

Chase had no intention of halting. Mere touching her was intoxicating. He eagerly resumed his divine mission, stoking and teasing with his tongue. With her fists clenching the covers, he claimed dominion. He slid his lips across her smooth belly toward her full breasts. After gathering a handful, he suckled and nipped, reveling in her cries of ecstasy. He planted a trail of kisses along her neck and over her upturned chin, and then found her mouth again—wet, sweet, trembling.

He lifted his head and braced himself on either side of her, surveying his possession. Beneath him lay a treasure far more valuable than anything resting on the ocean floor. Anything he might have imagined.

Wordlessly, she roped one hand around his neck and guided him against her shoulder. She raked her fingers down his side and spread them over his hip. While her hot breath blew currents across his ear, her free hand slipped between their bodies, inspecting the level of his hunger.

His pounding heart skipped a beat. He eased back and gazed down at her sealed eyes—eyes that had never failed to claim his during their ardent exchanges. His chest tightened. Why wasn't she looking at him?

"Chase..." she breathed.

The sound of his name on her lips relaxed his brow. He realized that he was being foolish. She wouldn't be there if she didn't enjoy his touch, if she didn't have feelings for him.

"You're amazing," he said, his voice ragged in his own ears.

A soft smile played on her lips. He leaned down and devoured them, his tongue urgent and insistent. He shifted his hips between her legs. With one swift motion, he drove his fully erect shaft deep inside her.

"Ahhh..." she exhaled. She slipped one leg and then the other around his waist. She drew in a deep breath and clamped down, sending a fresh wave of desire over him.

Chase began a steady rocking rhythm. He gradually increased the tempo, thrusting harder and faster. Tension mounted with his blowing breaths, his rapid movements. His heavy panting matched hers as sweat eased their back-and-forth motions. They were meant to be together. Why couldn't she see that?

Say it, Rachel. Say I love you. "Love you..." Did he say that aloud?

"Mr. Cohen...Mr. Cohen..."

Chase opened his eyes slowly, adjusting to the bright light in the room. An unfamiliar, bristle-haired nurse was standing at the side of his bed, staring down with a dour expression.

"Your breathing's erratic," she said. She pressed her thumb to his wrist to check his pulse and then lifted his chin to check his eyes.

"What...where am I?" he mumbled.

"You're a patient at San Palo General Hospital. You were brought in complaining of chest pains and dizziness two days ago. Dr. Miles was planning to transfer you to Ventura County, but your symptoms seemed to be improving. He indicated on your chart that you were being kept an additional night for observation, but if you'd like me to call the doctor—"

"No...no, I'm fine. Just woke up a little...confused, is all."

Rachel knocked at the door and leaned in. "Hi, it's me again. Can he have visitors yet?"

"I suppose it's all right, Miss Lyons. But I'd like to remind you to keep Mr. Cohen calm. As you're fully aware, he's been through a lot."

As soon as the duty nurse was gone, Rachel approached his bed. "I know you're tired, Chase, so I won't keep you long."

He gazed up at her with a lazy smile. "I don't mind."

She looked around for a place to sit. Discovering none, she eased onto the edge of the mattress. "I'll make this quick and painless," she said. "First off, I checked on Blaine and he came out of surgery just fine. He was actually alert enough to recommend a new book on computer science...not that I'd ever read it. I also met with Wade down at the marina. He wanted me to assure you that everything's been safely transferred from *Stargazer* to a bank vault, pending your release from the hospital. The chief of police even loaned out some of his men to help."

Chase studied her with renewed interest. He never realized how confident she'd become. How cool and businesslike.

"Dr. Bailey also gave me fantastic news about Allie's test results. When you're up for it, I'm sure he'd like to share them with you. Oh, and Professor Ying arrived home early this morning. Eleanor said he's on his way to a full recovery."

"That's great news," Chase said. He noticed the minor scrapes on her arm and asked, "What about you? Looks like you had an altercation."

Rachel smiled. "You wouldn't believe it if I told you."

"I'm listening."

"Maybe another time. Anyway, I wanted to let you know before you heard it from someone else. I got a job offer and will be leaving town soon."

Leaving? Surprise must have shown on his face.

"Don't worry, Chase. I'll make sure my work is done before I go. And once a new director's been appointed and Dr. Ying returns to work full time, you'll get the kudos and rewards you truly deserve. In fact, even after everyone takes his fair share, you're going to end up with more money than you'll ever know what to do with."

She was rising from the bed, leaving him in more ways than one. He swallowed hard and placed his hand over hers.

"I'm sorry I wasn't there for you, Rachel. I should have been... I know that now. The treasure was at risk and all I could think about—"

"Believe me, there's no need to explain," she said. "You had your men to take care of and a tough job to do. Now that it's all over, you'll have time to consider those great offers you're going to be receiving."

"What about you, Rachel? You're really going to leave...just like that?"

She shrugged. "I got an invitation from the CEO of BioGlobe to head up his research team in Hawaii. It's pretty tough to turn down a job like that...especially when you've spent your whole life working toward that goal." She moved away from his hand and stood. "It's been a great adventure, Chase. One I'll never forget. But now you need to follow doctor's orders and concentrate on getting well. You've got a beautiful daughter to think about. I'm sure we'll see each other soon."

She was walking toward the door, taking his heart with her. Leaving him far behind.

Chase struggled to get untangled from the sheet. "Rachel... wait!" He brought his feet to the floor and stood, his thigh braced against the bed. "Listen to me," he pleaded. "There's something I have to tell you...something important."

She didn't move. She didn't say a word. But curiosity must have piqued her interest, as she glanced over her shoulder and slowly walked back. She lowered her chin, emphasizing her point. "OK, you've got exactly five minutes, and then I have to go to work. And you'll need to get back to bed where you belong."

He sat on the edge of the mattress and patted the place beside him. With a slight hesitation, she bent her knees and looked up at him, stirring his emotions once more. In the span of three minutes, he told her about the fight that had ensued under the ocean. About Zane's final seconds and the bad mix he'd inhaled. "I thought I had it all handled. Didn't even think to check my pony tank. Have to say, I honestly thought I was done for when I saw her…this incredible angel. The same one you must've seen. She looked me straight in the eyes and laid her hand on my heart. And in that moment, I knew. The heart of the dragon isn't in a box. It isn't buried in a ship under the ocean. It's the person you love from the depths of your soul. Beyond all reason…all doubt."

Rachel stared down at her hands. She gnawed on her bottom lip.

"For Captain Brunelli, it was Mai Le. He was the dragon in Mai Le's life and she was his snake." Chase smiled. "Her heart belongs to him for all eternity. Just like my heart belongs to you, Rachel. You're the heart of this dragon, and I'm begging you… don't go. I need you in my life, now more than ever."

He lifted her downturned chin with his thumb and gazed into her tear-filled eyes.

"Sweetheart, I love you. Tell me you feel the same way and I promise I'll never disappoint you again. I'll be the man you've always wanted. I'll do whatever it takes to make you happy," he said. "I just can't stand not knowing how you feel."

A single tear trailed down her cheek. "Chase…I…I've been wanting to tell you—"

"Hate to be botherin' ya." Ian was standing in the doorway with a cockeyed smile. "Would ya both mind following me down the hall? Ya need to see what Allie and her little friend have been up to."

"*Now?*" Chase asked.

Ian nodded.

Rachel stood. She glanced down while Chase put on his slippers and wrapped himself in a robe. They walked solemnly, side by side, without saying a word. When they reached room 310, they filed past Ian as he held the door open. Allie was sitting up in bed smiling, her cheeks flushed with color. The tube that had been in her nose was gone, as was the monitor that had been stationed at her side. Shishi was sitting on the upper right corner of her bed with a sheepish look on his face.

"Goodness, Allie," Rachel said. "You're looking considerably better today."

Chase smiled at his daughter. "Isn't she, though?"

Allie giggled, scrunching her covers tightly under her neck.

Chase noticed a bump under her blanket. "So, whacha got there, Peanut?"

From the playful smirk on her face, she wasn't about to surrender an answer…or anything else, for that matter. Ian crossed his arms and gave Allie a pinched evil eye.

"Gator…member yer promise."

Allie's smile evaporated. A crease drew her tiny brows together. She peeled back the sheet and thin blanket, revealing her treasure. To Chase's amazement, a black, lacquered box covered with red chrysanthemums appeared. A silver lock was fastened to the lid Sam had found, hiding whatever remained inside the box.

Rachel gasped. "It was *you*?" She picked up the box with both hands.

The hurt in Allie's face was instantly apparent. Rachel's eyes softened. A gentle smile curled her lips. "Why, you little dickens," she teased. "All this time I thought your father had taken it to get even with me."

Chase stared at her, puzzled. "Even?"

"For telling…you know, a little white lie."

"Little?" he huffed. "Since when is battling pirates a *little* thing?"

Allie's eyes shone. "Pirates?"

Rachel had to give Chase points for that one. "All right…it wasn't little. But there wasn't any reason to involve you when I already had—"

"You've got to be kidding. *Really*?"

Ian held his hand in the air, silencing the feud between them. "Enough. Let's get to the gist of this. Our fine young lad, here, has his own little secret ta share. Don't ya, Shishi?"

The young boy moved from his hiding place and stood before Rachel. "We were only playing with it," he said, his voice cracking.

"With what?" she inquired.

"This." He pulled his right hand out from behind his back, revealing a tiny, tubular key. "We didn't hurt anything. Honest."

"How did you get that out of the lock?"

Shishi demonstrated by pulling the bow of the key back and twisting it to the right. Then he inserted it into the lock's keyway. It clicked into place, locking the box once again.

"Oh…I see."

"But what's inside?" Chase asked. "After keeping it a secret all this time, surely you're going to share it now."

Rachel's smile thinned. "Of course." She turned the key and extracted the bronze snake. She handed it to Chase and waited for his reaction.

"Wait a minute. Wasn't this the first piece you brought up when we were diving?"

She nodded and half shrugged. "At the time, I had no idea it was Mai Le's gift. It's probably worth fifteen thousand at the most. But I don't think the price will matter to Dr. Ying."

"That's not all," Shishi said. "Watch this."

He spun the box around on Allie's bed and inserted the key into a tiny hole masked by the painted design. With one turn of his small wrist, a hidden drawer sprung open, exposing a shimmering red diamond.

Everyone's breath caught. The room was perfectly still. Rachel took the gem from its post and held it to the light, allowing it to refract light into all corners of the room. The diamond was astonishing. It was close to six carats in weight. Its approximate worth…unimaginable!

"So *that's* the heart of the dragon," Ian chimed in. His eyes gleamed like polished emeralds as he held the diamond captive in his gaze. He stepped closer, drawn by its luster. Its mysterious, magnetic appeal. "Can I touch it?" he asked.

Rachel's protective instincts appeared to have kicked in. "If you don't mind, I'm going to put this away for now," she said, as if speaking to an adolescent. "We wouldn't want anything to happen to it, now would we?" She kept an eye on Ian, waiting for his head to wag back and forth. With his attention still fixed on the diamond, she returned it to its secret compartment, locked the box, and pocketed the key.

"So, what do you think it's worth?" Chase asked, watching her eyes more intently.

She cleared her throat and delivered a viable answer. "I'll know for sure when Dr. Ying has a professional jeweler examine it. In the meantime, why don't we agree to keep this between all of us? Like a buried treasure?"

Allie and Shishi were all smiles. "A pirate's treasure?" Allie asked, gushing with enthusiasm.

Rachel smiled. "Yep. And I know this is a bit of a stretch, but just out of curiosity, Shishi, what does your name mean…if I were to translate it into English?"

He puffed his chest, exuding pride, and announced his answer loud and clear. "My papa named me Lion because I'm so brave and strong."

Rachel exploded in laugher, crushing the joy in Shishi's face. She regained her perfect sense of propriety and drew him into her arms. She assured him that the joke wasn't in his name at all.

"You're miraculous," she told him, boosting his spirits. "A genuine, four-hundred-year-old prophecy. In fact, it's pretty phenomenal, when you think about it. Allie's family originally came from Portugal; yours came from Asia. Allie wants to be a sea captain and you enjoy adventure stories. Together, you discovered the heart of the dragon and kept it safe. It seems to me that destiny has a great sense of humor, don't you think?"

While everyone's eyes remained fixed on Shishi, Chase reached for Rachel's hand.

"Outside," he whispered.

"You know, on second thought, maybe we should call the professor," Rachel said. "Although he'll probably have a coronary when he hears the news."

"Outside," he repeated.

She followed him through the doorway and looked up at him, confused.

"What do you think *we're* worth, Rachel?" he asked.

"I don't understand. What are you asking me?"

"Back in my room, you were hesitant to answer, so I'm asking you this final time. I know destiny brought us together...just like Mai Le and her captain. No matter what your decision might be, I'll love you forever, sweetheart. But I need to know, for better or worse: are you willing to give us another shot?"

She exhaled a deep breath and looked into his eyes. "I don't want anyone but you, but I don't want to feel like I do. You're asking for the truth, and here it is. I fell in love with you the moment we met, Chase Cohen. But I'm not that person anymore. I'm like an iceberg on the ocean, adrift and unsure of what lies in store for me. No matter how hard I try, though, I'm never going to stop feeling. I'm never going to stop longing for you."

Tension was pulling him in all directions. His heart was aching. "Why does that sound like a curse?"

"Because it is," she assured him. "You've touched my heart, my mind...the deepest part of my soul. I can't imagine my life without you. Is that what you want to hear? Is that what you need to know?"

He looked down, hoping for more. Trying to settle for less.

"Can't we just focus on now?" she said sweetly. "We can always worry about tomorrow later."

Chase threw on a crooked smile. He roped her into his arms, and while Ian and Shishi stared in astonishment from the Allie's doorway, he fixed his mouth on Rachel's in a long, demanding kiss, leaving her gasping for breath.

"I'm going to make you say it, angel," he breathed in her ear. "No matter how long it takes."

EPILOGUE

Six Months Later…

Chase stood across from Dr. Ying with Rachel's arm draped around his neck. He was beaming with pride. The new museum wing, appropriately named after Sam Lyons, was now complete. All the relics collected from the Chinese merchant ship, including a duplicate of the Mai Le diamond, were on display. A poem titled "Severed Threads," about souls separated and then reunited, was inscribed on a metal plaque and mounted below it. An excited crowd was gathering outside, eager to view the amazing *Wanli II* collection.

"I just heard some remarkable news," Dr. Ying told Rachel. "Were you offered the directorship of San Palo University's new oceanography program?"

Her smile broadened. "Yes…it's true. I have to admit, it's more than I ever hoped for. Without your encouragement, it would've taken me a lot longer to realize that I belong under the water and not behind a desk." She squeezed Chase's neck and whispered in his ear, "I believe I owe you, too."

"I'll be collecting on that tonight."

"Excuse me, Miss Lyons," Eleanor interrupted. "Your brother called and is waiting for you at the marina."

"Oh, I completely lost track of the time." She leaned up for a kiss and smiled. "I promise we'll be home for dinner. That is, if I can get Devon away from the engine room long enough. With his new interest in keeping Dad's pride and joy in top condition, it might take a little persuasion from Mika and her pan-fried noodles to unplug him."

"You sure you don't want me to go with you?" Chase asked.

"I'd love for you to come, but this is something Devon and I need to do. I hope you don't mind."

Chase smiled. "Of course not. Just get home safe, OK?"

"I will."

As she strode toward the exit, Rachel couldn't stop smiling. She drove through town and parked in the marina's freshly paved lot. As soon as she boarded *Stargazer,* Devon pulled out into the harbor. While he maintained their heading, she used Chase's map to navigate their course. All the while, a gold metal canister sat on the floor between them.

They arrived at their destination an hour later. On the horizon, the sun painted the heavens in a multitude of colors: orange, red, lavender, pink. It was the kind of night sky their father had loved. When the moment was right, Devon joined Rachel at the gunwale. She opened the gold urn, and together they spread their father's ashes over the sea, bidding Sam Lyons a final farewell.

Rachel blew out a tearful sigh. "He would have loved this, you know. Both of us here, seeing his dream realized." She glanced at Devon, who was staring out to sea. "I'm sorry about Selena… that you lost her, too."

Devon flashed a rueful smile. "Crazy as it sounds, I loved her. I really did. But people aren't always what you make them out to be. Hearts can't always pick who they choose to love. That's not the case for you, Rachel. You've got a good man who would do anything in this world for you. He makes no bones about the way he feels."

She looked up at the stars filling the sky.

"I had no right to get involved," he said. "But now I'm offering you some brotherly advice. I'm hoping...no, I'm praying you'll take it. Life is *so* short. You'll never know the joy or sweet pain that comes with true love unless you're willing to open yourself to it. There's a port waiting back there for you and a captain who wants to guide you for the rest of your life."

She cast Devon a sad, sidelong glance.

"Take a chance," he told her. "Tell Chase you love him. You'll never regret giving your heart away, just like I never will."

As he turned the ship and headed back toward shore, Rachel stood on the afterdeck, considering her brother's advice. *Perhaps he's right*, she told herself. It was time to move on. To trust her heart. To believe in love again. As she watched their wake spread beyond the *Wanli's* tomb, a flicker of light off to the right captured her attention. In that moment, she witnessed the gossamer woman swimming away under a rolling wave. The image morphed and became two descending dolphins. She stared at the astonishing sight and wondered if Mai Le had found her captain and was finally at peace.

After a long, romantic night in the cottage, Monday morning came sooner than Chase had anticipated. He helped Rachel into his truck and slid into the driver's seat. Then he turned to her with a smile. "Now remind me. What were those three little words you said after I climbed into the shower with you?"

"Pass the soap?"

Chase laughed. "Real cute."

"Who, me?"

"Definitely."

Rachel leaned across the seat and whispered up close. "I love you?"

"Is that a question?" He held her face and kissed her gently, relishing the softness of her lips. "OK…time to get on your side of the truck, young lady, or I'll have to take you back upstairs and have my way with you."

Rachel sat back in her seat smiling while Chase checked his side mirror. He was about to pull away from the curb when Reverend Yamada showed up, blocking their exit. He circled the front of their vehicle and stood outside Chase's open window.

"I had an opportunity to go to the museum yesterday with Mika and Shishi," he told them. "I've been hearing all about your success on television and in the newspapers and wanted to compliment both of you on your miraculous discoveries. God's definitely been blessing you two. I never would have expected anything so extraordinary to turn up right off our coastal waters."

"Thank you," Chase said. "I don't mean to be rude. It's just that I promised to meet Allie and Ian for breakfast…"

"Oh, I have no intention of keeping you. But if you don't mind, there is one specific question I'd really like to ask."

Chase looked at Rachel and sighed.

"Don't worry, honey," she said, smiling. "I'll text Ian and let them know we're running a little late." She picked up her phone and began tapping away.

"All right," Chase told the pastor. "But can you please make it quick? If I'm not there to stop him, Ian will have Allie eating chocolate pancakes with fudge sauce along with a seven-layer piece of cake."

Reverend Yamada chuckled. "I understand, believe me. My son's the same way. I was just hoping to enlist your help in finding a valuable heirloom that went down in a capsized yacht off the coast of Japan. Believe it or not, my brother's a Buddhist priest and good friend of Dr. Ying's. His premonitions are highly regarded in Japan and were responsible for my bringing Shishi to California and reuniting him with Allie."

Chase couldn't help but smile. The man obviously had his own take on their friendship.

"My brother's recent dreams told him that you and Miss Lyons were the chosen ones to help us with this difficult task," the pastor insisted. "I assure you, he will cover all your expenses in addition to providing a sizeable reward for finding the Templar's Stone."

"*Templar*?" Rachel's eyes sparked with excitement. "You *do* know what that means?"

Chase angled a look. "What?"

She crossed her arms and jutted out her chin. "You're now looking at the newest member of Trident Venture's international salvaging team."

"Who?"

"Me, of course."

Chase laughed and pulled her close.

With her ear pressed against his chest, she listened to his heart and then whispered, "I love you, Chase Cohen."

He smiled and kissed the top of her head. Rachel Lyons had become a fascinating, daring creature—so complex and full of surprises. With her at his side, there was no doubt in his mind that their greatest adventures were about to begin.

ABOUT THE AUTHOR

Linda Yoshida, aka Kaylin McFarren, is a rare bird, indeed. Not the migratory sort, she prefers to hug the West Coast and keep family within visiting range. Although she has been around the world, she was born in California, relocated with her family to Washington, and nested with her husband in Oregon. Besides playing an active role in his business endeavors, she has been involved in all aspects of their three daughters' lives: taxi duties, cheerleading coaching, script rehearsals, and relationship counseling, to name but a few of her duties. Now, she enjoys spending free time with her two young grandsons and hopes to have many more.

Although Kaylin wasn't born with a pen in hand, as so many of her talented fellow authors were, she has been actively involved in business and personal writing projects for many years. As director of a fine art gallery, she assisted in furthering the careers of numerous visual artists through promotional opportunities in national publications. Eager to spread her creative wings, she has since steered her energy toward writing novels. As a result, she has earned more than a dozen literary awards and was a 2008 finalist in the prestigious RWA® Golden Heart contest.

Kaylin is a member of RWA, Rose City Romance Writers, and Willamette Writers. Receiving her associate's degree in literature at Highline Community College originally sparked her passion for writing. In her free time, she enjoys giving back to the community through participation and support of various charitable and educational organizations in the Pacific Northwest.

Inspiration Behind the Story

Kaylin has been involved in the business of collecting and selling Asian antiques for more than a decade. Because of her interest in this field and her fascination with the undersea world, she was inspired to write a story about the recovery of a Chinese concubine's cursed treasure from a sunken ship, a feat that helps to heal a woman's damaged soul. Kaylin spent four months researching scuba diving, trade routes, famous battles, and the natural disasters that befell Spanish galleons from the fifteenth to the seventeenth centuries. It is her hope that this action-adventure romance will entertain readers and honor the dedicated salvaging and exploration companies that have contributed remarkable discoveries and cross-sections of history to museums and institutions around the world.

More Stories by Kaylin McFarren

Buried Threads – Book 2, Threads series: Rachel Lyons and her partner Chase Cohen accept a contract to recover a lost priceless treasure in the Sea of Japan. However, upon arriving in Tokyo, they soon discover their mission is more complicated and dangerous than they originally believed. In order to prevent a natural disaster from striking Japan and killing millions, they must form an alliance with yakuza members, dive into shark-infested waters and recover three ancient cursed swords before time runs out.

Flaherty's Crossing– Award-winning inspirational romance: Successful yet emotionally stifled artist Kate Flaherty stands at the deathbed of her estranged father, conflicted by his morphine-induced confession exposing his part in her mother's death. While racing home, Kate's car mishap leads her to a soul-searching discussion with a lone diner employee, prompting Kate to confront the true reasons her marriage hangs in the balance. When her night takes an unexpected turn, however, she flees for her life, a life desperate for faith that can only be found through her ability to forgive.

Available at Amazon.com, Barnes & Noble, Powell's Book Store and Independent Outlets

WWW.KAYLINMCFARREN.COM

AUTHOR'S NOTE

I've often been asked, "What inspires you to write?" Most authors have a pat response. It might be the people they've known, the circumstances in which they find themselves living, books they've read over the years, a favorite movie, or their desire to live in another time and place—a romantic, undaunted, and unpretentious era. For me, oddly enough, stories develop in the recesses of my mind, becoming a pageant of dreams and often recurring and continuing, like a weekly series on television. I find that I'm compelled to write because my brain keeps me up at night with possibilities. Unfortunately, there isn't an on-and-off switch. Once I have a story in my head, I'm completely consumed by it. This might sound egotistic and self-promoting, but if I don't put it on paper or on my computer, I'm convinced I'll be haunted by the failed opportunity to affect other people's lives—to provide insight into resolving broken relationships and damaged emotions. However, by no means does this qualify or allow me to advise and counsel the public. There are accomplished specialists trained to address those specific needs. My purpose is simply to entertain and to open the mind's eye, allowing a glimpse inside the average woman's thought process. I've simply been given the gift of a vivid imagination that takes me on journeys better shared with good company.

To the man who's always in my corner and never lets a day go by without reminding me how much I'm loved—this one's for you, baby.

Made in the USA
Middletown, DE
04 April 2016